LAXDALE HALL

LAXDALE HALL

A Novel by

ERIC LINKLATER

JONATHAN CAPE
THIRTY BEDFORD SQUARE
LONDON

FIRST PUBLISHED 1951

PRINTED IN GREAT BRITAIN IN THE CITY OF OXFORD
AT THE ALDEN PRESS
BOUND BY A. W. BAIN & CO. LTD., LONDON

To

ISMAY and *DONALD ROSS*

with my love

LAXDALE HALL

CHAPTER ONE

'IF I were a writer,' said Mr. Crantit, 'I would write, in times like these, only small, restrained and agreeable books. I would insist, though quite unobtrusively, on being civilized. Especially if I were young, for youth should always attach itself to some impossible, high purpose — if only for the sake of exercise — and certainly the great lost cause of this interesting century appears to be civilization.'

'What,' asked General Matheson, 'do you mean by civilization?'

'Not exactly what you mean perhaps,' said Mr. Crantit, putting down his glass. 'Your ideas, I fancy, would be too strenuous for my taste, and your view too rigid. You see it, I dare say, as victory exacted from the darkness, and I shan't complain of that. But I want a long perspective. I don't want a victory so recent that we are still patting each other on the back. Self-congratulation is a vulgar gesture, and civilization, to escape vulgarity and be worthy of its name, must have forgotten its sense of achievement. It should, indeed, have begun to go down hill a little. — And there, a mile or two below the crest, in the mellow but declining rays of afternoon, how charming it can be!'

'When it's already decadent,' said the General gruffly.

'When its flavour is ripe,' said Mr. Crantit. 'When people have exchanged their harsher virtues for a certain grace. When we remember the lost heroism of our fathers with admiration but without regret. When we teach our children to keep their balance rather than their virtue: to keep their balance on the downward slope lest they descend too far, and in the shadows lose their manners and their happiness. — Yes, that's the climate I prefer, and the light that should illuminate our present books: a gentle, post-meridian glow.'

'But you haven't any children, have you?' asked Catriona Matheson.

'Nor are you a writer,' said Olaf Swanson.

Mr. Crantit drank a little more sherry and gently smacked his lips, as though to applaud its flavour. His brown eyes were magnified by the thick lenses of his rimless spectacles, and his acquiescent smile raised little hillocks of geniality on his rough-skinned, sallow cheeks. 'As the Reader in Greek at an ancient university,' he said, 'I am almost without employment of any sort. I entertained last term five students, two of them women without the intellect to be scholars or the appetite to be amused; and of my three men, one was a mere eccentric, the others were destined for the Scottish Church. — Not that I underrate them on that account, you mustn't think that, no, not for a moment. What I do deplore is the little use that our clergy make of their learning. I gave up going to church when I lost hope of being daunted by the sermon — for surely a sermon should put us in our place? It is difficult, perhaps impossible, to be civilized without some apprehension of status.'

'You must speak to our Mr. Macaulay about that,' said the General, looking at his watch.

'Is he coming to dinner, or to stay?'

'I told him he'd better stay. His housekeeper went off in the steamer this morning, she's going to Inverness to get her teeth out — she's always been a bit fanciful — and Macaulay can't possibly look after himself. So I asked him to come here.'

'Father likes taking charge of people,' said Catriona. 'Do have some more sherry, Mr. Swanson.'

Catriona Matheson had the linear beauty, precisely drawn, of Botticelli's sea-born Venus; but she was sun-burnt, weather-tanned, hers was no Florentine complexion. Her chin was a dimpled narrowing of her slender jaw, her eyebrows curved and pointed down to a nose alert and exquisite; the deep space between eyebrows and eyelids was of equal measure with her upper lip. Her hair, of a ripe harvest hue, looked too heavy for such delicate features and a neck so small and smooth; and her eyes, sea-grey, were a little melancholy, like harbours of some unknown regret. She had had a conventional education, but was seriously minded in spite of it. She wore a green silk dress, country-made, that did her scant service except to cover her; and even her friends admitted that she had no sense of humour.

'Mr. Macaulay only became a minister because father insisted on it,' she said, 'and he still has trouble with his conscience, especially when his back is hurting him.'

'It was lucky for him I was here at the time,' said the General. 'He was in very poor shape when he came home, he thought his life was ruined, poor chap. — Just because he'd been shot down with a few shell-splinters in his back and a broken leg,' he explained to Mr. Crantit. 'He was in the Fleet Air Arm, and got shot down somewhere in the south of Italy. Bari, I think. — Well, I told him he'd have to give up his notion of being a political journalist, which was what he'd been thinking of, and settle down to something quiet and orderly. "You'd better go back to the university," I said, "and take your degree in divinity. We'll be needing a new minister here before long" — old Chisholm was over eighty and showing his years by that time — "and I'll see to it that you get the parish as soon as you're ready for it." His mother took to the idea at once, there's a very good manse, and she used her influence too. I'd known the boy all his life, of course, for his father was my estate-agent till he died. A nice fellow, though far from able. I do all his work myself now, and make quite as good a job of it as he ever did. — Well, the end of it was that young Macaulay took my advice, and old Chisholm died a week after he graduated. So here he came, and on the whole he's settled down quite well.'

'Except when he's in one of his moods, and worrying about his back,' said Catriona.

'You've got to make allowances,' said the General. 'He's easily upset, I grant you that, and he takes himself a bit too seriously perhaps. — His mother couldn't get on with him, and went off to live with an unmarried daughter who's a teacher in Paisley, poor girl. That's why Macaulay had to find a housekeeper, and a bad choice he made, if you ask me. She'll be worse than ever when she comes back from Inverness with a great shining set of false teeth in her mouth.'

'What is he like, this minister of yours?' asked Swanson in a voice that seemed oddly constrained and dry. 'In appearance, I mean?'

'Tall,' said the General, 'and well built. Black hair, and a long white face. A rather lugubrious expression. Did you meet him in Italy? You were down in the south at one time, weren't you?'

'Yes,' said Swanson, now manifestly uncomfortable. 'It's the same man, I think.'

'It was in Italy, during the war, that Mr. Swanson met father,' said Catriona to Mr. Crantit. 'But that was in Ravenna, wasn't it?'

'What were you doing?' asked Mr. Crantit. 'Lecturing to the soldiery? Restoring their morale with timely excerpts from the Bard?'

'I was in the army.'

'Of your own volition?'

'Yes!'

'I beg your pardon. I didn't know that you combined the profession of arms with your practice of literature. Though *Tam Marti quam Mercurio* is, of course, an old diversion.'

Mr. Crantit's astonishment was understandable, for Olaf Swanson did not look like a soldier; even a retired soldier. He had, indeed, no aptitude for war nor natural gifts for military employment, being of a timid and imaginative habit, night-blind, and even in broad daylight given to losing his way. He was unmethodical, and had so erratic a memory that he had often failed to recognize his own batman, and forgotten his battery commander's name. He had never mastered the army's system of accountancy nor overcome his horror at the sight of blood, and he found it difficult to understand the working of even the simplest mechanical instruments. But in spite of these disabilities he had spent some nine of his fifty-one years in uniform, for his boyhood had been inflamed by a romantic patriotism, a romantic view of military life; and the uneasiness of his century – the climacteric of Europe – had given him two wars in which to suffer for his folly and his faith.

Paradoxically, it was the first of the great wars which had created his unsoldierly appearance; for while serving at an early age in the ranks of a Highland regiment he had been struck by a shell-fragment and lost the greater part of his chin. A series of skilful operations had repaired some of the damage, and for several years his face had worn, clearly enough, the angry scars of battle. But because he was young, and his tissues healthy, the scars had gradually been absorbed, and his chinless countenance, so mild of aspect, so irresolute in implication, was presently accepted as the work of nature; or, by the more perceptive, as the consequence of some country doctor's impatient use of forceps at his birth. – His cheeks were rosy and his hair, grey only at the temples, still grew thickly; he looked ten years younger than his age, and that, in his second war, had saved him some embarrassment when six years' service brought him promotion only from lieutenant to captain.

Too old for the infantry, he had joined in 1938 a Territorial anti-aircraft regiment raised for the defence of his native islands, the far-northern archipelago of Shetland, and after two cold winters there had served successively in Palestine, the Libyan Desert and Italy. Seconded in the winter of 1944 to the Allied Military Government, he had worked for some months under General Matheson, and now, six years later, mere chance had renewed their acquaintance. The General had been shooting grouse in South Uist, Swanson fishing for sea-trout there. The same cottage had given them shelter from heavy rain, they had dined together, and when the General discovered that Swanson was alone, had been alone for a considerable time, and from some unknown cause was worried and unhappy, he had insisted on taking him back to Laxdale Hall with the promise that he should catch a salmon there; and mend his spirits.

Two days ago, when they came ashore from the island steamer, the prospect of spiritual recovery had been fair enough; for though the river was too low for fishing, the General's house was handsomely situated in a picturesque and many-coloured landscape, and there was abundance of comfort indoors. But now a coldness, a little draught of foreboding, seemed to invade the library where they sat drinking sherry and waiting for the dinner-gong and Mr. Macaulay. It was a warm and pleasant room, used for hospitality rather than scholarship, but the light reflected from its walls, from the long shelves filled with tawny calf and the brighter book-binding of recent years, held now, for Swanson at least, a sinister quality, as though it were a flare thrown down to see what darkness had kept hidden; and a great silver cup, a challenge-cup retired from conflict, winked malevolently at him from a little table.

The General and Mr. Crantit were talking at cross-purposes about Ravenna — the one of civil administration, the other of mosaics — when the door was opened and Mr. Macaulay came in. He stood for a moment, uncertain of himself, a tall parti-coloured figure, dark of hair and clerical suit, white of face and clerical linen, and then with a Highland accent spoke in a deep baying voice like that of a noble but melancholy hound. 'I am late,' he said, 'and I am sorry to have kept you waiting. I had my duties to attend to.'

'Come in, come in,' said the General. 'You're in plenty of time for a glass of sherry, dinner's not ready yet. — You haven't met Mr. Swanson, have you? He's an old friend from our Italian days, and he's going to catch a salmon or two, as soon as there's any rain.'

Macaulay turned to see his fellow-guest, and recognized him at once. He drew back a little, his arms stiffening, his fingers spread and extended as though he were an old-fashioned actor in a melo-drama; and Swanson, who had risen, grew pale of face.

'Oh, but yes, yes!' said Macaulay. 'We have met before, and more than once. Yes, more than once!'

'You're looking very well,' said Swanson with a nervous flicker of a smile. 'You made a good recovery.'

'That will be a disappointment to you, no doubt.'

'Now what's all this about?' asked the General.

'Twice he tried to assassinate me,' said Macaulay, 'with great guns at his command! Many a time since then have I remembered him, with prayer that some day I shall be granted the grace and compassion to forgive him. But that day has not yet come. No, not yet!'

'I still don't understand,' said the General.

'Is your back hurting you?' asked Catriona. 'Would you like to go to bed?'

'I will have a word with Mr. Swanson first,' said Macaulay, 'for we have never had an opportunity to discuss this matter that lies between us.'

'I gave you an opportunity when I came to see you in hospital,' said Swanson, 'and you know what happened then. I've got the mark of it still.'

'A little scar upon your forehead! Do you complain of that and expect me to keep silent about a shattered leg and twenty wounds on my back? — He came to see me, in the hospital at Bari, to pretend he was sorry, and to gloat over his good marksmanship in shooting me down into the sea . . .'.

'No, no!'

'I was wrapped in bandages from top to toe, like an Egyptian mummy, and my left leg shattered in two places — and now you are grumbling because I struck you on the head with a small table that stood by the bedside. You are no gentleman, Mr. Swanson!'

'Come, come,' said the General, 'it won't help you to lose your temper, whatever happened. And I want to get this clear. — Was it, in actual fact, Swanson's battery that shot you down?'

'It was.'

'Not intentionally,' said Swanson. 'It was an accident, and I wasn't entirely to blame. There was low cloud over the harbour, and he came in without sending recognition signals.'

'The apparatus was out of order.'

'You couldn't expect me to know that.'

'So you have said before, but you are not talking to a Court Martial now. You are talking to the man you tried to assassinate not once only, but twice. — Yes, twice he did it, and it is a great wonder that I am alive to tell the tale!'

Deeply agitated by his emotion, Mr. Macaulay entirely forgot his manners and snatching the decanter of sherry from its tray, poured nervously an overflowing glass and drank it at a gulp; poured another and quickly drank that too, as if to forestall the clutching hand of death; filled his glass a third time, and spilt it when suddenly from the hall came the brazen din of a gong that had been forged beyond the Himalayas to frighten devils from a Tibetan monastery.

'Dinner!' exclaimed the General with relief. 'Come along and have something to eat, you'll feel better then.'

'Food would choke me!' said Macaulay.

'Oh, nonsense. Food's just what you need. There's a lot to explain yet, I realize that, but it can wait till we've had our dinner. We'll be a lot calmer then. — Go along, Catriona. Come on, Mr. Crantit. And don't look so worried, Swanson. We've all had our ups and downs.'

' "Ups and downs" is good!' said Macaulay bitterly, but for forty minutes he submitted to the General's authority, and without adding to the conversation ate hare soup, roast grouse, and an abundant savoury of scrambled eggs and soft herring-roes.

Conversation, indeed, was little more than a monologue delivered by Mr. Crantit, with a few interjections by the General and Catriona. Swanson, still rather pale, was manifestly ill-at-ease. Catriona had listened to Macaulay's loud and still mysterious wrath with the calm detachment of one to whom human emotion was often a puzzle; and her father had exhibited the habitual patience of the commanding officer, long accustomed to anger and the incoherence of witnesses to any sort of crime. But Mr. Crantit had enjoyed every moment of the dispute. Mr. Crantit had a great appreciation of comedy however it presented itself, and his affection for human beings depended largely on their capacity for making statements that seemed to him absurd, or for creating situations that would entertain him.

Stimulated by the revelation of ludicrous mishap, and pleasantly tickled by the promise of more to come, Mr. Crantit discovered a fertile theme in the General's casual statement that Macaulay's vanished housekeeper stood only five feet two; and thereafter delivered a remarkable address on the natural authority of small women, mentioning in particular Justinian's Empress Theodora, the Dowager Tsz'e Hsi of China, and Queen Victoria. His dissertation, with occasional interruption, lasted until the port was put upon the table, and Catriona got up to go. Then Macaulay also rose, and declared, 'You will excuse me, General, but I am in no mood for the idle talk that commonly accompanies the passage of the wine. With your permission, I shall go with Miss Catriona.'

'Well, well,' said the General, when the door had closed, 'perhaps that makes it easier. Macaulay, I may say, has always refused to speak of his — let's call it a misfortune — but you'll tell us all about it, Swanson, won't you?'

Warmed by a sufficiency of good claret, and thus fortified to some degree against the ineluctable brutalities of life, Swanson was able to make his confession. 'I can't deny it,' he said. 'I gave the order to fire, and what we brought down was a Swordfish of the Fleet Air Arm. The navigator wasn't badly hurt, but Macaulay had a broken leg.'

'He mentioned another occasion of the same sort,' said Mr. Crantit.

'It was a remarkable coincidence,' said Swanson. 'He was flying a Walrus the first time. That was in Shetland, in 1940. We had a lot of air-raid warnings after the Germans invaded Norway, and perhaps we got a little too sensitive about them. A little too ready to shoot. And one morning, before it was really light, I opened fire on an unidentified aircraft — and when we went out in a boat to see what we'd got, we picked up Macaulay.'

'Oh, no!' said the General happily.

'But he wasn't hurt that time. He was very lucky really.'

'Twice!' exclaimed Mr. Crantit. 'To do it *twice*! Oh, my dear Mr. Swanson, you literary men live lives quite different from the humdrum existence of us ordinary folk! Especially when you join the army.'

'It was merely a coincidence,' said Swanson.

'Oh, ho ho!' exclaimed the General, and wiped his streaming eyes. 'Poor Macaulay! But I can't help laughing. To do it twice! Oh, for God's sake pass the port.'

'I've never told anyone before,' said Swanson. 'I mean I've never made a story of it.'

'But you should!' said Mr. Crantit. 'It's a perfect story, because the pattern is traditional but the detail new. — Repetition has always been the clown's technique. He suffers mishap, or contrives mishap, and his audience is titillated. But to satisfy his audience and get a belly-laugh, he must do it again.'

'Our purpose, at that time, wasn't amusement,' said Swanson coldly.

'But now,' said the General, 'looking back at it — well, if it had happened to anyone else, you'd laugh, wouldn't you? My God, I think it's funny! Especially knowing Macaulay as I do, poor chap.'

Some ten minutes later Catriona returned to the dining-room and said, with a severe expression on her face, 'Mr. Macaulay has gone to bed. He heard you laughing, and got very offended.'

'Oh dear,' said the General, 'I'm sorry about that. The last thing any of us wanted to do was to hurt his feelings. But when you see the funny side of a thing —'

'I don't think it was funny at all,' said Catriona. 'Mr. Macaulay told me the whole story, and I do sympathize with him. I don't blame you, Mr. Swanson, but to do it twice —'

'Yes,' said the General, 'that's just what we were discussing. To do it twice!'

'History always repeats itself,' said Mr. Crantit. 'Little events are continually re-iterated, and the largest events habitually recur. But no one has ever discovered the purpose of repetition. That humanity has failed to profit by example is clear enough, and we can therefore dismiss the motive of instruction. But what are we to infer if we assume that the Author of all history has merely been indulging his sense of humour?'

'Sit down,' said the General to his daughter, 'and have a glass of port with us. Mr. Crantit's in no hurry to move, and neither am I.'

CHAPTER TWO

LAXDALE HALL was a handsome building of classical design that still, after a hundred and fifty years, looked out of place against its romantic background. The little hill behind and the little bay below could not properly support so large and civilized a structure. Two storeys high, above a sunk basement, it had been built by a pupil of Robert Adam, and the pediment and the seventeen windows of its south front were in perfect proportion to the whole. It was, indeed, the perfection of its design, even more than its size, that gave it an alien look amid the splendid irregularities, the mingled bareness and brilliance of Highland scenery. Below its west wall a peacock sea broke upon a beach of cream and sparkling sand, and to the north-west rose a hill, as ragged as a cock's comb hewn from the rock, that birches, heather, and bracken brightly coloured. A plantation of trees half-girdled it from north to east, and from the terraced lawns in front a bridge across a tumbling stream led to a walled garden that more trees encircled. But for its graciousness, that precluded all thought of conflict, it might have seemed a forgotten outpost of civilization still defending itself against time's ruinous assault and the wild alliance of the mountains and the sea; but it was, in fact, so gently handsome, so blandly big, so unassertively correct in the wrong place, that it more resembled an eccentric, huge and gifted visitor who had blissfully forgotten to go home.

It was the creation, as might be expected, of a vigorous and imaginative Englishwoman. The Highlander in his own country has rarely been capable of constructive thought or action — he must cross an ocean or the Scottish border before he can see that life challenges him to amend it — and but for their replenishment from

England and the United States, and especially the incursion of strong-minded women, the Highlands would be even lonelier and more desolate than they are. It was a Miss Phipps, the daughter of a banker in Middlesex, who had commissioned Robert Adam's pupil to build Laxdale Hall when she married the great-great-grandfather of General Matheson, a handsome and amusing man whose health had been undermined by tropical fevers. He had spent several years in the Far East, and almost alone among his English and Scottish contemporaries there, had failed to make a fortune. But Miss Phipps had inherited half a million, and immediately after her marriage she discovered that generous enthusiasm for her new surroundings which the English so often feel for picturesque and backward countries, such as Scotland and Southern Arabia; and having great wealth to enforce her will, she had compelled her husband, much against his inclination, to live in his own country. Their sons, brought up by Gaelic-speaking nurses, had been taught to kill deer and salmon as soon as they had opened their Cicero and Xenophon; and as Miss Phipps, with her father's money, had bought some eighty thousand acres of adjacent moor and mountain, the boys found great pleasure in their heritage and grew up as devoted to the Highland scene as even an Englishwoman could wish. And when, after three generations, the estate became impoverished by the addiction of a late Victorian Matheson to baccarat, the present laird – the General, that is – had fortunately won the love, in exchange for his own, of a Miss Bagot from Boston. She, as serious and lovely and intent on well-doing as her English predecessor, had like Miss Phipps been extremely well-off, and professed an equal attachment to her husband's country. She had paid the debts he inherited, borne him three children, fallen a prey to melancholy, and died. Most of her fortune had pre-deceased her – for riches today, like modern art, are only a surface-growth, without roots – but enough remained, for the moment, to let the General pay his taxes and live in reasonable comfort.

The parish of Laxdale had been less fortunate than Laxdale Hall. A blunt peninsula, rising to grandeur in the clouds and lapsing into idyllic charm beside little brooks that ran among yellow irises and granite boulders, it thrust itself like a clenched fist into the Atlantic, and where the sea did not surround it, was almost isolated by rugged hills. Its population, in a century and a half, had shrunk from about fourteen hundred to little more than three hundred, though there had been none of those evictions under duress which, in other parts, drove out the noise of human tongues to let in the melancholy cry of sheep. It was benevolence, not tyranny, that first began to dislodge the people from a barbaric culture and their immemorial contented poverty; for Miss Phipps did so much to improve the material conditions of their life that when she built a pier, where no pier had been before, and made a road over the hills, their sons and daughters took advantage of easier travel to go and look for wider fields than Laxdale knew, and the opportunities that a larger world now offered. Many put to sea and in Canada settled down to harder work than their grandfathers would have considered tolerable, and won rewards which their grandmothers would have found irrelevant or burdensome. Many went to Glasgow, and while a few of these prospered exceedingly and built large villas in Helensburgh and Wemyss Bay, the majority lived meagrely in slums darker than a Highland winter and died of drink or consumption. Between 1840 and 1940 several hundred lively young men joined the army, and having fought with gallantry in the Crimea, the Punjab and the Sudan, on the Kabul river and the Modder river, the Somme and the Rhine, at Gallipoli and Ypres and Knightsbridge-in-Libya, and many other places from Burma to Dunkirk, were buried where they fell and remembered in their mothers' grief and the battle honours of their regiment. More obvious and substantial rewards had been won by a score or two of successful doctors, professors, clergymen, and commercial magnates in the East; but the successful emigrants were by success as far removed from Laxdale as those who had died in the deserts of Asia and Africa. And many young women, who left the parish to teach and nurse and cook, found husbands whose demands were almost as exigent as regimental honour or a great position in the world.

In one way or another, then, the world took more from Laxdale than nature could make good with the diminishing forces at her command, and people who regarded the over-crowded streets of industrial cities as a normal or desirable condition of life were now truly shocked by the silence of its shores and the desolation of the hills. Its three hundred and twenty-four remaining inhabitants, however, regarded the local scene with deep affection, and most of them were tolerably contented with their lives. Though they had their grievances, and were always ready to discuss them, and though their material comforts were small in comparison with European cities and non-existent on the American scale, they probably found more to interest them and less to complain of than the inhabitants, for example, of Leeds and Leicester and Dundee, of Lyons and Milan and Milwaukee. Poor men in Laxdale had such leisure as even rich men in cities could not afford, and no one worried because time fled too fast or went too slow. A crofter on the hillside commanded as much space as a millionaire could buy, and though he had to carry his water from the well, he bore no burden of plumbers and electricians on his budget, he was never worried by the inattention of waiters and taxi-drivers, and his entertainment cost him nothing; for all his neighbours gave it free, though sometimes with reluctance.

Death brought them tragedy, and every funeral was a drama that all attended. Love came with whispering, closely watched, and pipers played the parish to the wedding dance. Sometimes the midwife arrived before the minister, and while women deplored a girl's improvidence the young men mocked a young man's heat and folly. A sheep died on the hill, with its throat torn out, and everyone looked to his own lambs and listened for the barking of his neighbour's dog. A new fishing-boat came into the harbour, and for a week there was high debate on commerce, finance, the migration of herring, and the advantage of diesel engines. The growth of every field was everyone's concern, and half the parish would be gratified, half jealous, if a neighbour won a prize for hammer-throwing at the Strathpeffer Gathering, or a neighbour's son took a scholarship at Glasgow University, or a neighbour's daughter went into service at Laxdale Hall. Because in all that happened everyone was in some degree involved, life was continuously interesting and often it pulsated with urgent, large excitement.

At this moment in the history of Laxdale there was indeed almost an embarrassment of interest. There was so much to talk about that the prospect of an early harvest, which could not fail to interfere with conversation, was widely regarded as a grave injustice. — In the first place, there was the old question of communication with the outer world; which, in the enormities of the winter climate, ceased to exist. This was the most serious of local grievances, and the only one that evoked united indignation.

From the east there was no way into Laxdale but Miss Phipps's mountain road through the Larig Dubh; and from the sea there was no landing except at Miss Phipps's pier, which was, in fact, no better than a jetty. The road, in the course of time, had fallen into disrepair, and now in places it hung from the hillside like a shelf on broken brackets, and elsewhere was worn down to native rock; every winter it was blocked by snow. The pier, good enough when it was built to take little coasting smacks and fishing-boats, was no use to modern trawlers and steamers that needed proper accommodation. For years the Laxdalers had been sending their petitions, to local authorites and to the Government itself, for a new road, and in even more urgent language for a longer pier. But though many a deputation of solemn and important gentlemen, County Councillors and Civil Servants and even Members of Parliament, had come to hear their complaints, and see for themselves what was really required — and though all had agreed that something must be done — the years had gone by, year after year, and nothing at all had been done.

So at last the Laxdalers had been driven into small but open revolt, and all those in the parish who owned motor-cars — there were five of them — had refused to pay any tax or licence until they were given a road fit to drive on. The rebellious motorists had not as yet been prosecuted, for the ordinary process of the law had twice, by curious mishap, been frustrated; but their spirited behaviour had attracted so much interest that the most recent of the Laxdale petitions to Parliament, which had been delivered only three years before, was now said to be receiving urgent attention. A new deputation was already on its way to examine the situation, and the utmost excitement had been aroused by the news that its leader was Mr. Samuel Pettigrew.

By name and repute Mr. Pettigrew was known to everyone in the parish, and nearly everyone was confident that his visit would ensure the happiest results. For his maternal grandfather had been a Laxdale man, and Mr. Pettigrew himself was not only a politician of redoubtable vigour, but a self-made millionaire whose influence extended far beyond the House of Commons. Hope rose higher still when it became known that he was bringing a wife with him— there was some doubt as to whether it was his second or third — because her company suggested a quality of sentiment in the occasion. He must be bringing her, it was thought, to show her with pride and affection the land that had nurtured his mother's people; and in such a mood he might be generous indeed. So rich a man need not wait for Parliament's authority, but could build a pier out of one pocket, a road from the other, if sentiment persuaded him to dip his hands deep enough.

And how, thought the Laxdalers, could sentiment fail to move him, who was almost one of themselves, when he saw the evening light upon the hills, and the grass-green sea that lapped their shore? They were reasonable and deserving people — this they were sure of, and sure that anyone with a grain of understanding would instantly perceive it — and what they asked for would be of advantage, not only to themselves, but to the larger world. For a road and a pier, or even a pier alone, would let visitors come in, to be rewarded with beauty and the Atlantic air, while on the outward journey went cattle-beasts and eggs and sheep to hungry people who needed them, and would doubtless pay for what they got. There was in their case both sentiment for the heart, and commercial argument for the head; and because the sentiment was sound enough, the combination, thought the Laxdalers, would be irresistible to Mr. Pettigrew.

The second great cause of excitement was the recent invasion of the parish by an organized gang of poachers from some town as far distant, perhaps, as Glasgow. In the mere act of poaching there was, of course, nothing new, and nearly every grown man in the

24

parish had at one time or another shot a hind in the back-end of the year, or taken an occasional salmon from the General's river. One or two, such as Nicholas McLeod, who was a County Councillor and kept the village shop, were persistent poachers, artists of the game, and like artists everywhere — if they are great enough — had won from their fellows a reluctant admission of the privilege to indulge their temperament; though Nicholas, unlike painters and poets, dared not publicize his talents, but had to exercise them in the manner of a diplomat who achieves his triumphs under a mask of innocence, behind a façade of virtuous inactivity. — It was the grossness of the poachers from outside, the impropriety of their outrageous destruction, that had roused the whole parish to fierce resentment.

An unknown number of men, well prepared for their task and trained in its execution, had crossed the mountain road and emptied a river that was teeming with salmon newly come from the sea in a summer spate. There had been a mighty run of fish, and for a day the brown waters were turbulent with their dark shoulders and swift, powerful movement. But the next day the river was lifeless, and here and there a dead fish, washed on to a bank of shingle, had torn gills and a narrow bruise across its head for evidence against the net which had caught and killed it. On a cart-track that crossed the moor from a ruined bridge on the river to Miss Phipps's road, someone found the wheel-marks of two cars that had halted, many footprints, and a crumpled, greasy sheet of newspaper; and these signs of invasion from the busier parts of Scotland — it was a Glasgow evening paper in which the enemy had wrapped his sandwiches — were regarded with indignation and a curious unease. They were the leavings of something uncouth and violent, the footprints of men foreign to Laxdale; and because they had come once, they would probably come again.

Everyone in the parish had been shocked by the brutal efficiency of the poachers, by the unnaturalness of total destruction, and many women were obscurely frightened by the thought of strangers moving in the darkness on their hills. But the General had told his young game-keeper McKellaig exactly what he was to do if the

25

invaders returned, and while the General felt comfortably sure that he would catch them the next time, McKellaig watched the mountain road and lost a lot of sleep.

McKellaig was a tall young man, handsome in profile but less pleasing from in front. His face was curiously narrow, his eyes close-set, his mouth small and rather girlish; his disposition was gentle, his habit of mind — not without reason — mournful. He led a troubled life, and the worst of his troubles was his widowed mother, who kept house for him. She was a cross-grained, envious, domineering woman with a bitter tongue. An incomer to the parish, she had been born and brought up on the colder side of Scotland, in the uplands of Angus, where for a few years McKellaig's father had been employed as a shepherd. He had taken her home to Laxdale as soon as they were married, and from the beginning she had shown her contempt for the lack of industry and the gentler habit of life that she found in the west; and when her husband died she felt less of sorrow than a sense of grievance. Her grievance hardened with time, and discovering that age conferred a certain authority, and a little immunity from criticism, she grew old beyond her years; though she had something to build on, for she had not married till she was thirty-three. She had a stiff leg, and walked with a limp, a stoop and a stick; and in the freedom that her pretended age conferred she sometimes used her stick upon her son's broad but uncomplaining shoulders.

The third of the major sources of excitement in the parish was a play that Catriona Matheson was producing, and against his mother's wishes McKellaig had accepted a part in it. It was no ordinary play, none of the homely little comedies that Laxdale, like every other parish in Scotland, was accustomed to perform when winter nights grew long and called for common pleasure; but a play which few could understand, and many had read with a superstitious dislike that only a series of evening sermons by Mr. Macaulay had been able to dispel.

Mr. Macaulay himself had had the gravest doubt about its propriety, but he, since General Matheson decided he was to enter the ministry, had been more troubled by doubt, and in more various fields, than anyone else in Laxdale. The difficulty of reconciling the state of the world with the benignity of the Christian promise perplexed him; but in that he did not differ from the majority. His particular problems were more recondite, and often he lay sleepless to wonder what precisely had been the heresy of the Albigensians, those good fellows of Provence who hated priests and may have had reason on their side. The Manichaeans worried him, he was gravely exercised by Mithraism, and the cult of the Magna Mater often wakened untimely thoughts. His powerful sermons filled the church week after week, perhaps because they were so clearly the evidence of his wrestling with faith, and week after week he would go to the General for comfort and re-assurance.

The General would listen, patiently and with genuine sympathy, for an hour but no longer; and then would give his opinion, which seldom varied.

'There may be something in that,' he would say. 'You never can tell. But don't make too much of your difficulties, Macaulay, and don't exaggerate your own private responsibility in the matter. Our intelligence is very limited, you know, and the surest way of making some fearful blunder is trying to be a bit too clever. Stick to a few facts and a few beliefs — the fewer the better — and try and be content with them. And now let's have a glass of sherry, and tell me what's the latest gossip in the parish.'

Major-General Aeneas Matheson, C.B., D.S.O., had spent most of his military career in regimental employment, and never wished for anything better. He had a natural liking for his fellow-men, without undue faith in their virtue, and a confidence in his own judgment that was wholly free from arrogance. He was brave without display, physically robust, and his mind was lively enough to take an amateur's interest in history and natural history, and literature within reason, as well as in regimental sports, and weapon-training, and agriculture. In his company, when he commanded a company, and in his battalion, when he was promoted, there had always been a singular absence of crime; and until he rose to General's rank, in 1941, the only derogatory remark about him, in his military record, had been that he lacked ambition. In the

Western Desert, however, he had revealed his romantic belief, at odds with the circumstance of the times, that riflemen could successfully oppose German tanks; and after being seriously wounded for his faith, he had been relegated to the Allied Military Government in Italy. But Macaulay and many others still came to him for advice, and Macaulay had been persuaded, after anxious searching of his conscience, that a minister of the Church of Scotland could advise his flock to support and act in a heathen play, and should set an example by accepting a leading role.

It was a play by Euripides, in a new translation by Mr. Crantit, that Catriona Matheson was producing.

CHAPTER THREE

NORMAN MCKELLAIG had spent the night in the Larig Dubh, on the summit of the road out of Laxdale into the wider parts of Scotland. It had been cold on the high ground, cold and windless with a little frost after midnight; and the growing moon had been hidden by dark clouds. But neither darkness nor cold had worried him, and loneliness was much to his liking. He had, in the last war, been a prisoner for some eighteen months, and in the inescapable close company of his fellow captives he had longed, not primarily for freedom, but to be alone; and on the hill-road, far from his mother's scolding tongue, he enjoyed the comfort of solitude. His conscience still troubled him a little, for he was again betraying his trust; but so fiercely and insistently did he feel the need of money that he gave hardly more attention to the protest of his inner voice than to a professional beggar's unconvincing tale of hardship.

The day was just breaking, with a whistle of wind out of the pallor in the east, when up the rough road from Laxdale came a small motor-lorry, and twenty yards behind it a shabby saloon car. Neither of them showed any lights.

McKellaig stood in the middle of the road and signalled with a weak torch, using his left hand as a shutter. The lorry stopped, and in the dark cab two cigarettes glowed like fireflies behind a cracked windshield. The driver spoke in a surly Clydeside voice: 'He's in the caur ahint.'

McKellaig nodded, and walked to the shabby saloon. There were four men in it, and one of them in the back seat pulled down a window and looked out. 'Well, that was a bloody waste o' time,' he said. 'That was juist the waste o' a good night's sleep. We'd ha' done better to bide at hame.'

'I did not think there would be any fish tonight,' said McKellaig. His voice was soft, and in the Highland rhythm of politeness there seemed a note of true regret.

'Hauf-a-dizzen, that's all. And what's the bloody use o' that?' said the man in the car; and opening the door, got out and stood on the road, facing McKellaig, his head thrust forward in the style of one long addicted to shouting and blustering, and used to getting the best of a bargain. He was of middle height, broad-shouldered and running to fat. He wore a tweed cap and a dirty raincoat, unbuttoned, above a dark suit that was apparently too tight for him; for he stooped to ease it under the crutch, and a couple of buttons were missing from his waistcoat. There was a certain quality in him, a coarse unruly vigour, that clearly gave him command over those with him. They were lank and pale, younger than their leader, and they sat in a glum silence, staring at McKellaig with the vague hostility of city hooligans to whom anyone from another street may be an enemy.

'I told you the river was low, Mr. Gamlie,' said McKellaig. 'We have had no rain since you were here before, and there have been no fish coming up.'

'There was plenty o' rain in Glasgow last night,' said Gamlie indignantly.

'But there was none here. I would have let you know if there had been.'

'Ah, weel, I wasn't too sure I could trust you. So we took a chance, and after coming a' this bloody way we weren't going back without wetting the net.'

'I gave you good advice, and gave it in plenty of time, three weeks ago,' said McKellaig reproachfully. 'You can rely on me to do my best for you, Mr. Gamlie.'

'I thought the whole country would've got a drenching last night. I tell you, it was coming down cats and dogs in Glasgow!'

'And it will be raining here before long, you can be sure of that, and then there will be salmon by the hundred for you. They are down there in the sea, just waiting for the chance to come up.'

'Then see you and give me the wire when the weather breaks. Just send me a telegram to say your auld mither's feeling better, and you'll be writing tomorrow; or whatever time you think we should come. That'll do it — and God help you if we dinna get a good haul.'

'You did very well the first time, Mr. Gamlie.'

'And so did you, McKellaig! But neither you nor me's going to make a fortune out o' this night's work. It's been a dead loss to me, and that's all you're getting.'

From a thick pocket-book he took a pound note and gave it to McKellaig.

'It is not very much in return for what I am doing,' said McKellaig.

'But I'm no' the only one that's paying you. You've got your own boss, McKellaig, and you're no' doing much to earn his money.'

Stooping a little, heavy-shouldered and formidable as an old bull, he glared at McKellaig as though he resented the thought of money passing through any hands but his own; and after a moment or two of uneasy silence, finding nothing else to say, eased himself under the crutch again, cleared his throat and spat on the road, and in a grumbling voice said to his pallid, lean subordinates, 'Come on, lads, we canna bide here all night.'

He shouted to the lorry-driver, and got into the car again. None of his companions had spoken, but all had watched McKellaig with a surly interest and cold, unchanging regard. — 'You'll be here when we come?' he asked.

'Yes, yes,' said McKellaig mournfully. 'You will be safe enough.'

He watched the shabby vehicles go eastward, downhill and out of sight. He put the pound note in an inner pocket, and walking a few yards took his bicycle from a hollow behind a granite boulder. Stiffly, for now he felt the cold in his legs, he mounted and rode slowly to the west, keeping close to the side where the surface was smoother.

From behind him the rising sun was dispelling the last shadows over Laxdale, carving anew the line of its shore, and lighting its fields with a hesitant candour, with colours that promised in a little while the clear radiance of emerald and amethyst and topaz, on grass and root-crops, on heather and ripened oats. Here and there an early chimney was already smoking, and mist like a lingering smoke lay on the turquoise sea. To the north-west, from the island of Skye, a sombre foundation of darkness wreathed in clouds, rose the Gothic heights of the Cuillins into the stillness of an immeasurable blue air; and from an old march-stone by the roadside a short-eared owl went sidling with heavy wings into cover. Far below the road, to the north beyond a rough moor still dark, brown-purple scarred by peat-banks, the river shone in intermittent pools, in a gleam of quicksilver or the shimmer of oyster-shells.

Holding hard on his brakes, McKellaig came down into the low-lands that narrowly bordered the sea, and when he was in sight of the village turned right, along a grassy road that led presently to the cottage where he and his mother lived. He rode more slowly as he approached the house, wondering if his mother was already afoot. He was setting his bicycle against the wall of the byre — a byre for one cow and its calf, with an open cart-shed adjoining it — when the door of the house was abruptly opened, and his mother appeared, her stick tapping on the pavement, her voice sharp with anger.

'And whaur hae you been a' this long night?' she demanded.

'On the top of the hill, Mother,' he said. 'You know as well as I do that I have to watch the road.'

'A fine excuse!' she exclaimed. 'And only a man wi' no naitural feeling in him would think o' making it! For wha's to look aifter me when you're stravaigin on the hill?'

'I have to do what I'm paid for, Mother.'

'And when you come hame in the morning, one fine day, and find me deid on the kitchen flair, a cauld corp wi' nane to help her, you'll still be canty and crouse because you've done what you were paid to do! — Could you no fetch me a pail o' watter afore you gaed oot tae the hill, you muckle, doited, hertless Hieland stot that you are?'

'Had you no water in the house?'

'Would I be as dry as a stane and drouthy as an auld sack left oot i' the sun, for want o' me cup of tea, if you'd put a pail o' watter ahint the door afore ye gaed oot?'

'I am sorry, Mother —'

'And muckle need for sorrow, you snipe-nebbit, thowless fathom o' misery! Tak' up the pail and bring the watter, and let me mask a pot o' tea.'

The old woman, bent over her stick, with which in her tantrum she beat upon the ground, was a picture of wilful and deliberate malignity. She was thin, flat-chested, small of stature; but in spite of her age and her wrinkled cheeks she gave the impression of something more than a sufficient vitality — of an old mischievous energy — and her eyes, red-rimmed in a narrow, yellowish face stained russet about the cheek-bones, were as blue as winter lakes beneath a frosty, sunlit sky. She had a new set of teeth, great prim-rose-coloured teeth, got free by the Government's beneficence; and her thin purple lips, which could not quite cover them, made a daunting frame for them. — Norman McKellaig, quailing before her anger, went to pick up the bright, two-gallon pail that stood by the door of his cottage, and as he passed his mother she suddenly raised her stick and struck him vigorously across the shoulders. He stooped and faltered, she struck him again, a glancing blow; and then, as he went with the pail to the well, she limped indoors, and set about making their breakfast, nodding her old head in satisfaction and showing now a sort of grumbling equanimity.

They took their porridge in silence, but while they drank their tea and ate their bread and butter they exchanged a few words, they spoke briefly of local events and domestic matters, in a mood that was almost amiable; and Mrs. McKellaig made no complaint when Norman, after breakfast was finished, filled a china mug with hot water and retired to the closet where he slept. In memory she still heard the fine whack of her stick coming down on his shoulders; and she washed the dishes in a tolerable contentment with life.

There was a gleam of cleanliness on everything in the house, and the old woman had a taste for bright colours. There were yellow roses on the curtains of her box-bed in the kitchen, and red roses on the linoleum that covered the ben-room floor. In the middle of the room a polished table glittered coldly beneath an enormous Bible and a bowl of red and yellow tulips ingeniously made of china. A Victorian sofa and armchair, of yellow mahogany upholstered in black horse-hair, looked grim as a winter funeral and appeared to rebuke the frivolous window-curtains, which cherries and cherry-blossom profusely decorated. Photographs of Mrs. McKellaig and her late husband, horribly enlarged, frowned from the fireplace wall on either side of an elaborately carved over-mantel with a slightly distorting mirror in it; and on the opposite wall a steel engraving of a defiant stag, after a painting by Landseer, hung between framed texts in red, white and black crewel-work. McKellaig's closet, which opened off the ben-room, was sparsely furnished with a small iron bed, an iron wash-stand, a sheepskin rug on a bitterly scrubbed floor, and a long shelf on the inner wall. On the shelf was an old-fashioned portable writing-desk, of mahogany with brass on the corners and for decoration, that had belonged to his grandfather.

He took off his coat and rolled up his sleeves. Slowly, interrupted by other thoughts that let the soap dry on his cheeks, he washed and shaved. Then, still slowly, but with what appeared to be resolution, he took down the writing-desk and carrying it into the ben-room, set it on the glittering table. He pushed away the Bible and the china tulips, unlocked the desk, and from its crowded interior took the photograph of a girl with downcast eyes, which he propped against the tulips, and a pad of thin, ruled writing-paper. He contemplated the photograph for several minutes, and seemed to make a decision. Not hastily, but without further pause for reflexion, he wrote a letter and addressed an envelope. From his pocket he took the pound note that Gamlie had given him, and two others from a little drawer in the writing-desk. He put them into the envelope, and licked the edge. Then he heard his mother's voice, angry and imperative. — The little season of her amiability had passed, and she was exigent again, demanding service. He must bring in some peats, fetch more water, shift a tethered ewe,

34

and shoot a black-backed gull that was threatening her pullets. — He locked the writing-desk, put the letter in his pocket, and went out to do her bidding.

It was still early when, on his bicycle, he rode into the village, and found it waking leisurely to another day. The sun, bright on the rough white-washed walls of the cottages, was skipping and leaping on the blue waters of the sea-loch beyond. Smoke rose in the first fullness of a newly kindled fire from a few chimneys; and there a door was opened, a cat put out. A little boy, blue-jerseyed and bare-footed, ran out of a narrow alley and stopped to shout beneath a dormer window; another small boy came out, and together, talking seriously, they went down to the shore. A stout man in shirt and trousers looked up at the clear sky, yawned prodigiously, and scratched his ribs.

On the pavement outside the principal shop in the village Christina McLeod was trying to take down the shutters, and, as usual, finding it difficult; for the hinges were old and stiff. She was a cheerful, stoutly built woman, broad in the beam, with plump and rosy cheeks; but her arms were short and her height was small. From the door of the shop she shouted inward, 'Morag! Are you there, Morag? Will you come and give me a hand, like a good girl?'

But before her daughter could obey the summons, an untidy, pretty, thin-faced girl came across the street — her hair unbrushed and lank, her stockings wrinkled, sleep in the corners of her eyes — and in a gentle voice exclaimed, 'It's a fine morning, Mrs. McLeod.'

'It is indeed, Mary, and you're up early to enjoy it.'

'Could you let me have a half a pound of tea, if the shop's open?'

'It's half-open, anyway. Just wait till I get the shutters down. — Reach up to it, Morag, will you?'

Morag, her daughter, came out, already dressed for school. She was neat and trimly shaped, as pretty as wild narcissus in a Ligurian spring, but demure and composed as a Victorian bride. Her seeming gentleness concealed a strong self-confidence. She greeted her untidy neighbour, and tried to lift the shutter from its unwilling hinges. Then McKellaig, having posted his letter, came down the

35

street, and Mrs. McLeod called him to help. He came readily enough, good-looking in his gillie's tweeds, and with easy strength took down the shutters.

Mrs. McLeod thanked him, and the untidy girl, to draw attention to herself, said: 'It's a grand life you have, Norman, just walking about like a gentleman all day.'

'And sometimes all night too,' said McKellaig. 'I haven't been in my bed since yesterday.'

'Were you led astray?' cried Mrs. McLeod, her red cheeks plumping with the joke.

'Ah, tell us who it was!' said the untidy girl. 'It wouldn't be Morag, would it?'

'That is no way to be talking!' said Morag indignantly.

'It was nothing of that kind at all,' said McKellaig, ill at ease.

'I'm sorry to hear it,' said Mrs. McLeod. 'For there's plenty of girls would be glad enough to hear you whistling at the end of the house, even though Morag said no to you —'

'Will you be quiet, Mother!' cried Morag. And with a trim display of temper, with an affronted look and a twirl of her skirt, she danced into the shop and left them.

'She's proud,' said the untidy girl, stooping to pull up her stockings.

'She is that,' said Mrs. McLeod.

'I was wondering,' said McKellaig, 'if Nicolas is in?'

'He is,' said Mrs. McLeod, her voice less friendly now, 'but you can't see him, Norman. He had a touch of lumbago when he woke up, so he's taking the morning in bed.'

'I am sorry to hear that,' said McKellaig. 'It's a sore thing, the lumbago.'

'I'll tell him you were asking for him.'

'Well,' said McKellaig, 'I had better be on my way — and I'll see him another time.'

'Goodbye, Norman,' said the untidy girl.

He got on his bicycle and rode off down the street, and Mrs. McLeod said softly, 'I hope to God Nicholas will always see you before you catch sight of him.'

'Is he bad with the lumbago?' asked the girl.

'He was out and away to the river an hour ago,' said Mrs. McLeod, 'but I wouldn't be telling that to Norman McKellaig, would I?'

'He's not so bad, when you know him,' said the girl. 'It's just a pity he won't get married.'

'Ho, ho!' said Mrs. McLeod, genial again. 'You can put McKellaig out of your mind! He's been disappointed once in the village, and he swore that never again would he try his luck with any girl in Laxdale; for there's pride in the man, though you mightn't think it.'

'It's not me that has any interest in him,' said the girl.

'And why should you?' asked Mrs. McLeod.

'It was just his old mother I was thinking of.'

'Ay,' said Mrs. McLeod, 'she's a warrior, that one. Well, come in and get your tea.'

CHAPTER FOUR

T H E General and his guests were still at breakfast. The General, a man with fewer affectations than most people, believed that the old Highland usage was to eat porridge afoot, as though alert for the day's business, or sudden enemies; and while the others sat conventionally at the table he walked up and down, supping his milk and meal, somewhat noisily, from a silver bowl. He wore an old tweed jacket, cut round in front and short to the haunch, a faded kilt ragged at the edge, and a shabby leather sporran: Catriona said he would not sit down, at that time in the morning, because their leather-seated chairs were too cold for one so clad. But the General declared that he maintained an old custom because the custom was sensible, and a useful aid to digestion. He could, moreover, look at the view when he was tired of listening to the conversation. Mr. Crantit was already talking with distinguished fluency.

'The newspapers and the radio,' he was saying, 'are much to blame for the present unhappiness of the world. For as they thrive on horror, fear, and vulgar frivolity, so they are eager to disseminate them, make the most of them, and propagate them more and more. And evil communications corrupt good manners, as everybody knows. — Or does everybody know? It is difficult to gauge the growth of ignorance since education became scientific.'

'Mr. Macaulay preached on evil communications last Sunday,' said Catriona.

'And you thought I was speaking about bad roads,' said Macaulay gloomily.

'I hope,' said Mr. Crantit, 'that you told your flock where

the quotation comes from? St. Paul, you know, was quoting Menander.'

'Menander?' the General inquired.

'A Greek dramatist,' said Mr. Crantit, 'of great interest at this crisis in our history; though not, I suppose, very widely known. He lived and wrote when Athens, like Britain, was embittered and impoverished by war; a diminished city with melancholy recollections of her former greatness, and a disenchanted knowledge that pride's heir is poverty and the fruits of political reform may be small and nauseating. But in spite of catastrophe and disillusion, Menander's temper was genial and polite. He was a cheerful, civilized man. It was he who discovered that they whom the gods love die young; but he comforted himself by taking a kindly interest in their survivors, less worthy though they might be, and stoutly declaring that nothing in humanity was alien to him, since he himself was human. — Yes, a charming person; and what a pretty choice a play of his would have been for our production here!'

'Then why aren't you doing one of his?' asked the General.

'Only fragments of his work survive,' said Mr. Crantit sadly.

The General, who had been contemplating through the long window the aspiring hills of Skye, turned and said to Swanson, 'Would you like to walk up the river this morning? There's no use trying to fish, of course, in weather like this; but I could show you the pools. Will you come, Catriona?'

'I don't think I can spare the time,' said Catriona. 'I want to rehearse Mr. Macaulay and some of the Chorus in the scene where the Second Messenger arrives. — You must make that long speech more interesting, and hold their attention,' she told the minister.

Macaulay wiped his mouth and folded his napkin. For a moment or two his hands lay flat upon the table, and with downcast head he seemed to be meditating some grave decision; perhaps even praying for strength to announce it. Then, slowly looking up, he gazed at Catriona with melancholy eyes and spoke in pulpit tones. 'In the sleepless watches of the night,' he said, 'I have been searching my

39

conscience; and what I found must be declared without hesitancy or equivocation, though it will not please you to hear it.'

'What are you going to say? You can't —'

'I can, and I must,' said Macaulay sadly. 'It is a play about idolaters, and even for your sake I cannot act the part of an infidel.'

'But you said you would! You promised. And now, with only ten days to go, the whole thing will be ruined!'

'I have been weak and foolish, I am much to blame,' said Macaulay. 'But it is a great mercy that I discovered my mistake in time. I might have continued in error, believing I was justified in playing the part, until the very morning of the performance.'

'Come, come!' said the General. 'We've been through all this before, and discussed both sides of the question. You knew perfectly well what the play was about when you agreed to act in it, and you can't let Catriona down now!'

'My conscience was sleeping,' said Macaulay, 'but now it is wide awake and speaking like a trumpet. I am truly sorry for the inconvenience I am causing, but the trumpeting of conscience cannot be silenced and must not be ignored.'

'That's all very well,' said the General, 'if you've got a conscience you can rely on to be sensible. But you haven't, and you know it.'

'You're not really going to let me down?' said Catriona, pleading with eyes as troubled as the minister's.

'It may be,' he said, 'that you will be making a fearful mistake if you perform this play. My conscience has warned me against it, and perhaps the warning was meant for more than me alone. A heathen play in Laxdale could have fearful consequences —'

'Now, now,' said the General, 'that's going too far. You can't expect other people to listen to your damned silly trumpeter.'

'After all the trouble I've gone to,' said Catriona hotly, 'do you think I'm going to give up the play now? Just because you couldn't sleep last night, and got up in a bad temper?'

'Nor can you deter us by talking about consequences,' said Mr. Crantit. 'It's our intention, or at least our hope, to provoke consequences.'

'Let's talk things over coolly and rationally,' said the General, 'and see what we can do to save the situation.' He drew up a chair and with an air of purpose seated himself beside the minister; Mr. Crantit moved to his other side, and Catriona, half indignant but half inclined to tears, sat opposite. Swanson stayed where he was, at the other end of the table, and listened to the argument with somewhat less than his whole attention.

Swanson had troubles of his own, from which, in a rather haphazard way, he had been trying to escape when the General found him in South Uist; and the shock of his re-introduction to Macaulay, with its painful reminder of his unfortunate gunnery, had reinforced his feeling that the world was a sorry place and kept him awake, disconsolate, for half the night. Sleepless, he had heard Macaulay in the next room tossing and turning on a noisy bed; and lying so near the victim of his ill-timed marksmanship, after so many years, he had felt that life was nothing but a baited trap. It was, then, with imperfect sympathy that he listened to the argument about a Greek tragedy.

Catriona's project was remarkable in more ways than one. To produce a play by Euripides, with village actors whose only dramatic experience was in little rural comedies, presented difficulties that no one could be blind to; and to produce it in the open air required such a faith in West Highland weather as few could hold. But even more impressive than her courage, and faith, and imagination — or lack of imagination — was her singular disregard of an audience, and her manifest contempt for publicity. The production had, indeed, been announced in two or three Highland newspapers, but with no more display, and at no greater length, than the simple tidings of a birth in this village, a death in that. Nowhere was the play advertised save on two small notice-boards which had been set up, one east of the pass on the hill-road into Laxdale, the other on the little jetty where, on Tuesday, Thursday and Saturday of one week, on Monday, Wednesday and Friday of the other, passengers might come aland from the steamer that lay anchored off-shore. Hand-printed by Catriona, the notices read:

41

At

LAXDALE HALL

on Friday, September 15th

at 2.30 p.m.

(weather permitting)

the

BACCHANALS of EURIPIDES

will be presented

in a new English translation

by

THE PEOPLE OF LAXDALE

A semi-circle of flat meadow-land, between a half-ruined water-mill on the river-bank and a solitary, steeply rising little hill called The Drum offered a natural amphitheatre and a picturesque background for the performance; but the only seating accommodation was two old garden benches and half a dozen deck-chairs that lay meanwhile in the lower storey of the mill. 'We'll keep them for old people,' Catriona had explained, 'and the others can sit on the heather. They'll bring rugs and macintoshes, I suppose, and if the weather's really bad, we'll put the play off for a day or two.'

Her lack of concern for an audience was deliberate, not due to forgetfulness; and to her father she had explained her theory very seriously. 'They've got to realize it's the play that's important,' she had said, 'and not them! I always feel that far too much is done for the general public, whether inside a theatre or out, and that's why I'm not going to put myself about for people who simply come to be entertained. If they do come, we'll be glad to see them, but they'll have to make all their own arrangements and not expect to be pampered. After all, we only want people who're really interested in the *Bacchanals*, and if they are interested, they'll make their own inquiries and be willing to put up with a little discomfort, won't they?'

'Don't you think you ought to advertise here and there?' the General had asked. 'Otherwise I don't see how people are going to

42

hear about the play — even the sort of people who make rather a point of being interested in Euripides.'

'The news will spread,' Catriona had assured him. 'Real news goes by word of mouth, and travels very quickly. The very fact that we don't advertise, and don't try to cajole people, will make the play talked about, and do more than anything else to bring the sort of people we want. We'll be something of a mystery, you see, and make them curious. — Oh, I'm not being fanciful, I promise you that! I really want a big audience, as big as we've room for, but I think the best way to get it is to say as little as possible about what we're going to do.'

'Well,' said the General, 'it's your affair, and you may be right. I haven't enough imagination, I suppose, to see it as you do.'

'Perhaps,' Catriona had added, after due reflexion, 'you had better shoot a few stags. If we get a big crowd, and the weather turns bad and they're stormbound, we shall have to feed them . . .'

She had taken no thought, however, to provide understudies and guard the play against a storm of temperament; and now Macaulay's defection seemed likely to wreck it. He would listen to no argument, though Mr. Crantit reminded him of the sermons in which he had defended Euripides' claim to Christian respect, and the General promised to accept all responsibility, both in this world and the next, for his appearance on a heathen stage. Macaulay could not be moved, nor his conscience answered; and Catriona, her cheeks a fevered pink, sat in a stricken silence of anger and dismay.

He got up, and went heavily to the door. Then, his hand upon the knob, he paused and turned, and pointed to Swanson. 'There,' he exclaimed, 'is a man with no scruples whatever! Ask him to act in your play. It will not worry him to play a heathen's part, for he is well used to it.'

He closed the door behind him, more loudly than he need have done, and Catriona said, 'So that's the explanation! It wasn't his conscience at all, it was just spite against Mr. Swanson — and we've got to suffer for it!'

'I think you've over-simplifying,' said the General. 'He's ill-balanced, poor fellow, but he's not wilfully dishonest.'

'It's spite,' repeated Catriona, 'nothing but spite, because Mr. Swanson told you about shooting him down, and made you laugh at him.'

'That wasn't my intention,' said Swanson unhappily, 'and it isn't my recollection of what happened. I thought you were laughing at me.'

'I'm not blaming you,' said Catriona, 'but what are we going to do?'

'Take Macaulay's advice,' said Mr. Crantit, 'and persuade Swanson to play the Messenger.'

'Will you?' asked Catriona.

'But I can't act! I haven't even tried to, since I was at the university, and I don't think I was any good then.'

'You have a loud, resonant voice,' said Mr. Crantit, 'and in Greek costume your figure may show to better advantage than in tweeds. Since you've been a soldier, you must have learnt how to stand still. A short beard will give you dignity — and there's all the equipment you need.'

'That would certainly get us out of our difficulty,' said the General, 'but I don't know what your plans are. Could you make arrangements, do you think, to stay here for another ten days?'

'As it happens,' said Swanson thoughtfully, 'that would suit me very well indeed.'

'Well then,' said the General to Catriona, 'there's your man!'

'Will you do it?' she asked. 'Oh, please say yes! I wouldn't ask you — I really wouldn't — if there was the slightest chance of finding anyone else. But there's no one here who'd be suitable!'

'Now there, surely,' said Mr. Crantit in great delight, 'is a plea that compels acceptance!'

'You'll get some good fishing if you stay,' said the General.

'I should like that,' said Swanson frankly; and thought of running water falling in an amber curve over granite boulders or flowing in a ponderous stream, rain-fed and curiously graven, down a long pool where salmon watched for gaudy flies, and felt their muscles flex, and laved their silver skin. — 'I should like that very much indeed!'

CHAPTER FIVE

F R O M a dark loch high on the moor, deep and gloomy where the hill rose steep above it, the Laxdale river tumbled over rocky falls into a long, slow-moving pool with open banks, and thence, by rapids where a copse of pines leaned eastward from the wind, ran in a serpentine channel that sometimes carried the stream over small beds of shingle, sometimes in swifter movement between rock walls that ferns and alder overhung; or roared through a granite linn under yellow plumes, then circled slowly in deep cauldrons and scoured round basins in the rock. Birch and rowan trees grew from its softer banks, and here and there, on drier ground, a single twisted pine spread its rough branches and gave the honeyed air a sharper scent. Some distance above a little pool called The Cruive a smooth granite ledge confined a bend of the river, and below the pool, for a mile or more, it ran like a lowland stream, past the ruined mill, and between green banks to the bridge that carried the road from the village to Laxdale Hall; and below the bridge it grew wide and noisy among great boulders, and met the tide, and with the Atlantic ebb was sucked into the sea.

On this fine morning, while the General and Catriona were arguing with Mr. Macaulay, Nicholas McLeod lay full-length on the rocky shelf above The Cruive, as still as stone, his gaze intent on a dark shape in the clear green water of the stream. Under a heather-bush that overhung the ledge was a silver grilse of six or seven pounds weight, with a little blood about its belly, that he had gaffed half an hour before. The fish he was watching, waiting for it to come into the shadow of the rock, was about the same size.

Nicholas McLeod, who owned the village shop, kept a motor-car for public hire, and represented Laxdale on the County Council, was a man of lean but massive build, with a combative strong jaw, the mobile lips of an orator, and light blue eyes that looked as frank and open as a child's. His hair still grew dark and curly, though grey now threaded it, and on his right arm, bared for fishing, a writhing snake had been tattooed. He was fifty-four, and all his life he had lived with much enjoyment and without offence except in one particular: he had the passion of a drunkard for poaching, and the artist's excuse that he excelled in it.

He had been a sailor in the merchant navy for some years, and served in both wars against Germany. From a submarine he had seen the coasts of Marmora and the Baltic in the first round; and in the second, in frigate or corvette, survived mischance and kept his watch from the White Sea to Java Head. When his father died, in the middle 'twenties, he had inherited a small general shop that sold paraffin and boiled sweets, boots for little boys and aprons for their grown sisters — tin-tacks and baked beans, flour and sugar, sauce in bottles and patent medicines — and retiring from the sea, had promptly married and settled down with the liveliest satisfaction. His young wife Christina grew angry when twice within the first month of marriage he stayed out all night, and she was a little frightened when he brought home his first salmon and, in November, a hind he had shot. But nothing could keep him from the river or the hill when the mood was on him, and presently she learnt to recognize the signs of an approaching foray — the imminence of the mood — and would resign herself to a night's anxiety. Though often suspect, Nicholas was never caught; yet she never ceased to be anxious.

In 1945, after his second war, Nicholas once again settled down to village life, as promptly as before, and when by a large majority he was elected to the County Council, Mrs. McLeod thought her troubles were over and his new dignity would keep him safe at home. But before darkness fell, on the very day of his election, he had shot a thirteen-stone stag, and by the next dawn he had brought it home and was expertly cutting it up to present collops of venison to his supporters. General Matheson, retired from the service, came home about the same time, and a year or two later appointed McKellaig to be his keeper. Nicholas and McKellaig disliked each other, and Nicholas found a new relish in poaching when he could do it under McKellaig's nose. His forays became the deliberate assertion of his superiority to the keeper in field-craft and knowledge of the chase, and grew bolder with the years; though not more frequent, for there was no greed in his enthusiasm.

For more than a month he had not taken a fish — not since the poachers from outside, by their wholesale thievery, had given everyone in Laxdale a revulsion against poaching of any sort; and the good weather, indeed, had made it difficult. But the day before, walking peacefully along the river bank, he had seen a pair of grilse in the run beyond The Cruive, stayed there by the shallowness of the stream, and the temptation had been too strong. The bend of the river where they lay was only a couple of miles from the village, and less than that from McKellaig's cottage: to take the fish, in broad daylight, would be as risky as stealing the spoons from a policeman's table, and need planning as well as dexterity. But Nicholas had made his plan, and all his attention was concentrated now upon the second fish.

Head to the slow current, it wavered in the stream, now drifting down a little way, now with a ripple of its tail shooting forward and with minute flexure of its fins holding the ground it gained. But slowly, yielding to a lateral pressure of the current and the attraction of the shade, it came nearer to the granite ledge; and in still water, dark as a figure in a room at dusk, the grilse lay motionless. Gently breaking the surface the steel hook of the gaff went down, and Nicholas's hand, the writhing serpent on his forearm, dipped deep into the river and slowly travelled forward. A quick pull, and the calm was shattered. The darkened glass of the water broke into bright fragments, and the placid strength of the fish became a molten fury in the maelstrom of its desperation. The quiet water splashed in sudden fountains, the surface of the run broke into wild eddies, and for a moment, pulled off his balance, Nicholas came near to falling in the pool. But the weight of his body re-asserted itself, the strength of his arm brought up the fish, and

47

its bending pain was quickly stilled. For a moment he admired its silver plumpness, stroking its cold side, and then, rising to his knees, searched the rough slopes beyond the stream with quick, far-sighted eyes. He had heard, far off, a young dog barking, and recognized its voice. Before leaving home he had told his youngest child, a lively boy of twelve called Peter, to keep an eye on McKellaig's house, and warn him if McKellaig, newly back from the hill, showed untimely interest in the lower reaches of the river. Peter had a black and white collie, nine months old, that would bark or be quiet, go this way or that, as he commanded; and its shrill out-cry was clearly a warning.

Putting the two fish into a sack, Nicholas forded the river at the upper end of the run, and moving swiftly through the heather came unobtrusively to a little knoll from which he could see much of the land between the river and the village. A mile away, or rather less, he perceived McKellaig, with one uplifted, minatory arm, signalling to someone unseen; and now the dog was silent. Peter had done as he was told, and having surprised McKellaig was protesting his innocence and showing to the keeper's anger a face of childish bewilderment; while his collie, crouching at his heels, watched with bright eyes, its pink tongue pendant from black lips.

Presently McKellaig, with long determined steps, moved down towards the meadows, and the shortest way from the road to The Cruive; and Nicholas, after a little thought, took an opposite and nearly parallel course, using every bank and hillock and bush for cover, towards the upper part of the village and the school where Morag taught, that stood at its landward end.

CHAPTER SIX

A
N hour or so later the General and Swanson were walking slowly upstream on the south side of the river. Exposed by nearly a month of drought, long banks of dazzling white shingle reflected the morning sun, and over the diminished water in a secluded pool dragonflies darted in iridescent flight, or poised in the still air as though suspended on gossamer. Through the leaves of an old birch tree, with a thick gnarled trunk of tarnished silver, the light fell in golden drops that sank into the stream and seemed to light it from below. On a strip of sand a wagtail ran, dipping its stern, with quick, high-lifting steps, and from the heather a hundred yards away a cock-grouse called. Between turf and bracken, and tall heather in flower, the narrow track climbed steeply where the river tumbled over a rocky linn, and they stood to look back at the blue Atlantic sea and the islands anchored in its depths. The sea enclosed them on the one side, and in front of them rose the rough mountain that divided Laxdale from the rest of Scotland.

'I'm very glad,' said the General, 'that you're going to help Catriona with this play of hers. I don't think she'll make a success of it — I only hope it won't be an utter wash-out — but she's set her heart on doing it, and I want her to get what satisfaction she can out of it.'

'It's a curious choice for a village production,' said Swanson.

'It's not what I would have suggested, but then I haven't got a mind like hers. She went to the university for a year, you know. She'd had enough of it by then, of course, but that's where she met Crantit.'

'I've heard him talking on the wireless,' said Swanson.

'He could talk anywhere, I should think. — Well, Catriona persuaded him to make a new translation of this play, and come here to help her with it; and I couldn't say a word against it, because it was just the sort of thing her mother might have done. She had a serious mind too. She was American: a Boston family with a good deal of money, all gone now, and a great sense of responsibility that's still alive. Americans of that sort are full of good intentions. I suppose they're the only idealists left in the world: they still believe that people can be improved.'

'When the contemporary view,' said Swanson, 'is that they can only be drilled.'

'But I'm not sure,' said the General, 'that they're right in setting so much store on the pursuit of happiness.'

'They go into training for it,' said Swanson.

'Yes, that's the real difference between us! They're earnest about things, whether they're right or not, and we aren't. And Catriona, in that respect, is very American. — I live here in Laxdale, you see, because I like it. I like the country, and I'm fond of the people. I get all the amusement I want, and I do what I can to look after my property and keep people comfortable. — But that's not enough for Catriona. She's just as fond of Laxdale as I am, but she wouldn't live here if she'd no better reason than that.'

'She does a lot for the village, does she?'

'Yes, a great deal — and some of it's very useful.'

'I suppose people should be encouraged to live fuller lives,' said Swanson, 'but I wonder if it helps very much to give them intellectual tit-bits off other people's plates?'

'Now don't misunderstand her,' said the General. 'That's not her plan at all. Here in Laxdale we *are* living a full life — so she says — and she thinks it her duty to attract attention to it.'

'Then this play of hers — '

'So far as I understand it,' said the General, 'the theme is that you can't ignore nature, without nature having its revenge. Well, Catriona thinks the world has taken the wrong turning — you may have heard that before — and all this herding into big cities, the regimentation of politics and industry, are sterilizing human life and inciting nature to take reprisals.'

'So humanity, to save itself, must acknowledge the power of earth and air, and the old simple rule of the seasons?'

'That's about it; and the reward, she says, will be a new zest in life and the sort of joy that only primitive people have retained. But there, of course, she's thinking like an American: about the pursuit of happiness.'

'If everyone went back to nature,' said Swanson, 'you might find Laxdale uncomfortably crowded.'

'That has occurred to me,' said the General, and stopped to light his pipe. Swanson, uncertain to what extent his host was in serious agreement with Catriona, looked at him with a puzzled expression, and the General said, in his mildest voice, 'I daresay you had some extravagant ideas when you were young.'

'I live in the country myself,' said Swanson hastily. 'I think there's a lot in what she says.'

'There may be,' said the General, 'I'm not so sure. I know people who've lived all their lives among open fields, and still they've got minds like a continental slum. — But the thing is that tomorrow, when this fellow Pettigrew and his wife arrive, and the rest of the party, I want you to be on Catriona's side if they choose to poke fun at her. There's bound to be some talk of the play, and they may think it rather an odd thing to do. Which, of course, it is.'

'It's a good choice of a play for her purpose, and if I'm to take part, I certainly shan't laugh at it.'

'We may have a week of rain,' said the General for his own comfort, 'and then the performance will be indefinitely postponed. — But there's going to be no rain today, is there? Look what the drought's done to this pool. This is the White Pool, and a very good one too, when the river's in order.'

'Is that a dead fish over there?'

'It's improbable — but it does look like one, doesn't it?'

At the far end of the pool, where the bank had fallen in and a drift of leaves and broken twigs moved slowly in a listless eddy, a salmon palely floated, and when they had pulled it in they saw that it had not long been dead, and from the bruised line on its head and the torn gills it was clear enough how it had been killed. The inference was clear, but puzzling. No one in Laxdale had a net — the General felt sure of that — and certainly no one in Laxdale would take the risk and go to the trouble of netting the river when there were so few fish in it. Therefore poachers from outside, perhaps the same gang who had previously invaded the parish, must have been at work again. They had gone to the Long Pool, probably, three or four miles upstream, and the salmon, breaking free of the net, had been carried down by the current till the eddy caught it. — But the poachers who had cleaned the river before were experts at the game. Why had they returned when the water was so low? And what had McKellaig been doing, who should have been watching the road?

The General sat on the bank with a sad, abstracted air, and as if to comfort it, patted the dead fish. 'Poor chap,' he said, 'it's a damned shame to have been caught like that. You'd have fought like a hero, wouldn't you ? — That's what makes me really angry with these filthy, commercial poachers: they don't give the fish a chance! Oh, I resent their spoiling the river, and robbing me of my fun, but what I loathe them for is their lack of sportsmanship. They're brutes. They're impercipient, degraded brutes. I'm not a fanciful sort of fellow, and I don't believe that the death of any of God's creatures, from a six-ounce trout to a six-foot Guardsman, is necessarily an outrage against the established order of things. But I do believe in decency. I believe there's a proper way of fishing, and a proper way of going to war. A natural, decent way in which the fish gets a chance to escape, if he's good enough, and victory goes to the chap with the better eye, and a better appreciation of the ground, and the guts to earn it. What's ruining us all is commerce and machinery: everything gets turned into money nowadays, and any cad can drive a motor-car. There's no respect for natural order, and the world's turning into a factory whose only rulers are production-experts and chartered accountants. These poachers are typical of the whole process: they're so damned efficient they can make hundreds of pounds by a night's work, and leave desolation behind them. And they care for nothing because they know nothing — nothing except how to drive a motor-car and find a market for stolen goods.'

Swanson, a fisherman himself, sympathized with the General's emotion, but was surprised and a little embarrassed by the scale and depth of his feeling. He was almost as indignant with the spoilers of the world as were the Bacchanals, in the play his daughter was producing, with the foolish king whose rationalism, so long ago, had stopped the sap and robbed the joy of life. Scratch a soldier, thought Swanson, and find a mystic. Sandhurst and a good regiment give him the disguise of fine manners, but there's the essence: the birds and beasts he kills are part of his life, and he not only loves but respects them.

The General mastered his distress, and searched his pockets for the piece of string he always carried. He found a stout twig of birch, and made a handle to carry the fish. 'Let's go and look for McKellaig,' he said, 'and see what's he got to say for himself.'

They set off down-stream, with no more talk. The General went at a shepherd's pace, and Swanson was hard-pressed to keep up with him. They found McKellaig, apparently idle, at the rocky ledge above The Cruive; and he told a circumstantial story of walking far afield, the night before, to investigate a rifle-shot he had heard from the northern slopes of the hill.

'But you found nothing?'

'Nothing at all.'

'And you were away from the road for two or three hours?'

'It was maybe more.'

'So the poachers got in and out again, without interference.'

'It looks like it indeed.'

'Well, there's no other way to explain this fish, is there?'

'The poachers from outside,' said McKellaig slowly, 'are not the only ones. I asked to see Nicholas McLeod this morning, and Christina told me he was in bed with the lumbago. But then I met Willy John Watt, and he had seen Nicholas out for a walk. So I thought I would take a look along the river, and Nicholas's boy, Peter, came after me with a young dog he has. I waited for him and told him to go home; and the dog set up a barking you could hear a mile away.'

'I don't see anything very suspicious in that.'

'It may have been intended for a warning. For there was no one here, when I came, but there on the rock, if you will look, there are two spots of blood.'

'It may be blood,' said the General. 'I'm not so sure. — Do you know if there were any fish in this run?'

'I had not seen them, if there were; but Nicholas has the sharpest eye in the parish.'

'It seems a pity I haven't got him for a keeper, instead of you.'

'That would suit him very nicely,' said McKellaig.

'Well, there's one thing I'm sure of,' exclaimed the General, 'and that is that he wouldn't use a net. He may take a fish or two now and then — I've no doubt he does — but he doesn't take them wholesale, like those brutes from outside.'

'You could go and have a word with him,' said McKellaig. 'You could ask him about his lumbago.'

'I suppose I ought to,' said the General doubtfully. 'I've got no grudge against Nicholas, but it's rather too much of a good thing if he's taking fish from one end of the river, and that Glasgow gang's robbing the other. — What are you going to do?' he asked Swanson.

'I promised to see Crantit and have a talk about the play.'

'Yes, that's a good idea. You haven't too much time, have you? — Here, McKellaig, you take the fish. Take it down to the house, will you? And I'll go to the village.'

CHAPTER SEVEN

BECAUSE of the prevailing scarcity of teachers, and the disinclination of town-bred young men to live in so remote a place as Laxdale, Morag McLeod had been in sole charge, for the last six months, of the twenty-nine children who attended the village school; and it was fortunate for them, as well as for herself, that considerable strength of character underlay the sweet demureness of her look. She could have sat as a model to Greuze, or set an example to pioneers. Mr. Crantit, when he first saw her, had been moved to singular enthusiasm: 'A proper little honeypot!' he said. But the honey was spiced with sharper flavours, and here and there a peppercorn lay buried. She found no difficulty in maintaining discipline, and she succeeded in giving a measure of instruction to twenty-nine boys and girls whose ages ranged from six to fourteen.

The school consisted of two classrooms divided by folding doors, which now stood open to make one fairly spacious room. The smallest children sat in front, and the cleverest of the elder ones gave half their time to coaching them. Morag would begin the day by allotting separate tasks to each of her classes, and divide her attention between them as might be convenient. She was unceasingly busy, but usually she maintained an air of unhurried ease and gentle composure. This morning, however, there was a frosty sparkle in her eyes and her voice was sharp and unfriendly.

She had remembered, on her way to school, that she had forgotten to lock the large teacher's desk which stood, like a pulpit, in front of the shabby rows of little desks; and because she was pleased to think herself methodical, she had rebuked herself for carelessness. She kept a strap in the desk, and to steal the teacher's strap would be a very pretty exploit for some bold boy. But when she arrived, though half the children were there before her, the strap was safe enough; and in such security as the desk afforded lay two freshly caught grilse of about six or seven pounds weight. For a moment she stared at them, bewildered, and then with sudden comprehension, and anger as quick, slammed down the lid and turned the key in the lock. But her brother Peter was late, and two other boys with him, and she had to unlock the desk again to find the strap for them. Two of the smallest children began to cry in sympathy, and lessons began, under an air of constraint, to the sound of sniffing.

By half-past eleven Morag's temper was calmer, but the children were still wary of her and unusually quiet; and at half-past eleven there was a knock at the door and the General came in. He bade her good morning and, a little gruff with embarrassment, inquired if she could spare him a few minutes of her time.

'Stand up, children,' said Morag, and put her hand on the desk to make sure it was locked. 'Stand up, and say good morning politely.'

Solemnly the children rose: moon-faced infants, little girls with sharp eyes, little girls who tittered nervously, a clumsy boy who let his slate fall with a clatter, pale-straw-thatched boys and a boy like a Spanish gypsy, hobbledehoys and sensitive, startled children and girls old enough to be self-conscious and wriggle in their tightening frocks — and the General, benign but a little shy, smiled and made some pleasant, jocular remark; whereupon they all looked more solemn than before.

'Do you think you can leave them for a moment?' he asked. 'I shan't keep you long, but — well, I'd rather speak privately.'

Warning the children to be quiet, Morag went out into the small playground, and the General, after commenting without much interest on the fine weather, inquired, 'Have you seen your father this morning?'

'No, not this morning,' said Morag carefully.

'I'm in a difficulty, Morag, and I think I ought to have a word with him. But he isn't in the shop, and your mother didn't know where he'd gone.'

56

'He is maybe taking a walk.'

'McKellaig,' said the General, 'thought he might have been taking a walk along the river.'

'Then he was doing no harm along the river,' said Morag hotly, 'or he would never have let McKellaig see him!'

'McKellaig didn't actually see him, but there were signs, or possible signs, of a fish being taken out of that little run above The Cruive; and quite certainly there was someone using a net last night, farther up the river.'

'It's not my father who would be using a net!'

'No, I don't think he would — but I should very much like to know what he has been up to.'

'My father,' said Morag, 'has never done anything to spoil the river or hinder you from catching all you need! And if he likes a little sport from time to time, it's because he is just the same as yourself when it comes to salmon and suchlike.'

'But I've offered him a day's fishing again and again, and he always refuses.'

'It would be a mean thing,' said Morag, 'to go fishing in the morning, at your invitation, and go out at night too, without your knowledge.'

'And if he has to make a choice, he prefers darkness and his own methods?'

'Perhaps he did, when he was a young man. But that is a long time ago now.'

'Well,' he said, as though reluctant to make so unfriendly a point, 'there's someone poaching: there's no doubt about that.'

'Then surely it is McKellaig you should be talking to? It is his business to look after your salmon, not mine!'

'Morag, my dear' — for the first time there was a hint of temper in the General's voice — 'if there's one thing I'm thankful for, it is that I'm not a helpless little boy with you for my teacher. But if I were an old reprobate like your father, I'd be pleased, I admit, to have you as a daughter. Good morning!'

He turned at the gate, however, and shouting 'Hey, Morag!' came quickly back. Morag waited for him on the steps.

'There's one other thing,' he said, 'that I meant to speak about. The public meeting tonight. If you could help with the arrangements —'

'You should see my father about that. It is he who is the local representative on the Education Committee of the County Council, and responsible for the school.'

'But you're the teacher, and all I want you to do is to get some of the bigger boys to take out the desks, after you're finished this afternoon, and bring in the benches we always use for a meeting. You can do that, can't you?'

'Whatever is right for me to do, I shall do with pleasure,' she said, her voice still hard. 'The school will be clean and tidy when you come.'

'You're a good girl,' said the General with a sigh. 'It's reaction, I suppose. Well, goodbye, Morag, and thank you.'

A little tremulous after her bold display, a little unhappy after the expense of so much spirit, she waited on the steps till she could control her feelings; and with reviving strength felt anger growing against her father, who had soiled her desk with his shameless, glittering plunder, and left her, with intolerable unfairness, to shield him from suspicion and disarm inquiry with a look of innocence! Her cheeks grew pink with the renewal of her wrath, and already rehearsing some good, wounding phrases for the domestic argument she anticipated when she went home, she returned to the classroom.

She opened the door, and halted by astonishment, stood upon the threshold. — The children had come crowding forward, some laughing, some gravely fascinated, to stare at a large globe of the world which had been lifted from its usual corner by a tall man, of lean but massive build, who now, with a gleam of honest enjoyment on his brown face, stood behind it and with arms outstretched, like an orator in his passion or a cheapjack on a fair-ground, was telling his entranced audience, 'Laxdale, I say, is the very centre of the world, and you ought to be proud of living here! We're in the middle of everything, and all the great, important places of the earth just dangle round us on what is called the circumference. And if there's anyone here who doesn't believe me, I can prove it in half a minute!'

'What new mischief is this?' demanded Morag.

'Is it yourself, Morag?' said Nicholas, turning to greet her with a smile of welcome and a portentous wink. 'I saw you colloguing with the Laird out-by, and I wasn't wanting to interrupt you; so I came in by the other door, and to pass the time I asked the children a question or two in geography. And they're backward, Morag. They're very backward.'

'Do you not think you have given me trouble enough for one day?'

'I am here,' said Nicholas, 'in my capacity as local representative on the Education Committee of the County Council. Be patient, like a good girl, and I'll talk to you in a minute. — And now watch carefully, children, and I'll prove what I was saying.'

He took a drawing-pin from the desk and a piece of white tape that Morag had used for tying a bundle of exercise-books; and pinning one end of the tape to what was approximately the position of Laxdale on the globe, described a circle from his arbitrary centre.

'Look there!' he said. 'There's the bottom end of Greenland, where the whole sea's alive with cod-fish, and the polar-bears get so hot with chasing them, they have to sit on icebergs to cool themselves; and here, the very same distance away, is Moscow, the capital of Russia, and it's full of cod too, and Russian bears; and down here, still at the same distance, is the Rock of Gibraltar where the Union Jack flies at the entrance to the Mediterranean. And right in the middle of those three places is Laxdale, where I'm talking to you now! — And look at this, will you? There's New York, the biggest, richest city in the world; and there's Basra, one of the hottest places in the world, where the oil comes from that takes the New Yorkers to work in the morning; and there's Bathurst, the capital of Gambia, which was the very first colony we ever had in Africa. And all those places are the same distance from Laxdale, and here's Laxdale in the middle. — And now we'll take more of the tape, and we find a place called Okinawa, where the Americans and the Japanese had a great battle; and here's the Nicobar Islands, where they use coconuts for money, as I know very well, for I was shipwrecked there in the war; and here's Kimberley, where they dig diamonds like we dig potatoes; and Rio de Janeiro, the capital of Brazil; and Callao, which is in Peru, where I once had a fight with a policeman. I hit him on the jaw with my closed fist, and he went sailing across the whole breadth of the street, and landed on the opposite wall like a drop-scone on a girdle —'

'That's enough of your nonsense!' cried Morag angrily. 'I'm not going to have the whole day wasted!'

'Rouse their imagination,' said Nicholas, 'and they'll learn their own lessons. I'm saving you trouble, Morag. — And now, children, look at the globe for yourselves, and study it out, while I have a word with your teacher.'

He took her by the arm, and leading her out, closed the door behind them. 'Have you got the key?' he asked.

'The key's in my bag,' said Morag, 'and there it'll stay!'

'I couldn't get home with the fish,' said Nicholas, 'for McKellaig was after me, and if I'd tried to go back to the shop he'd have seen me. But there's an easy way to the school —'

'So you took the risk of getting me into trouble, to save yourself.'

'What trouble could you have?'

'What did the Laird come for, do you think? And do you suppose I enjoyed myself, pretending I knew nothing about it, with a couple of grilse in the desk, and a blackguard of a father that I told him was quite the reformed character nowadays?'

'Did you tell him that?' exclaimed Nicholas in delight.

'I implied it,' said Morag with dignity.

'It's what I would expect of you! And now, to be on the safe side, give me the key of the desk, and I'll come back when it's dark and get the fish.'

'It is my desk,' said Morag hardily, 'but I have no proof that the fish are yours.'

'And what will you do with them,' asked Nicholas, 'if I leave them where they are?'

'I haven't made up my mind yet. I may tell Norman McKellaig to come and get them.'

'Indeed,' said Nicholas, 'that would be a fine way to encourage him.'

'It's a couple of years since Norman lost interest in me, Father. It's only you he's interested in now.'

'And I feel the same way about him as you did: he's better kept at a distance. — Be sensible, now, and give me the key.'

'I will not!' said Morag, and returning to the classroom, slammed the door in his face.

CHAPTER EIGHT

MR. MACAULAY had written a dignified letter to say that in the circumstances he had thought it better to return to his manse; where, despite the lack of a housekeeper, he could make himself comfortable enough for a man with simple tastes. He was grateful to the General for his offer of hospitality, he said, but a guest who had so greatly disappointed his hosts in one respect, could hardly fail to displease them in others. — The General and Catriona agreed that it was a pity he regarded the breach so seriously, but without much debate decided to let him have his own way. And at dinner Catriona interrupted Mr. Crantit to say, complacently, how much tidier the table looked with only four people. 'I like even numbers,' she said.

'We'll have eight tomorrow, won't we?' said the General. 'The four of us, Pettigrew and his wife, Marvell, and the chap from the Scottish Office.'

'We can give Mr. and Mrs. Pettigrew a bathroom to themselves,' said Catriona, 'and Mr. Crantit is sharing father's. But Mr. Marvell and Mr. Flett will have to use yours, I'm afraid,' she told Swanson.

Swanson said he thought that could be arranged without undue discomfort, and Mr. Crantit resumed, a little impatiently, the discourse which had been so unnecessarily broken off.

'As a teacher myself,' he said, 'though teaching as little as may be to next to nobody, I am appalled — but quite appalled! — by the monstrous burden that lies on the very pretty shoulders of the girl called Morag McLeod. I went to see her this afternoon, and found her in charge — the spiritual trustee and appointed mentor — of twenty-nine children, the youngest of them dribbling babes, and the eldest incipient ploughmen with great knuckled hands and the eyes of young satyrs. That girl is a heroine, and may well become a martyr!'

'There were two teachers till six months ago,' said the General, 'but old Ross, the headmaster, died, and we haven't been able to replace him.'

'What a sinister humbug education, as we know it, is!' said Mr. Crantit. 'What a grandiose and frightful swindle! — The great majority of the tax-payers who finance it still believe that education, as prescribed by government, is designed for the individual benefit of every child who submits to it; though it is, of course, designed for no such purpose. It's designed to cut and shape poor children into useful, nicely fitting little pieces of machinery in the vast work-shop of the modern state. And teachers, mark you, admirable teachers with wisdom and benignity in their hearts, are equally enslaved by stultifying ordinances, and perpetually harassed by itinerant foremen whose only interest is to see that human infants are reduced to a mechanical specification in a statutory space of years.'

'Schools can't be wholly bad,' said Catriona sensibly, 'or some-body would have discovered it before you.'

'One thing only,' said Mr. Crantit, 'prevents our established system of education from crumbling into the dust and ashes of the minds which devised it, and that is the stubborn virtue of individual teachers. Teachers who, under-paid and over-worked in a revolting environment — breathing daily the inspissated odours of boyhood and unclean clothes — stand like missionary saints against the hypocrisy of their present employment and the barbarism of tomorrow!'

'Morag,' said the General, seeking in personalities a refuge from the pessimism of general topics, 'is over-worked. We all know that. But she's a young woman of great character — she put me in my place today — and I really don't think her responsibilities weigh too heavily on her.'

'What would you do to reform education?' asked Swanson.

'I should make it very difficult to acquire,' said Mr. Crantit promptly, 'and thereby stimulate an appetite for it, and enhance the respect paid to it.'

'Surely it would be wrong to abolish compulsory education,' said Catriona.

'There's no such thing, my dear girl. No one has ever been educated except by his own volition, and the fortuitous impact on it of a superior, procreative mind. What is compulsory, unfortunately, is the dispatch of helpless children to ugly schools where they are forcibly fed on pasteurized language, pasteurized history, and nowadays, at eleven o'clock in the morning, on pasteurized milk; thereby destroying every scrap of resistance, whether instinctive in the soul or bacillary in the gut, and gradually softening their minds to receive whatever impressions our ruling caucus may wish to print upon them.'

'You're condemning education because it's systematic,' said Swanson, 'but can you imagine education without a system?'

'Easily,' said Mr. Crantit. 'If education were regarded as a creative art, which it is, the dedicated teacher would set himself up as an artist does, and apply for custom. The brilliant teacher would be surrounded by a swarm of pupils, the man of talent would gather a respectable following, and the worthless, uninspired preceptor would very properly starve.'

'There'd be glib fellows,' said the General, looking at his watch, 'who'd talk a lot of nonsense and draw the biggest crowd of all.'

'The naturally gullible, those who by temperament are addicted to the spurious, would attend the glib fellows,' said Mr. Crantit, 'but they would never ripen in any case. They would be no loss.'

'Well, that may be so — but it's twenty past eight, and we've got to go to the meeting.'

'It was advertised for half-past seven,' said Swanson.

'Yes, meetings always are. But no one expects them to begin till about half-past eight; or later than that if it's a concert or a dance. But I think we should make a start.'

The evening was mild and still, the sky not grossly dark, and they walked through the village to the school; Swanson with the

General, and Catriona, still anxious to learn new theories of education, with Mr. Crantit.

'Crantit,' said the General, 'got quite warm tonight.'

'Very warm,' said Swanson. 'Morag's an extremely pretty girl.'

'Do you think she was at the back of it all? That talk about teachers being saints and missionaries?'

'He began with an admiring reference to her shoulders.'

'So he did, I'd forgotten that. Well, really, that's rich. I'd never have thought of it! But an idea's got to start somewhere, I suppose, and quite a lot, I dare say, started with pretty girls. And perhaps as many with plain women. — How old do you think he is?'

'Rising forty?'

'Yes, about that; and a bachelor. You never know what's going on in a man's mind at that age; or at any other age, unless he's a hunting man. They just think about horses. — Well, well, I am pleased about that! I'll have to keep my eye on Crantit.'

Delighted by the thought of sentiment flowering in so unsuspected a hothouse as Mr. Crantit's scholarly mind, the General walked more briskly, chuckling at intervals, until he reached the school; where he greeted a little group of elderly men who, gossiping contentedly, waited near the lighted door. Crantit and Catriona arrived; and Catriona and the General, at once engaged in conversation by people with whose affairs they seemed to be intimately acquainted, moved slowly into the classroom where, beneath the slightly swaying light of two paraffin lamps, hung from the ceiling, some forty people already seated on long backless benches were exchanging the news of the day with great liveliness and volubility. Catriona and the General, as much inclined to gossip as any of their neighbours, greeted one after another of the audience to inquire about their beasts and their harvests, their boats and their broken fences, their sons and their daughters-in-law; and no one showed any impatience to begin the business of the meeting.

Nicholas McLeod, however, in a little group at the back of the room, was quieter than usual, and took care to avoid the General's eye and keep as far from him as he could; while Morag spoke to no one, and by her appearance of unnatural calm provoked the suspicion, among several of her neighbours, that the dignity of being a schoolmistress had gone to her head. They looked at her sideways, and whispered together, and said she was too proud by half. But the truth was that Morag was unhappy, and a little frightened.

In her anger with her father she had put off reconciliation until, having changed her frock for the meeting, she found her temper also changing; and by then it was after eight o'clock. She gave him the key of the desk and Nicholas went hurriedly to the school, but found half a dozen early arrivals comfortably seated in the lighted room. So the grilse were still in the desk, and Morag was praying that the General would not become too animated when he rose to address the audience. For the lid of the desk was loose at the hinges, the lock was none too strong; and should he emphasize a point with too forceful a hand, there might be an embarrassing disclosure.

Swanson and Crantit had remained outside to smoke their pipes. 'We have plenty of time,' said Mr. Crantit, 'for here, where modern comfort has hardly made its appearance, the primal luxuries are unimpaired.'

The dark air was still warm, and in a sky that few clouds obscured bright stars drew attention to yet more distant swarms of light. The road lay fifty feet above the sea-loch, and slowly they walked beside it as if on the deck of a ship sailing quietly through a deep and kindly sea.

'Tell me,' said Crantit, 'what sort of life you lead.'

'A fairly normal life, I think.'

'Oh, no, no! That's quite impossible. You're an author, a successful novelist —'

'Indeed I'm not. I've never been farther from success — in the common meaning of the word.'

'Surely that goes to show your life can't be normal? You've written a dozen or so novels, all of them popular, I believe, and some of them justly so. You've earned success — in the common meaning of the word.'

'Thank you.'

66

'I don't pretend,' said Crantit in his kindliest voice, 'to have read all your books, but I have read two or three. And though historical novels are not my favourite fiction, I was favourably impressed by the orderly and civilized style of your writing. You write English — and that is something of a distinction nowadays.'

'One owes a certain respect to words,' said Swanson gruffly. He disliked, and even feared, discussion of his books; for though in private he thought highly of them, he was too diffident to be sure of his opinion when others questioned it.

'One does indeed!' exclaimed Crantit. 'Words demand the utmost of our respect, and how seldom they get it! Because, of course, respect isn't easy. It implies close attention and devotion to its object. From time to time, at least, an exclusive devotion. The author who treats the raw material of his trade with the respect that's due to it must shut himself away from the world and live like an anchorite. And there's the paradox, for of all men the author is most closely involved in life, and yet to be an author he must live like a monk remote from life! Now you can't pretend that that's a normal existence, can you?'

'What I meant,' said Swanson, 'is that I'm married, I have a family — '

'How many?'

'Five. Three girls and two boys.'

'Good God!'

'They're quite young,' said Swanson apologetically. 'I married in 1938.'

'And do you live with your family, the year round, on your — forgive me saying so — your brumous Shetland isle?'

'Usually, yes. Since the war, that is. I've been away for the last two or three months, but not by my own choice.'

'You alarm me,' said Crantit, 'and I'll tell you why. — It has long been obvious that man has only a limited faculty for being good. Probity has its frontiers, respectability is never complete. Men of the worthiest appearance live hidden lives — you can think of examples for yourself — and it seems to me that an author, such as yourself, whose regard for good form is lavished on every page, must exhaust his goodness in his writing and lead, for the rest, a dissolute, reprobate and quite unruly existence. It was in the hope of such a revelation that I inquired the manner of your life. I certainly didn't expect to hear of bourgeois felicity — five children in twelve years does smack of fidelity — and I don't believe you have told me the whole story yet.'

'The General,' said Swanson, 'lives in Laxdale because he likes it. I live in Shetland because I like it. You needn't look deeper than that for a reason.'

'But where's your outlet? What are your vices? You're a scrupulous writer, a philoprogenitive householder: and they're activities that must drain respectability to the very dregs. Well, what's the other side of the picture? Your life can't all be sterling effort and the reward of an easy mind.'

'Whatever the effort was,' said Swanson, 'that isn't the reward. I've got a coolie's load of worry on my mind — and if you really want to know, I've been on the run for the last three months.'

'My dear Swanson, you've no idea how relieved I am! Your life becomes credible, the good manners of your style are comprehensible, and your next book, I'm sure, will be a masterpiece. Tell me more.'

'No, I don't want to. Other people are involved.'

'They always are, that is inevitable. But you can trust my sympathy. Like our good Menander I confess humanity and admit that nothing man does can be alien to me.'

For a minute or two they walked in silence on the starlit road. Then Swanson, clearly troubled, stopped and said, 'I didn't mean to give myself away like that. It slipped out because I've been worrying too much; and like a little boy who wets his trousers, I lost control for a moment. But you won't say anything, will you?'

'Most assuredly not. It is secret between us, locked in my bosom; but if on reflexion, you think I can help you — with advice, I mean — you have only to ask. I have had trouble myself: even I, an inoffensive don.'

'We ought to turn and go back, or we'll miss the meeting.'

'I had forgotten all about it. Such is the charm of conversation! But you're right; or our host will be offended.'

They were a full mile from the village, and having turned, they walked more briskly; and both, for some little while, were silent. Then Crantit said, 'This delegation that's coming tomorrow, these politicians and their followers, may be unwelcome to you, if you are very strictly in hiding here. — What a good place it is to hide in!'

'No, they won't affect me. They won't be staying more than a few days, and it isn't generally known that I'm — well, in difficulties.'

'The hue and cry hasn't yet been raised?'

'Not yet,' said Swanson grimly.

For several minutes Mr. Crantit was happily engaged in speculation on the probable nature of Swanson's plight; and then, in a very friendly and confiding manner, said: 'It's a good thing, you know, that Macaulay has left us. He might have made things very awkward. Oh, I realize that he's unbalanced, poor fellow, and bears quite a foolish grudge against you for shooting at him. But such people can start all sorts of trouble. I had a little talk with him this afternoon, before he went — he's going to preach from the Book of Amos on Sunday; we must hear him — and he told me I oughtn't to associate with you. He said you were dangerous. He's convinced — poor Macaulay — that you're a criminal type.'

'If you find it worth your while to listen to him — '

'I listen, but I don't believe. No, no!' said Crantit with a worldly chuckle. 'I don't believe a word he says — even though I realize that men like you, who've served in two wars, aren't likely to set so high a value on life as mild civilians like myself. *Homo sum; humani nil a me alienum puto*, as Terence says, quoting from dead Menander — '

'If you think I've committed murder, you're wrong!' said Swanson angrily. 'I'm the victim of gross injustice, and that's all!'

'Don't labour the point, I beg you. Don't tell me you're perfect,' said Crantit earnestly. 'That's all I ask, for that's the only thing that could estrange me. — But listen! We're very, very late. That is the voice of a man in the full tide of oratory.'

69

They had returned to the school, and through an open window they could hear, without distinguishing his words, the agreeable but slightly booming tones of the General's voice.

'There's a back door,' said Swanson. 'We can slip in quietly.'

'Wait,' said Crantit, 'here's someone else coming.'

A small car drove into the playground, and a brisk woman in blue uniform got out, and walked confidently towards the main entrance.

'Nurse Connachy,' said Crantit. 'An excellent woman. We've discussed midwifery together. Come along: we'll take the rear approach, and she can cover us.'

They entered unobserved, and stood behind a row of tall, dark-suited men. The General, caught in a maze of conditional clauses, welcomed the late appearance of Nurse Connachy with relief, and retiring from a syntactical position that was no longer tenable, addressed himself to her.

'Good evening, Nurse,' he exclaimed. 'I hope you'll forgive us for starting without you? We were rather late as it was.'

'I am sorry I couldn't get here in time,' said Nurse Connachy earnestly. 'It's with Mrs. Willy John Watt I've been. She is always terribly slow.'

'I hope it isn't another girl?'

'Another girl it is. That's five of them now.'

There was a buzz of interested conversation, and in the front row an elderly crofter, of mournful aspect, remarked with wonder in his voice, 'Would you not think a man like him would know better?'

'Who are you to be talking?' demanded a vigorous woman nearby. 'Have you not five daughters of your own?'

'Yes, yes,' said the crofter, 'and everyone of them welcome when she came. But it's not me that has the second-sight, like Willy John.'

This new topic threatened to engross the attention of the whole audience, and the General had to call for order. He turned to Nurse Connachy again, and said: 'I was about to put a resolution to the meeting, Nurse, and I'm very glad that you're here to add your authority to it — for I've no doubt it will meet with general approval. Now I'm not going to make my speech all over again, but I think I should tell you that I began by informing the meeting of the imminent arrival of the Parliamentary delegation that we've been expecting for so long. It is, in fact, coming tomorrow, and we are, of course, particularly interested in it because it is led by the redoubtable Mr. Pettigrew, who himself has strong ties with Laxdale.

'Now there is no doubt, in my mind, that the arrival of these gentlemen is due, in some degree, to our own action. We who are motorists here — there aren't very many of us, but five resolute people can still make their voices heard — we motorists refused to pay our road-fund licences until we had a road fit to travel on; and the authorities, as you know, have made some effort to bring us to book for our bad behaviour. They have, in fact, summoned us to appear before the Sheriff Court at Inverness; and when we declined the invitation, on the ground that the road between here and Inverness was unsafe, I was privately informed that we had laid ourselves open to a charge of Contempt of Court; which, of course, is a very serious offence, but one that we are not frightened of.

'Well, now, what happened next may well be deemed miraculous. On Thursday of last week, a fine day as we all remember, the postman from Scatwall came over the hill, and some little distance from here met our friend Nicholas McLeod. He told Nicholas that he had a new set of summonses, for us old offenders, and was so obliging as to show them. And at that very moment, while he held them in his hand, there came a gust of wind of extraordinary violence, from a clear sky, that blew the summonses from the postman's grasp, and scattered them far across the moor. We have Nicholas's own word for it — '

The General had already told this story, which was indeed, by much repetition, familiar to everyone there. But everyone was delighted to hear it yet again, and laughed happily and vigorously applauded; while Nicholas in the back row stood with a solemn look on his face like that of a man who has seen wonders enacted.

'The conclusion, then, is fairly clear,' said the General. 'We have shown that we are not to be trifled with. We have a good case, and because we are determined to defend it, we have compelled the authorities to take notice of it. We have proved already that determination pays, and when these Parliamentary gentlemen arrive we're going to show a united front. We're going to insist on our elementary right to decent communications, and until we get our rights those of us who are motorists will persist in our refusal to pay any tax or licence for amenities that don't exist. Our motto, in short, is No Surrender — And that's as far as we had got, Nurse, when you came in. I was, in fact, trying to phrase a resolution to put to the meeting; but that isn't as easy as you might think. Perhaps you could help us, and put into words — quite briefly and clearly — what we all feel?'

Everybody looked at Nurse Connachy with grave attention or lively expectancy; and Nurse Connachy pursed her lips and stared very hard at the nearer of the hanging lamps, which had begun to smoke a little. Then an old man in a fisherman's blue jersey — an old man called Rory Mackenzie, whose thin brown face was deeply lined, who had listened throughout with a gnarled old hand cupped to his ear — stood up in the middle of the room and spoke in the strong rhythm of the Gaelic speech to which he had been bred.

'I have seen many of these delegations that come to Laxdale from time to time,' he said. 'County Councillors, and Members of Parliament, and very important men: I have been seeing them ever since I was a small boy. They come, and they promise to do this for us, and that for us, with smiling faces. And then they go back to their parliament, and nothing is done. Nothing has ever been done! And mark my words, this new lot will be like all the rest of them. They will talk a lot, they will shake us by the hand like friends, and smile at us like old friends. And they will go away, in their own good time, and do nothing.'

This unequivocal blunt pessimism roused immediate protest, and half a dozen people, warmly indignant, drew attention to the enormous difference, between the coming delegation and all the previous ones, that the presence of Mr. Pettigrew would make: Mr. Pettigrew whose own grandfather had been born and brought up in Laxdale. Then, as Nurse Connachy was breathing rapidly and plainly suffering under the strain of finding words for a resolution, a confident-looking man with a red moustache proposed his own; which was found inadequate in every respect. A dozen others followed, none of which was received with general favour, though several were seconded, and amendments were proposed to nearly all of them. Most of the amendments were seconded, and some of the resolutions were withdrawn when amendments had made them unrecognizable. Nurse Connachy, after the General had called for order three times, got up and said in a strained voice, 'That in the opinion of this meeting a good road is necessary, and a good pier too if we can get it, but one or other of them, or else — ' And then, after a long pause, with a look of deep embarrassment, sat down again.

Finally, after half an hour of the most animated discussion, the General again called for order and said: 'We all know what we want, and we're going to do our utmost to get it. We're going to show a united front to the Parliamentary gentlemen, and we motorists aren't going to surrender our position. — Will you accept that as your resolution?'

'I second that!' exclaimed Nicholas, and it was passed with loud acclaim.

'Well, then,' said the General, 'that, I think, concludes our business, and thank you all very much for coming here, and showing such understanding of our common cause and sympathy with it. Good night, everybody.'

With a murmur of self-congratulation, and many a satisfied comment on the achievements of the evening, the audience divided and through the noisily opened doors moved slowly into the darkness. Morag McLeod, who had been manifestly nervous whenever the General called for order, was now almost blissfully relieved, for the desk had withstood the heavy impact of his hand, and the grilse were undiscovered. Nicholas waited patiently for the audience to disperse, and as soon as the last man had gone, he bolted the back door and taking the key of the other door from Morag, told her to go home. He closed the windows and turned out the lamps. Then, in darkness, he unlocked the desk and tidily concealed the fish by slipping them inside his trousers, where he secured them, one down each leg, by pushing a tag of his braces through mouth and gills, and re-buttoning it. The fish had stiffened, and gave a certain clumsiness to his gait; but he relied on the darkness to cover that.

In the playground small groups of people were still talking, reluctant to go home, and when Nicholas came out he found the General waiting to thank him for seconding the resolution.

'It was a good meeting,' said Nicholas. 'There's no one like yourself for carrying a meeting with you, and getting business done without loss of time.'

'Well, I don't know about that, but it did go well, I think. It made a good finish to a day that began rather badly. I suppose Morag told you about last night's poaching?'

'She said something, indeed.'

'And McKellaig, you know, thought he'd seen you at the river this morning. Down by The Cruive.'

'He may well have done that, for I took a walk on the bank and thought to myself there was nowhere on the face of the earth I would rather be, than here in Laxdale on a fine day like this.'

'Did you see any fish in The Cruive, or in the run above it?'

'What good would it do me to go looking for fish? I would hardly know the difference between a salmon and a cod-fish, if I saw them together.'

'Now, now, Nicholas! That's a bit steep, even for you.'

'Excuse me, General. There's the Nurse having trouble with her car again.'

Nurse Connachy's Austin Seven was twelve years old, and seldom started without assistance. She was duly grateful to Nicholas, and thankfully gave him the starting-handle. He stooped to put it in, and discovered that with a six-pound stiffened grilse down each trouser-leg, he could not bend his knees.

'What's wrong with you, Nicholas?' she asked.

'Nothing, nothing at all, Nurse. It is just a touch of lumbago that has been bothering me.'

'Then I'll do it myself. Give me the handle.'

'No, no, I can manage fine.'

'What's the matter, Nicholas?' asked the General, coming to see what was going on.

'He's got a touch of lumbago,' said Nurse Connachy.

'A very painful thing too. I had it myself once. Here, Nicholas, I'll do that.'

But Nicholas, with his feet planted widely apart, and bending stiffly from the waist, swung the handle strongly and the engine started. 'Where there's a will there's a way,' he said, and bade the Nurse a warm good night.

'I wish,' said the General, 'that you and McKellaig could get on together.'

'That McKellaig,' said Nicholas, 'is just a busybody, and an idle busybody at that, which is the worst kind. And even if he was speaking the truth — which he couldn't do if he tried — well, what's a fish or two between friends?'

75

CHAPTER NINE

BOLDLY painted, business-like, the red-funnelled *Lochbois-dale* rounded the rocky point of Ardewe, and raised a long smooth wave that broke against the steep shore with a running flourish of foam, an ever-opening fan, and a sibilant, hoarse murmur. There was no movement on the shining waters of the Inner Minch but the small, arrow-shaped billows of the steamer's progress, and the creaming at her bow, the flurry at her stern. The air was still, the sun supreme; and the scarred hills of the mainland, the fantastically patterned heights of islands seemingly desolate, were coloured, as if in some confusion of the seasons, with the tenderest hues of spring and the gentler shades of autumn — harebell-blue and turning leaf, new beechen-green, the tarnished copper of old bracken, and faded purple from a dowager's forgotten cupboard. The air was fresh, as if new-blown from the first kindliness of spring, but the hill-slopes in the middle distance were covered, as it seemed, by the golden varnish of old pictures, and the farther heights, immutably still, were the decoration to an ancient and forgotten tale of epic bravery and simple splendour, simple folly. — The passengers, leaning on the starboard rail of the steamer, confused their neighbours and impressed themselves with their inaccurate memories of Highland feuds. It was there, said one, that the McLeods assassinated a parcel of Mackenzies, or the other way about; and there the piper of Mhic Iain Ruadh had blown his stirring tune what time a foray of the Macdonalds smoked-out a rag-tag of Campbells from the sea-cave in which, after rape and murder, they had taken cowardly refuge. — Or did the Campbells light the bonfire? No one knew.

In a haze of wonderment, under the still Atlantic sky and between the gently shining ramparts of the west, the passengers were deeply moved by the beauty of the scene. Watteau might have coloured part of it, Mantegna the starker views — and in their hearts there stirred heroic, melancholy thoughts, and a hunger they could not identify for a happiness beyond recall. Even the English tourists admitted to their minds an unusual sensation of something lost, or to be found, that Nice and Naples, Table Mountain and Nuwara Eliya had never given them; and the third Mrs. Pettigrew, standing between Mr. Marvell and Andrew Flett, said quite simply, 'I don't think I like it. It seems to touch you, and you can't tell what it is. I don't like things to touch me.'

This statement was not wholly true, for Mrs. Pettigrew had very pretty hands, and to come to terms with her world habitually relied on the sensation of touch, and, in certain cases, on the reciprocal sensations it aroused; when she stroked a fur coat or a silk dress, her hands were not only visibly pleased by the contact, but quick with appraisal, sensitive to value; and her finger-tips on a porcelain dish or Boulle marquetry revealed quite honestly their calculation as well as their enjoyment. She would put her hand on the arm or the knee of the man she was talking to, not provocatively — or not always provocatively — but simply, as though physical contact was necessary to understanding; and when circumstances gave any encouragement, she would lean against his shoulder, or press her thigh to his, apparently in the instinctive belief that contiguity pro- moted well-being. — Now, on the steamer-rail, with passengers on either side, she stood so close to Marvell that he felt, as it were, the emanation of her weight against him, from the shoulder to the knee; and her hand lay lightly on his fore-arm.

She had large grey eyes, a look of innocence, a pretty mouth and chin. It was difficult to guess her age, for though she had left girlhood well behind her, the years had not wrinkled or coarsened her skin, and time had made little impress on her mind. Her skin was white and very smooth, and her flesh had such a quality of softness that most men thought her fragile; though she was fairly tall and plumply made. Her voice, too, was soft and caressing; there was a

77

note of waiting laughter in it, and the hint of some provincial accent.

'It's lovely,' she said, looking at the view, 'but somehow or other it gives me the creeps. It's too still, and there don't seem to be any people about.'

'There's an old woman,' said Flett, pointing to the shore.

'Leading a cow by a rope! That's not what I call social life.'

'An American woman,' said Marvell, 'of the old-fashioned, liberal, globe-trotting sort, once told me that for natural beauty the Western Highlands were second only to the Vale of Kashmir.'

'Then I don't suppose I'd like the Vale of Kashmir either,' said Mrs. Pettigrew. 'But Sam ought to be looking at this. Where is he? I haven't seen him since breakfast.'

Alone, in the deserted saloon where a strong odour of coffee and kippers lingered with a slight smell of oil, Mr. Pettigrew was drinking gin and tonic-water. He was a heavily built man, of solemn mien, and his cheeks depended a little over the deep lines that ran down and outwards from his generous nostrils. His solemnity was an acquired appearance. It had begun to threaten him — as though at a party someone had pressed a mask upon his face — when he made his first hundred thousand; and by the time he had made his first million, the mask was firmly in position. The look of melancholy he now wore was due to a relaxation of his normal expression: a look unguarded, for a little while, by his consciousness of power and importance.

On deck, after breakfast, he had been accosted by an elderly, respectable man of the artisan sort, who had said to him, 'I didn't recognize you, Mr. Pettigrew! It was the wife that spotted you, and at first I just thought she'd made a mistake. Man, you've changed a lot since the old days!' — Pettigrew had talked with him for ten minutes, then abruptly left him; for his old friend had inconvenient memories, and with loving admiration had recited a list of the unusual luggage he had taken on his first honeymoon.

'Two Spanish guitars, a ten-pound medicine-ball, a parrot and a spare leg!' he said. 'It was in all the papers, and photographs of you and the bride in that wee car you had. It wasn't politics that

78

made you famous, not in the first place, and it wasn't money either; it was just two Spanish guitars and a spare leg.'

The accidental loss of a leg, in the furniture factory where he worked, had given Samuel Pettigrew, at the age of seventeen, the capital and the leisure he required. He lay for six months in hospital, and on alternate days studied the works of Karl Marx and his disciples, and the columns of the *Financial Times*. He became a convinced and eager Socialist, and with the £750 which he had been awarded in compensation for the loss of a limb, he gambled shrewdly on the Stock Exchange, and doubled it by the time he could walk. He went bankrupt at nineteen, but three years later he had paid his creditors in full and was making cheap furniture in his own factory. At twenty-four he stood for Parliament in a rowdy by-election, and by skilful organization and the exuberance of his attack almost won a reputedly safe Conservative seat. On the day the result was made known he married a girl of his own age, a fellow-member of a social club he had joined, and undismayed by political defeat, set off on his honeymoon with certain effects whose seeming oddity appealed to the reporters who had been covering the election; and in a season of little important news, his luggage received more attention than the Conservative victory.

Pettigrew's loud vitality and genuine good-humour, at that time of life, protected him against embarrassment and disarmed ridicule. 'I lost a leg once,' he had said, 'and I never mean to be short of one again. We're going to make life one long duet, we're going to keep young and beautiful, and teach the parrot to say we're not at home. We've got just the luggage we need.'

The duet, however, lasted no longer than eighteen months, and after his wife's death Pettigrew addressed himself seriously to the complementary tasks of making money and a reputation. In the course of time he acquired an interest in a chain of cinemas, he became a director of a crematorium and two dog-racing tracks, he bought derelict estates and stripped them of their timber, he owned a large hotel and two smaller ones, his furniture factory grew into one of the biggest in Britain, he made paint and varnish, he marketed a remedy against lost virility, and exploited a patent for manufacturing a dark, unpleasant-looking crockery out of slag-heaps. He became a Member of Parliament before he married again, and adding a weekly paper to his other properties, preached Socialism with force and ingenuity. His fortune grew steadily, but though he was effective in debate and a great source of strength at elections, he was never given office, or, indeed, the confidence of his Party leaders. His interpretation of the Marxist gospel had never been quite orthodox, and latterly he had begun to develop a variant doctrine which was loosely described as 'Socialism Plus'.

His second marriage ended in divorce, and the less amiable of his acquaintances believed that his interest in the third Mrs. Pettigrew was due, in some degree, to her having been the widow of a wealthy promoter of football pools. They had spent their honeymoon, in great luxury, at Montego Bay; but their luggage had not included a parrot, a medicine-ball or Spanish guitars, and their month in Jamaica had largely been occupied with negotiations for the purchase of a coffee-growing estate.

Mr. Pettigrew called the steward and ordered another gin-and-tonic. He was not a man devoid of sentiment, nor indeed immune from sentimentality. Generosity had first inspired his politics, and for much of his life he had felt truly indignant that poverty should still be widespread in a world where it was so easy to make money, and there was so much to be made. All his employees drew good wages, and were handsomely treated. He had served on many committees, and devoted much time to public causes that he might have spent, with greater profit, on his own affairs. He had under-taken his present mission because he felt it his duty to help the little backward community of Laxdale, and he had devoted considerable thought to a plan of his own for improving the condition of the simple people from whom he was descended. He had found himself unexpectedly moved by the prospect of seeing, for the first time, the remote peninsula where his maternal grandfather had been born; and in such a temper he had been unusually vulnerable to memory's attack. Damn and confound the fellow, he thought; and sorrow-fully sipped his gin.

The man who accosted him had been a foreman in Pettigrew's

first factory, and while it hurt a distant tenderness to be reminded of the parrot and the two guitars, it wounded an ever present vanity to hear that time had so defaced his youth that he was no longer recognizable by the companions of his youth. — A man, thought Pettigrew, a man like me should be protected from people who knew him when he was young. And letting the gin create a little anger against the unfairness of circumstance, he armed his spirit with ill-humour.

Flett came into the saloon and said, 'We're in sight of Laxdale now. Mrs. Pettigrew thought you would like to come up and see it.'

Mr. Pettigrew resumed his proper expression of grave importance, and slowly — with his little finger extended from the glass — finished his drink. 'Very well,' he said and went on deck. But now there was no pleasant expectancy in his mind, and sentiment had been put down.

Over the gently throbbing deck he pushed his way through a gathering crowd of passengers to where his wife and Marvell leaned upon the rail. The steamer was heading towards an arc of greenery, and shining sand, and small white houses that the hills with ragged crests enclosed. On the one hand a sea-loch, turquoise-blue, divided a majestic confusion of many-coloured heights; and on the other the alpine pinnacles of Skye grew abruptly from the ocean-bed. The sun, now lightly veiled at the top of noon, was reflected, as it seemed, from old enamels, precious metals and jewels with scarred facets casually inlaid in the mountain-sides, in the rock-faces, and the long pale beaches.

'Well, there it is,' said Mrs. Pettigrew cheerfully; 'and if you ask me, the best thing your grandfather ever did was to get out of it.'

'There's this to be said,' declared Marvell in a conscientiously business-like voice, 'that with decent communications you could develop the tourist industry. The Norwegians have capitalized their northern fjords, and there's no scenery in Norway to better that.'

'I don't approve of scenery,' said Pettigrew gruffly. 'Fine scenery's just an excuse for wasting time.'

'That may be so, but tourists will go a long way to look for it; and if this place were better known, and easier to get to, a lot of them could come here.'

'There'll be rain tomorrow, there always is,' said Pettigrew. 'And tourists don't like rain.'

'They do if they're fishermen,' said Flett, who, leaning far over the rail, was trying to accommodate hills and beaches in the view-finder of his camera.

'I'm not interested in idlers, Mr. Flett! And while fishermen make a philosophy of idleness, tourists have turned it into a trade. What the people here need is honest work; and if they want to enjoy the benefits of civilization, they'll have to work harder than ever before.'

'This air,' said Marvell with a midday yawn, 'isn't conducive to so stern a view.'

'You get tired of work sometimes,' said Flett in the blunt confidence of his youth. — He had been a Civil Servant only for three years. — 'Especially the sort of work we do.'

'That remark, Mr. Flett, is unworthy of you! You are engaged on public duty, and public duty should be its own reward. You should, at any rate, never speak lightly of it.'

'You're not to bully him, Sam!' said Mrs. Pettigrew warmly, and laid a protective hand on Flett's nearer sleeve. 'I know just how he feels, and it's only natural. I feel the same myself.'

An open motor-boat, about twenty-five feet long, was now approaching the ship, and three hundred yards offshore the engine-room telegraph rang *Stop*, the *Lochboisdale* turned her nose to the last of the flood, and idly drifted. The boat from the shore made fast alongside, a large double port on the lower deck was opened, and a numerous cargo of small packages, parcels, bales and boxes was transferred from the larger vessel to the smaller. By far the most conspicuous article was a new perambulator, a shining thing of chromium plate and cream enamel.

A civil steward informed Mr. Pettigrew that his luggage had been put aboard the Laxdale boat, and it was time for him to follow. Mr. Pettigrew exchanged a dignified salute with the captain of the

Lochboisdale, who stood upon the near wing of his bridge; and followed by his party, descended to the lower deck.

They were the only passengers for the shore, and the remaining voyagers lined the starboard rail, and leaned over it and looked down to see them disembarking, with the solemn air of those who take farewell of pioneers, desperate adventurers, exiles to a foreign shore.

CHAPTER TEN

O n the semi-circle of green turf where the War Memorial
stood — between the row of five diminutive cottages called
Shore Street and the jetty that was still known as Miss
Phipps's Pier — about a hundred and fifty people were waiting to
greet the Members of Parliament. All the school-children were
there, for it was a Saturday, and as they ran foolishly to and fro,
waving small flags, their excited voices rose in shrill explosions
above the deeper sound of their elders' conversation, and the soft
pounding of the tide on the beach. The *Lochboisdale* lay off-shore,
with the Laxdale boat alongside, and all eyes but the childrens' stared
seaward in a concentration of expectancy. It was the children who
turned the general gaze about. Gathered like starlings in a flock,
their chattering voices quieter and more urgent, with a sudden,
solemn interest they faced the other way; and watched the dark
approach of an unexpected addition to the scene.

Round the corner and down the short slope from the village street
came the parish hearse, with Willy John Watt at the wheel. It was
a large vehicle, of antique pattern and sombre hue, that Willy John —
the local joiner and undertaker — had made himself, by building a
wooden body on the chassis of an old Austin. Each of its panelled
walls, painted black and glossily varnished, rose to a cornice from
which grew a patriotic row of wooden thistles, that Willy John had
carved with pride and care; and from the angles of the cornice
sprouted huge aigrettes of black horsehair, which could be detached
and put away for safe keeping. The driver's seat was open to the sky,
but was protected by a heavily framed, vertical windscreen.

Silence and consternation fell upon the little crowd. There had

84

been no recent death in the parish, nor was death feared — not imminently feared — in any house. But Willy John, of course, would be one of the first to hear of calamity, or its nearness; though news of that sort could not quite explain why he had brought his hearse to the pier.

The momentary silence broke into whispering, muted inquiry, and with one impulse the crowd moved towards Willy John; who had got down from the driving-seat and was wedging a stone under a back wheel of the hearse, the brakes of which were unreliable. Everybody could see that he had put on his dark suit, the one he wore to funerals, and felt a little draught of foreboding.

It was General Matheson who put the questions that all were so anxious, but reluctant, to ask. The General, with Catriona and the several dogs that usually accompanied her, had been standing apart from the crowd, to rehearse in his mind the arrangements he had made for the entertainment and instruction of his visitors; and he moved with more decision than the others.

'What's the meaning of this, Willy John? What's this out for? Your wife's all right, isn't she?'

'She is well, thank God, and so is the child,' said Willy John in a lugubrious voice. 'It is my old father in Glasgow.'

'What's happened to him?' asked Catriona.

Swiftly the news was repeated, in a murmuring of voices: It is not the wife, it is his father in Glasgow. The old man . . .

Willy John was tall and lean, mournful of aspect, with a long sad nose and a drooping moustache. His father was remembered, clearly enough by the older people, as a squat and burly man, quick of tongue and temper, a grizzled reprobate who had spent his youth in sailing-ships and retained at sixty most of the vigour of youth and the habits he had learnt on the west coast of South America. He had been a scandal and a nuisance in Laxdale, and had fled to the city, eight or nine years before, to avoid trouble with the police and a man as hot-tempered as himself. But Willy John was devoted to his father, and would often speak of him with pride and affection. 'There was no smarter sailor in the nitrate trade,' he would declare. 'He could pick and choose the ship he would sail in.'

85

The crowd pressed closer to hear his reply. 'I have heard no details,' said Willy John, 'but I had the sight of him last night, and I think his body will be aboard the steamer there.'

'But surely if he was ill,' said the General, 'he'd have written to say so?'

'No, no! He was always a very bashful man about himself. He would never talk of his own affairs.'

'What did you see last night?' asked Catriona.

'He stood at the foot of the bed,' said Willy John impressively. 'He laid his finger to the side of his nose, and tapped it three times. He looked at me with the light in his eye that I have often seen, and then he turned to the door, as though someone was calling him. He fetched a deep sigh and blew out his cheeks before he went — and then he was gone!'

'I don't think that can mean very much,' said the General. 'You had a dream, I suppose — '

'Willy John has second-sight,' said Catriona reproachfully.

'Well, he needs spectacles for it,' said the General impatiently. 'It's failed you before now, hasn't it, Willy John? Cheer up, man, your father isn't the sort to die in a hurry.'

Willy John, unconvinced, shook his head, and his audience debated his vision with lively interest. Some were persuaded of its mortal tidings, but others recalled occasions when his premonition had been wide of the mark; and while they were still balancing probabilities there came a cry from a party of the children: 'They're here! Here they are!'

The boat, indeed, had come ashore unobserved. Mr. Pettigrew and his party were already on the jetty, and Mr. Pettigrew, offended by the lack of attention, was standing on his dignity. With his head erect, his shoulders square and his hands lightly clasped in front of his stomach, he waited to be received. The General, annoyed with himself for his discourtesy and with Willy John for provoking it, hurried to greet his visitors, and Catriona and her dogs followed close behind.

The General and Mr. Pettigrew shook hands. Mrs. Pettigrew, Mr. Marvell and Mr. Flett were introduced. Catriona was introduced. The visitors were told how eagerly their arrival had been awaited, and to polite inquiries about their voyage made gracious answers. Their luggage, said the General, would be looked after, and the sea air, he expected, had given them an appetite for lunch. He had not brought a car, he said, for on so fine a day he was sure they would enjoy the short walk to Laxdale Hall.

Mrs. Pettigrew looked down at her plump feet encased tightly in high-heeled shoes, and made a face. But the General did not see it, and Mr. Pettigrew had become aware of an audience. There were now nearly two hundred people on the green in front of Shore Street, or pressing forward to the jetty, with a dozen school-children waving small flags in the foreground.

Mr. Pettigrew stepped forward, and took off his hat. He made an impressive if sombre figure in his black city coat and striped trousers, and there was an almost evangelical warmth in his voice when he raised his hand and said, 'My friends!'

There was a mutter of applause. 'My friends!' he repeated, 'I am deeply honoured by this demonstration, this spontaneous demonstration, of your goodwill towards the Parliamentary delegation that I am privileged to bring here. Yes, I am honoured, but your presence here, in such numbers, fills me also with a warmer feeling, that I think should not be hidden from you. I have, as perhaps you can guess, a very special feeling for the people of Lax-dale. It was in earliest childhood that I first heard the name of Laxdale, from the lips of my saintly mother. Her father was born here, and tilled its soil, as many of you still do. It is because of that memory, that sacred memory and dear association, that I have come here to help you if I can. And I do think I can! My colleague and fellow Member of Parliament, Mr. Marvell here, and Mr. Flett of the Scottish Office, are just as ready as I am to give you the benefit of their knowledge and experience, and it is the hope of us all that this very hour will long be remembered, by all of you, as the prelude to a new and happier era in your lives!'

This speech elicited loud exclamations of pleasure, and Nicholas McLeod, who, to honour the occasion and his status as a County Councillor, had put on his best suit, pushed his way to the front of the crowd, and waving his cap round his head called in a heart-stirring voice for 'Three cheers for Mr. Pettigrew, M.P.!'

'Thank you, my friends, thank you!' said Mr. Pettigrew, his equanimity now fully restored, and with the General walked slowly up the jetty while the crowd respectfully made way, and his party obediently followed.

They drew level with the hearse, and Willy John standing beside it. Fearful of the confirmation of his vision, and a coffin in the boat, he was waiting in a quivering impatience for the crowd to disperse.

'You have had a loss in the parish?' asked Mr. Pettigrew sympathetically. 'Some poor family has been bereaved? Not of the bread-winner, I hope.'

'We don't quite know,' said the General. 'We're not sure what has happened.'

Willy John, touching his cap, approached them and hoarsely inquired, 'Was there a body aboard the boat?'

'There were about a hundred and fifty bodies, so far as I could see,' said Pettigrew.

'*Dead* bodies?'

'They were all alive when we left the ship!'

'Then my father wasn't there?'

'I must explain,' said the General — but before he could begin his explanation there came an imperative shout from the end of the jetty, where the boatmen were unloading the last of their cargo from the *Lochboisdale*.

'Willy John! Is Willy John there?'

'What is it?' cried Willy John, and hurried to see.

'There's this, that's addressed to you,' said the boatman, and lifted on to the jetty a smart new perambulator, shining with chromium-plate and cream enamel.

A wave of delighted laughter swept the crowd, and its backwash was loud with mockery and consolation for the latest failure of Willy John's supernatural gift. The women pressed forward to examine the splendid perambulator, and the men acknowledged their relief that it was something for the nursery, not an item for the churchyard, which the steamer had brought. Mr. Pettigrew and his party were left, not wholly unattended, but with a much diminished following.

The road to Laxdale Hall ran northwards, away from the village, with the beach and a broadening strip of *machair* on the one side, cultivated fields on the other. Mr. Pettigrew led the way, between Catriona and Nicholas McLeod; the General followed, with Mrs. Pettigrew; Marvell and Flett were already deep in conversation with three or four of the villagers; and a dozen children trotted behind, still drawn by the fascination of the strangers.

Mr. Pettigrew was being deliberately obtuse. He could not understand, or so he pretended, why Willy John had expected his father's body to be aboard the ship. He would not believe that Catriona was serious when she spoke of second-sight, and he refused to accept the indisputable evidence of it that Nicholas offered. He was rudely incredulous, he proposed exasperatingly rational explanations of the tales they told; and Catriona grew increasingly dogmatic as her claims became more fanciful, and Nicholas vouched for the truth of everything she said. They were within easy reach of abuse when the argument was interrupted by the high-pitched frenzy of a cocker spaniel.

Four dogs had followed Catriona to the pier: a tall and handsome greyhound, his plebeian-looking but intelligent lurcher son, an elderly and massive golden Labrador, and a young black cocker. The Labrador and the greyhound walked sedately on the road, the lurcher was roving the *machair*, and the spaniel had been lost to sight in a field of turnips. But now, shrilly barking, its butterfly ears wildly flapping, it sprang into view as it broke through hedge after hedge of tough green leaves in fierce, hopeless pursuit of a hare.

Almost as excited as the cocker, Catriona at once gave tongue, and made nearly as shrill a noise. 'Yooie, yooie!' she cried. 'Yooie, yooie, yooie!' And pointing in the direction the hare had taken, gave the wandering lurcher a lead, and with long, leaping strides herself set off in pursuit. The greyhound, in a swift-flowing gallop, was already half way across the turnip-field, and the Labrador, breathing heavily, followed gallantly behind. The children, shouting and screaming, tumbling and getting up again, scrambled through the roots and over the furrows with breathless determination and scarlet faces, and the Laxdale men who had been discussing roads and piers with Marvell and Flett hesitated only a moment before joining the chase; they were still young enough to course a hare, the oldest being only fifty-eight. Marvell and Flett, a little doubtfully at first, looked at each other, and Marvell said, 'Come on!' They followed gamely, and quickly overtook the oldest of the villagers.

The General, aware of his duty to Mrs. Pettigrew, still gave her the support of his arm, but his attention was on the chase; and when he saw that Catriona was leading the chase in the wrong direction — for the lie of the land was such-and-such, and the hare would surely go the other way — he could no longer restrain himself. Brusquely disengaging from Mrs. Pettigrew he cupped his hands to his mouth and bellowed, 'No, no, *no!*' With a sweeping movement of his right arm he set the course nor'-nor'-west, and clearing the ditch with a leap that lifted his kilt like a ballet dancer's skirt — 'Oh, my!' said Mrs. Pettigrew admiringly — went pelting over the furrows, still shouting and waving .

Painfully startled, at first, by the sudden clamour, Mr. Pettigrew was now utterly bewildered, and turning to Nicholas McLeod, who alone of the natives remained on the road, inquired in hollow tones, 'Well, what's the meaning of that? Have they all gone mad?'

'It was a hare that got up,' said Nicholas with a touch of impatience in his voice; for he was eagerly watching the chase, and had stayed with the Pettigrews only in deference to good manners. 'A fine young hare. Did you not see it?'

'It looked like a rabbit to me,' said Pettigrew.

'No, no, it was a great hare with long legs on it that'll run like a stag!'

'I still don't see what all the excitement's about. I don't go careering over the fields every time I see a rabbit — even if it is a hare.'

'It would do you such a lot of good,' said Mrs. Pettigrew. 'Look at the General, he's still running. At his age!'

'We are all great sportsmen here in Laxdale,' explained Nicholas.

'Indeed, it's a grand place you have come to, Mr. Pettigrew, with stags on the hill, and fish in the river, with grouse in abundance and the wild duck in their season, and hares for anyone that has a good dog and legs to follow them. It would be a paradise on earth if only we had a few miles of good road and a decent pier that a ship could tie-up to. And that is why we are so glad to see you— not that we don't welcome you for your own sake, oh, we do indeed, and Mrs. Pettigrew too — but our pleasure is much greater to think you will be telling us tonight how to get a new pier and make a new road!'

'Is that what you think I've come to do?'

'What else would you be doing? Except to enjoy yourself where your own grandfather was born, and show the beauty of the country to Mrs. Pettigrew?'

'He's fallen!' exclaimed Mrs. Pettigrew. 'But he's got up again!'

'Who?'

'The General.'

'A fall is nothing to the like of him,' said Nicholas. 'A strong man, supple for his age, and a great sportsman.'

'Has it never occurred to you,' said Pettigrew, 'that it would be unjustifiable use of public money to build roads and piers in the West Highlands when what they would cost — and that would be a large sum — might otherwise be spent for the benefit of the whole community?'

'Are we not part of the community?'

'Only a small part, Mr. McLeod. A remote and inaccessible part, and a part of very doubtful economic value.'

'There are other values than economic values, Mr. Pettigrew.'

'There are indeed! Of course there are, and who knows them better than I? There are spiritual values! Spiritual values such as —' For a moment Mr. Pettigrew's mouth remained open. He frowned, and closed it, and appeared to search a sector of the western sky for the missing words. He coughed, tentatively at first, then with such violence as required a handkerchief to conceal it. He blew his nose, and resumed. — 'As I was saying, there are spiritual values in plenty, and moral values too. Oh, we mustn't forget the moral values!

But what we have always got to remember, Mr. McLeod, is that we're living in the twentieth century, and in the twentieth century people have more to do than chasing rabbits!'

'The twentieth century, Mr. Pettigrew,' said Nicholas gently, 'has not been altogether faultless, and perhaps it could learn as much from Laxdale as we can learn from it. It was not a rabbit, moreover. It was a hare!'

The hunt was out of sight, but from beyond the ridge of rougher ground that hid it there came suddenly, muted by distance, the high, ecstatic yelping of a dog.

'They have caught it,' said Nicholas. 'That is the lurcher speaking, a clever little dog. However they are bred, and though all are brought up in the same way, there is always one in the litter that is cleverer than the rest.'

CHAPTER ELEVEN

A T half-past two that afternoon forty-three of the sixty-five performers in the Greek play were ready to begin a full rehearsal. They were all in costume, and Mrs. Pettigrew, who had come as a spectator, was greatly impressed by the handsome appearance they made, and gave Catriona the warmest commendation for it.

Mr. Crantit had friends of the intellectual sort who hovered about the ardent flame of the theatre; and friends of the aesthetic sort, who understood but did not commit themselves to the sterner passions of the intellect. He had made use of both, and by combining adroitly their sometimes antipathetic advice had provided Catriona with admirable designs for costumes coloured boldly enough to show their bass and treble hues, and middle notes, against the orchestrated colours of a Highland landscape. Catriona, throughout the preceding winter, had kept the members of the Laxdale Women's Institute hard at work, cutting and stitching himation and peplos, chlamys and chiton and so forth. All the costumes were made of sensible material, and were, in consequence, not only acceptable to the scholar and pleasing to the aesthetic eye, but agreeable to those who might have to wear them on a chilly Highland day.

No attempt had been made to rebuild the ruined water-mill which stood as background to the play. It was a dignified piece of masonry, broad and high — though the roof had gone — and Mr. Crantit and Catriona had agreed that it could represent, well enough, the castle of King Pentheus of Thebes that the stage-directions called for. It had a large doorway which had been dignified, for the occasion, by the addition of stone pillars that supported a heavy lintel; and immediately adjacent to the mill was the deserted garden overgrown with honeysuckles that the last miller had planted, in which the ruin of his cottage now represented the sacred Tomb of Semele, and would emit a little smoke when required.

The mill, some three or four hundred yards below the good salmon-pool called The Cruive, was sufficiently whole to provide dressing-rooms for both men and women, and an upper storey with a good floor accommodated stage-properties. A little flat meadow in front of it made a natural stage, and south of the meadow, in the curious, arbitrary geology of that part of Scotland, rose the small hill called The Drum to provide an auditorium. — Mrs. Pettigrew, alone on the hill, again applauded a casual gathering of the costumed actors on the meadow. 'It's wonderful!' she cried. 'It doesn't matter what you do, or what you say, it looks wonderful!'

Catriona, darkly clad and white-wigged as Agave, the mother of King Pentheus, felt her first, instinctive dislike of Mrs. Pettigrew melt and vanish; and concealed the contrary tide of emotion by describing, in detail, the shaping and sewing of the costumes, and the difficulties the Laxdale Women's Institute had had in following Mr. Crantit's extremely clever but often impractical designs.

By a quarter-past three seventeen other members of the cast had appeared, and all the principals being present, it was decided to begin. Swanson read his part, but the rest, surprisingly, were word-perfect, and recited their lines as quickly as possible. The rehearsal was completed with remarkable speed, but the dramatic effect was negligible.

At half-past four the actors, now numbering sixty-one, sat down to a hearty meal of tea, mutton-sandwiches, oatcake and cheese, home-baked scones, pancakes and jam, paper-girt confectionery from Glasgow, and boiled sweets; and Catriona, after congratulating the principals on their mastery of so many words, and the choruses on their proper entrance and graceful movement, said unhappily, 'But you went far too quickly, didn't you? The play didn't sound as though it meant very much, though it does, in fact, mean a great deal. You've been very clever about learning the words, which are difficult, but you don't seem to understand what is happening, which is really quite simple — though, of course, it's not the sort of thing that has ever happened in our own experience. But every woman, I think, must sympathize with the *feeling* of the play, because we have experienced that, and you all know how angry you get when some really clever man suddenly becomes quite appallingly stupid, as they so often do. — But Mr. Crantit can explain things much better than I, so please go on with your tea, and I'll ask him to tell us all once more, as simply as he can, what the play is really about. — Mr. Crantit! Mr. Crantit!'

Mr. Crantit, a ham-sandwich in one hand, an empty cup in the other, was walking with Olaf Swanson on the bank of the placid mill-pool that lay, like black glass, deep and still. 'You've got a good voice,' he was saying, 'and, of course, the knowledge of how sentences are constructed. That makes a tremendous difference to the manner in which the actor speaks them. You're going to be all right, Swanson, if you keep your head up and stop being self-conscious about your beard.'

'It's because I have no chin,' said Swanson, 'that I feel my beard uncomfortable.'

'War, in the last half-century,' said Mr. Crantit, 'has deprived everybody of something. You're very lucky if you've got off with the loss of nothing more important than a chin. — Think of poor Macaulay, who's lost his sense of proportion. — Have you heard anything new from Shetland? Is the hue and cry coming closer?'

'No,' said Swanson with sudden irritation. 'That's not likely. At least, I don't think so. Not yet.'

'You can depend on me,' said Mr. Crantit comfortably, 'if trouble comes. The artist is known by the trouble he keeps, and I, for one, shall be sympathetic.'

'Mr. Crantit! Mr. Crantit!' came the loud, clear voice of Catriona.

'Bless her heart,' said Mr. Crantit, hurriedly finishing his sandwich. 'Isn't she beautiful? I wish I could fall in love with her. I should like, above all things, to live here — in sufficient comfort, of course.'

'Mr. Crantit,' said Catriona, approaching them with a hurried, ineffable grace in her wine-dark peplos, her knees breaking its dusky flow like otters playing under the moon. — 'Mr. Crantit, you must come and speak to them! You must tell them again what it all means. I do think they know, really, but they won't trust their own feelings. Please try to make them realize, and show some conviction, before we rehearse again!'

'A pedagogue,' said Mr. Crantit, 'is not, perhaps, the best evangelist. You must not expect me to preach the pure milk of Orphism or the mystical centrality of the Dionysiac orgy. But a summary of Euripides' intention, and some remarks on the enduring significance of his play, I can supply if that's what's wanted. Where is my hapless audience?'

Mr. Crantit, portentously crowned and robed in a ruby-bordered himation of dove-grey, played the part of old Tiresias in the drama. A long white beard subdued his lively face to a proper solemnity, but his rimless glasses, which he insisted on wearing, gave him the look of some high-ranking Baptist minister rather than the archaic authority of a Theban prophet. His fellow-actors, however, had been deeply impressed by his learning, and thought highly of his personality.

He stood in front of the pillared doorway of the ruined mill, and looked benignly upon them as they sat in rows before him, still eating buttered scones and drinking cups of strong tea. 'I could talk to you,' he said, 'for days on end about Euripides and this play of his, but I'm not going to, because you wouldn't listen as long as that. Euripides was a Greek dramatist who was born nearly five hundred years before Christ, and one of the things he said, that has often received favourable comment, was that a woman suffered more in child-birth than a soldier in the front rank of infantry in two hard battles. Well, that isn't true, of course, but it shows he had a nice, warm feeling for humanity, and good feeling is sometimes worth more than scientific accuracy. And a dramatist who makes a silly remark isn't thereby prevented from being a good dramatist; or we wouldn't have any dramatists at all.

'Now this play called the *Bacchanals* is about common sense, and women, and religion, and clever men who go too far and think they can put a stop to what's right and natural by substituting what they consider reasonable and expedient. King Pentheus, I've no doubt, had some very good reasons for trying to put down the worship of Dionysus. He may have thought the women of Thebes would work harder if life was made less enjoyable for them. Or perhaps he was jealous of Dionysus: it isn't humble people who are moved by jealousy, it's people half way up the ladder. And perhaps he objected to the way in which the Bacchanals killed his deer.

'But whatever his reason, King Pentheus, that dull, clever rational man, declared war on Dionysus, and got the worse of it. The women, of course, were on Dionysus' side, and so were the two old men, Tiresias and Cadmus, who were sound Conservatives and enjoyed a glass of wine. The worship of Dionysus wasn't entirely a matter of drinking, however; it was rather a recognition of the fact that a great many products of the earth, and of life itself, are available for enjoyment, and the price that has to be paid for them is reverence. Now the impulse to worship is as natural as the impulse to pleasure, and the women of Thebes, being doubly frustrated by the reforming zeal of their silly king, were quick to take their opportunity for revenge.

'They take a terrible revenge, and some of you, I know, still feel uncomfortable about the scene where Agave, the mother of Pentheus, comes down from the mountain with the head of her rationalist son in her bloody hands. . . .'

Mr. Crantit's lecture, though very enlightening, perhaps went on too long; and in spite of what he had said to Catriona, he dealt at some length with the mysticism of sacrifice and the spiritual rewards of Orphism. His audience, alert and interested to begin with, fell into a kind of torpor before the end; and the second rehearsal lasted three times as long as the first, because the actors were all so impressed by the importance of what they were saying and doing that the principals were frightened to speak and the choruses afraid to move.

Catriona was much cast-down, but Mr. Crantit assured her that troubled rehearsals were merely the rough voyage to a harbour of great promise; and hurried into that part of the mill which the male actors used as their dressing-room. He changed from Greek himation to Britannic tweeds with great celerity, avoiding conversation with his fellow players, and then, on the meadow without, strangely loitered. Catriona, having also changed, came out and invited him to walk home with her. But Mr. Crantit excused himself. A point had occurred to him, he said — a matter of interpretation — that he wanted to discuss with the Leader of the First Chorus.

'With Morag McLeod?'

'Yes, it is Morag, isn't it? She's very good, I think — or will be — but she hasn't quite got that note of ecstatic conviction which, at one point, we should hear in her voice.'

'Morag's a very sensible girl,' said Catriona.

'Yes, that's the trouble, perhaps. But I thought, if I spoke to her, she might at least see what I meant.'

'Oh, I'm sure she would!' said Catriona earnestly. 'But here's Mr. Swanson, I'll go back with him — and there's Morag, with those other girls. Morag! Mr. Crantit has something he wants to say to you.'

In a modest tweed suit, with a cotton handkerchief tied over her head, Morag was less beautiful than she had been, a little while before, in a coronet and belt of velvet ivy, a saffron robe, and a deerskin cape whose rough texture showed off the milky smoothness of her arms; but Mr. Crantit, through his rimless glasses, beamed at her with unabated pleasure, and found grace as well to turn and beam his gratitude to Catriona.

'Shall we walk up the river, and then across to the schoolhouse?' he suggested. 'It's the long way round to the village, but much the pleasanter way.'

'It is the way my father sometimes goes,' said Morag.

'A remarkable man, your father. He's going to make a splendid Cadmus, as soon as he feels himself in the part.'

'He has a good, strong voice.'

'Oh, but all the voices are splendid! You all speak beautifully. The West Highland intonation gives such a richness to the lines, especially in the choruses. You yourself I find *almost* enchanting.'

'I am sorry if I am not as good as I should be.'

'It's because you're already very good that I want you to be even better,' said Mr. Crantit. 'You must learn to let go — if you understand? I'm sure you appreciate the Dionysiac flavour of the play, and know what it means; but you don't, as yet, persuade us that you know.'

'It is a strange play to be doing here in Laxdale,' said Morag.

'Is it? Do you think so? I should say that Laxdale is one of the few places where the *Bacchanals* can be played with real conviction. You have such a strong, sensible attitude to life here, and so much relish for enjoyment.'

'We do not run wild upon the mountains, however, nor murder people because we disapprove of them.'

'But sometimes you feel you would like to, don't you?'

'Sometimes,' admitted Morag, after a pause for consideration.

'I was sure of it. Quite sure. Women, in all the northern countries, have passionate, turbulent natures. Throughout history they've dominated their men-folk, though, until recently, they were clever enough not to insist on public recognition of their power.'

Mr. Crantit took Morag's hand and gave it a conspiratorial squeeze. His eyes twinkled roguishly behind his spectacles, and his voice grew arch. 'I remember a friend of mine — a man of great experience – once telling me that Scotswomen, especially in the Highlands, were the most passionate in Europe; and the most discreet.'

Because the path by the river was narrow, a mere sheep-track, Morag with a skip and a run took the lead, and for the next two hundred yards walked briskly and in silence. Then, relenting a little, went more slowly and said over her shoulder, 'My mother read the play, and did not like it at all, though she thought you were very clever to have translated it so beautifully But it was a heathen play, she said, and none of us would have acted in it, if it had not been for Mr. Macaulay and what he preached from the pulpit.'

'Oh, dear!' said Mr. Crantit. 'Oh, dear, oh dear, oh dear! We are now in danger, my dear Morag, of getting into very deep water. I'm not going to ask you what you mean by *heathen*, because I know the answer you'd give me, and it would, I think, only beg the question. But tell me the opposite meaning: what should we strive to be, and how should we behave? How do you behave?'

'I think,' said Morag slowly, 'that we ought to be good. But I think we should be clever too, and able to enjoy ourselves. It is like an isosceles triangle, if you know what I mean.'

'I do,' said Mr. Crantit, 'yes, I do. But don't you think it should be an equilateral triangle, with goodness and cleverness and enjoyment all equally situated? All equally important?'

'One of them must be at the top, however you look at it.'

'Well, suppose, for the sake of argument, that enjoyment has pride of place. What then?'

'I would spend all my salary on it!' said Morag seriously. 'I can hardly resist going to a dance, if I know there will be good fiddlers playing. I like a concert, and whenever I am in Inverness I go to the cinema, though I do not always enjoy it, and I will eat two or even three ice-creams at a sitting. I am very fond of my food, and good stockings. I was once in Inverness, and bought a new hat for £2. 5s., and I went to the Station Hotel, all by myself, and had dinner and half a bottle of white wine, just for greed of the good food and showing myself off. — Oh, if pleasure was at the top, I would be ruined in no time! But that is not what you were wanting to hear, is it?'

'If your nature,' said Mr. Crantit, 'prompts you to enjoyment, can it be wrong for you to yield to enjoyment?'

'It would be very wrong!' said Morag indignantly. 'For no matter what one's nature wants, it is necessary, as I told you before, to be good!'

The path narrowed again, and Mr. Crantit took the lead, thinking deeply. 'Let us go back to your triangle,' he said, 'of goodness and cleverness and enjoyment. Let us suppose it is a Triangle of Forces. Do you know what that means?'

'I heard of it,' said Morag, 'in the Training College.'

'Take Goodness as your apex,' said Mr. Crantit, 'and if the

adjacent sides of your triangle represent, in magnitude and direction, the forces of Goodness to Cleverness and Goodness to Enjoyment, then the third side will represent their resultant: Cleverness to Enjoyment is the end and purpose of it all.'

'You are being too clever for me,' said Morag.

'I don't want to be,' said Mr. Crantit humbly.

'You like being clever.'

'I have a brain, that must be admitted, but I have never used it for vulgar advantage; or not often. I have used it, almost exclusively, for my own entertainment, and in one or two areas it has become tolerably sensitive, and responsive to superlatives if to nothing else. At this moment its afferent fibres are buzzing with the news of your beauty, the whiteness of your arms, and the anthropophagy of your eyes!'

Morag removed her hand from Mr. Crantit's rather clumsy hold, and said severely, 'You are still trying to be clever.'

They had turned away from the river, and taken the path to the schoolhouse that Nicholas, burdened with a brace of stolen grilse, had taken the day before. They had passed the schoolhouse and turned eastward along the road that ran parallel with the sea-loch and above it, and they had come to a corner of the road where the loch closely girt the land and a wall had been built to withstand the tide. The dusk had fallen, and the water was a darkness that caught the remnant light of the sky only where it leapt and ran, on the little peaks of movement. The landward hills were black as Bible-boards, but in the west, a little to the north of west, a thread of cathedral-window hue remained to mark the setting of the sun.

Mr. Crantit, turning his back upon the loch, sat on the sea-wall, and drew Morag down beside him. 'There is a time,' he said, 'when the faculty of speech means very little in comparison with muscular activity of a less delicate and complicated sort. I know a lot of words, and in many circumstances they serve me well. But what I want to do now is what a ploughman does with instinctive knowledge and a physical assurance that the scholar can't push beyond his inkpot. If my arms were as clever as my vocabulary — '

'No,' said Morag, disengaging herself.

'Oh, please!' said Mr. Crantit, and agonized his desire by holding, for a clumsy moment, her neck with his fingers.

'You are too clever,' said Morag, 'to be doing this sort of thing.' And moved decisively away from him.

'You don't like me?' asked Mr. Crantit sadly.

'I like you very much! But not in this way.'

'Not at all — in this way?'

'No,' said Morag, thoughtfully.

'Oh, God!' said Mr. Crantit.

'I am sorry. I am very sorry.'

'You're an angel.'

'Oh, no, I am not!'

'You are.'

'No, no!'

'You are — you are!'

'It is no use saying that, Mr. Crantit. I am *not* an angel, and it wouldn't suit you if I were!'

CHAPTER TWELVE

'SOCIALISM,' said Mr. Pettigrew, 'was a good thing, a very good thing. More than that, it was a necessary thing, for society had to be reorganized in order to consume what industry was capable of producing, and encourage it to produce more. Labour, in particular, needed reorganization. Capital wasn't in too bad a shape, but labour had to be stabilized, and given more purchasing power, in order to stimulate consumption and keep it at a high level. Full employment was a humane ideal, of course — we made the most of that — but also, don't forget, it was the only way to keep the wheels of production turning; and production means profit, however it's distributed. And that's where my policy has a lot to say: in the distribution of profit. That's where the weakness of orthodox Socialism is most clearly seen; and it's my opinion, which is shared by a number of forward thinkers, that orthodox Socialism has had its day. It's time to substitute what I call "Socialism Plus".'

'Plus what?' asked the General from the other end of the table.

'The easiest way to answer that,' said Mr. Pettigrew, 'is to show you a little equation that I've worked out. I'm going to publish it in my paper one of these days. Do you read *New Classes* here?'

'I'm afraid not.'

'You ought to. It's good.'

Mr. Pettigrew had pushed away his soup-plate, and on a blank page in a pocket-diary was carefully inscribing, with a gold-cased pencil, the equation:

$$SOC + \frac{I^2}{SPR} = SUC$$

The diary was passed to the General, who looked at it gravely, but without comprehension. Mr. Pettigrew, after allowing him a little while for consideration, then explained that SOC meant ordinary Socialism, I^2 was Individuality multiplied by Initiative, and SPR represented a Sense of Personal Responsibility. SUC, as anyone could see, meant the resultant of Success.

'Well,' said the General, still rather puzzled, 'I'm not much of a politician, but that does seem to raise questions, doesn't it?'

'It's my intention to raise questions!' said Mr Pettigrew, visibly elated by this tribute to the energizing power of his theory. 'And the first question, and the most important, that will be raised —'

At this point, unfortunately, he was interrupted by the belated arrival of Mr. Crantit, who looked unusually serious and rather pale. With extreme formality he apologized first to Catriona, then to the General, for his tardiness; and explained that he had had a long and difficult conversation with a member of the cast. Some lines in one of the choruses were perhaps obscure — he had tried to clarify them — it was, essentially, a problem in interpretation. He wasn't hungry, he added. He didn't want any soup.

'I was about to say,' said Mr. Pettigrew —

But quickly, with the fluent ease of custom, Mrs. Pettigrew smothered his ponderous beginning with a little cloud of questions, a flocculence of airy comment, and politics had to yield to drama and the players. Who, she wanted to know, were the young men who played Dionysus and Pentheus? What a god-like figure was Dionysus! So tall, so lovely, and such eyes! And a voice, with its Highland accent, to rock a woman's heart in a cradle of delight.

'That's Hector McBride,' said the General. 'He's a shepherd.'

'He looks like a poet,' said Mrs. Pettigrew with a sigh. 'Not a real poet, of course, but what you think a poet ought to be.'

'He is a poet,' said Catriona, 'but he won't let anyone read his poetry. He's too shy.'

Mr. Pettigrew snorted with a double impatience, of poets and their shyness, and the General said: 'The other fellow, the chap who's playing Pentheus, is my keeper, Norman McKellaig.'

'He looks sad,' said Mrs. Pettigrew, 'but he's got an interesting face.'

'He is sad,' said Catriona, 'and not without reason.'

'There!' cried Mrs. Pettigrew. 'I was right again! I've always said I could read character, and it's very seldom I make a mistake. You, of course, are just an open book — '

'Oh come, come!' said the General.

'But you' — and she turned to Swanson, who sat on her other side — 'you're much more difficult.'

'We were discussing,' said Mr. Pettigrew harshly, 'a very interesting political question.' — And Mrs. Pettigrew, her grey eyes wide with wonder as she contemplated the problem beside her, let mockery for an instant enliven them, made a quick, conspiratorial grimace, and to emphasize her understanding of Swanson's sympathy, lightly squeezed his hand.

He, encouraged by such flattering attention, leaned a little forward and challenged Mr. Pettigrew. 'Don't you think,' he said, 'that we hear too much of politics? And talk of them too much, and trust in them too much? Every age has its heresy, and our contemporary heresy is politics.'

'Nonsense,' said Mr. Pettigrew.

'Oh, goody!' whispered Mrs. Pettigrew.

'Is it true that every age has had its heresy?' asked Marvell. 'The Victorians believed in Industry, the French Revolutionaries believed in Perfectibility, and the Eighteenth Century in Benign Autocracy; at the Reformation they believed in Religion, at the Renaissance in Man, and in the Middle Ages in God.'

'Surely it can't be a heresy to believe in God?' asked Catriona.

'At the mediaeval pitch of belief, it probably was.'

'What Swanson means,' said Mr. Crantit, 'is that heresy, or what he calls heresy, is created by excess. And how right he is! He is arguing from a solid foundation of belief in the classical mean. He and I are on the same side, brothers in arms against that contemporary dinosaur, the modern state, and barbarous too-much-ness!'

Mr. Crantit was feeling better. He had drunk, rather quickly, two glasses of excellent claret — 1934, he observed: it had all the good manners and assurance of maturity — and he was sipping a third. The saddle of mutton had been delectable — oh, there were advantages in living in the country! — and meat and wine had consoled his spirit, restored the ravages of emotion.

'I often think,' he said, 'that there is no fault in us, no sin, but excess. Murder itself could be condoned, under guarantee that all murderers were moderate, discreet and judicious men. Blasphemy, within the limits of politeness, is a great help to reverence. A miniature gluttony is only good appetite, and occasional intemperance a seemly refusal to be strait-laced. — But how fearful and destructive are the virtues that grow too big! Patriotism inflamed with pride must go to war; righteousness that's arrogantly aware of itself will listen to no excuse; articles of faith become regulations by the police and make a moral desert all around them. The great sinners, the lustful conquerors, the maniacal reformers grew up, as if in some moral Debrett, with the Best Intentions; and made havoc of their worlds because they grew too big and went too far. Nature, that abhors a vacuum, abominates a nimiety: a too-muchness, that is. Consider the brontosaurus —'

'Good God!' exclaimed Mr. Pettigrew. 'Do you see what time it is?'

'A quarter-past eight,' said the General. 'There's no hurry.'

'But the meeting was advertised for half-past seven!'

'Yes, meetings always are, but they never start then, and the more important the meeting the later it is. People like to talk things over among themselves first, and that often saves time in the long run.'

'A community that lives as haphazardly as that,' said Mr. Pettigrew severely, 'is just asking for trouble!'

'Oh, I hope not. You'll find them a good audience, very attentive, and quite intelligent. — But perhaps you want to look at your notes, before going along?'

'I never use notes,' said Mr. Pettigrew, 'because I don't need them. I keep my facts at my finger-ends, and I know how to explain them. You'd have seen that, if I'd been given a chance to say a few words about Socialism Plus. I could have given you an outline of the whole theory in ten minutes or so. Distribution, for example —'

'The port is beside you,' said the General.

'One of the lessons that Socialism has to learn is that very large incomes — in the proper hands — are not inimical to general welfare.'

'How much do you think teachers should be paid?' asked Mr. Crantit.

'It's an honourable profession,' said Mr. Pettigrew. 'It deserves proper remuneration.'

'In my opinion,' said Mr. Crantit, 'their minimum salary should be £1000 a year.'

'I'm not prepared to be facetious,' said Mr. Pettigrew stiffly, 'about so grave a matter.'

'Good God!' cried Mr. Crantit. 'Do you think I'm joking? Have you ever wondered what a teacher has to do in these dishevelled times? Or should do? When the Church has lost its authority, and parents have thankfully abandoned theirs? All that the Church once did, all that responsible parents did, is left to poor teachers now. The teachers in elementary schools, where the very elements of decency and good manners have to be taught as well as arithmetic and English grammar; the teachers in secondary schools, where shreds of common sense, common humility before the unknown, common reverence before the unknowable, have to be slipped in, as time permits — time rationed by Government regulations — between Pythagoras' Theorem and the date of the Treaty of Utrecht. That's what teachers have to do, because other people have failed in their tasks — and you think I'm joking!'

Catriona caught Mrs. Pettigrew's eye, and the ladies got up. 'We'll be ready as soon as you are,' said Catriona, and smiled graciously to Marvell, who had hurried to open the door.

Swanson moved into Mrs. Pettigrew's chair, and the General said to Flett, 'Come up here beside me, Mr. Flett. I haven't heard a word from you tonight.'

'And there's more to it than that,' Mr. Crantit continued. 'Under the new benevolence of our state the teacher has also become a kitchen-servant: he has to serve meals to the pupils whom he is hired to instruct in the English language, elementary physics, and the mathematic art. Curate to an absentee Vicar, deputy-Parent, over-burdened Pedagogue, and Canteen-waiter all in one. Now tell me how much you'd pay him!'

'He get's pretty warm about teachers, doesn't he?' whispered the General.

'He's quite right,' said Flett, speaking for the first time that night. 'I was a teacher myself once, for a few months, and no one ever thanked you for what you were doing. There was no future in it, so I gave it up.'

'I am not accustomed,' said Mr. Pettigrew slowly, 'to being addressed in the tone of voice that you have seen fit to use. I am not prepared to admit that the Church has lost its authority, and most certainly I don't accept your statement that parents, in this essentially home-loving country of ours, are indifferent, or could be indifferent, to the manners and beliefs of their own children. Your manner is injudicious, and your arguments, Mr. Crantit, lack substance.'

'I've always thought it unfair and illogical,' said Marvell, 'that a teacher, who has to look after a child's mind, should be so poorly paid in comparison with the doctor who looks after its body.'

'And what,' demanded Mr. Crantit, 'does the young doctor of today do for his money? He gives his patient an injection of penicillin, and if that doesn't cure him, sends him to see a psychiatrist!'

'I think,' said the General, 'that we have just time for another glass of port, and then we must go. — Here's to a good meeting, Mr. Pettigrew! We're all looking forward, with the greatest interest and expectation, to what you have to say, and I hope that none of us will be disappointed.'

CHAPTER THIRTEEN

THE school was so closely filled for Mr. Pettigrew's meeting that between the platform-party — for whom, indeed, there was no platform — and the audience that faced them, there was barely room for a well-fed child to pass. Tightly packed on narrow benches, the knees of those behind pressing on the buttocks of those in front, shoulder to shoulder — fat women overflowing on to thin men, shrivelled spinsters hardly visible between burly neighbours — the people of Laxdale sat listening to Mr. Pettigrew with strained attention; and round the walls, two or three deep, as grave and motionless as figures on a frieze, stood those who had come too late to be seated, but in time to be uncomfortable. The air grew hot, a glaze of sweat varnished rosy faces and sunburnt faces, the lamps burnt a little smokily; but no one stirred in protest, no one complained. Their attention was concentrated on Mr. Pettigrew.

Mr. Pettigrew had not vainly boasted when he said he had no need for notes. He was an accomplished speaker, with a brimfull river of words in his head, and the skill to keep them within stiff and purposeful banks. His manner was confident and down-to-earth, but sometimes lacked sympathy; and his voice was now, perhaps, a little harsh and brusque, not only with the remnant irritation of his argument with Mr. Crantit, but because he could not walk up and down, as he usually did on a platform, without stumbling over the feet of the people in the front row. From time to time, for no reason they could divine, he would pause for a moment and scowl at those who so vexingly restrained him.

On the wall behind him was fastened a large coloured chart,

entitled DRUMLIEDUBBS, which, before Mr. Pettigrew's arrival, had aroused a lot of confused speculation in the audience; but for some considerable time Mr. Pettigrew made no reference to it. He began his speech by reiterating his deep, personal interest in Laxdale, but though he spoke at some length about his saintly mother and her formative influence on him, his audience, still thinking about the chart, were less responsive than he had expected them to be. It was not until he began to summarize the history of Laxdale that he won their whole attention.

Broadly, but with some lively detail, he drew its picture as it had been when Miss Phipps of Middlesex bought the estate. He was scrupulously fair to her and all her works — praised her, indeed, for her benevolence and good management — but then showed how, from her time onwards, the population had decreased, and the old self-sufficiency of the parish had almost disappeared. It used to have its own smiths and millers, coopers and weavers and tailors, shoe-makers and boat-builders; but where were they now? 'The shoes you're wearing now,' he said, 'were probably made in North-amptonshire, your clothes in Yorkshire, and your boats on the Moray Firth.' The old days when a parish lived not only on its own milk and meal and meat, but on its own manufactures, had gone for ever; from Laxdale as from everywhere else. They could no longer depend on themselves, but had to buy what they needed from places where clothes and shoes were made cheaply and efficiently. But could they, in fact, afford to live like that?

Mr. Pettigrew, who had clearly gone to a great deal of trouble to acquire so much information, then told them how many old-age pensioners there were in Laxdale, and how many people in receipt of pensions for sons and fathers killed in war. He told them, with embarrassing accuracy, how much a crofter could expect to earn, and the whole value of the cattle and eggs and sheep exported from Laxdale. He calculated for them, with impressive ease, the Government subsidies, direct and indirect, which enabled them to maintain their present manner of life — and then, with a sudden change of voice, with a sudden access of emotion, he demanded, 'And what, after all, is the manner of your life? And what is it worth?

'You are living a life of mediaeval hardship,' he declared, 'in circumstances almost as stark and poor as the Middle Ages! Your menfolk work from dawn till dusk to wring a meagre return from an unrewarding land or a stormy sea, and your women-folk work harder than the men. Yes, that is true! For here in Laxdale the housewife has none of the advantages that housewives, in all other parts of the country, have long considered an essential, indeed a natural part of existence. You have no running water in your houses, no sanitation, no gas-stoves or electric cookers to make the preparation of a meal not only an easy task, but a pleasant occupation! No laundry-van calls for your washing, no municipal dust-cart to remove the waste and discards of domestic life. And when the hard day's work is over, are there buses and trams passing your doorstep to take you swiftly to a warm and comfortable cinema where you can forget the toil and heartbreak of your day? No! Because there is no cinema to take you to!'

Mr. Pettigrew, warming to his theme, painted so drab and miserable a picture of life in the parish — beaten upon by Atlantic storms, poverty-stricken, far from dentists and plumbers — that his audience grew more and more unhappy. A deep sadness fell upon them, self-pity crept into their minds. Never, until now, had they realized the wretchedness of their lives, or seen the stark injustice under which they lived. 'And think,' said Mr. Pettigrew, 'of your children. What is their future to be? What hope can you offer them, who have no hope yourselves?' — Here and there a woman murmured in the pain of her heart, and the close-packed ranks of people stirred uncomfortably.

'But you say,' Mr. Pettigrew continued smoothly, 'that if you had a good road to the east, and a serviceable pier for steamers, the material conditions of your life would be immeasurably improved, and the value of your work would also be increased. Well, that brings us, without any question, to economic considerations. Now such a road as you want would cost many thousands of pounds, and a pier might cost more. But the whole value of Laxdale, as I have already shown you — its exportable value, its value to the rest of the community — is negligible. And therefore, on economic grounds, what claim have you on the rest of the community? Why should it spend vast sums of money on you when it cannot possibly get any return for its money, either in goods or service? Laxdale, my friends, is not an investment that I, or any honest man, could recommend. And you, honest, God-fearing people though you are, in your present mode of life are not an asset to Britain, as you should be, but a liability!'

A profound and awful gloom descended on his audience, and Mr. Pettigrew, perceiving the effect he had created, immediately became more cheerful.

'But don't despair!' he exclaimed. 'Don't give way to pessimism! I've come here, because of my inherited interest in Laxdale — because of my instinctive hatred of waste of time, waste of effort, waste of human material — I've come here to tell you how this sad and dreary picture can be reversed, quickly and decisively, to show upon its other side a scene of bright and prospering industry, of cheerful modern homes replete with all the luxury that science and technology can provide, and a community, inspired with new hope and purpose, that will achieve happiness by consecrating its labour to the general good! Look at this plan upon the wall, the plan of a new town that might well have been called the New Jerusalem, but, in deference to local opinion and the long-established name of the vicinity, is in fact to be known as Drumliedubbs.'

Mr. Pettigrew then explained the coloured chart that hung behind him. It was the plan of a new industrial estate — as he described it — in which the houses of the workers were to be scientifically designed for their health and comfort, and so economically situated as to be within easy reach, on the one hand, of the factories where both men and women could earn a living, and, on the other side, of the cinemas, public parks, and popular restaurants where they might forget the toil and weariness of their labour. *That* way, he said, was the way to earn good wages; and *this* way the way to spend what part of them they could properly afford to spend. Labour would turn into ready money, money meant security and pleasure, and comfort was guaranteed by a house or commodious flat with a refrigerator and a washing-machine in every kitchen.

Nor was this, as they might suppose, an idle dream of happiness but reality already visible; for the drains were dug in Drumliedubbs, the houses were going up, and the foundations had been laid of a furniture-factory, a paint-and-varnish factory, a lesser factory for the making of brushes, and a mill for the making of imitation textiles from coal-dust and seaweed — in all of which he, Mr. Pettigrew, had a personal interest and a large investment. It was because of this that he was able to offer the people of Laxdale a solution of their problem that would be advantageous to one and all.

'In the words of an old revivalist hymn that my sainted mother often sang to me,' he said, ' "Leave the poor old sinking ship, and pull for the shore"!'

Mr. Pettigrew drew his handkerchief and wiped a glaze of sweat from his forehead and his cheeks. 'Because of the influence I have,' he said, 'because of the large investment I have already made in Drumliedubbs, and because of my affection for Laxdale, I can promise to all of you homes in this new and splendid industrial estate, profitable work for all who are capable of it, part-time work for boys and girls, and the older people too, work in such abundance and continuity as you have never dreamt of, and rewards for work passing your understanding! And here, in a single sentence is the advice I give your from my head, and the help I offer you from my heart: abandon Laxdale, poor, worn-out old Laxdale, and come to Drumliedubbs with its glorious future of hard work and high wages, and a significant part to play in the morrow of the modern world!'

Mr. Pettigrew, with an impressive gesture, waited for applause. He sat down and looked about him, expectant still, but with a slowly deepening frown of bewilderment and disappointment. The audience avoided his eyes. More bewildered than he, they sat in silent consternation. General Matheson cleared his throat, but found it difficult to comment on what Mr. Pettigrew had said without discarding his impartial, chairmanlike manner; and on the close-packed benches there were such tumultuary feelings, so many cross-tides of sentiment and loathing, so many overfalls of instinctive knowledge and eddies of sudden doubt, that no one could find a tenable position from which to refute Mr. Pettigrew and his argument, until a small, rosy-faced, bald-headed, rather simple-minded crofter from the uppermost limits of cultivation rose and began a rambling discourse, that gradually, by its general incon-sequence, restored a measure of ease, if not of confidence, and infuriated Mr. Pettigrew by the speaker's obvious failure to grasp the meaning of his careful discourse. The rosy little crofter con-cluded his remarks by asking, 'And what will you say, Mr. Petti-grew, if we reply to your very generous offer by stating, quite simply, that we do not want to go and live in Drumliedubbs?'

'I shall say, in that case,' said Mr. Pettigrew, losing his temper, 'that beggars can't be choosers!'

Like the in-drawing of the wind before the burst of a winter squall, or the suck of the open sea before the tumble and fall of an Atlantic billow, there sounded harshly through the room the note of impending storm, and a youngish man, white of face, with a dark mane of hair like dry seaweed on a sunlit rock, rose and cried, 'Do you call me a beggar, Mr. Pettigrew, because I draw a pension for *this*?'

He raised the stump of his left arm, six inches of sewed-in sleeve, and spoke like a cracked trumpet: 'I lost that with the Cameron Highlanders on Cameron Ridge on Keren Hill, and it wasn't for Laxdale only I was fighting, but for all of you in the big cities! And my father was killed on the Somme in 1916, and my mother drew a pension for him — was she a beggar too? Her father was killed at Tel-el-Kebir! Oh, we haven't worked for you in your dirty factories, that's true enough, but by God, we've fought for you, and there's none fought better!'

Suddenly, quite suddenly, the temper of the meeting changed. The melancholy, the sense of failure and futility that Mr. Pettigrew had created, was blown away, and stormy defiance supervened. Dead men were remembered, battle-fields recalled, and vaunted names were passionately tossed towards the platform. Are we beggars, they cried, because we draw the wages of bravery?

Mr. Pettigrew sat grim and unresponsive. His face, as rough as granite, was carved in the bold lines of granite sculpture; and Mr. Crantit regarded it with proper admiration. Mr. Crantit had been deeply moved by the sudden display of popular sentiment, but he was also capable of respect for Mr. Pettigrew's resistance to it. He observed, with interest, that the anger shown by a score or so of elderly women in the audience was peculiarly dreadful: they showed their teeth, snarling, like great primeval beasts, and Mr. Crantit was both pleased and perturbed when he realized that all their teeth were artificial. They had been supplied, free of charge, by the benevolent service of the new Department of Health, the establishment of which Mr. Pettigrew had undoubtedly supported. — He saw, with concern, the flush of indignation on General Matheson's face, and was surprisingly perturbed by fear that he would speak inadvisedly.

It was with proportionate relief that he saw Nicholas McLeod rising to address the audience.

'I am not a clever man, like Mr. Pettigrew,' said Nicholas gently, 'and therefore I am not going to challenge him on matters of sentiment and such-like, where a clever interpretation of the facts is necessary. I am just going to ask him one or two questions on simple, straightforward economic lines. Mr. Pettigrew, you will remember, sympathized with us because we have no up-to-date and proper form of sanitation; and then he complained that we were a burden to the general community, and cost the Government of Britain more than it received, or could ever receive, from us. — But I would ask Mr. Pettigrew how much of our taxation is spent on the removal of sewage from the great cities of London and Liverpool and Glasgow, and Manchester and Birmingham and all the rest of them, that enjoy indoor sanitation? How much, indeed, does it cost to look after any big city, and supply it with rent-collectors, and policemen and firemen, and a civic administration; with chartered accountants, and district railways, and electric light; with barbers, and cinemas, and ice-cream shops, and billiard-saloons, and all the other things that we can do without? There is not one of those big cities that is not a greater expense to all Britain, and a more wasteful use of its resources, than Laxdale! I say we are the cheapest and most economical parish in the Kingdom, we have less spent on us than anybody else, and everything we export for the benefit of the larger community is practically free, gratis, and for nothing! It is no more than the claiming of a debt when we ask for a road and a pier!'

Now, in the clamour of voices, the note of anger was replaced by a sound of triumph: Nicholas had scored against the enemy and taken revenge, not only for his insults to Laxdale, but for the intolerable disappointment of his speech. They had expected him to be on their side, and without warning he had turned against them! The insults had hurt them, but the betrayal of their confidence hurt them more, and Nicholas's counter-attack had sweetened their minds in consequence. They cheered him loudly, and defied their adversary as they applauded.

Catriona rose, white-cheeked with anger, and speaking very quickly, said, 'It seems to me that Mr. Pettigrew overlooked a lot of things when he was telling us all the advantages of going to live in Drumliedubbs. It's true that nobody here earns much money, but everybody has a great deal of freedom, and plenty of room to move about, and the best view in the world! And those are things that only the wealthiest people can usually enjoy!'

Morag McLeod stood up, and startled Mr. Crantit by the lovely fierceness of her voice and look. — Like a Maenad! he thought. — 'And our time is our own!' she cried. 'We live our own lives, we are frightened of no one, and if we don't have bathrooms in our houses, we don't miss them as the people in big towns would do, because we don't get so dirty!'

'Bravo, bravo!' cried Mr. Crantit, clapping his hands, and again there was much applause.

A dozen others put the case for Laxdale, some with force and coherence, some with indignant or sentimental ineptitude; and then the General rose and said, 'I think it is time, perhaps, for me to try and summarize what has been said on each side —'

'We haven't heard what Mr. Marvell has to say!' cried a man at the back of the room.

The General turned inquiringly to Mr. Marvell, who, with manifest unhappiness, stood up and said, 'I came here without any pre-conceived ideas. I didn't come to try and persuade you into any particular course of action. I came to see for myself the conditions of your life, and to observe your reaction to Mr. Pettigrew's pro-posals. I am not, I hope, being disloyal to Mr. Pettigrew when I say that I am not committed to his policy, and I hope I shan't be raising your hopes unduly when I say that I want to see more of your country, and hear more of your arguments, before I accept, or dismiss from my mind, what may in fact be a justified demand for better communications. I have an open mind, ladies and gentlemen, and that being so, I must keep my lips closed.'

There was a rough murmur of sympathy, and the General, rising again, was about to speak when Mr. Pettigrew asked permission to say a little more.

'I want, first of all,' he said, 'to apologize for my unfortunate reference to beggars. I give you my word that nothing was farther from my mind than any lack of gratitude to those who fought for us, of reverence for those who died. If I have hurt anyone's feelings, I apologize without reserve. And secondly, I wish to congratulate Mr. McLeod on a very clever speech. Mr. McLeod pretended to deal with the economic facts of the case, and very skilfully threw dust in our eyes. But economics is a subject to which I have given considerable study, and you must allow me to clear that dust away. The true facts of the case are these ...'

For five minutes Mr. Pettigrew marshalled facts and figures on the one side, figures and supposed facts on the other; and con-clusively proved — proved too quickly to be easily refuted — that he was right and Nicholas wrong. He spoke easily and without any sign of ill-feeling. He repeated his arguments for the abandon-ment of Laxdale and the colonization, as he called it, of the more fruitful land of Drumliedubbs, and said that history could supply many examples of people who had recognized the proper moment at which to change their traditional way of life, and prospered as a result of change; and as many contrary examples of people who had refused to see the facts that stared them in the face, and perished in consequence. 'Laxdale is going down the hill,' he said, 'and

Drumliedubbs will march to the summit. All I ask is that you should choose, before it is too late, which slope to live on. And if you choose the upward slope, I pledge you all the help and favour I can command!'

Again a silence fell on the close-seated, unhappy audience. Unwillingly they were impressed by Mr. Pettigrew's confidence, and the acrobatic assurance of his figures. They searched their minds for an answer — they knew there must be an answer — but they could not find it; and slowly, miserably, they felt their case going by default. And then, in the middle of the room, an old man got up who had been listening, with difficulty but patient attention, to everything that was said, a gnarled brown hand cupped to his ear to catch the words. He was Rory Mackenzie, the fisherman who, at the General's meeting a couple of days before, had been sceptical about all Parliamentary delegations.

He stood up and said, in his high-pitched Gaelic voice, 'I have been very much impressed by all the advantages that Mr. Pettigrew has offered us, and I am wondering if Mr. Pettigrew will be very kind and tell us something more about this fine new town of Drumliedubbs.'

'I'll tell you all I know,' said Mr. Pettigrew bluffly, 'and that's as much as anyone knows.'

'Well, to begin with,' said Rory, 'how much land will you be giving us with these fine houses?'

'Land?' said Mr. Pettigrew. 'What do you want land for?'

'How else can we live, if we have no land?'

'You'll be given a job, I tell you! A good, sensible job of work to do, and good money for it at the end of every week!'

A neighbour, with better hearing, had to repeat Mr. Pettigrew's answer before Rory thoroughly understood it; and after a moment or two, for taking thought, he asked, 'Will we be able to see the Cuillins from this new town?'

'The Cuillins?' said Mr. Pettigrew. 'What have they got to do with it?'

'The Cuillins,' said the General, 'are the high hills we see on Skye. On the island of Skye.'

'Yes, yes, I know that. But I don't get the relevance of the question. — In Drumliedubbs, my friend, you'll be nearly two hundred miles from the Cuillins, and even with a telescope you couldn't see them.'

'Well, well!' said Rory, shaking his head in disappointment. 'But there will be a fine river in this new place. What is it called?'

'There isn't exactly a river,' said Mr. Pettigrew. 'There's a canal, a mile or two away, and there's going to be a public park with a pond in it — for little boys, you know, to paddle in.'

'Can they not paddle in the sea?' asked Rory.

'Well, they're not within thirty miles of the sea — '

'Thirty miles from the sea?' cried Rory, in his old, crackling voice. 'And no hills to look upon, no river! And no land to work! Man, I would as soon go to live in Hell as a place like that!'

Shriller and more voluble, leaping higher in delight, the cries of commendation came in Gaelic now, and all the audience rose to cheer the old man who, unmoved, had resumed his seat, and was listening — his hand to his ear — as patiently to acclamation as he had to Mr. Pettigrew's argument. Now they were convinced, by the pure simplicity of his reasoning, that they were right and Pettigrew wrong, and from their applause of Rory Mackenzie the rougher part of the audience turned to jeer at Pettigrew and shout their hatred of all he had said. The old women with artificial teeth were especially vociferous, as Mr. Crantit observed, and once again he looked with admiration and alarm at their large and gleaming fangs. — But before the audience got out of hand, and before Mr. Pettigrew (who was ready to do so) could rise and more deeply exacerbate their feelings, the General, tall and grave, was on his feet and with a perfect composure was saying, 'Well, that concludes our meeting, and while I think it unnecessary to call for a show of hands, to decide whether opinion is for or against the scheme that Mr. Pettigrew has so ingeniously propounded, you will, I am sure, all agree with me that Highland courtesy and the custom of the parish demand a vote of thanks to a speaker who, while not arousing general favour, has at least stirred our interest more deeply than any of our political visitors for some considerable time. Ladies and gentlemen, I declare the meeting at an end, and ask you to accord Mr. Pettigrew a very warm vote of thanks for his kindness in coming here tonight!'

The clamour died. Mr. Pettigrew, still full of fight, stood up and was about to renew his argument. 'Not another word!' whispered the General fiercely, and led him out. A patter of applause followed them, civil and obedient, and inhuman as castanets.

CHAPTER FOURTEEN

'POOR Sam!' said Mrs. Pettigrew, 'he does ask for trouble, doesn't he? He gets carried away by his own ideas, that's his weakness. But he wouldn't be worth two and a half million without it.'

'Is he really?' asked Swanson.

'Within a couple of hundred thousand, this way or that.'

'Oh, God! You live in a different world!'

'Don't be so silly! A person like you oughtn't to say things like that. We're all men and women, there's no other difference that really matters — and if anyone complains about that one, there's something wrong with him.'

'Have you always been rich?'

'What, me? Don't make me laugh. My mother kept a boarding-house in Blackpool, and I might have been there still if it hadn't been for Jim Poppledyke.'

'Who was he?'

'Didn't you ever hear of Jim Poppledyke? He was one of the first to start football pools. He used to come and stay with us in Blackpool, he was a sanitary engineer then — plumber, they used to call it — but he had ideas. He got ideas about me, too.'

'A visionary plumber. An aspiring plumber thinking also of the heart's convenience —'

'Oh, don't talk like an intellectual! I read one of your books once, it was full of words, but if you got past them there was plenty of fun and games in it.'

'I have never,' said Swanson, a little nervously, 'had fun and games with anyone worth two and a half million pounds.'

'Well, you're going to now,' said Mrs. Pettigrew, and clasping him firmly in her arms, planted a generous kiss on his startled lips.

Immediately after the meeting Mr. Pettigrew had climbed into the General's elderly Daimler, and said in a rough, determined voice, 'I want some brandy, in a claret glass. Let's go home.'

The General, seeing none of the other members of his house-party near at hand, had decided it would be tactful to do as Pettigrew wished, and then return for the rest. He had driven off, and Marvell, seeing him go, had said to Catriona, 'What a wonderful night it is! Shall we walk back?'

Mr. Crantit, watching the turbulent edge of the crowd like a scrum-half behind the tense forwards at a throw-in from touch — Mr. Crantit, waiting for Morag McLeod to be expelled from the audience as a rugby football from a line-out or a scrum, by destiny hooking in his favour — had, to his intense chagrin, seen her go off with the bullet-headed, insignificant Mr. Flett. A tea-drinking, pen-pushing, paltry little Civil Servant with a Scotch accent and a soul untaught by the passion of Greek poetry, the beauty of a Greek vase! A barbarian had defeated him, a young barbarian had dispossessed him of his desire; and Mr. Crantit's face, with sunken jaw and darkness reflected in his spectacles, had put on the likeness of a tragic mask.

Brought together by accident, Mrs. Pettigrew and Olaf Swanson had observed his discomfiture and been united by the social malice which, nowadays, is quicker than kindness to make the whole world kin.

'Poor Mr. Crantit!' she said complacently. 'But he's far too old for her. He's got brains, of course, but brains don't count for much with a girl of twenty-two. What she wants is glossy hair and a nice profile, or someone who can dance the samba, or looks like an all-in wrestler in his bathing-pants. I was just the same myself at her age. The first boy I ever fell for played the tenor sax. in a dance-band: God, what a fool he was! And mean. But he'd lovely hair, and when he played his solo bits my heart would turn to milk, and I wanted him to lap it up, like a kitten. Then I went off the deep-end with a harrier. You know, they go out on a Saturday afternoon and run for twenty miles, and come back again. He was dark, with a sort of Italian look, and he used to show me how much he could expand his chest. — Oh well, we've got to live and learn, and Jim Poppledyke taught me a bit of sense. I began to realize, then, that a man ought to have brains as well. Let's go back by the beach, shall we?'

Swanson, who was usually frightened of women, was in a mood of unnatural audacity. Speaking little at dinner, except for his brief attack on Pettigrew, he had drunk a lot of the General's good claret, and the meeting, at which he felt no responsibility for either side, had excited him. The fine fresh air of the moonlit night, after the paraffin-fumes and human smell of the schoolroom, had put a top on his exhilaration like the cream on a champagne glass, and he had been delighted to lead the softly yielding Mrs. Pettigrew across the *machair* to the shining strip of beach that led to Laxdale Hall. He had put his arm about her before they began to speak of Sam Pettigrew's millions, and while palpable surrender pleased his fingers, the perceptible excitation of her heart had flattered his thoughts. — But now, when she stopped and turned and lustily embraced him, his thoughts grew faint and fled from what they had seen far-off, like an island discovered in a telescope, whose distance was its temptation. — He retreated, or tried to, from her grasp. He stumbled over a tree-root, fell; and brought her down on top of him.

They had reached the northern end of the beach, and for the last fifteen or twenty yards had been walking heavily through the loose, dry sand that bordered the frontier of the General's plantations. The outermost trees of the little seaside wood were Corsican pines, growing from an evergreen mat of soft, resilient moss that wind-blown shells and the dropping of scented cones enriched. It was the root of a Corsican pine that tripped them, the evergreen moss that received them.

'Well!' cried Mrs. Pettigrew, twisting away from him. 'I didn't expect that, I must say! You intellectuals don't waste time, do you?'

'I'm so sorry!' said Swanson, sitting up 'I tripped —'

'So you say!'

'I did really!'

'Well, you found a good place to trip, I'll say that for you. At least it's soft and dry. — Oh, don't look so solemn!'

Swanson was again swept by enclosing arms, by a demanding mouth — swept as the stern of a trawler, driven ashore before an Atlantic gale, is swept by breaking waves — but the wave suddenly receded, and Mrs. Pettigrew sat upright, sighed and was thoughtful for a little while; and she spoke of what seemed to her the strangeness of life in Laxdale. It didn't make sense, she said, but she liked it; and the very air, she thought, induced a feeling of irresponsibility.

'Your husband will be wondering where you are,' said Swanson uneasily.

'Not he!' she answered. 'After a good meeting he's wrapped-up in himself for hours, thinking how clever he's been, and after a bad meeting you can't speak to him for a whole day, because he's wondering what went wrong. At this moment he'll be drinking the General's drink, and telling the General how stupid the audience was not to understand him; and he'll go on doing that as long as anyone listens.'

'Why did you marry him?'

'Well, I was left a widow at twenty-nine, and that's not a natural state, is it? I had a good time with Jim Poppledyke for five or six years — oh, a lovely time! — and then he began to get worried about his business. It got bigger and bigger, you see, and there was more and more money coming in, and he had heavier and heavier responsibilities every year, and that meant ulcers, of course, it always does, and just after he'd bought a country estate and made up his mind to breed cows for safety, one of them perforated and he was dead in ten days. — Well, I went to London, for a change of scene, and six months later I met Sam. He'd more money than Jim, and lived in a more sophisticated way, and that's what I thought I wanted. So I married him. But I don't know. It's all right in one way, and everybody respects him — except these people in Laxdale. But it isn't what I'd hoped for. At least, I don't think so, though I've half-forgotten what I did hope for.'

A little of Swanson's courage returned, at the prospect of conversation, and he began to talk, entertainingly enough, about the meeting in the school. Mrs. Petttigrew listened with diminishing attention, and suddenly, by means of a neat and agile movement, was leaning comfortably against his shoulder.

'You don't even know my name,' she said reproachfully.

'I've heard your husband call you Lucy.'

'It's Lusitania, really. After the ship, you know. My father was a steward aboard her when she was sunk, and I was born a month after.'

Swanson, at a loss for words, but feeling that some expression of sympathy was called for, rather tentatively stroked her hair.

'Last year,' she said, 'Sam and I went to America in the *Queen Elizabeth* — top-price cabins, of course — and my bedroom-steward had been a pantry-boy aboard the *Lusitania*, and remembered dad. It makes you laugh, doesn't it?'

'Well, in a way, perhaps.'

'It ought to! And it would, if you looked at things properly and didn't worry too much about them. But people are forgetting how to laugh, if you ask me. — You haven't got ulcers, have you?'

'No.'

'Well, why can't you enjoy yourself when you get the chance? Are you frightened of women? Or just of me?'

'That's putting it too simply,' said Swanson unhappily. 'I am, I think, rather frightened of the consequences — oh, not physical consequences, it's more than that. You see, everyone is a sort of island in the world, an island with certain rights and, I think, a natural expectation of privacy. But if someone comes ashore, he leaves footprints on the sand —'

'And the next tide washes them away.'

'Not if he goes too far.'

'Well, even if he walks all over the place, and lights a fire, and prepares to settle down for a bit, what does it matter? The fire won't burn for ever, and the grass'll grow again.'

'I don't think every island recovers as easily as that.'

'You take yourself too seriously.'

'I'm taking you seriously.'

'That's only another way of saying you're frightened. Oh, it was just the same in America! We were there for a fortnight, and twenty-three men tried to make love to me when they were too drunk to have any real interest in it, but only one had the guts to make a pass at me sober. He was a truck-driver, and asked me to go to Skaneateles. Well, I didn't want to go to Skaneateles, but I was grateful to him for not being frightened.'

Swanson had often tried to rationalize and rid himself of his fear of women; but though he could explain it, well enough for his own satisfaction, he could never drive it away. He had had a series of unfortunate experiences early in life, of which the memory was too deep to be erased. — An elder sister, a sturdy, jealous child, had tried to drown him in his infancy, and at twelve or thirteen he had had to run for his life from a huge, crop-headed young woman, a crofter's simple-minded daughter, in whom the full moon occasionally roused a frenzy of desire. And in his first war, when he was a pretty boy of seventeen with a delicate complexion, he had been attacked and roughly handled by a drunken corporal in the Women's Auxiliary Army Corps. A less sensitive mind would certainly not have been permanently affected by such trivial accidents, but Swanson, with the receptive imagination of the artist, still saw in many of the women he met a significant likeness to the shameless corporal, the single-minded simpleton under a Shetland moon, or the murderous innocence of his sister. — His wife had won his love by a shyness exceeding his own, and her demure resemblance to Fouquet's Virgin of Melun; which seemed to set her somewhat apart from ordinary womanhood. — But Lucy Pettigrew, ignorant of this troubled history, assumed a simpler reason for his fear.

'I've often seen men looking at me,' she said mournfully, 'in a way that ought to mean something; but it doesn't, because when they look at me, they see Sam and his two and a half million. And they're probably hoping to get something out of Sam, and don't want to give offence; or they're employed by him, and won't risk getting the sack; or they've just got a superstition that it's unlucky to find yourself on the wrong side of a rich man. So they give themselves a bit of a shake, and look somewhere else. — I'd all the fun I wanted when I was poor, but now, except for the clothes I wear, I might as well be in a convent.'

'I am not in the least frightened of your husband!' said Swanson with deep annoyance. 'I want nothing from him, and he's got no power to harm me.'

'Where are your books printed?'

'Somewhere in Middlesex.'

'He could buy-up the printing-works; or start a strike. He's done both in his time.'

'I think you're exaggerating his power — but in any case I am not, I repeat, frightened of him.'

Proudly, to prove his words, Swanson put an arm round her shoulders and kissed her on the lips, firmly enough, but without much warmth or promise. Lucy sighed, and waited. But Swanson was thinking more of the need to justify himself than of the occasion to comfort her; and after half a minute of awkward stillness and complete silence, he began once more to explain his theory of the island-personality and the sanctity of its shores. But Lucy was not listening.

She stood up, and stooped again to brush her skirt. 'Come on,' she said. 'Let's go back and have a drink. There's plenty of that here, whatever else you go short of.'

She looked round her, at the little wood of twisted pines, their tufted branches black against the moon, and the running silver of the moonlit sea. 'But it does seem a pity,' she said, 'on a night like this.'

CHAPTER FIFTEEN

'I'VE never been to church in my life,' declared Mr. Pettigrew, 'and I'm certainly not going to start now.'

'We got married in a registry office,' explained Mrs. Pettigrew.

'I always get married in a registry office,' said Mr. Pettigrew testily.

'Did your saintly mother not take you to church?' asked Mr. Crantit.

'She never had the time! No, nor time for idle luxury of any sort. Work from morning till night, and from year's end to year's end, was all her share of life.'

'There's no great luxury in going to church in Laxdale,' said the General. He stood with his back to the breakfast-table, contemplating the morning's weather while he supped his porridge. 'The pews are far from comfortable.'

'I am looking forward to the sermon,' said Mr. Crantit. 'I told you, I think, that Macaulay is going to preach from the Book of Amos.'

'Who was he?' asked Mr. Pettigrew.

'In spirit, at least, a man of our own times,' said Mr. Crantit. 'An angry man, who came out of the desert and denounced people. His language is more elegant than that of our contemporary prophets, but his manner is very like the snarling vilifications with which, in the last few years, we have become so wearied and familiar. I am most anxious to hear what Macaulay will make of him.'

'I haven't seen Mr. Macaulay since he left here,' said Catriona.

'He wasn't at the meeting,' said the General. 'He ought to have come — even at the risk of sitting next to Swanson — and I'm going to tell him so.'

'I think we ought to have another meeting early next week,' said Mr. Pettigrew. 'I want to give these people a chance to reconsider their opinion.'

'He's a glutton for punishment,' said Mrs. Pettigrew admiringly.

'I'm going to talk to a lot of them individually, first of all,' said Mr. Pettigrew. 'Two people, talking alone, will listen to reason and common sense; but in a crowded meeting you're at the mercy of emotion.'

'It ought to be the other way about, oughtn't it?' said Mrs. Pettigrew, wide-eyed and innocent; and Swanson felt his cheeks grow warm with discomfort.

'I'm going to start this morning,' Mr. Pettigrew went on, 'while you're at church. A good lot of women have to stay at home, I suppose, to look after their children and cook the dinner; well, I want to look at their houses, and ask them some questions; then I'll restate my argument, briefly and simply, but quite unanswerably. And if Mr. Macaulay wants to know why I couldn't come to church, tell him I had a job of work as a missionary.'

The General, though little inclined to help Mr. Pettigrew in his new enterprise, was impelled by courtesy to offer the loan of his car; but Mr. Pettigrew declared his intention of walking. He had needed resolution in the beginning, and plenty of exercise thereafter, to accustom himself to an artificial leg, he said; but by strength of will and daily use he could now walk five miles as well as most people.

'And he never falls,' said Mrs. Pettigrew, smiling kindly, to Swanson.

'It's going to be a very warm day,' said the General, looking through the window at the morning mist that hung, with a faintly golden braid, over a pale, unmoving sea. 'You people from the south think we never see the sun in Scotland, but wait till that mist rises: you'll almost need a solar topi this afternoon, Mrs. Pettigrew.'

Later that morning, a little while before noon, Mr. Macaulay stood up, tall and gaunt, in his pulpit, and said in his deep baying voice, that echoed vaguely from the plain white walls of the church,

'You will find the words of my text in the Book of the Prophet Amos, in the seventh chapter, at the seventh and eighth verses: "And, behold, the Lord stood upon a wall, with a plumbline in his hand. And the Lord said unto me, Amos, what seest thou? And I said, A plumbline. Then said the Lord, Behold, I will set a plumbline in the midst of my people Israel."'

The church was full, and the congregation settled down to listen to his sermon, as comfortably as was possible on narrow, un-cushioned pews, with a mutter of creaking woodwork, subdued coughing, and boots scraping on the floor. The General cleared his throat, Mr. Crantit crossed his legs, and here and there was a rustle of paper, a faintly audible smacking of the lips, as some of the older members fortified themselves with hard peppermint sweets. Mr. Macaulay waited for silence, and began his address quietly, in a conversational tone.

'To the frivolous,' he said, 'to the shallow-minded, and to those who have no great faculty of imagination, it may seem that there is nothing very terrible about a plumbline. It is, after all, only a piece of cord with a weight at one end. It cannot, you may think, have added much to the foreboding of people who had already suffered a plague of grasshoppers that devoured the growth of their fields, and a plague of fire that consumed the sea itself. There was much wickedness in Israel, and Amos was not the man to overlook wickedness, or spare the feelings of proud sinners, obdurate in evil.

' "Wailing shall be in all streets," he said, "and they shall say in all the highways, Alas, alas!" Their wickedness had been found out, and now there was to be no escape from punishment. Neither rich nor poor could avoid the punishment that always follows sin, though sometimes it is long-delayed, and often the sinner will plume himself, and strut in his pride, to think how clever he has been in concealing his sin. But sin cannot be concealed for ever, and punishment will come before the day is done. "He will smite the great house with breaches," said Amos, "and the little house with clefts," and though the guilty may flee from their just and proper doom, they will not escape. No, not one! They may run through the streets, and think for a little while they have outstripped the

130

pursuit, but all the time their doom is waiting, and will come upon them when they least expect it, in some shape or manner they have never anticipated: "as if a man did flee from a lion, and a bear met him."

' "Woe to them that are at ease in Zion!" said the Prophet, and no one reading the history of the times can doubt that woe was what they deserved; no one reading the history of that day and generation can deny that woe befell them. Wickedness was punished indeed — and what, you are wondering, was the significance of the plumbline? What was its place and purpose in the apparatus of punishment?

'Well, what was a plumbline used for? It was used by masons to try the straightness of a wall, and make sure it was vertical. Or you may think of it as a deep-sea lead, that sailors and fishermen still use to measure the depths of unknown waters, when they are lost in a fog or benighted by storm. Think of it in both ways, and you may guess why the Lord went with a plumbline among the people of Israel. Was it to try the rectitude of their lives, or to sound the depths and profundity of their faith? Or was it both? It was both, I think.

'Now, that, you may say, was more merciful than to afflict the whole population with an indiscriminate plague of grasshoppers, or to amaze them with the general terror of a plague of fire. But I am not so sure of that! For where punishment is general, the particular sins and the private vices of the individual will escape notice and avoid the shame of discovery; but if everyone is measured, man by man, against the undeviating narrow judgment of the plumbline, then all our faults and weaknesses are revealed, we are stripped naked to the scorching gaze of truth, and even the comfort of self-deception is swept away. The plumbline is more terrible than fire, more merciless than grasshoppers, for who can stand beside it and lay claim to perfect rectitude? Who can suffer it to sound the troubled waters of his soul, and be sure that the lead will find no angry reef or shoal of doubt, and the tide of faith receding from the shallows of our insufficiency?

'Look there upon the wall, and see the shadow of a plumbline!

See how straight it is, and how narrow, and say to yourselves: Against that straightness must I be judged!'

In the south side of the church, on either side of the pulpit, there were two tall windows, reaching to the roof, of small, leaded panes of plain glass, and the light of noon, shining through them, threw upon the opposite wall the shadows of two brass chains, descending from brown-varnished rafters, on which, in winter-time, paraffin-lamps were hung. Their dark shadows looked stiff as rods, and the congregation, turning stiffly, turning creakily to see this dramatic illustration of Mr. Macaulay's theme, were visibly impressed by it. But then, their gaze returning to the south wall and the pulpit, one half of them — those on Mr. Macaulay's right — stiffened in angry astonishment at the sight of a man's figure, who was staring in at them through one of the long windows. Mr. Macaulay, yielding to curiosity, leaned far out over his pulpit to see what had surprised them, and in a sidelong view perceived a stranger in a black coat and hat who, it was apparent, had mounted a convenient flat tomb-stone to get a view of the congregation. Though Mr. Macaulay had not met Mr. Pettigrew, he guessed at once the stranger's identity, and in his unsettled state of mind felt a surge of anger against the inquisitive face that pressed its nose upon the church's glass.

'Woe to them that are at ease in Zion!' he cried. 'We here, who must be judged by the justice of eternity, are now being judged upon a temporal plane by judges from without! But they themselves are not exempt from higher justice! They also, when their time shall come, must stand against the inerrable plumbline and submit their seeming righteousness to examination. And if their righteousness fails their punishment will be more terrible than ours, who are simple people, and humble in our simplicity. Yes, for them it may be said, "I will make a wailing like the dragons, and mourning as the owls!"'

Mr. Macaulay, for the next ten minutes, was a little incoherent, but the whole congregation, after some whispering along the pews, was aware of that which had caused his perturbation, and sympathized with him; and many enjoyed his somewhat reckless use of the imagery of the Prophets. He recovered his self-command,

and command of his theme, in time to deliver a stirring peroration in which he recapitulated his arguments for the unbending sternness of the plumbline, and after the concluding hymn pronounced the Benediction slowly, harshly, and with apparent reluctance.

'I think,' said the General to those who shared his pew, 'I should stay and have a word with him. The poor chap's worried. You go along, and don't wait for me — but I'll be back in time for lunch.'

Crantit and Marvell and Flett, Mrs. Pettigrew and Swanson, obediently filed out, and Catriona, who played the unmusical harmonium, said she would join them in a moment or two. The high sun struck them with an almost tropical warmth as they went out, and Mr. Pettigrew rose from an ancient, horizontal gravestone to greet them. Because of the heat he had taken off his coat and loosened his tie; and he was smoking a cigar. The congregation had deviated from the gravelled path that led past his seat, leaving a space between them as though he were a leper, and now, in angrily muttering groups, they stood beyond the wall that enclosed the church and the graveyard of leaning stones, and looked back at the interloper who, in his shirt-sleeves, appeared to them like one who wilfully was committing sacrilege. Their shyness and their Highland courtesty forbade them to rebuke him; but they quickly drew away, and looked back across their shoulders with horrified surprise.

'Oh, Sam!' cried Mrs. Pettigrew. 'You shouldn't have peeped in through the window — and please put on your coat!'

'I've had a very useful morning,' said Mr. Pettigrew complacently. 'I've been in five different houses, and what I've seen is almost unbelievable. Then I had a look-in at this mumbo-jumbo business of going to church, and there's no doubt about it that Laxdale's an anachronism: an insanitary anachronism!'

CHAPTER SIXTEEN

Before lunch, the house-party at Laxdale Hall changed the dark respectability of Sunday clothing for the lightest garments they possessed, and immediately after lunch most of them went off to look for coolness in the little wood that bordered the sea-beach. From hour to hour the heat of the day became more oppressive, and the languid sky grew paler as the sun, without loss of ardency, veiled itself in luminous mist. The General confidently predicted a storm before night, and though there was no visible evidence of its approach, the air was heavy, as though with the imminence of thunder.

Swanson, taking seriously his responsibilities as an actor, went to the library to read Gilbert Murray's *Euripides and his Age*, and the articles on Orpheus and Dionysus in an elderly edition of the Encyclopaedia Britannica. The General's library was surprisingly varied, and included several shelves of classical texts and commentaries as well as all the Badminton volumes and eight or nine hundred books on fishing in the more temperate parts of the world, on big-game shooting in mountainous or tropical areas, on military history, and exploration from Hakluyt to Gino Watkins. — He settled himself comfortably between two open windows and prepared to consider, with a critical mind, Mr. Crantit's assertion that the play was essentially a contest between King Pentheus, an excessive and inopportune rationalist — a reformer, destructive in the fashion of his kind — and the innate conservatism of the Theban women, who rebelled against him when he proscribed the worship of Dionysus, not only because he robbed them of the emotional satisfaction of worship, but because they saw in his rationalism a cold enmity to their natural enjoyment of the world. 'It is essentially a modern play,' Mr. Crantit had told him. 'Change the names and the scene, make a tactful alteration of the circumstances, and it might have been written in the 1870s; after the introduction of compulsory state education, that is.'

Within rather less than an hour Swanson was half-encircled by open volumes of the Britannica, of Murray, and Frazer's *Golden Bough*, of a Dictionary of Classical Antiquity, and a ponderous work entitled *Prolegomena to the Study of Greek Religion*; and was passing from intent analysis to a phase of contemplation that would soon have lapsed into slumber, had he not been startled by the opening of the door and the unexpected appearance of Mrs. Pettigrew.

'Hullo!' she said, with drowsy sweetness in her voice. 'Reading?'

'I've been trying to.'

'All these books!' she said, looking round the room. 'Don't you think they're depressing?'

'They keep one humble.'

'I don't see why.'

'Do you know anything about biology?'

'Only what I've learnt by experience.'

'Coral reefs are created by enormous colonies of things called polyps. The great mass of them consists of the skeletons of dead polyps, some of which are very beautiful. Only living polyps are found near the surface, and they don't stay there long. They become dead coral on which new polyps build. And that's what a library is: a coral reef. And an author's just another polyp. Would you find that humbling, if you were an author?'

'It depends on how beautiful he's going to look when he's dead — but it's long odds, I suppose, against his ever being noticed.'

'Long odds.'

'I could write a book if I'd patience to sit down to it,' she said, 'but it wouldn't be worth the trouble.' She sat herself on a sofa facing the stone fireplace. 'I went up to my room to write some letters a little while ago, but if I'd said all I wanted to say they'd have been so long that no one would have read them. So it didn't seem worth the effort. — I wish I'd brought a bathing-suit.'

'You forget where you are. They're very strict about sabbath-observance here.'

'What difference does that make?'

'They wouldn't approve of your swimming on Sunday.'

'I never heard anything so silly!'

'We all observed conventions before we were ruled by Acts of Parliament.'

'For God's sake don't start talking politics,' said Lucy Pettigrew, and swinging her feet on to the sofa, stretched herself, yawned, and lay in comfort. 'I'm sick to death of them.'

There was silence, for a little while, that Swanson found embarrassing; and unwisely he said, 'I'm glad you came in. I wanted to tell you how sorry I am for being such dull company last night.'

'It's too late to think of that now.'

'I wasn't trying to re-create the situation!' he said hurriedly.

'Well, why talk about it?'

'To say I'm sorry.'

'You should never apologize to a woman: haven't you learnt that yet? If you hit her, and then say you're sorry, she's got you on toast; and if you let her down, and say you're sorry for that, she'll give you hell. I don't, because I'm good-tempered; but you can't rely on everyone taking things as easily as I do. It's a rarer quality than you might suppose, and I'm not sure it's appreciated as it should be.'

'I do appreciate it — '

'Well, read to me. I like being read to.'

'I don't think this sort of stuff would interest you.'

'Try it and see. Reading aloud can't be against your principles.'

Swanson, annoyed, stooped and picked up the nearest volume of the Encyclopaedia Britannica, and began to read the first paragraph his eye fell on: ' "The rules of the Orphic life prescribed abstinence from beans — " '

'I'm on their side, whoever they were,' said Lucy. 'Go on.'

Swanson obediently recited a synopsis of Orphic faith, ritual and history, and in five or six minutes became aware of such a stillness in the room that he felt himself not merely alone, but lonely. He read more slowly, in a softer voice, and heard upon the western beach the drowsy obbligato of the sea. He heard, too, like a miniature of the score on tissue-paper, the slow, relaxed breathing of Lucy Pettigrew; and gently closing his volume of the Britannica, laid it silently on the floor and stood up.

Her right arm upon a cushion, her head on her arm, she lay — he thought — like an enchantress in a mediaeval tale of sorcery and dwarfs and forest-rides. Her eyelids were a little moist, with unguents or the heat of the air, and the light caught an infinitesimal liquidity in the sea-shell curl of her nostril. Her left knee was slightly bent, her left thigh sloped down to the knee and seemed to caress its underlying fellow. Her free hand, with widespread fingers, lay upon her breast, and her lips were almost imperceptibly parted.— Swanson stood for a long minute, looking down at her, and felt increasingly afraid. Asleep, she was all womanhood, and lovely as the orchid that catches flies for its supper. He stared, bemused, till he felt his pulse quicken with something like the airy panic of a dream, and as though in a dream he felt, for a moment, that he had been smuggled into a Sultan's harem for butterfly-bliss and its inevitable termination by the eunuch's bowstring. A rivulet of sweat ran coldly down his neck, and with infinite caution he tiptoed to the door, opened it with tremulous fingers, went out, and closed it soundlessly.

Though still intent upon escape, it now occurred to him that he must find some excuse for flight. He went quickly, but on tip-toe through the almost empty house, to his bedroom, and found his acting-copy of the *Bacchanals*. He ran down again by the servants' staircase, and out of the house through the side-door by the gun-room; and was well on his way to the river before it occurred to him that he had been uncommonly foolish.

This was no new discovery. It had punctuated his life since, at the age of fourteen or so, his adolescent consciousness had come to birth. His memory was full of impetuous advances followed by ignominious retreat, of ebullient confidence suddenly calling for help from an unexpected quicksand, of footholds in the firm snow failing in irrational thaw. In a superficial way he had been successful — he made a handsome living by his authorship — but every year of his life was commemorated by private humiliation, and his innermost desire, for a soldier's aptitude and military honour, had achieved nothing but getting his chin shot away in one war, and hitting the wrong target in another. The only aeroplanes his anti-aircraft battery had ever brought down were those that Macaulay was piloting. — I have survived my half-century, he sometimes told himself, not because of any inherent gift for living, but by reason of a mere desire to live: which, as a reason for living, has the increasing value of rarity. I have fought, he would say in such a mood, a rearguard action for thirty years and more, and I am still capable of counter-attacking twice a week with a plump and seemly hope. I persist in optimism because I believe my repeated failures are due only to my own folly, which I cannot suppose to be incurable. Though, I must admit, it shows no sign of being cured . . .

I have run away, he now told himself, from nothing but enjoyment; and I don't know why, unless I am a slave to heredity. My Norse ancestors were more frightened of their own womenfolk than of their roaring, sword-swinging enemies — every chapter of the Icelandic sagas reveals that — and the tax on my inheritance is that I am frightened of them both, and plagued by remorse on either side. I don't think it's fair; but life, of course, isn't fair. — Oh, that little shimmer of greasy light on her eyelids, and her breast lying soft under her fingers! I am a bloody fool! And she'll tell me so, once again, very sweetly. Because she's a nice woman, and that makes it all the worse. Oh Christ I'm a fool!

Head down and hands in pockets, the play-book under his left arm, he shambled across the meadows like a village hobbledehoy, and told himself repeatedly what a poor-spirited oaf he was, and unhappily recalled how often he had uttered the same complaint. But comfort came in upon the heels of denunciation: 'I am an author,' he exclaimed, 'and I can use my discomfiture to fill a chapter. I can draw a royalty of twenty per cent on folly — and that's a higher rate than gallantry or virtue wins. The clown lives on, and the clown has recompense — but he's got to learn his part . . .'

He opened the play-book and began to read the long speech he must deliver as Second Messenger in the drama of revenge. He had a hundred and fifty lines to speak, and in those lines he must declare how Pentheus, driven mad by Dionysus' spells, had taken to the mountains, and there, fleeing from the Bacchanals, had climbed a great tree to escape them; but all in vain, for the women in their frenzy had pulled him down and torn him limb from limb.

He read it twice, in Mr. Crantit's translation, and felt the heat of the sun on his head; for he had left Laxdale Hall without waiting to look for a hat. But a couple of hundred yards away stood the old water-mill that would be the background of their play, their green-room, and headquarters. In its shelter, he thought, he could more comfortably rehearse his part.

There were two staircases to the upper floor of the mill, a flight of stone steps at the west end, and a solid wooden ladder from the ground floor. Near its eastern wall some parts of the roof had fallen in, and the great cog-wheel which transmitted power from the water-wheel to the upper millstone that ground upon a nether circle of smooth granite, was broken and fouled with bird-droppings. A partial ruin at that end, it was still a solid shelter at the other; and Swanson, climbing the outer staircase, stood for a minute or two to admire the larger view that height afforded, then sought the inner coolness of the floor where once the sacks of grain, the harvest of the parish, had been stored.

He sat down on an old three-legged stool that chance had left there, and read again, and yet again, his lines that told of doom for human arrogance. He tried his memory in a whisper, then got up, and with a flavour of the theme to heighten his delivery, began to recite:

'And we listened, and heard the song
Of the Maenads beyond the trees,
And Pentheus, hotly impatient, said to our guide —
A guide who gleamed like a god —
"That is a shameful sound, of revelry unashamed,
But I cannot see them from here,

I cannot discover their shame!
I must climb through the leaves to the topmost branch of a
tree . . ." '

To and fro he walked, from the doorway that opened on the
outer staircase to the darker end of the floor where the wooden steps
came up from below.

'And the voice of the god ran clearly,
"O maidens and wedded wives,
White arms in the forest!
Here is he who banned your revels
And forbade you to worship me!
Now you can beat and torment him, as long you have wanted
to do,
And as he deserves," '

he recited, and turned again. His voice grew louder as he
approached the climax of his speech, and pausing for a moment at
the western door, declaimed:

'Agave, drunken huntress,
Drunk on the god's enchantment,
Saw in the broken branches not him, but a lion,
And setting her foot to his side,
Tore him asunder . . .'

Then turned, and forgot his lines. For slowly mounting into sight,
on the wooden steps at the other end, came the Reverend Mr.
Macaulay, black-suited and white of face; and aslant on his right
shoulder he carried a great two-handed sword, whose dull steel
caught a grey light from the broken roof behind him.

CHAPTER SEVENTEEN

GENERALMATHESON, after morning church, had gone to the vestry and found Macaulay standing gaunt and rigid, almost as rigid as an epileptic in his seizure. His dark eyes shone fiercely, and perhaps by reflexion from the red cloth on his table, they seemed, for a moment, to hold the colour of old garnets.

Harshly he exclaimed, 'That man! The man at the window! He has committed sacrilege!'

'Now, now,' said the General, 'you mustn't exaggerate. It was disconcerting for you, I know that, coming as it did in the middle of a very good sermon — one of the best I've ever heard, my dear chap. I do congratulate you — but you shouldn't make too much of it.'

'Sacrilege,' said Macaulay again.

'Our Mr. Pettigrew,' said the General, 'is a man of exceptional ability, of unusual imagination. A man of great gifts. But he has, I admit, a streak of vulgarity in him, and vulgarity can sometimes be extremely offensive, and yet as innocent as a child of any intention to offend. That's a thing we've all got to remember nowadays, when vulgarity's on the increase.'

'You are a kind man,' said Macaulay after a pause for consideration. 'It is doubly kind to minimize the offence by excusing the offender. It is kind to me, as well as to him. It was very upsetting to be interrupted in my sermon.'

'Come and have lunch with us,' said the General. 'I don't think you're being properly looked after.'

'No, no! There is a meal waiting for me. Mrs. McLeod of the shop — Nicholas's wife — found a girl to come in and cook for me while my housekeeper is away.'

141

'You should have stayed with me,' said the General. 'I'm a little bit offended by your desertion.'

'It was impossible!' said Macaulay earnestly. 'I could not sit at the same table as Mr. Swanson, and digest the good food you gave me. It was more than my stomach would bear to see the man who shot me down as if he had been fighting for the Germans — yes, twice he did it! — to see him sitting opposite, and eating out of the same dish.'

'Well, we've talked that over,' said the General, 'and nothing more can be said about it except that when large forces are committed to battle, there are bound to be accidents.'

'What a man does is what he has to do,' said Macaulay gloomily. 'His actions are like planets revolving round his personality — and there are personalities in the world that are clearly malignant.'

The General, refusing to be drawn into a discussion of Swanson's motives, or his gunnery, repeated his opinion that Mr. Pettigrew's irreverence had been unintentional, and advised Macaulay to think no more about it. He invited the minister to supper, and the minister glumly refused.

'Well,' said the General, putting on his hat and picking up his stick, 'if you want a talk at any time, or a glass of sherry or a whisky and soda, you know where to come for it. Goodbye, Macaulay, and many thanks for a damned good sermon. Keep your heart up!'

Macaulay walked slowly to his manse, and hardly seeing what he ate, scarcely tasting it, took his lunch. The girl whom Mrs. McLeod had found to cook for him was a happy-go-lucky, sixteen-year-old slut, and she had given the minister three slices of bully-beef from a tin, a few half-boiled potatoes, and a pudding concocted of some farinaceous dust that tasted only of the cardboard in which it had been confined.

Three-quarters of an hour later Macaulay felt a vague discomfort in his stomach, a tension in his bowels, and physical unease brought back unhappiness to his mind. Like an aeroplane flying unexpectedly out of cloud, a sentence of his own sermon crossed his memory: 'Who can be sure,' he repeated, 'that the lead will find

142

no reef or shoal of doubt, and the tide of faith receding from the shallows of our insufficiency?'

Doubt, on the instant, rose like a half-tide rock from a treacherous sea, and in perplexity, as though stumbling on the edge of the cliff above, he asked himself if he believed — he himself — in what he had so lately said from a pulpit built for faith.

He remembered reading an article, in some popular magazine, in which it was claimed that the insoluble problems of the cosmic mathematicians had been solved, at last, by the discovery of an ever-expanding universe. A universe fed and fattened, and presumably created, by a persistent fountain of hydrogen whose bubbles — after certain electronic, atomic and molecular developments that he could not clearly recall — coalesced with an equal facility into such familiar but unpredictable shapes as household furniture and professional philosophers, a *nova* of the first magnitude and a nosegay at a rural flower-show. — Gas, all was gas, a consubstantial vapour.

The word evoked an older problem and his earnest though untutored study of the great heresies of the past. Suddenly, as if it were a dive-bomber descending from the blindness of the sun, the shade of Arius the Libyan crossed his mind. Arius had nearly split the Church with the subtle wedge of his misunderstanding. Arius had disputed the consubstantiality of the Trinity, and divided the theologians of the western world, and their obedient flocks, into those who voted passionately for *homoousian*, or the identity of God in his Trinity; and those who, with an equal temper, plumped for family likeness, or *homoiousian*. — But where was the essence of dispute if all was hydrogen? Not faith alone, but valiant heresy dissolved in a metagaseous mist, and a man could not even feel the satisfaction of being wrong. — Macaulay remembered the name of Epiphanius, an Aegean Greek who had written a treatise against no fewer than eighty heresies. But now, in the anarchy of his despair, he perceived four-score heresiarchs inscribing their gaseous misconstructions on mere vapour, to be blown away by a draught of hydrogen over which, in aery symbols, the name of *Epiphanius* floated.

Never before had his doubt gone so far as to question the validity of doubt. Hitherto doubt had rung like a hammer against unseen rock, doubt had been the clapper in a bell of faith; but now bell and clapper both melted into aery nothing, and poor Macaulay, tormented in mind and body, was more tormented when he tried, and failed, to make distinction between his pain and his bemoaning consciousness of pain.

In a semblance of immobility, he sat at the heart of a cyclone. Then he became a vortex, and all around was motionless. He propped himself up on the arms of his chair, and tried to recover sanity by movement. He dared not sit still, and went out to walk in the fields. The heat of the veiled sun fell upon him, and in the appearance of a familiar view he saw no reality. He looked with scepticism at the grass, at his long pale hands with incredulity. He considered the short, white-washed steeple of his church, and said: 'It is not only a memorial to delusion, it is delusion!' In a fiction of sullen rage he kicked a stone, and hurt his toes; and wondered why clotted hydrogen should make them sore. A suspicion entered his mind — but did not lodge there — that the American inventor of the hydrogen theory was but the latest heresiarch: a mischievous avatar of Arius the Libyan.

'I know nothing,' he said aloud, 'but I have the sensation that I've been betrayed.'

Aimlessly, only half-seeing where he went, he walked on until the discomfort of the sun persuaded him to look for shelter, and the nearest building he saw was the old water-mill. He strode more quickly then, and on its lower floor was grateful for the shade.

He sat down, on a grey worm-eaten bench, and looked about him. Leaning against the opposite wall he saw a pair of great two-handed swords, six feet long, with heavy cross-guards. — Mr. Crantit had found them in Laxdale Hall, and though there was nothing Grecian in their shape, he had decided they were so noble and dramatic in appearance that the sentinels who stood before King Pentheus' palace must carry them. They had been brought to the mill, and left there with other properties needed for the play. Idly they rested against a cobwebbed wall — idly until Macaulay looked at the nearer, and saw it, with its long cross-guard, in the shape of a crucifix.

Doubt fell from him, like snow from the tree-tops in a sudden thaw. Hydrogen was nonsense, *homoousian* and *homoiousian* stood distinct and wide apart, and the American chemist was but a Yankee heresiarch. The Crucifix was categorical, the Cross was a call to action . . .

Here — here on his own soil — there was manifest heresy, he told himself. How wrong he had been to allow a heathen play to be performed! To idle thought and superficial understanding the worship of Dionysus might seem attractive indeed, and a performance of the *Bacchanals* could sow the seeds of so monstrous a misbelief as had never been known since the old rule of paganism, or the chattering imperium of Mount Olympus. And it was not yet too late to put a stop to it . . .

His turbulent thoughts were stilled by the sound of footsteps overhead. He listened, and presently heard a voice reciting rhythmic lines. The voice grew louder, and with a surge of anger he recognized it. He stood up, and listened more closely. The voice grew louder, and his ears caught a phrase or two — a heathen phrase — that he had heard before.

He felt the pulse beating in his temples, an excitement in his chest and his arms, and in the orchestration of his blood recognized a theme of high purpose. He took one of the great two-handed swords, and stepping quietly up the oaken ladder to the higher floor, astonished the unlucky Swanson by the fearsome spectacle he presented, and the strangeness of his utterance.

'Samaria shall become desolate,' he declared, 'for she hath rebelled against her God. They shall fall by the sword, their infants shall be dashed in pieces, and their women with child shall be ripped up!'

'What on earth are you talking about?' asked Swanson nervously.

'The heathen shall be disconcerted,' said Macaulay, coming slowly towards him, stepping short and somewhat unsteadily under the weight of the long sword. 'They shall be destroyed in the land, or driven from its borders.'

Swanson retreated to the doorway at the west end of the mill, and Macaulay followed without haste — almost with reluctance, it seemed — until they stood face to face on the small platform at the head of the outside stairs.

'We know each other!' said Macaulay, bending a little forward and staring at his old opponent.

'Of course we know each other,' said Swanson, his voice unsteady, 'but why are you carrying that sword?'

Macaulay, as though he had forgotten his burden, looked sidelong at it, then clumsily reversing it, set it point-downwards and leaned upon the cross-guards. 'It is the sword of Gideon,' he said.

Convinced that the minister had gone mad, and deeply perturbed by his apparent hostility, Swanson admitted that he himself must be responsible, in part at least, for the collapse of his mind; and conquering his not unnatural fear, wondered what he could do for the poor man, and how, for his own good, a maniac might best be mollified. But imagination failed him, his gift of invention was bankrupt, and before he could even find some easy phrase with which to start a general conversation, Macaulay was again describing the unfortunate episode at Bari, when his seaplane had been shot down by Swanson's guns.

'I can see the scar on your brow,' he went on, 'that the little table made when I hit you on the head in the hospital at Bari; and I will not deny that the sight of it gives me satisfaction. But it reminds me, too, that I have only hit you once, and you hit me twice. And though I am a minister of the church, I am also a Highlander, and a Highlander does not like his enemies to get the better of him.'

'I'm not your enemy!' exclaimed Swanson. 'For God's sake get that idea out of your head! I've suffered mentally as much as you've suffered physically from that frightful mistake I made —'

'So you say!' said Macaulay. 'So you say, but you have not the marks of shell-splinters on your back to prove it — and if I could mark you again, to be quits with you, I think I would be a happier man!'

'That's not exactly a Christian attitude,' said Swanson, and with one hand on the iron rail, descended a couple of steps.

'What right have you to talk of Christian attitudes?' demanded the minister, closely following him, and trailing the long sword, which clapped on the stone. 'You who are taking part in a heathen play that may turn all Laxdale from the true Faith — yes, and could turn the whole of Scotland to pagan rites and a justification of the sensuality its people are so terribly inclined to! But I will not suffer it. No, I will put a stop to the whole procedure!'

'You'll have to talk to Miss Matheson about that,' said Swanson, and carefully went down another three steps.

'I will talk to her at the proper time,' said Macaulay, 'but it seems to me that this is a good opportunity for talking to you — about the play for one thing, and about your mischievous and malignant gunnery for another.'

Swanson, still facing the minister, went backwards down the staircase more quickly now, and the long sword, trailing in his pursuer's hand, clattered loudly from step to step as Macaulay followed him.

'Let's go back to Laxdale Hall,' said Swanson desperately, 'and put our case to the General, and ask him to arbitrate.'

'No, no!' said Macaulay. 'The General has a great handicap: he is a gentleman. He would tell me to let bygones be bygones — and that is philosophical, I know, but it doesn't satisfy a Highlander like me. If I could mark you once again, Mr. Swanson, I would be easier in my mind, and that, I believe, is the only way to make me easy.'

They stood on the ground now, and Macaulay, the fierceness of his expression dissolving, of a sudden smiled with a curious, genial innocence, and putting both hands to the hilt, swung the long sword up.

'No, no!' cried Swanson. 'Oh, for God's sake don't be such a fool!'

'Thou shalt not take the Name of the Lord thy God in vain,' said Macaulay severely, and stepped heavily forward.

'Listen! What's that noise? What's happening?'

From some little distance away, up-stream and beyond the mill, came a raucous din of voices raised in anger. A woman's voice, harsh and cracked with age, dominated a chorus of ill-temper, and

Swanson, his fear diminished by surprise, thought eagerly that even the worst-natured company might save him from Macaulay and his vengeful sword. He turned, and ran round the corner of the mill.

Macaulay followed, crying, 'Stop! Stop!' — but stopped too, revenge momentarily forgotten, when he found Swanson halted by amazement at what he saw; and looked and felt the same amazement.

Above the mill, on the far bank of the mill-dam, grew an immense and ancient willow tree with a bifurcating trunk. At a height of five or six feet one arm leaned earthwards and grew parallel with the ground, while the other, inclining a little to the opposite direction, soared to a high cupola of pendant leaves. — And while they stood, and stared, the naked figure of a man climbed desperately from the lower limb to the bending branches of the upright trunk, and on the bank below him some thirty or forty women, most of them elderly, stood and howled their anger. In the forefront of their array was Mrs. McKellaig, shouting abuse, and waving at the naked man what looked, from a distance, like a human leg.

CHAPTER EIGHTEEN

MR. PETTIGREW'S fortune included more than his material assets. He enjoyed a perfect assurance of the rightness of his own judgment, and a spirit so combative that he found real pleasure in defeating those who opposed it. The loss of a leg had given him a successful start in life, and since then he had often turned disadvantage to victory, and seeming loss to solid gain. In spite of initial rebuff, he was still convinced that the proper way to deal with Laxdale and its problems was to evacuate the whole population and re-settle it in Drumliedubbs — he must find workers somewhere for his new factories — and if he were given a little time, he felt sure that he could persuade these backward people to see the wisdom of his plan. On his morning walk he had looked into several houses, and had some interesting conversations; and discovered, to his satisfaction, fresh proof of the poverty and discomfort of life in the remoter Highlands.

After lunch he slept for half an hour, and decided to explore farther. Like the others he had changed into holiday clothing, and in coffee-coloured flannel trousers, a pale green shirt, a white linen cap and sun-glasses, he made a conspicuous figure. Not far from Laxdale Hall he passed a little group of seven or eight women, who did not reply to his greeting, and a couple of hundred yards away he noticed, but paid no attention to a somewhat larger group. He left the road and took a footpath that led towards McKellaig's cottage. He walked slowly but strongly, with the help of a stick, and showed no sign of being handicapped by an artificial leg. His mind was pleasantly occupied by a rehearsal of new arguments for the migration to Drumliedubbs, and he was unaware that the women he had seen were following him . . .

McKellaig's fierce old mother was entertaining half a dozen elderly, female friends — not, indeed, with solid fare, but with intemperate comment on Mr. Pettigrew — when her cat, crying to be let in, took her briefly from their company; and standing for a moment in her doorway, looking this way and that to see what might be seen, she perceived in the distance, but coming towards her cottage, a figure whose walk she recognized, though his clothes were strange and unfamiliar. Sharply she called to her friends, and hurriedly the old women came out of the kitchen. There was shrill exclamation, a little cackle of talk, and then with a hobbling gait they all ran across to the opposite building, the byre and cartshed, and hid behind it.

Mr. Pettigrew's behaviour, on his morning walk, had caused great offence. He had been seen going into empty houses — empty because the whole family was at church — and the women with whom he had had his useful conversations had been scandalized by the questions he asked. Questions about their personal habits, how much money they spent on groceries, when their blankets had last been washed, and if they had matrimonial difficulties . . . Then, after church, the story had quickly spread of his abominable interruption to the sermon, of his impudence in sitting on a gravestone, smoking a cigar in his shirt-sleeves.

The women were more deeply angered than the men by his behaviour, and when they gathered to talk it over their anger grew. Some of them went towards Laxdale Hall, with no specific intention, but drawn by wrathful curiosity, or a vaguely defensive feeling that they should keep watch on their enemy. Others met in a neighbour's kitchen, and with infinite repetition told of their morning encounter with Mr. Pettigrew; or listened, irate and horrified, to tales of his intrusion. Old Mrs. McKellaig's visitors had been discussing with relish an improper question he was alleged to have asked a youngish, newly married woman, when Mrs. McKellaig gave unexpected warning of his approach; and overcome by a sudden reluctance to meet such a monster face to face — but curious to see what he would do — they ran, in an elderly flutter, to hide from him, and disposed themselves as well as they could to watch.

Mr. Pettigrew knocked at the door, and got no answer. He stooped and stared through the nearer window, and then went boldly in. With a quick, appraising eye he looked round the kitchen, lifted a lid off a pot that stood on the stove, and picked up a pair of Norman McKellaig's boots, that were drying beside it, to examine the quality of the leather. He went through to the ben-room, admitted to himself that it was clean, but pursed his lips and shook his head to see how old-fashioned were its furnishings and scanty ornaments. Quietly he opened the door of the closet where McKellaig slept, and was surprised to see him in bed. McKellaig woke and sat up, alarmed by a visitor so strangely dressed. 'A young man like you should be up and about, not lying in bed on a fine afternoon,' said Mr. Pettigrew severely; and left him.

The old women, peering from behind the byre, drew back and avoided discovery; and Mr. Pettigrew, with more evidence of sloth and poverty to consider, decided to walk to the river and look at the old mill. It was too late, of course, to think seriously of using water-power to promote some local industry, but it would be interesting to see what power there was.

He took off his linen cap, and mopped his head. It's as hot as the south of France, he thought. Why didn't I bring a bathing-suit? A swim, and a long drink: that's the programme for an afternoon like this. And I've earned my pleasure, too. I've done a good day's work. It's been a useful day, and now I'd like a swim. And a long gin-fizz. By God, it's hot! I'd never have believed it possible.

He came to the mill, but did not go in. His attention was taken by the smooth water of the dam above, and the shade of a huge willow tree that grew on the farther bank. — He found a long, dead branch and tried the depth of the water. He looked round him, and saw no one in the wide landscape that only the small steep hillock that was to be the dress-circle for a Greek play occluded. It's deep enough, he thought, and there's nobody about. A swim's just what I need.

Quickly he undressed, and unbuckled the straps that secured his artificial leg. Cautiously he lowered himself into the cool water, and with a powerful breast-stroke swam across the pool, turned and duck-dived, lay and floated. He had taught himself to swim, after his accident, as soon as he had learnt to walk, and he took great pride in his accomplishment. He had a broad chest and powerful shoulders, and though he looked clumsy in the water he swam strongly and with perfect confidence.

For several minutes he swam slowly up and down the length of the dam, turning and returning, lifting his head from the pleasant coolness only high enough to breathe; and he was startled as rudely as if shaken out of sleep when a piece of turf fell with a splash a yard or so from him. He looked up, and with indignation saw on the bank a crowd of women, most of them old.

The several groups who had cautiously been following him, reinforced on their way by Sunday idleness and normal curiosity, had gathered, during the last few hundred yards of his approach to the mill, behind the hillock called The Drum; and from its shelter watched him, in a rising clamour of scandal and excitement, while he undressed. They had seen him sit down on the bank, and disappear as he took to the water; then, bright in the sunlight, the water-drops thrown up by his first lusty strokes. And with a single mind, without dispute or hesitation, and in a silence broken only by their heavy breathing and the creaking of their stays, the old women hurried to the dam to feed their horror full, and keep their anger fierce, by closer inspection of the uncouth stranger who had come to desecrate their Sabbath. It was Mrs. McKellaig who threw the first clod.

Mr. Pettigrew, for once in his life, was disconcerted by an audience and failed to be eloquent. 'Go away!' he shouted. 'Go away at once!'

'What for did ye come here?' screamed Mrs. McKellaig in her rough voice of the eastern Lowlands. 'Was it for anything better than tae brak the Sabbath day?'

'You are bre-e-aking the Sa-a-abbath!' came the shrill chorus of her Highland neighbours.

'Tak your muckle, naked hurdies oot o' the watter!' yelled Mrs. McKellaig, shaking her stick.

'Shame upon you, and shame on your nakedness!' bellowed a

short, stout woman with a drill-sergeant's lungs, whom Mr. Pettigrew had insulted by a question about the price of her under-clothes.

'Shame! Shame upon you!' howled the chorus.

Mr. Pettigrew began to feel frightened, and shivered in a colder air. There was a light breeze blowing now from the south-west, and clouds marching into the sky behind it. He was almost ignorant of the sensation of fear, but the anger of the women on the bank was so concerted, their old faces were animated with such hate — many of them had new sets of artificial teeth which gleamed with an almost wolfish threat — that he felt the first fluttering of an impulse to turn and run; but could not yield to it because he had left his leg on the bank.

'Be quiet!' he shouted. 'Be quiet and listen to me. Give me a chance to get dressed, and I'll answer any questions you like to ask. I don't know what I've done to offend you —'

'He does not know what he has done to offend!' cried a tall, gaunt woman with an ivory skin and an eagle's beak of a nose. 'He has done nothing but offend — he sat on a tombstone to smoke a cigar, he came poking into our houses, he called us beggars, and now he is breaking the Sabbath day — but he doesn't think he has offended us!'

'Let him bide where he is, and droon!' cried Mrs. McKellaig, and tearing up a piece of turf, threw it at Pettigrew. 'Let him droon!' she screamed.

Excited by her example, and exasperated as much by Pettigrew's helplessness as by his immunity in deep water, the others also stooped, and picked up clods and handfuls of sun-baked earth, and pelted the swimmer with all their strength.

A little pebble hit him on the head, a lump of turf missed him by half an inch. He turned and swam to the far side of the dam, but was slow in climbing out.

'After him!' yelled Mrs. McKellaig, and dropping her stick, picked up the light framework of Pettigrew's artificial leg. Already some of the old women were running with ungainly speed to the mill-lade that fed the dam, and the plank-bridge that crossed it

Pettigrew, now frightened indeed, hesitated only a moment before pulling himself on to the lower limb of the ancient willow that overhung the water, and from it, with some difficulty, climbed to a fork in the upright trunk . . .

That was the state of affairs when Swanson and Macaulay came round the corner of the mill, and forgot their own dissension before the unusual spectacle of a Member of Parliament, naked among the branches of a tree, while thirty or forty elderly women, of sober habit and good repute in the village, stood below and howled abuse.

Accustomed, by his study of the Old Testament, to violent episode and bizarre occasion, Macaulay was quicker than Swanson to master his astonishment, and with the long sword sloping across his shoulder strode solemnly along the bank, all scarred by the old women's fingers, and across the lade by the little bridge, to make inquiry and get such an explanation of the disturbances as was due to him. Swanson, lingering on the near bank, felt a little light-headed after his sudden release from the menace of the sword, and for a minute or two enjoyed the scene without sympathy for Mr. Pettigrew's evident discomfort.

The first fringes of the approaching clouds now covered the sun, and the breeze blew stronger. The smaller branches of the willow bent and bowed before it, and all their myriad leaves, pointing the same way, fluttered like little pennants, as though the old tree were dressed for some arboreal review. But pink among the grey-green leaves could be seen the large incongruous body of Mr. Pettigrew, and, almost as incongruous, Macaulay stood below him with a two-handed sword aslant upon his shoulder, and listened gravely to the chattering explanation of the episode that two-score of his female parishioners competed to give him.

Not until he had taken his aesthetic pleasure did Swanson feel compunction for his indifference to Mr. Pettigrew's sufferings; and then, briskly crossing to the other side, heard Pettigrew interrupt the confabulation below with an angry statement that he was getting cold, and an urgent appeal to Macaulay to get rid of those damned women. — Mr. Pettigrew had regained some of his courage with the arrival of Swanson and the minister; but Mrs. McKellaig was not daunted by their presence.

'Come doon, ye thummart!' she cried, brandishing his leg at him. — O mutilated Pentheus! thought Swanson. — 'Come doon, ye mangy tod, and I'll buff your beef!'

'Quiet, woman, quiet!' exclaimed Macaulay, and raised his sword, not indeed as if to strike her, but as though to exorcise anger and dissension.

'I'm getting cold, I tell you!' shouted Mr. Pettigrew; for the sky was darker now, and the first drops of rain were already falling.

'Keep your tongue between your teeth and your nakedness behind the leaves!' cried Macaulay. 'I'll deal with you in my own good time. — And you,' he told the women, his voice baying like a hound, 'get home with you, and down on your old bony knees, and ask forgiveness! I had not thought to see such shamelessness in my parish, as women chasing a naked man, and pursuing him to the very tree-tops! In very truth, a sword is needed in the land, to cleanse iniquity and strike impiety with fear. There is a harvest still, a harvest of thistles and of tares, for the sword of Gideon!'

'Oh, for God's sake don't be such a bloody fool!' cried Pettigrew, shivering with cold as the wind whipt him with wet leaves and bending twigs, and the rain fell steadily. 'A sword's no use to anyone, I want an umbrella!'

Swanson was so foolish as to laugh. He laughed loudly, coarsely; and a few of the flighty old women cackled in sympathy.

Doubly insulted, Macaulay turned and remembered his old enemy. The sacrilegious man had called him a fool, the man who had filled his back with shell-splinters mocked him, and the fickle old women were laughing too. — He still held the sword aloft, in a proud hieratic pose, and now, swinging the point down and round, he struck tremendously at Swanson.

The ponderous blade came round like a hammer in the hands of a hammer-thrower at a Highland Gathering. Swanson jumped away from it — he was standing at the edge of the mill-dam — but the sword by a fraction of a second was quicker than he, and touched him as he fell.

He fell with a wide-spread, resounding splash on the flat of his back; and when he found his balance and stood up, shaking his head — there was little more than four feet of water at that side — a trickle of diluted blood was colouring his right cheek. The minister's great buffet had cut the tip of his ear and left a little red wound about the size of a ladybird.

Macaulay seemed strangely pleased with the success of his blow. He stuck the tip of the sword into the bank, and leaning on the cross-guards looked down at his victim. The white fury had vanished from his face, and in his long cheeks appeared the dimples of a reluctant geniality. His voice, when he spoke, had a soft and purring note:

'Vengeance is mine, saith the Lord, I will repay! In other words, Mr. Swanson, *Tit for Tat!*'

A deeper sound came from his lips, a series of convulsive, barking noises, and his face was curiously contorted. It became evident that the minister was laughing, and the old women, who had momentarily been dismayed by his violence, now saw the joke — or part of it — and relieved that nothing worse had happened, cackled with simple enjoyment of Swanson's discomfiture. He stood shoulder-deep in the water, among the little fountains that the rain threw up, and with a wet hand tried to staunch the flow of blood from his ear, and on his mild, round face there was a look of ludicrous un-certainty, like the expression of a boy who has fallen on the ice, and cannot think how it happened, and still wonders if he is hurt. — He had not seriously been hurt, but he had no intention of coming ashore until it was safe to do so.

He had not long to wait. The old women's laughter reminded Macaulay of his responsibility in the parish, and he rebuked them sternly.

'Go home,' he bade them, 'and mend your ways. Pray for a better understanding. To take pleasure in the sight of justice being done is one thing; but wanton relish in the spectacle of human downfall is another thing altogether, and not to be condoned. Get home with you, and think shame of the ill nature that's in you!'

He drove them before him like a flock of dark-feathered geese, cackling still but now more quietly, and when they had crossed the lade Swanson, looking over his shoulder, came slowly ashore.

'Will you fetch my leg for me?' asked Mr. Pettigrew, his teeth chattering.

He had come down to earth again, and stood on the lee side of the willow, his leg and arms patched with a chilly blue. No one had paid any attention to him for the last few minutes, and he, shocked by Macaulay's assault on Swanson, had thought it prudent to keep quiet until the minister had gone. He had still to suffer a final insult, however, for Mrs. McKellaig, before she left, had thrown his leg into the mill-dam.

The light framework had not sunk, and Swanson, returning for it, had only to swim a stroke or two. He brought it ashore, and taking a sodden handkerchief from his trouser pocket, folded it against his ear.

Mr. Pettigrew sat down on the wet turf, and began to strap on his leg. 'Do you think this sort of thing often happens here?' he asked.

'No, I should say it's exceptional. Quite exceptional.'

'Those damned women! I'm not easily frightened, by God, but they frightened me.'

'What had you done to upset them?'

'Nothing at all. They're a pack of old fools, and that's all there is to be said of them. But that minister of theirs — he's a maniac!'

'There were special circumstances in his case. He's had a trying time lately, and I'm partly to blame for it.'

'What did you do?'

'It's too long a story.'

'He ought to be certified.'

'He may feel better now.'

'But where did he get that sword? He doesn't always carry it, does he?'

'It's one of the properties for the play. Are you all right now?'

They crossed the lade by the little bridge, and Mr. Pettigrew gathered his clothes and walking-stick from the other bank. He went into the mill to dress, and Swanson took off his sodden shirt and trousers, wrung them out, and put them on again. He made a pad of his handkerchief, and Pettigrew lent him another with which, in a rakish style, he tied the pad to his wounded ear. The rain fell heavily now, slanting before the south-west wind.

'Is it going to clear up, do you think?'

'There's no sign of that,' said Swanson.

'Well, we can't get much wetter than we are — and we shan't have to explain why we did get wet. I don't intend to say anything about what happened — I'm not in the habit of climbing trees — and if you take my advice, you'll keep quiet too.'

'The old women will talk. We can't keep them quiet.'

'It'll take time for the story to reach the Hall. Do as I say, and we shan't have our dinner spoiled — not tonight, at least — by that fellow Crantit making clever remarks about us.'

'Well, if that's how you feel . . .'

They walked steadily towards Laxdale Hall, soaked and shivering, and Pettigrew said fiercely, 'I'm not beaten yet! What happened this afternoon just proves that I was right from the beginning: these people aren't responsible, and nothing can be done to help them till they're taken in hand and properly managed. The whole world needs management — discipline, order, overseers with proper power and whips if necessary — but by God, there's nowhere needs it so much as Laxdale!'

CHAPTER NINETEEN

'WHAT was Nietzsche's great discovery?' asked Mr. Crantit. 'He discovered that God was dead. And that, I suggest, is typical of the German habit of exaggeration. For what he really meant was that Man was seriously ill.'

Mr. Crantit had had little interruption during dinner, and he was, perhaps, unduly inclined to assert himself. He had come to a decision of some importance, about two and a half hours before, and was still pluming himself on his good sense and resolution. — In spite of the rain he had been about to go to evening church when he met Andrew Flett, also dressed for public worship, and realized that their purpose was the same. Neither was really intent on singing hymns and listening to Mr. Macaulay, but both were hopeful of meeting Morag McLeod and walking home with her. Mr. Crantit, however, remembered previous disappointment and his public discomfiture; and looking at Flett's well-washed, shining face saw upon it a gloss of complacency, a detestable assurance. — Youth will be served, he thought bitterly, though youth has nothing more to commend it than a lack of years; and harshly putting from his mind the delectable image of Morag's proud and pretty head, he decided to stay where he was and talk to the General instead. — For more than an hour they had drunk sherry together, and discussed the absorbing subject of British rule in India; and Mr. Crantit was now happily aware, not only that he had shown a sufficient grasp of Viceregal policy from Dalhousie to Halifax, but a worldly wisdom that demanded his own congratulation, though by its nature it could expect no wider tribute.

At the dinner-table, none of the others was in a mood to compete with his assertions. The General was listening to the rain on the windows, and hoping that the river would rise enough to bring the salmon up, but not in so heavy a flood that they would all run without a pause through the seven miles of rocky stream to the loch above. — Catriona's mind was occupied with a dress-making problem, for she had come to the conclusion that the chorus needed a more emotional colour-scheme; and Mrs. Pettigrew, long accustomed to tedious discussion, could remain deaf for long periods when general topics were debated. Pettigrew, though determined that a pack of old women should not interfere with his plans, thought morosely of the indignity he had suffered; and Swanson, whose wounded ear was now cumbrously patched with sulphonilamide gauze and sticking-plaster, felt uneasily that his explanation, of a loose slate falling from the roof of the mill, had been received with some scepticism. Mr. Marvell, who as well as being a silent Member of Parliament was a journalist and a well-known broadcaster, was composing a sonnet about Catriona. And Andrew Flett had not come in to dinner.

Mr. Crantit, therefore, continued without interruption: 'The irony of the situation is that Germany, after resounding defeat in two major wars, has infected the rest of the world with her own distemper and seen the triumph, elsewhere, of her own ideas. Nationalism, a chronic disorder of the mind, had become acute in Germany; and now it has spread its fever from Bahia Blanca to Bangkok. The peculiar unhappiness of German philosophy fertilized the subsoil of Russian unhappiness, which has grown crops of unexampled nastiness ever since. The Germanic passion for tidiness and order carried its contagion to the dear, casual shores of Britain, and we, who had no previous experience of order — we, who had always relied on general principles and a sense of form — now live in a sort of waste-paper basket, stifled by regulations and amendments to regulations, by Orders in Council and Acts of Parliament tossed out like confetti, by licences and revocations of licences, all execrably written in a language that looks like the sloughings of language, like dandruff brushed from old decrepit dictionaries.

'But the most important, the most spectacular growth of the

Teutonic seeds of good and evil can be observed, of course, in the United States of America. German efficiency, the Germanic addiction to work for work's sake, and the German passion to expand — to blow every little balloon of an idea to its utmost circumference — have all taken root and prospered there beyond belief. The exuberance of Whitman and the frontier, the virtue of Lincoln, the idealism of Jefferson, the zest of cowboys and Mark Twain, the Tory assurance of Washington and the ingenuity of a nation of pioneers have all been canalized — if I may change the metaphor — to drive a psycho-electric power-system that can only be regarded, I think, as the Baron Münchhausen's posthumous masterpiece. And nobody can stop it.

'Nor, indeed, should we try to stop it. We should take what advantage we can from an historical process that appears to be inevitable. The Americans enjoy working, they enjoy making more and more steel, motor cars, washing-machines and bubble-gum to create new records in production. They are poets, in a way, and records are their verses. But their economists have discovered that, in order to go on practising their national art, they must give away every year many thousand million dollars' worth of tractors and cosmetics, of corn and cannon-shells, of bacon and beans and comic books — and we benefit accordingly. The chief argument against federal union with the United States is that, if we became incorporated in their society, we should lose that benefit. We should be expected to work as hard as their own people, and become as reverent of salesmanship.'

'Well,' said the General, who had not been listening, 'that's very interesting. Very interesting indeed. But what's the weather going to do? It's stopped raining.'

Catriona and Mrs. Pettigrew had left them to their port, and getting up, he drew the curtains and looked out at a misty, moonlit sky. 'We want more rain,' he said, 'but not too much. What do you think about it, Swanson?'

Mr. Crantit drank a third glass of port while they discussed the weather, and when they joined the ladies felt so animated that he marched across the room like a conqueror and loudly invited Mrs.

Pettigrew to come for a walk with him. The magic of the West Highlands, he declared, depended upon the moisture of the atmosphere. There was often too much, he admitted, but now beneath the moon the air was exquisitely lucid, the islands were a silhouette of romance in black velvet, and the sea whispered veracious tidings of Tir nan Og.

Surprised by his ardour, Mrs. Pettigrew raised a slim leg, pointed to an insubstantial, pretty slipper, and said she was neither shod nor clothed for walking.

'It will only take you a minute to put on a coat and thicker shoes,' said Mr. Crantit impatiently

'Don't forget an umbrella,' said the General.

'There's not the smallest occasion for an umbrella. The sky's clear, and the moon is climbing it with the utmost confidence.'

'Well . . .' said Mrs. Pettigrew, still doubtful.

'You are too young to sit by the fire,' said Mr. Crantit, 'and a moonlit night after rain is too precious to be wasted.'

'Well, just for a little while,' said Mrs. Pettigrew more briskly, after looking first at her husband, who grunted in his chair, and then with some kindliness at Mr. Crantit, who stood in the operatic pose of a tenor-singer inviting his soprano to adventure.

A few minutes later, with her usual need of physical contact, she took his arm; and Mr. Crantit, much encouraged, promptly squeezed her hand.

'I should like,' he said, 'to be loved for my money alone. It would, in the first place, imply that I had some money. And in the second place it would give me confidence; for so long as I was properly generous, my love would be secure, and when I grew tired of it I could bring it quickly to an end by cutting off supplies. But you cannot possibly enjoy such good fortune; for though you're rich enough to attract a score of venal lovers, you're so beautiful that all of them would, inevitably, fall victims to sincerity.'

'I like compliments,' said Mrs. Pettigrew, 'but I don't like them to be too clever.'

'Why do you distrust cleverness? It's not nearly so dangerous as stupidity.'

162

'Oh, I'm not afraid of danger. I just don't like having to think too much.'

'How right you are! Sensation's worst enemy is the intellect.'

'I don't hanker for anything sensational, either!'

'No, no! I only meant that *feeling* — the natural movement of the heart, the instinctive response to your beauty and your finger-tips — can be ruined by excessive thought.'

'But you do like to think-out a line of retreat from my beauty and my finger-tips, just in case you get tired of them?'

Mr. Crantit disengaged his arm from hers, and stepping back a yard or so, looked at her with admiration. They stood on the soft turf of the *machair*, between the beach and the road, and the moon through a gossamer cloud shed its light upon her. 'Now I am truly in peril,' he said. 'I was prepared to succumb to beauty, but I hadn't expected to fall captive to wisdom.'

'Oh, I'm not so dumb as you think.'

'You are Pallas Athene in Aphrodite's flesh!'

'No — no!' she exclaimed, as Mr. Crantit somewhat clumsily tried to encircle her in his embrace. 'My God, this place is open as the day, and in any case — well, I'm a little worried tonight.'

'About what?'

'What was Sam doing this afternoon?'

'He went for a walk with Swanson, they got caught in the rain, and came back soaked to the skin.'

'He had a whisky-and-water when he came in, and said he was going to have a bath. When he was in his bath he shouted to me, and said he wanted another drink. I brought him another whisky, and his arms and his leg were all covered with little scratches. I asked him what he'd been doing, and he told me to mind my own business. But he asked me to unpack his other leg — he always carries a spare — because the straps on the one he'd been wearing were wet. Well, they were more than wet. There was mud in the buckles. And Swanson, who was with him, comes back with a bite out of his ear. — Well, what were they doing?'

'My dear Mrs. Pettigrew — may I call you Lucy?'

'Oh, call me anything you like.'

'It amounts to this, my adorable Lucy: that whoever comes to Laxdale is involved in the oldest entanglements and terrors of the world, because Laxdale has not, as yet, broken the silver cord of tradition. He was probably attacked by Harpies.'

'Harpies?'

'A Greek word for an eternal peril. The major perils do not die, and the primal joys are equally indestructible.'

'Oh, stop it, do! This place, I tell you, in the moonlight, is open as the day!'

'We should be less conspicuous if we sat down.'

'But the grass is wet.'

'The air is warm, and my waterproof is at least damp-proof.'

'Well, just for a few minutes.'

'No common minutes, but a little overdraft on eternity.'

'Was it learning Greek that made you like this?'

'Are you flattering now? Am I a credit to classical education?'

'Well, you're worse than I'd expected. Much worse. — Oh, damn!'

'What's the matter?'

'It's raining again!'

'Mist, mist. Highland mist. No harm in it at all.'

'It's raining, I tell you!'

'A passing sprinkle.'

But Lucy Pettigrew was right. A black cloud, carried by a draught in the upper air, had come swiftly out of the south-west, and at sight of land had begun to discharge. A fleet followed, similarly laden, and the moon was darkened. The first few scattered drops, cold and heavy, were quickly followed by a downpour of growing intensity, thin shafts of rain swiftly thickening, and filling the whole air with their sibilance.

'Come on!' said Lucy, scrambling to her feet.

'Take this,' said Mr. Crantit, proudly courteous, and threw his waterproof about her shoulders.

'Oh, God!' she said. 'I might have known this would happen.'

'In the wood, perhaps, we should be tolerably sheltered.'

'You don't know what this dress cost — and my hair's going to be like a bird's nest. Oh, damn you intellectuals!'

'Don't blaspheme, dear Lucy.'

'Shut up — and let's run.'

They ran, jog-trot, and the rain fell heavily from a darkened sky. Lucy Pettigrew hated discomfort. Mr. Crantit's exuberance dissolved in the misery of disappointment. She was wet and he was sodden when they reached Laxdale Hall, and with only a perfunctory good night she ran up to her room. He picked up his waterproof that she had dropped, and hung it in the cloak-room. He stood in the lavatory, rubbing his hair with a towel, and heard the front door open and close again. He put on his spectacles, and going out met Andrew Flett who, pink-cheeked and with shining eyes, was unbuttoning a serviceable oilskin.

'You're very late,' he said severely.

'I stayed to supper at the McLeods'.'

'Even so, you're late.'

'I went for a walk with Morag —'

'I hope you realize,' said Mr. Crantit, 'that love is not merely the most painful of the venereal diseases, but the only one for which there is neither prophylaxis nor remedy.'

CHAPTER TWENTY

A GREY morning showed a sagging sky in which the clouds
hung like wet canvas, and a desolate small wind made a
mournful whistling. By breakfast-time it was raining again,
lightly at first and as though haphazardly. But slowly the rain grew
heavier, and seemed to acquire, with increasing weight, a sullen
purpose. The sky was shuttered by its fall, the land lost shape and
colour, the sea lay invisible behind thick curtains that the clouds
had dropped. In a half-drowned world — or so it appeared — only
the rain had will, and the rain's will was malignant. Faintly gleaming, loudly percussive on slate roofs and soundless on yielding
grass, the ceaseless rods of water beat upon the vanquished earth in
perpendicular attack; for even the wind had now been crowded
from the sky. There was no room for anything but rain.

A few minutes after ten o'clock the Mathesons' car stopped in the
village street beside Mrs. Mackenzie's general shop, one counter of
which was the Laxdale post-office; and Catriona, who had been
sitting close-pressed in the back seat between Marvell and Flett, got
out to buy some stamps. The General, with Mr. Pettigrew beside
him, filled his pipe and said, 'It takes five minutes, at least, to buy
stamps; and that depends on your having the post-office to yourself.
Mrs. Mackenzie's very fond of conversation, and if there are two or
three other people there, you won't get what you want under
half an hour. But she's a good soul, and well-meaning.'

No one replied, or offered comment on what he had said. His
visitors were dismayed by the apparent malignity of the weather,
and like prisoners in their cells, staring hopelessly at grimy walls,
they looked through the misted windows and saw nothing but the
occluding rain.

Comfortably the General smoked his pipe, and thought: This is the very day to show them the road. They won't see much, but what they do see will be horrible. Even Pettigrew may admit that we're entitled to a little comfort . . .

His meditation was interrupted by the passing of an oilskinned figure on a bicycle, and suddenly opening his window he shouted, 'Hi! Hi, McKellaig, come here!'

McKellaig dismounted and wheeled his bicycle alongside the car.

'Where are you going?' demanded the General.

'I was coming to ask if I should open the sluices and let out the dam.'

'Oh, yes. Yes, certainly. You ought to know that for yourself.'

Though the water-mill was no longer worked, the dam and the sluice-gates were kept in repair to scour the lower parts of the river of the weed that sometimes choked it in a long period of drought.

'The rain may stop as quickly as it started,' said McKellaig.

'That's not likely, not at this time of year. Have you seen the river yet? Is it rising too quickly?'

'It may indeed, if the rain goes on.'

'I could have told you that myself!'

'Hullo, McKellaig!' said Catriona, coming out of the post-office and returning to her seat between Marvell and Flett. 'I'm sorry to hear your mother's been ill. Is she really better again?'

'She was not exactly ill,' said McKellaig, stammering a little, disconcerted by the question. 'It was just a shortness of breath, I think. She said her heart was beating too much.'

'But she's better now?'

'Yes, yes. She is all right.'

'You ought to have told me,' said the General, 'and I'd have come to see her.'

'Oh, she wasn't bad enough for that,' said McKellaig, ill-at-ease.

'Let me know if there's anything I can do. Tell your mother I was asking for her, and get those sluice-gates opened. There's no point in storing water with Noah's Flood coming down.'

'Whatever you say,' answered McKellaig obediently, and the

General, pressing the starter, let in the clutch and drove eastwards towards the Larig Dubh.

'I shouldn't have said that!' exclaimed Catriona, a moment or two later. 'I mean, about his mother being ill. It was Mrs. Mackenzie who told me. She said McKellaig came and knocked at her door before the shop was open, and asked her to send a telegram to someone in Glasgow to tell him his mother was getting better. But he asked her not to let anyone know that she'd been ill, for she didn't want to be bothered by people coming to see her; and Mrs. Mackenzie said she wouldn't have told anyone but me, but she knew that we would feel responsible. — And then I saw Norman, and I just forgot that what I'd been told was confidential.'

'I don't suppose it matters,' said her father. 'Nothing remains confidential for very long in this place.'

He stopped the car a few hundred yards short of the summit of the pass, and invited his guests to get out and consider the state of the road. They stood for some minutes, very unhappily, in a pearly mist through which the rain, attenuated now, fell in a wiry, cold descent; and gloomily contemplated the parent rock that obtruded through the road, the runnels that swept away its remnant surface, and the surrounding fog of mist and water.

They drove farther, a mile or two beyond the summit, and again got out. To the one side rose a darkly gleaming rampart of wet rock, on the other a drenched anarchy of stone and heather descended to a long inlet of the sea. The rain was gentle here, a sparser fall; and a glimmer of light came through the clouds above and divided the clouds beneath. A metallic light, yellowish and silver, like old Sheffield plate, was reflected from the sea that pushed a long arm behind the Laxdale peninsula, sixteen hundred feet below them. Mr. Pettigrew looked down at the hairpin corners of the road that descended to the shore, and said gruffly, 'Only a fool would live in a place like this.'

The General turned his car, where rock had been quarried from the roadside, leaving a space of level ground, and when they had re-crossed the top of the pass he stopped for the third time, and though here the sky was pouring a monsoon flood upon the hill, again made his guests get out to inspect a particularly impressive example of erosion.

They stood miserably, enduring the rain like cattle with drooping heads and their rumps against the weather, and listened dumbly. The General grew eloquent. He lived much out-of-doors, and was indifferent to physical discomfort. The road was a subject of the deepest interest to him, and a well-governed passion gave force to his words, while abundant knowledge of its history and the probable cost of repairing it provided substance. He spoke of Miss Phipps and conduits, grading and surfaces, estimated labour requirements and the use of bulldozers, while his hearers grew colder, wetter, and more unhappy, and Mr. Pettigrew remembered a visit to Niagara Falls.

The General, indeed, was only beginning his economic survey when he was interrupted, from somewhere on the almost invisible hillside, by the report of a rifle.

He turned sharply, eyes questing, and exclaimed, 'You heard that? A rifle-shot. How far away, do you think?'

'It's difficult to estimate, in weather like this,' said Marvell.

'That's the direction.'

'A little to the right, I think.'

'I'm allowing for the wind,' said the General, and with a swift purposeful step strode into the grey obscurity of the moor.

'Oh, father!' cried Catriona. 'You'll never find him on a day like this! You'll only get lost!'

But the General paid no attention, and Mr. Pettigrew said, 'Well, I'm not going to stand here any longer.' He returned to the car, slammed the door, and sat in a glum silence. The others followed, and Catriona said sensibly, 'I think we should put our coats in the boot. We'll be more comfortable then.'

'Very comfortable indeed,' said Mr. Marvell a few moments later, as he felt Catriona's shoulder pressed against him. 'We've had a most interesting demonstration — don't you agree, Pettigrew? — and I hope your father doesn't get lost.'

'The more I see of this place,' said Mr. Pettigrew, 'the more certain I am that all its inhabitants are mad. What sane man would want to go shooting on a day like this? And who in his senses would care if he did?'

'We're not mad enough,' said Catriona with spirit, 'to be frightened of a little rain! And if somebody was shooting one of our stags, father naturally wants to know who. — And I don't really think he'll get lost.'

Only Mr. Marvell enjoyed the half-hour they had to wait for the General's return, but he, with Catriona so close beside him, felt a physical comfort that hovered with exquisite trepidation on the border of luxury; and suddenly into his mind there fell, like a legacy from the Elizabethan past, the sugared but resounding lines of the concluding couplet he needed for his unfashionable sonnet.

Red-faced, a little steam of bodily heat about him to repel the rain, the General came out of the brumous mist, walking briskly up the road, and said, 'I couldn't find him! I quartered the ground like a pointer — there's a little corrie down there, and there were deer in it not very long ago — but I couldn't see him, nor anything he'd killed. But in weather like this there might have been a dozen chaps there, lying quiet, and I wouldn't have spotted them. I wonder who it was?'

Slowly he drove back to Laxdale, and shortly before they entered the village said, 'I wonder if it was Nicholas? Do you think I should stop at his house, and see if he's in?'

'It would be rather awkward,' said Catriona, 'if you caught Nicholas poaching just at present. He's got a very important part in the play.'

'And it might be a little unfair,' admitted the General. 'If it was Nicholas, he beat me on the ground, and to go spying into his house mightn't be quite the thing — what do you say?'

'No,' said Catriona.

'All right,' said the General. 'Let's go home and forget about it; and have a glass of sherry.'

In the library they found Swanson and Crantit and Mrs. Pettigrew, very comfortable before a large fire, extremely hilarious, and already drinking sherry. Mrs. Pettigrew had spent some time in the kitchen, where she had heard the whole story of her husband's flight into a willow tree and Swanson's descent into the mill-dam. The story had by now spread through the village and most of the parish, and Mrs. Pettigrew, after the first shock of surprise and a sort of delayed consternation, was as much pleased by it as everybody else who heard it. Mr. Crantit was even better pleased, but bitterly deplored his absence from the scene. He made Swanson relate the whole tale of his conflict with Macaulay — Mrs. Pettigrew knew nothing of their war-time encounters — and when Swanson, for Mrs. Pettigrew's benefit, had demonstrated, by falling on to the sofa, the manner in which, for the cost of getting wet, he had avoided the minister's sword-stroke, his misadventure seemed to him as funny as it did to the others. They were particularly pleased to hear, from Mrs. Pettigrew, that the old women had greatly admired Macaulay for what they described as his masterful manner.

But when the General and his guests came in, and Mrs. Pettigrew began to explain what they had been laughing at, she soon perceived that her husband saw the episode in quite a different light; and neither the General nor Catriona was inclined to laugh at it.

CHAPTER TWENTY-ONE

Aʙᴏᴜᴛ two o'clock in the afternoon, Willy John Watt stopped his hearse beside Nicholas McLeod's shop, and climbed down from its exposed driving-seat. He wore a dark cap and a long black oilskin, with a velvet edge to the collar, that already glistened wetly with the rain, though he had driven no more than a hundred yards. He opened the door of the shop, with a sharp peal of the warning bell, and saw Mrs. McLeod behind the counter with three customers on the other side. There were two middle-aged women, one thick-set and comfortable, the other with a face of weather-beaten resignation, and an elderly man whose grave expression was in curious contrast with his trousers, a pair of dungarees so often washed that they had faded to a frivolous pale blue. All three were there for conversation as much as business.

'Is it raining still?' asked Mrs. McLeod.

'There is a mist on the hill,' said Willy John cautiously. 'I don't know if it will come to rain or not.'

'The corn is laid in my field, whatever,' said the old man.

'It will rise again, if there is no wind,' said one of the women.

'There will be wind.'

'For three weeks,' said the second woman, 'the weather has been like Paradise. It couldn't last.'

'It is the heaviest crop I have known for fifteen years,' said the old man. 'It will be ill to cut.'

'It will be cut in time, God helping,' said Mrs. McLeod. 'And what are you wanting, Willy John?'

'Is Nicholas in?'

'No, he's not. He went out some time ago.'

'And what time will he be coming back?'

'Oh, I couldn't say. No, I couldn't say. Is it for anything important you're wanting him?'

'I was wondering if he would come to Glasgow with me.'

'To Glasgow!' said one of the women.

'On a day like this!' said her neighbour.

'In Glasgow and the other big cities,' said the old man, 'they care nothing for the weather. They are not concerned with crops, they are only concerned with business; and rain or fine makes no difference to them.'

'But what are you wanting to go to Glasgow for?' asked Mrs. McLeod.

'It is my father,' said Willy John. 'I am worried about him. I had another sight of him, last night, and he was needing help.'

'Can you not wait for the steamer?' asked one of the women.

'It would be too late. I have the hearse outside, and I was thinking that Nicholas might enjoy the trip, and he would be company for me too.'

'But if you are worried about your father,' said Mrs. McLeod, 'can you not send him a telegram and ask outright if he is dead or not?'

'No, no,' said Willy John. 'That wouldn't do at all. He is not used to telegrams, and the shock might be fatal.'

'That is so, yes, that is so,' said the old man. 'I had a telegram once, and for three days I was frightened to open it. And by that time my son had come home with a girl he had married in Birmingham, and I wished the telegram had told me he was dead.'

'Well,' said Mrs. McLeod to Willy John, 'if you are going to Glasgow you will be needing something to eat. What have you got?'

'I have a bottle,' he said, 'but I would like some biscuits.'

'Will a pound be enough?'

'Oh, plenty, for all the drink I have.'

'Well, here you are. And I hope you have a good journey.'

'Give my kind regards to your father, if he's still alive,' said the old man. 'He was a ne'er-do-weel and a very bad man, but I was always fond of him.'

Willy John, with his bag of biscuits, returned to his hearse and drove eastwards out of Laxdale.

He was in bottom gear, climbing slowly the rough approach to the summit of the pass, when at the road-side, rising darkly in the mist, a figure appeared above an outcrop of rock and shouted to him to stop.

He halted and looked back. 'Is it yourself, Nicholas?' he said.

'Just so,' said Nicholas. He had a rifle under his arm, and he was shining wet as a seal in sou'wester and short oilskin jacket and rough knickerbockers. 'And where are you making for, Willy John?'

'I am going to Glasgow. I had another sight of my father last night.'

'What sort of trim was he in this time?'

'Bad, bad! I felt sorry for the poor man.'

'Well, it's a long way to go, Willy John.'

'I called in at the shop, Nicholas, to see if you would come with me and keep me company.'

'Did you indeed? Well, now, and that is an interesting suggestion, I must think about it. — Come down, man, and stand in the lee of the hearse, and we'll talk it over.'

Willy John switched off the motor, obediently got down, and stood with Nicholas in the shelter of the hearse. For half a minute or so neither spoke, and then Willy John asked diffidently, 'And what are you doing so far out on the hill, Nicholas?'

'I was just going to tell you. — There is a small thing of a corrie, over that way, and I have noticed that when there is wind and rain, and the wind is in this airt, there is usually a stag and a few hinds in it. And when I rose this morning I felt a great curiosity to see if they would be there again. But it seemed a waste of time to come all this way without the rifle.'

'It is not a day I would choose myself to go shooting.'

'You are no sportsman, Willy John, so you do not see the advantages of a day like this. The visibility is poor, I grant you that, and unless you know where to look for a stag you are not likely to find one. But on the other hand, if that busybody McKellaig, or the

General himself, take it into their heads that someone is poaching, there is little prospect of them seeing who the poacher is. And this morning, moreover, I knew the General would be busy with the Members of Parliament.'

'Did you shoot a stag, Nicholas?'

'I did — and it's a wonder I'm here to tell you of it! For no sooner had I put my gully to the throat of it, and whistled to Peter — I had Peter and the pony waiting, maybe a cable's length behind, or a bit more — when I heard someone slithering down a little slope of scree on the hill above, and I'd just time to pull a few great bushes of heather to hide the stag, and take cover myself, when there on a rock, looking this way and that, and no more than a hundred yards away, was the General himself!'

'Was he out for a shot at the stags too?'

'He had no rifle. No, I think he must have been here on the road, with the Members of Parliament, just at that very time — and if visibility had been a small thing better, he would have had me. But I lay as still as a corpse, and he came no nearer, and Peter had the pony under a peat-bank with his hand on its nose. So all was well in the end.'

'It was a fortunate escape, but you will be caught one day, Nicholas. — And now, are you coming to Glasgow with me?'

'I am, if you will take the stag as well.'

'In the hearse, do you mean?'

'It travels better with a load — I've heard you say so many a time!'

'But what would you be doing in Glasgow with a stag?'

'I would take it to a butcher, Willy John. We'll look for a quiet, discreet sort of man, and whatever the price he gives me, there'll be half of it for you.'

'Would it not be irreverent to take a stag to Glasgow in a hearse?'

'There's no irreverence in a man that doesn't feel irreverent. It's what's hidden in the mind that counts — and a man with a mind like yours, Willy John, is in no danger at all.'

'Well, that is a comfort, to be sure.'

A little persuasion still, a little more argument, were needed before Willy John finally agreed to accept so unusual a cargo, and then, with a whistle, Nicholas called his boy Peter from the outcrop of rock under which he had been sheltering, and Peter came leading a grey pony across whose back the stag was slung.

'We had meant to conceal it by the roadside, and come back for it at night, but this is a better plan altogether. Bring it round to the back door, Peter. — It is not a large beast, Willy John. I have made the gralloch, and it will weigh no more than ten or ten and a half stone.'

With no great difficulty they lifted and pushed the stag into the body of the hearse, and closed and latched the double doors.

'You will tell your mother, Peter,' said Nicholas, 'that Willy John and I have gone to Glasgow on business, and we'll be back as soon as we can find a convenient opportunity.'

'But you can't go to Glasgow this night, father! There's the *ceilidh*!'

'The *ceilidh*! My wits must be going, I forgot the *ceilidh*!'

'What *ceilidh* is that?'

'The *ceilidh* for the Members of Parliament. We'll be wanting some *port-a-beul* from you, Willy John, and I have to make the opening address.'

'I do not see why we should entertain them with a *ceilidh* after the way that man Pettigrew has been behaving.'

'The arrangements have been made — and we have to consider the tradition.'

'It is traditional, I know, to invite distinguished visitors to a *ceilidh* — but we expect them to behave themselves.'

'We are not responsible for their behaviour, Willy John — but we are responsible for the tradition.'

'And what will happen to my father if I don't go to Glasgow?'

'You can go at crack of dawn tomorrow morning, and I'll come with you. We'll keep a watch on ourselves at the *ceilidh*, we'll drink nothing at all — or very little — and we'll both be as sober as a judge when morning comes. We'll lose no time at all, and the stag will stay where it is, for no one is going to interfere with a hearse. — Oh no, we cannot miss the *ceilidh*!'

It was Peter, however, not Nicholas, who finally persuaded Willy John to postpone his journey. The lights on the hearse were out of order, and it was now five minutes past three. 'You wouldn't get to Glasgow before dark,' said Peter, 'and it's a policeman you'd be spending the night with, not your father.'

'The boy has a good head on him!' said Nicholas admiringly, and Willy John, after laborious calculation of times and distances and a lot of grumbling, consented to drive his hearse only a little way farther, to the opening of the old peat road that ran towards the river, where he could turn; and then go back to Laxdale and the *ceilidh*.

Nicholas climbed in beside him, and Peter mounted the pony. He rode bareback, but his knees were strong and confident. They overtook him within two or three hundred yards, and stopped beside him.

'Will you be all right by yourself?' asked Nicholas. 'He has an awkward temper sometimes, so don't try any tricks with him.'

'I'll manage fine,' said Peter, and asked if he could look in at the house of one of his friends, some distance from the village, whose father was building a new boat. Nicholas told him not to be too late, and Willy John, letting in his clutch, stepped heavily on the accelerator, and made a noisy, jarring start.

The frightened pony reared and swung round towards the hill again. He got the bit between his teeth, ducked his big hairy head and threw up his heels. The old rope-bridle broke at the bit, and arching his back the pony threw Peter into the ditch, and galloped for the top of the pass. Peter, unhurt, got up and followed.

Two hundred yards away the pony stopped, and began to graze where a little thin pasture grew among the wiry heather. Slowly Peter approached it, and the pony seemed to disregard him. But when he was almost within reach of the trailing, broken bridle it flirted its tail, flung up its heels, and bolted.

Peter, a determined boy, without loss of patience again pursued it.

CHAPTER TWENTY-TWO

CATRIONA had a well-developed sense of duty. She spent most of the afternoon rehearsing the *Bacchanals* in a long store-house behind Nicholas's shop — sacks of flour and oatmeal and barrels of paraffin-oil had been moved to one end to make room for the *ceilidh* at night — and then, though reluctantly, decided she must call on Mrs. McKellaig, whom she disliked, and inquire for her health.

She walked briskly from the village and knocked a little too loudly, with too peremptory a note, on the keeper's door. 'You're surely in a hurry, whoever you are!' came an angry voice from inside, then shuffling steps, and the door was half-opened, held half-open by suspicion, and round the edge showed the old woman's russet and yellow cheeks, her embittered and vivacious eyes. 'Oh, it's you, Miss Catriona,' she said grudgingly, and opened the door a little wider.

'I came to see if you are really feeling better, Mrs. McKellaig. My father and I were so sorry to hear you hadn't been well.'

'I havena been well for twenty years,' said Mrs. McKellaig with indignation in her voice. 'But that's no' your fault. Come in and sit doon, and tell me what's the news.'

'Just for a few minutes. We've been rehearsing in Nicholas McLeod's big shed — '

'What need has Nicholas for a shed as big as that? Is it tae keep his big conceit in?'

'Oh, don't be too hard on him. We're all very fond of Nicholas.'

'Norman's no fond of him, for one. He gi'es Norman mair toolies than a' the rest o' the parish put together.'

'Yes, I know they don't get on well. I wish they did.'

'Aye. So you say. And wha was it tell't you I hadna been well?'

'It was Mrs. Mackenzie of the Post Office — but it just slipped out in conversation. I'm sure she didn't mean to betray a confidence.'

'There's naebody would tell her anything in confidence! Na, na. It was open for all to hear. We were at the mill-dam yestreen, wi' a wheen o' auld, rigwoodie bodies like oorsels, and I took a cramp abune the hurdies, that was all. But God! we had the laugh o' yon fellow Pettigrew, hauling his bare bum intil a tree, and yon fusionless craiture Swanson, that writes daft books, they tell me. Have you heard what happened? It was a proper rant! Go you in tae the ben-end and I'll mask a pot o' tea, and gie' you the hale clash.'

'Is Norman in?'

'He's in the closet, sleeping. We'll no' disturb him. — Ay, I was there masel, and saw the Member of Parliament clambering in the muckle saugh as naked as the day he was born, and the fusionless body Swanson falling intil the dam wi' a skelp you could hear a mile away. — Go you tae the ben-end, Miss Catriona, and I'll hae the tea ready in three minutes, nae mair. And if you canna laugh at what I've to tell, you'll laugh at nothing!'

Catriona had never seen the old woman so pleased about anything before. To her ancient, ingrown malignity the spectacle of Mr. Pettigrew's discomfiture and Swanson's ludicrous collapse had been a whole festival of delight — her grudging soul had taken a seat in a cream-and-scarlet merry-go-round, her old lips had drunk the year's new vintage, she had pelted strangers with confetti, fallen in love, fought for balloons and heard brass bands and gipsy fiddles in her pendulous, yellow ears — and now her wrinkles danced, her fierce old eyes glittered with the purest joy, and even her artificial teeth seemed as genial as the yellowed keys of a bar-room piano. — Fascinated and a little horrified, disliking Mrs. McKellaig's company but incapable of refusing to hear her story, Catriona allowed herself to be shown into the depressingly well-furnished ben-room; where Mrs. McKellaig left her with a repeated promise of swift return.

Catriona, who knew the room and had no interest in its curious ornaments, sat down on the horse-hair sofa and wondered for a puzzled minute why Mrs. Mackenzie of the Post Office had been given a telegram by Norman McKellaig that reported his mother's recovery from some unspecified ailment, when Mrs. McKellaig herself complained only of a chronic state of ill-being . . . She moved an awkward cushion to make herself more comfortable, and behind it discovered a folded news-sheet, smaller than an evening paper, that bore on its front page, in a good, bold lettering, the improbable title:

THE HEART MART

Below that black and four-square announcement there ran, in much smaller type: *With which is incorporated The Hymeneal News.* Under that, dividing the page, were two photographs of wedding-groups. On the left a representation of a nervously smiling middle-aged man in a hired morning-suit, and a frankly beaming middle-aged bride in a costume excessively ornamented, with flowers carried, plainly without goodwill, by seemingly moronic children in white shirts and theatrical kilts. On the right a picture of a tall, very thin, bashful young man with mournful eyes and a protruding Adam's apple, and a plump young woman with a vacuous expression and innumerable teeth.

Beneath these photographs the caption stared: 'What brought happiness to these lucky bridegrooms and blissful brides? They advertised in THE HEART MART!' — In three-column width, set in a commanding type, the opening paragraph of an editorial depended: 'There is no need to be lonely,' it proclaimed. 'There is no need to eat out your heart in solitude. No matter what you are, or where you live, *The Heart Mart* can put you in touch with a loving partner-for-life . . .'

Catriona unfolded the paper to read more, and perceived that its deceptive bulk was created by a collection of large, glossy photographs, all of women. They were not beautiful women, but several of them looked good. The age of most of them, so far as she could guess, ranged from the early thirties, a group characterized by anxiety, to the late fifties, who without exception revealed unabated hope. The photographs were all of the same pattern, showing head and shoulders only, and from the style of hairdressing and such clothing as was revealed, they came from classes appreciably differing — to an acute, feminine eye — in both wealth and status. A few were eccentric, individual, beyond the easy classifications which divided the majority. There was a young negress, extremely pretty to the eyes of anyone wise enough to appreciate young negresses; and a comely young girl with her hair modestly done and a white blouse of almost sentimental simplicity, who had had her photograph taken as she looked down at some object unseen — so steeply down that her eyes were completely veiled by eyelids agreeably smooth and fringed with long lashes.

Catriona had sufficient curiosity to count the photographs: there were twenty-nine of them. She put them beside her on the sofa, and turning to the back page of *The Heart Mart*, saw that it was filled with small advertisements, under a banner-headline which read: 'Fair Play and Standard Conditions for all! First advertisement not to exceed Fifty Words. There is a standard charge: fee for first advertisement and subsequent introduction: £3. 0. 0. No Favouritism, no Bribery, no Reduction!'

In the mass of advertisements one had been framed with a blunt pencil, and read: 'Willing to go anywhere, but country life preferred. Miss A. M., 27. Brunette, small, lively, and affectionate disposition. Would much prefer really remote countryside. Good plain cook, economical. Fond of animals, children. No parents, non-smoker. Write Box LG 317.'

That's the one for Norman, thought Catriona, and picking up the collection of photographs to see if she could identify her, heard the inner door opening; and turning, saw Norman McKellaig, in shirt and trousers, staring at her with startled eyes, his mouth half-open, his chin drooping.

'Oh, Norman,' she said, 'did I wake you? I'm so sorry.'

'I think it was my mother,' he said. 'I think it was her voice I heard.'

'I came to ask if she was better, and she made me stay for a cup of tea.'

'It was the least she could do.'

'I haven't been poking and prying, Norman. I just moved the cushion, and found this paper and all these photographs behind it.'

'I forgot about them. It was from my mother I hid them — I keep them locked up — but she came in, after dinner when I was looking at them, and I was just going to bed, for I must be out on the hill tonight, and I put them behind the cushion, and listened to what she had to say — and that isn't often a very pleasant experience, Miss Catriona — and when she had gone I felt so miserable, I went and lay down just for the comfort of it.'

'I'm sorry, Norman. I know your mother's difficult; very difficult. — But tell me, why do you do this? Is it just for a hobby?'

'Oh, no, no! It is more than that.'

'And how can you afford it? It says here that each introduction costs three pounds.'

'It is a very high-class agency. I tried cheaper ones before, but they were just insulting to any man who has a little self-respect.'

'But, Norman — how *can* you afford it? Three pounds a time, and all these photographs?'

'At the beginning, Miss Catriona, I didn't think it would be difficult to find someone suitable. It's the long time it's been going on that made it expensive. For when I told them about Laxdale, and where it is and how we live here, they all renegued, and said nothing doing. Until last week, that is.'

'But why can't you find someone in the village who would marry you — if that's what you want?'

'I could find plenty. I could find a score of them tomorrow — '

'Well — '

'But there's no one in the parish of Laxdale that I will marry, though if anyone needs a wife it is me, just to save me from my mother. There is no one hereabout that I will take home.'

'Why not?'

'You are proud, Miss Catriona, and so am I. We are all proud, in the Highlands, though in fact we may have little cause for pride. — Two years ago last June I asked Morag McLeod to marry me, and she said no. And then and there I swore that if Morag would not have me, then there is no girl in Laxdale that I would bring to the house. There will be no second-best for me.'

'Are you still in love with Morag?' asked Catriona.

'A man who is a man doesn't fall in love more than once,' said McKellaig.

'I don't believe that's true!'

'But a man who's a man is prepared to make the best of things.'

'Well, among all these photographs, is there anyone who's capable of taking Morag's place?'

'The last one, I think.'

From the collection of photographs McKellaig took that of the girl who had posed for her picture with downcast eyes, and showing Catriona the advertisement he had framed in pencil, went to his bedroom for a letter she had written.

'She is honest, you will see that at once,' he said; and Catriona read: 'Dear Mr. McKellaig, I think I should tell you, in the first place, that the reason I am looking down in the photograph is to hide the fact that I have quite a bad squint . . .'

'Yes, she's honest, and I think she's probably nice. She lives in Glasgow, does she?'

'So she says, and I was thinking that will be why she is wanting to come to the country.'

'You'll have to go and see her.'

'That will be more expense, and there'll be a ring to buy, if she's suitable.'

'Nobody ever got married without spending money. You'll have to reconcile yourself to that — and marriage is often a good investment.'

'With a mother like mine, it would be a haven of refuge.'

'Will you open the door for me?' came the harsh voice of Mrs. McKellaig, and Norman, quickly gathering up his photographs, whispered 'I am still asleep!' and tip-toed back to his closet, and soundlessly shut the door.

Catriona let Mrs. McKellaig in, who came burdened by a tray on which, beside cups and saucers and a pot of tea, were a couple of boiled eggs, scones, butter and honey, and pancakes still hot from the girdle. Catriona expostulated — said she was ashamed of having put her hostess to so much trouble — but Mrs. McKellaig denied having gone to any trouble at all, and as soon as she had poured out the tea and made her audience secure with a boiled egg, began her story with infinite relish.

It became, in her shaping of it and with her vigorous telling, an heroic tale in which certain ruthless invaders of the land, who had trampled on the finer feelings of Mrs. McKellaig and her friends, and by their insolence deeply wounded them, were with an ever watchful courage and liveliest intelligence opposed, and at last surprised in an indefensible position or ambush — and then, by Highland dash and daring, attacked and routed, utterly routed, and their defeat made manifest to all. The taste of revenge lay sweet as honey on the old woman's tongue, and the great, clattering, rumbustious words of her Doric speech sounded in her narrative like boulders carried down the rocky bed of a stream in spate. — Against her will Catriona responded, shared the pleasure, felt the triumph, and laughed at the proper time; and almost unaware of their several flavours, ate her boiled egg, her buttered scone, her honeyed pancake.

It was unfair, she knew, to regard Swanson as an enemy, merely because he was a stranger and earned an unnatural living by writing books; but it was necessary, she recognized, because the hero of the tale, in Mrs. McKellaig's construction of it, was the Reverend Mr. Macaulay. It was he, finally, who had mastered both wings of the foe. The Member of Parliament cowering among the grey-green leaves of the willow tree, the unfortunate novelist floundering in the dam, and between them a holy man of wrath with a great two-handed sword stippled, at the very point, with a drop or two of blood! And to show forth the savage triumph they felt, she, Mrs. McKellaig, had hurled into the water the artificial leg of their more wicked victim. — Catriona shivered, and remembered what the Bacchanals had done to King Pentheus' head.

Hurriedly she finished her second cup of tea, got up, and said she must go.

'Wait, wait!' exclaimed Mrs. McKellaig. 'You havena heard the feenish o' it yet! For what did the meenister do then, good man, but rax up the muckle sword against me and the ither carlins, his e'en glowrin' like a houlet, and in a voice like the wrath o' God bade us all awa' hame, and repent. De'il a chance for anither keek at the man Pettigrew then! Na, na. The meenister was at the heels o' us, herdin' us owre the lea like kye comin' hame i' the gloaming, and the muckle sword on his shouther tae gar us scrieve. Och, wumman, he was grand!'

CHAPTER TWENTY-THREE

'C-E-I-L-I-D-H,' spelt the General for Mrs. Pettigrew's
sake, 'but it's pronounced *caylie*. The spelling, in Gaelic,
doesn't really mean very much. It's only a convention.'

'But what does *caylie* mean?'

'Properly speaking, it's a little party, quite informal, where someone tells a story, someone else sings a song or plays the fiddle,
just as the spirit moves them. But the affair tonight will be more
elaborate than that, because the *ceilidh*, as a means of entertaining
distinguished visitors, has become something of an institution.'

'Will there be any speech-making, or opportunity for it?' asked
Mr. Pettigrew.

'Nicholas McLeod is going to say something about your visit, and
what a pleasure it has been to welcome you — the usual thing, you
know — but it's not an occasion for political speech-making.'

'I should like,' said Mr. Pettigrew earnestly, 'to tell these people
something about myself. Not about the policy I propose for Laxdale — that can wait — but just about myself. Because, for some
reason which I can't fathom, they misunderstand me — and that
means they can't possibly understand my policy.'

'Well,' said the General doubtfully, 'I think we had better wait
and see how the evening goes. Sometimes a *ceilidh* is loud and cheerful, sometimes rather quiet and conversational. It depends on the
atmosphere that develops.'

'I think we're going to enjoy it very much,' said Mrs. Pettigrew,
with hope in her voice rather than conviction.

'The Highlanders,' said the General, 'have never been very
creative. They didn't build bridges or cathedrals, they didn't breed

a Rembrandt or a Donatello. But they evolved a social system that satisfied their needs, and they did develop some of the smaller arts; especially the considerable art of personal relationship. The *ceilidh* was part of their technique.'

'The poor Highlanders' great misfortune,' said Mr. Crantit, 'was that they never had a bourgeoisie. In the circumstances, I admit, there was no room for a bourgeoisie, but the lack of it was crippling. The major arts, as well as many useful virtues, are nearly all bourgeois products. The historian Dillinger, of Cambridge, himself the son of a wealthy grocer, goes so far as to say that 93.4 per cent of all the significantly creative minds of the last five hundred years are of bourgeois origin. So procreative are the loins of a brave burgess, so generous a nurse is his splendid wife! What would the world be without them? They, my dear Swanson, striving with ceaseless gallantry in the jungle of commerce to find respectability, and security, and a decent return for their money — they are the hero and heroine of true romance, if only you novelists had the wit to see it. But no, you prefer your picaros, your tousled beauties and buffoons.'

'The burgesses aren't consistent,' said Swanson. 'They've always wanted a big profit on everything they sell, and been content with a small profit from life; they've always had a high regard for other people's property, and now they're letting their own be taken without a protest.'

'Shallow, very shallow,' said Mr. Crantit. 'And what bad taste to jeer at them in their extremity! If a Labour Government, or any other, allows the bourgeoisie to perish, its name will be remembered amid the execrations of all good men with the Mongolian brutes who destroyed the serenity of China under the Sungs — with the Dorian savages (if Dorians they were) who wrecked the Minoan splendour of Crete — or even with the prehistoric vulgarities of the Iron-workers who obliterated the exquisite Age of Bronze. Why, good heavens, even the faults of the bourgeoisie, their little venial faults, are blessings in disguise, and the shallow contempt of the artists and intellectuals of the last half-dozen decades for what gave them birth and substance is truly intolerable!'

'But surely,' said Marvell, 'the artists were the first to rebel against bourgeois standards?'

'Precisely! A young artist always begins as a rebel — but a young artist doesn't want to get hurt. And against a comfortable, well-carpeted, plush-curtained, cosy domestic background he could rebel without any danger of serious injury — and then, in all probability, his philistine father gave him an allowance, or he got surreptitious help from his mother, to feed and clothe him in Bohemia. Oh, it's the perfect background for the young poet, the young painter, the young intellectual — and what they will do if their background is demolished, I can't imagine. They will, I'm afraid, cease to exist.'

'If I succeed in re-modelling the present theory and practice of Socialism,' said Mr. Pettigrew, 'I see a very fair prospect for the bourgeois element in society. Under Socialism Plus — '

'Ah, yes,' said the General. 'You told us about that before, didn't you?'

'I like to be fair,' said Mr. Crantit, taking swift advantage of the check to Pettigrew, 'and I don't want you to think that I am altogether hostile to a Labour Government. It was a mistake, I admit, to build a policy upon the discoveries of that unhappy scholar who — as much at sea as Columbus when he saw America before him — found one day a mysterious something which he christened "surplus value". For his followers and disciples, pursuing his discovery, fell upon "surplus value" with indiscriminate rage, and succeeded only in de-valuing all other values, except that of power, which has been wildly inflated. — Yes, it was a mistake to rely on Marx, but give Labour its due, and you must allow that, to some extent, it was pushed into its policy by a revival of that very curious phenomenon, English Puritanism. English Puritans are unlike other Puritans. They are more altruistic, perhaps. They would rather reform their neighbours than themselves. — But it is a large and complex subject, and I see the General looking at his watch.'

'It's nine o'clock,' said the General, 'and time to go. We mustn't keep Nicholas waiting. — Now who wants to be driven, and who would like to walk?'

Into the long storehouse at the back of Nicholas's shop a few chairs had been brought for the visitors, but the majority of the fifty or sixty people there sat on egg-boxes or bales of straw, and in the yellow glow and wavering shadow of several paraffin-lamps the scene had an apparent geniality, properly casual but warm enough for the occasion. There was, however, a constrained silence when the General brought in his guests, which was broken, and then dispelled, by the wholly unexpected ebullience of Mr. Macaulay.

He came forward to greet them, not exactly smiling, but with a conspicuous relaxation of gravity, and welcoming them in a hearty voice, vigorously shook their hands. To Mr. Pettigrew, indeed, he merely bowed, but Swanson he clapped on the shoulder, exclaiming, 'Well, well, Mr. Swanson, I am glad to see you here! You are none the worse, I hope, for your immersion?'

The sally brought grateful laughter from the audience, and the minister, confident of their good opinion, turned to them and explained: 'Mr. Swanson comes from Shetland, where they are all very hardy people. They are as much at home in the water as on dry land, for they intermarry with the seals, I am told. Ha-ha-ha!'

It was now the visitors' turn to feel embarrassed, for those who were strange to Laxdale found so much hilarity, on so small an occasion for it, surprising; and to the General and Catriona it was even more astonishing, for they had never heard Macaulay laugh before. But having had his joke, the minister was satisfied, and expressed the hope that Nicholas McLeod would now open the proceedings with his usual felicity.

Nicholas, however, was dull, and knew it; tried to retrieve his failure, and failed again; and went on too long. The first singer was a shy girl with a small but pretty voice, who, affected by the uncongenial atmosphere, forgot her words and sat down flushing miserably. A wauking-song was the next item, with a lively chorus; but very few people sang the chorus. The *ceilidh* grew more and more lugubrious, and Nicholas looked anxiously for Willy John. Willy John had a gift for *port-a-beul*, the mouth-music that sets a hailstorm of words to something like a piper's tune; and *port-a-beul* was unfailingly popular. But Willy John was not there. Two or three men, glad of the chance to escape, volunteered to go and look for him. In the whispering, coughing, boot-scraping quiet that followed, Mr. Pettigrew was heard clearing his throat, and the General, recognizing an emergency, followed the tradition of his calling and immediately got up to ask for volunteers.

'Come, now,' he said, 'let's put more spirit into it. This isn't a *ceilidh*, it's as dull as a meeting of the County Council — isn't it, Nicholas? Well, then, let's make a new start — and who'll give us a lead?'

But before a volunteer could be found, they heard a sound of hooves on the paved courtyard, and through the open door came a boy in sodden clothes, his boots muddy and his hands muddy, and a streak of mud across his face. He stood blinking in the light, and Nicholas, going towards him, exclaimed, 'Peter! What has happened to you, Peter? Where have you been?'

'The poachers are here,' said Peter, and pushed away his mother, who was trying to wipe his face with a handkerchief.

'Who told you so?' asked the General.

'I have seen them. They came down the old peat-road near the top of the hill. They're in two cars, or a car and a lorry perhaps. They had no lights, and that's how I knew they were the poachers.'

'What were you doing up there, at this time of night?' asked Mrs. McLeod.

The question cast a little shadow of anxiety on Nicholas's face, but Peter answered calmly enough, 'The pony got loose, and I went after him. He led me a proper chase, to the head of the loch and beyond. But I didn't want to come back without him, and I got a hold of him at last, though it was dark by then, and set off for home. And then I heard the cars coming, on the peat-road, and felt a wee bit frightened. So I hid till they were past. And then, when we came to the road itself, we galloped the whole way without a stop.'

'Good boy!' said the General. 'That's a very good boy of yours, Nicholas.'

'A chip of the old block,' said Nicholas complacently.

'Oh, Peter, Peter!' exclaimed his mother. 'You must be terribly tired.'

'Not me,' said Peter defiantly. 'But you ought to see the pony.'

'Well, now,' said the General, 'there are two things we've got to do, and we must do them quickly. I want to save the river, if I can, and we're going to round-up these fellows and put them in the bag. I'll take a party, the larger party, up the hill and down the peat-road till we find their cars. We'll immobilize them, and post a guard, at some distance from them. I'll take a patrol down the river, and I want you, Nicholas, to establish a base near this end, say at The Cruive, and lead a patrol up-stream to meet me. Is that clear?'

'A good plan indeed,' said Nicholas.

'The patrols may or may not make contact with the poachers. The likelihood is that they'll hear us coming and take to their heels. They'll go back to their cars, in that case, so I want a guard there strong enough to deal with the whole gang: there can't be more than seven or eight of them. — We have to find two parties, that is: a larger forward party and a small one at The Cruive, and two patrols. How many cars can we muster? Mine is here; and yours, Nicholas?'

'It's here too, but Nurse Connachy is away to North Bay, and Mr. Macaulay's won't take the road till it gets a new big end.'

'My big end is the very abomination of desolation,' said Macaulay, 'but I will come with you myself, General, for you may be needing a chaplain before the night's work is done.'

'Does the law entitle you to arrest poachers?' asked Mr. Pettigrew.

'That's a question that can wait till we have arrested them. — We need some younger men. Who'll go and look for volunteers? You — and you? Be as quick as you can, and tell them to bring their bicycles, and a stick if they feel inclined. — I can take five in my car, including myself, and you can put five in yours, Nicholas. But I want some more on bicycles. McKellaig isn't here, is he?'

'Will he not be on the hill?'

'No, he doesn't go out till about eleven as a rule. And it's only twenty minutes to.'

'Shall I go for him, father?' asked Catriona.

'Tell him to take his bicycle,' said the General, 'and look for me on the old peat-road. I want him to patrol the river with me. — Now I've got to go home and put on a pair of boots, so I'll leave you in charge of recruiting and administration, Nicholas. I'll be back in fifteen minutes.'

CHAPTER TWENTY-FOUR

T H E honest girl with a squint, who wanted to live in the country, had said in her letter that she would soon be having a week's holiday, and it had occurred to McKellaig that a double purpose would be served if she came to Laxdale for her holiday. She could see the country and decide whether she liked it, and he would be saved the expense of going to meet her in Glasgow. There was no inn or hotel in Laxdale — though Nicholas McLeod had a licence to sell whisky and beer — but in two or three cottages casual visitors, arriving on bicycles or afoot, could get bed and breakfast. And at one or other of them, thought McKellaig, she could spend a week well enough.

He had written a long letter, describing the several cottages and their occupants, to let her make her own choice, and was already sealing it when a tap on the window-pane surprised him. He drew the curtain, and against the farther darkness saw, dimly lighted, the face of Catriona close to the glass.

She stepped back, beckoning, and McKellaig in his stocking-feet went silently to the door and quietly opened it.

'Is your mother in bed?'

'She will be, by this time.'

'I've got news for you, but I don't want to disturb her.'

'She sleeps like a log, she'll hear nothing at all. Come in, Miss Catriona.'

Catriona went into the ben-room and saw on the table the photograph of the girl with downcast eyes, and beside it the letter newly written to her. She turned and said, 'The poachers are here again.'

'Oh, no! They could never be here already!'

'Why not?'

'It is too early. Too early for them, I mean. Men like that, Miss Catriona, don't go to work till the dead of night. And it is not yet eleven.'

'Well, they're here, whatever their usual habits are. Nicholas's boy Peter saw them on the old peat-road, and father's organizing a party to go out and capture them. Two parties, in fact.'

Catriona's mind was not much given to speculation, or suspicion, or even fancy; but even to her the consternation on McKellaig's face suggested guilt. But because she had no wish or liking for guilty explanation, she made no effort to solve the puzzle of his unease, but sharply said, 'You didn't expect my father to sit quietly at home and do nothing, did you? He wants you to join him, as soon as you can, on the peat-road.'

'I will put on my boots.'

Catriona, while he laced his boots, told him the General's plan, and repeated his particular instructions.

'I must go to the village for my bicycle,' said McKellaig. 'I left it with Alec Muir to get new brake-blocks fitted.'

'I'm ready, if you are. — Aren't you going to take your letter to the post?'

'I think I will not send it just yet.'

'You've got to make up your mind some time, and the sooner the better.'

'I will wait till tomorrow morning, I think.'

'Well, come on. We can't argue about it now.'

Half way to the village, Catriona said, 'Does your mother know that you sent a telegram to someone in Glasgow to say she was better?'

'No, no! There was no point in telling her.'

'According to her own story, she hasn't really been ill.'

'It was nothing serious, I told you so this morning.'

'Then why send a telegram?'

'Don't ask me that, Miss Catriona!'

The tone of his voice recalled the look on his face when she had told him of the General's plan to capture the poachers, and brus-

quely, with unusual irritation, she asked, 'What have you been doing, Norman, that makes you look so guilty and sound guilty too?'

For a minute or so he said nothing, and then, very miserably:
'You will be hearing soon enough. They will catch the poachers,
and then it will all come out.'

'You don't mean — you haven't been taking money from them?
Oh, you couldn't!'

With indignation, with a cold hostility, she listened to the shabby
story, and was repelled by the wretchedness of confession. She
listened to his excuses — she knew the truth of them, and a little
while ago had been warmly sympathetic — but now, when the
river and the lovely, running salmon were threatened with gross
destruction, and her father was hastening to their rescue, all her
sympathy was engaged in his cause and she had none for McKellaig.
She had a sense of duty, which she had exercised since childhood;
her sense of pity had been less employed. It shocked her to think
that McKellaig had forgotten his duty, and his betrayal of the river
was abominable beyond all her knowledge of abomination.

'There's no point in my saying anything,' she said harshly. 'It's
a matter for my father to deal with, and now, for your own sake,
you'd better hurry. He'll be waiting for you, and he doesn't like
to be kept waiting. — Is your bicycle here?'

They stood outside the house and workshop where Alec Muir,
one of the village's most useful inhabitants, mended bicycles and
sewing-machines, spectacle-frames and frying-pans and almost
everything else that could be broken and patched again. — But
McKellaig's bicycle had gone. 'There was a dozen of the lads,' said
Muir, 'running up and down the street, taking bicycles wherever
they could find them, without stay or hindrance from anyone. And
as soon as they were mounted they set off up the hill, the pedals
going like the hammers of hell. There's nothing left in the village
with wheels on it, Miss Catriona, but two or three old barrows and
Willy John's hearse in the shed overbye.'

'Then you must take the hearse,' said Catriona decisively. 'My
father,' she explained to Muir, 'is waiting for McKellaig near the
top of the hill, and there's no time to be lost. Is Willy John in?'

'He's away himself, driving Nicholas's car.'

'Oh, there you are!' said Mr. Pettigrew coming out of the darkness. 'I thought I'd been left all alone. Everybody seemed to disappear all of a sudden. I was very disappointed, I wanted to go too. I don't think your father's justified in trying to arrest these fellows, and if I was with him, I thought I might give him good counsel in time of need.'

'If you want to give him good counsel, or anything else,' said Catriona angrily, 'you'll have to go with McKellaig. He's taking the hearse.'

'Are you serious?' asked McKellaig.

'Of course I'm serious! My father gave me certain instructions for you, and I'm going to see that they're carried out.'

'Very well, Miss Catriona.'

'Well,' said Mr. Pettigrew, 'it's an unusual conveyance for anyone in my state of health, but I'm not superstitious, nor ever have been.'

Catriona did not answer. In the light from Muir's door she had seen the tears on McKellaig's face as he turned to obey her, and despite her hatred of his treachery she felt his misery. — She had two brothers, both of whom were in the Army, but neither of them knew as much of the history of their regiments as Catriona. Neither was so deeply attached to Laxdale as she, for it was she whose nature was most like her mother's. Catriona was more respectful of tradition than her father, and now, when her sense of duty had been so deeply outraged, she was reminded by incipient pity that men who fail in their duty may sometimes redeem it on the battlefield. A battlefield, indeed, was the traditional place for redemption, and within an hour or two the dark hillside between the river and the Larig Dubh might, in a small way, become a battlefield. Mr. Macaulay had offered his services in the expectation that a chaplain would be needed.

McKellaig backed the hearse out of Willy John's shed, turned and halted while Mr. Pettigrew climbed stiffly in beside him. Passionately serious, Catriona looked up at McKellaig, and said, 'This is your chance, Norman. I can't forgive you yet, but if you do well tonight, I'll see a different man tomorrow.'

'I will, God help me!'

'Then off you go. — And don't show any lights.'

'No fear of that, Miss Catriona. The lights don't work.'

At many doorways in the village street stood little groups of women and old men, talking quietly, who all fell silent to see the black hearse go by, and disappear into the darkness — and then, with livelier comment and new speculation, their voices made between the houses an excited sound as if a flock of starlings were wheeling and seeking a roosting-place.

'You'll be getting wet through, Miss Catriona, standing there in the rain,' said Muir. 'You'd better go away home and make yourself comfortable, for there's nothing more we can do to help them.'

Catriona had been so intent on her mission that she had hardly noticed the new shower of rain that was coming in from the sea and marching up the hill. But now with a shiver she felt the coldness of the drops, and said good night to Muir; and wondered, as she walked to Laxdale Hall, if she could still allow McKellaig to play his part in the *Bacchanals*.

McKellaig, driving as fast as he dared in the darkness, his eyes intent on a road that was hardly visible, paid little attention to Mr. Pettigrew's questions about the economic problems of a gamekeeper's life; and as the road grew rougher, and Mr. Pettigrew perceived that their journey was not without danger, he too was silent, and looked a little wistfully for chink or opening in the black curtains of the sky.

The darkness, indeed, was neither solid nor unbroken. Far to the north, like a barrier-reef with the surf breaking on it, a long thin cloud reflected the unseen moon, and in the south-west, over the sea, there was clear sky like a range of blue hills on the horizon, their heights obscured by a passing storm. But over the road lay blackest night, and as the hearse jolted and bumped, and lurched and swayed, McKellaig bent across the wheel, staring into the dark, and Mr. Pettigrew braced his legs and held as firmly as he could to the seat jumping beneath him.

They stopped, suddenly, and McKellaig said, 'We're at the peat-road now, I think. Wait you here till I make sure.'

He got down, and returned a little way, and came back on the other side of the hearse. 'It's the peat-road right enough. I saw the great puddle at the entrance to it as we passed. I can take the hearse no farther, Mr. Pettigrew.'

'Why not?'

'It is too dark on the peat-road, with the heather growing big on either side. We might get stuck, or break an axle — for it's a rough, rough road — and that wouldn't please Willy John.'

'Then how are we going to find the General?'

'We shall have to walk.'

'How far?'

'It will be two miles, maybe, or a bit more.'

'On a night like this, on a road too rough for driving? I'm not going to walk that distance!'

'Then you will just have to stay where you are, Mr. Pettigrew, for I must go.'

'And leave me here all alone? You can't do that!'

'You will be all right. I have put a big stone under the back wheel, so the hearse will not run away with you; and you will be seeing some of us before long.'

'Wait a minute, and I'll see if I can manage.'

'You will need to hurry.'

Mr. Pettigrew got down and stared dubiously into the dark. Even on the road his town-bred eyes could scarcely see a yard in front, and at the entrance to the old cart-track through the heather he would have fallen into the big puddle that marked its beginning if McKellaig had not saved him.

'I'm damned if I'll go another step!' he exclaimed.

'Indeed, I think you had better not try. Go back to the hearse and wait there comfortably — and we'll be seeing you before morning.'

'I refuse — McKellaig!'

But McKellaig had gone, and Mr. Pettigrew, breathing deeply with the agitation of anger and dismay, tapping the road before him with his stick, found his way back to the hearse; and in its solidity, amid the huge loneliness of night, recognized with relief a man-made thing. He discovered that he had been sitting on a long oilskin coat, which he wrapped about his shoulders, but instead of being grateful for such a useful addition, he thought only how wretchedly inadequate it would be against the cold. He saw the long hours before him as a sombre eternity of waiting, wet and sleepless; and his discomfort was much embittered by the obvious futility of spending a night in a hearse.

He felt for the switches on the dashboard. These Highlanders were utterly unreliable, and one never knew if they were speaking the truth or not. Perhaps the lights did work . . . He pressed several switches, but without effect. His searching hands, however, had found a large compartment in which there was a plumply filled paper bag. He pulled it out, and opened it . . .

Biscuits. Mixed biscuits. Well, he might be glad of them before morning . . .

He felt deeper into the compartment, and his hands came upon a cylindrical parcel. A bottle wrapped thickly in newspaper. A bottle . . .

He held it between his knees and searched in his pockets for matches. He struck a light and saw that his transient wild hope had not been mocked. It was whisky. It was, moreover, a bottle closed with a tin cap that needed no tool to open it . . .

He was unused to drinking his whisky neat, and he shuddered slightly as he swallowed once, twice, and again. But it was comforting to feel the warmth that immediately suffused him. He ate a biscuit, and took another mouthful. Much pleasanter. The biscuit served as a dry diluent, or perhaps the first swallow had slightly anaesthetized the tissues of his mouth against the shock. Another biscuit or two and a little more whisky medicined spirit as well as flesh. He found it possible, now, to take a wry pleasure in his situation, for against the probability he had snatched advantage from hostile circumstance. As he always did, by God. As he always would do. These damned Highland peasants weren't going to defeat him, and upset his plans. He'd teach them yet, make them see reason against their will, and when they drew their first week's wages they'd thank him for every penny. And admit they had been wrong . . . He found a ginger-biscuit, and washed it down with a little whisky. A curious flavour, very. But interesting. Rather attractive . . . He took another, merely to repeat the experiment. And thought even better of it. He would tell Lucy about it, perhaps, and at their next cocktail-party, instead of gin-and-nonsense and what the Americans called canapés, they might serve neat whisky and ginger-biscuits. It might catch on. But better try again, and see if it's as good as I thought . . .

With a growing apprehension of well-being, Mr. Pettigrew's mind became more and more indifferent to his present surroundings, more and more clearly perceptive of the rich and splendid future that awaited him when the industrial estate of Drumliedubbs should be fully established. He saw its factory-chimneys smoking, the pavements under the evening lamps crowded with the energetic figures of his prosperous employees, and a balance-sheet full of bold figures with a train of noughts behind them, as if they were opening their mouths in a delighted astonishment to see such profit. Satisfied clerks intent upon their ledgers, sturdy operatives eager at the lathe or keenly scrutinizing the full conveyor-belt, and in the foreground a balance-sheet as well composed and richly rewarding as a canvas by — well, any of those great classical artists whose work you saw at the National Gallery when you went there with a press-photographer to take your picture looking at a newly cleaned Velasquez.

There was nothing like a good balance-sheet. A proof of industry, a work of art, credit at the bank, and power in hand . . . There was nothing money bought that could compete with power. A little on the surface, but the great mass of it out of sight. A secret horde, a hidden dynamo, and men moving at your will, living by your grace — and living better, by God, than of their own poor wits they could ever hope to do. Samuel Pettigrew, Philanthropist, with a balance-sheet to prove the measure of his philanthropy and the profits that accrued . . .

He could see the figures on his imagined balance-sheet with a strange clarity. As if someone had turned on the light. A light as gentle but illuminating as the latest fluorescent tubes he was installing in the new factories . . .

He blinked, and shivered. It was still cold. But now, he saw, the raven's-wing clouds were flying apart, and between their drenched wings there shone a great island of blue sky, powdered with light, and in the midst of it a moon but one day's distance from perfection. The road before him gleamed like a strip of wet sand, dark with pools and bright with glittering shells. He could read the shape and direction of the road as clearly as a morning paper, and emerging from his vision of power, and the pulsing life of Drumliedubbs, he realized that he was still upon a naked mountainside, and saw his chance of getting down again. To Laxdale Hall and the comfort of his bed.

Where McKellaig had left the hearse there was no room to turn, but the General, that very morning, had turned in a roadside quarry a little beyond the crest of the hill. He could find the quarry easily enough in this good light, thought Mr. Pettigrew, and shuffled sideways into the driver's seat. As to the others, crawling in the heather he supposed — to hell with them. Poachers and the General's party too — to hell with them all.

The engine started, hesitantly at first, and Mr. Pettigrew approached the summit of the pass with care. He had drunk a lot of whisky, and drunk it too quickly. He admitted that, and felt proud of his ability to take an objective view. And with care, he told himself, he would be all right. Quite all right. There was no danger in drinking too much so long as a man realized he had drunk too much. And took care in proportion. All that was necessary, for perfect safety, was the strength of mind to acknowledge his condition, and put on the brake in time . . .

Mr. Pettigrew crossed the watershed and began to go downhill. He looked anxiously for the roadside quarry, but failed to find it. He stopped the hearse, and engaged his bottom gear before starting again. On the other side of the road, divided by the moon into shimmering descent and black declivity, he had caught a glimpse of the fearful depths below; and now, though he grew more cautious still, his confidence diminished. The road was more difficult to see. A shadow fell upon it, and the shadow deepened. Fold after fold of the returning dark obscured the road, and hid it from his view. In his imagination the precipice came nearer, he leaned away from it, and steered closer to the inner side of the road. His near front wheel slid into a shallow ditch, and braking hard he stopped the hearse and switched off the engine.

The raven-clouds had closed again, and there was no light in the sky. Mr. Pettigrew was now farther from home than before, and the comfort of his bed seemed immeasurably remote. Aloud, but with a tremor of something more than anger in his voice, he cursed his luck, and thought unhappily of the precipice. 'Why should I have to suffer like this?' he demanded. 'Why, why, why?'

He thrust his hand into the compartment in the dashboard and brought out the bottle of whisky that Willy John Watt had provided for his journey to Glasgow. He fumbled in the paper bag, and found a ginger-biscuit. Comfort came to his spirit less readily than before, but presently he grew sleepy.

CHAPTER TWENTY-FIVE

PATRICK JAMES ALOYSIUS GAMLIE, the son of a pious Irish mother and a stone-mason who had migrated from Angus to Glasgow, had lately described himself to the police as a dealer in scrap-metal. The police alleged, but without sufficient evidence, that most of the metal he bought and sold had been stolen from various shipyards; but this Gamlie indignantly denied, and with coarse and voluble protestation of his virtue declared he had been going straight for more than three years.

'It's a pity you don't keep better company,' said the sergeant, and reluctantly let him go.

Gamlie's occasional interrogation by the police, and his two prison-sentences, were not the result of inability to work, or of his fear of hard work; but of his discovery, early in life, that honest labour became tedious to a man who felt himself superior to his fellow men, whose appetites were larger and more exigent than theirs, and who nourished obscure ambitions. At eighteen, with the help of younger boys who acknowledged his authority, he was regularly stealing material from the shipyards and selling it to small fences on Clydebank. He spent his twenty-first birthday in prison, but a few years later, in the vast indifference to honesty that came with war, he was making a handsome income; and after the war, when the Government was selling, not always with sufficient scrutiny, its enormous accumulation of surplus stores and equipment, he became for a year or two a wealthy man. But because success had made him, not merely careless, but contemptuous of law and authority, he went to prison again; for a longer sentence this time.

His appetites and ambition survived misfortune, as did his

natural pleasure in excitement, and when, with ever-rising prices, the large-scale poaching of deer and salmon became a profitable business, he recruited a small company of tough, alert and dissolute young men — some of country birth and living discontentedly in Glasgow; some of them city-born, and skilfully reckless drivers — and for a couple of years took a handsome profit from the waters and forests of Dumbartonshire and the nearer parts of Argyllshire. But one evening in Glasgow a powerful young water-bailiff, whose river had lately suffered, met him by chance, recognized him, and taking advantage of the liberality of Saturday night, thrashed him soundly and warned him of worse to come if he ever lost another salmon.

Gamlie feared nothing but humiliation, and feared that deeply. He began to look for farther fishing-grounds, and in Inverness met Norman McKellaig. McKellaig had had three pints of beer, and being abstemious by habit, they had drowned most of his inhibitions. He heard the barman address Gamlie by name — Gamlie had been spending lavishly — and leaning confidentially towards him said, 'My mother's name was Gamlie too. Where would you be coming from?'

Gamlie paid for his next drink, and learnt with interest that he was a gamekeeper. With less interest he discovered that old Mrs. McKellaig had been born near Edzell, in Angus, where his own father had grown up, and that the young man beside him was his cousin; but to McKellaig this seemed a marvellous encounter, and before the night was done he had told Gamlie all his troubles, and the fearful expense he had been put to in looking for a wife.

'If it's money you're needing,' said Gamlie, 'I could maybe help you — if you'll do something to help me.'

Deeply shocked at first by Gamlie's proposal, McKellaig had yielded at last to many specious arguments, to the sentiment created in his mind by their relationship, and by the pressure of his need for more money to continue his search for a wife. He returned to Laxdale on the following day with a five-pound note as earnest of more to come, and *The Heart Mart* and the excitement of receiving new photographs stilled his fears and drugged his conscience.

But Gamlie did not trust him — Gamlie trusted no one — and now, when the rain had come at last and he got McKellaig's telegram that told him so, he decided, with no better reason than his distrust of all mankind, to arrive in Laxdale some two or three hours before the time they had appointed when they first made their arrangements. His decision had been sound, he thought, for they had reached the entrance to the peat-road when the sky was only moderately obscured, and without great trouble had driven some two miles down towards the river, to an open patch of hard ground, where they turned the car and the small lorry they used in readiness for their homeward journey. But because of their early arrival they had been seen by Peter McLeod; and that Gamlie did not know.

They unloaded their gear and went down to the river. There was some argument then as to whether they should fish the lower pools first, where, it was probable, most of the fish would be lying, and carry a growing catch upstream from pool to pool. But Gamlie insisted they must begin at the top and work downstream, dumping their catch to be taken up as they returned; for so early in the night there was danger of their being seen at the lower reaches. He had his way, and sent off two of the gang, one on each side of the river, to reconnoitre the banks for a mile or so, and when they returned and reported all clear, they went out again as guards or sentries, and Gamlie and the other three laid their net across the upper end of the Long Pool, the topmost pool in the river, and with a man on either side of the drag-rope, walked it slowly downstream. They felt, from time to time, the buffet and struggle of a captured fish, but the main fleet of the salmon had not yet come so high, and when, at the bottom of the pool, the far end of the net was brought across and the catch counted, there were eleven of them, with one great cock-fish of twenty-six or twenty-eight pounds.

They were quickly killed and put into a sack, and the sack was laid on the bank by an easily remembered mark. Gamlie whistled to his sentries, and they all went downhill to the next pool: a shorter one, broad in the middle, that was called The Birks after a rank of hardy, wind-leaning, silver birches on the northern bank. Cautious and workmanlike still, Gamlie sent his scouts out again to reconnoitre, while he and the others, in a hollow fringed by tall heather, lighted cigarettes in the rain and took their ease.

But their ease was broken when the nearer scout came running back, out of breath, to say he had heard, far down the river, someone shouting, and on the other bank seen, for a moment, the little glint of light of a match being struck. 'Christ Almighty!' said Gamlie. 'Is there trouble already? Back to the top pool, lads, and get that sack oot o' the way.'

Quickly, but not much perturbed, they retreated and found concealment for themselves and their gear in broken ground some two hundred yards from the river. Suspicious though his nature was, Gamlie had no fear that McKellaig had betrayed him; for McKellaig did not expect him before midnight. There might be local poachers at work, or — and this, he thought, was the likelier explanation — the General had been alarmed by their previous foray, and now when the river had risen he was taking care to watch it. But his watchers would not stay long on the job in dirty weather. They would certainly not spend the whole night by the river, and a little patience would defeat them. — So he told the sullen young men whom he commanded, and they, being well used to waiting at street-corners, or lingering unobtrusively till a foreman should turn his back, were unconcerned and settled without complaint in the damp hollow where they hid. But Gamlie went forward, half way to the river, to where he could see, though dimly, anyone who passed.

Had the sky not darkened he would have seen, some fifteen minutes later, Nicholas and two other men go by; but raven-clouds obscured the rainy glimmer of light on which he had depended, and he saw nothing of the patrol, but heard voices and a nailed boot striking on a rock. He waited for the river-watchers to return, and waited a long time. For three-quarters of an hour or so he was neither perturbed nor resentful. Like a Red Indian on the warpath or a leopard stalking its next meal he had an equanimity, in time of stress, that resembled, perhaps, the earliest matrix of philosophy. But after an hour he began to think, with irritation, of his street-corner gang. They, he knew, would be sleeping peacefully, relying on him to keep watch and wake them with their orders at the proper time. And he resented their easy comfort. But still he lay and watched. The sky was breaking, and it occurred to him that the river-patrol, having reached the loch, was waiting for better light to return.

Nicholas, impatient for action, had left The Cruive a little before his appointed time, and arrived at his rendezvous while the General and his party were still busy with their task of putting the poachers' cars out of action. They had found them on the peat-road without difficulty, but then an argument began as to the proper way of immobilizing them. The General said they must take off the distributor-heads, but as none of them was a mechanic, none of them knew where the distributor-head was to be found, and the General himself was not sure that he had the correct name for the piece. Some of them proposed the cutting of various cables, but others protested against wanton destruction; and finally it was decided to remove the sparking-plugs. Then the General posted twelve men in a position from which, though unseen so long as they lay still, they could closely watch the poachers' transport and quickly attack them when they should come to drive away. He was about to go down to the river when it occurred to him that his own car, and Nicholas's, should also be immobilized; they stood no more than fifty yards from the main road — Miss Phipps's road — where they had been left to avoid risk of alarming the poachers. So the General went to look for Willy John Watt, and told him what he must do, and walked a few hundred yards with him, repeating his instructions, until he was quite sure that Willy John understood his task. All this time the hillside was dark as a dungeon, and movement in consequence was slow.

The General left Willy John, and returned to the river. Before he reached it, he was overtaken by McKellaig, breathless and sweating with his speed, who told him that he had spoken to Willy John half a mile back. They approached the river, between the head of the Long Pool and the loch, and while the General was saying that it was useless to go downstream till the light improved — for they could see nothing beyond the reach of an arm — they encountered Nicholas and his two companions. Not a smell, nor a sound, nor a sight of strangers had they had, said Nicholas, and his neighbouring patrol on the other side of the river had made no signal of discovery either.

'We'll wait for a little while,' said the General. 'We've found their cars, and made them safe — and the sky's breaking.'

Presently the black wings of the clouds parted, and in the gulf between, a bluebell floor powdered with light, an almost perfect moon shone candidly. 'Now,' said the General, 'we can walk in comfort. We have no reason to conceal ourselves, because what we want to do is to keep them off the river and drive them back to their cars — where they'll be collared. McKellaig and I will come half way with you, Nicholas, and return. If nothing happens, we'll repeat the patrol.'

Gamlie, from his outpost, saw five men go past him on the river-bank, and was perplexed. He could not be sure, but he did not think so many as five had previously, in the darkness, gone up-stream. He could not recognize McKellaig, who was walking be-tween two others, but suspicion of betrayal moved strongly in him now, for it was long past midnight. And if McKellaig had turned traitor, and the river-patrols were coming from the top as well as the foot of the river, it meant that their cars had been discovered, and their retreat cut off. Their retreat, that is, would have to be fought for.

But not, thought Gamlie, in bright moonlight. He looked at the sky, and decided that the clouds would close again. He felt excite-ment in the stream of his blood, and forgot the profit on the salmon he might not carry off, in the ebullience of his resolution to escape the trap. They would fight their way out, and win a difficult vic-tory to offset the loss of five or six hundred pounds . . . But not yet. Not till the sky filled with clouds, and their approach to the cars could be made unseen. He waited patiently, and when the first veils of mist were clouding the bright sky saw the General, with one companion only, coming upstream again. And now he recognized McKellaig, and with a bitter stalk of heather between his teeth muttered obscene threats and dug his fingers into the spongy ground in the intensity of his anger.

The sky thickened, and he went back to the hollow where his lean gangsters slept. He woke them, and briefly described their plight. They heard it without fear or despair, and fingered the weapons they carried. The youngest of them had a length of bicycle-chain with a rubber-grip at one end, an iron bolt at the other.

They moved from their shelter, presently, and approached the level space on the peat-road, where they had turned their cars on a patch of gravel that gave firmness to the ground. They crawled to within seven or eight yards' distance, and lay, and watched. There was no one sitting in the cars, no sign that they had been discovered. Gamlie was in half a mind to discount his fear of treachery, and wait till the river-watchers should go home — in half a mind to believe that their cars had not been discovered — when from beyond them he heard a smothered cough. 'Come awa',' he said, 'and dinna leave the fish. If it's a fecht they're wanting, let the buggars have it.'

They rose, and ran to the car and the lorry behind it; and leapt in. The drivers switched on the engines, pressed the starters. Nothing happened. And from the hillside rose a dozen shadowy figures, who surrounded the vehicles and somewhat doubtfully called upon their occupants to surrender.

Neither side was immediately inclined to come to grips. The dissolute young men from Glasgow drew their illicit weapons, looked at the darkness, and wondered what haven they could find; while the Laxdale men, though intent on capturing and disarming the invaders, were naturally diffident about taking the lead against them, and making a display of valour. — The little period of hesitation, however, was concluded by the arrival of General Matheson and McKellaig.

'Come on!' cried the General. 'Get 'em while they're cold!' — And running to the lorry, assailed its driver, who had jumped down, with his stick. The driver was the young man who carried a length of bicycle-chain, but the General had a long Highland walking-stick, that he used like a foil to keep him at a distance and like a sabre to beat him about the head and ears. McKellaig, nervously resolute, his jaw slack but his mind in a mask of fortitude, ran to the saloon car, saw Gamlie get out, and with a desperate courage charged him. But Gamlie, in the purity of his rage, snarled like a tiger and with something of a tiger's swiftness stepped aside, and struck twice with a cosh: on the crown of his head, and, as McKellaig fell, at the base of his skull. Poised in fury, Gamlie looked swiftly round, and saw that his gang was outnumbered. He dealt a numbing blow to the forearm of a half-hearted attacker, and took to the cover of darkness.

A young man from Shore Street, in the village, being lightly cut on the back of his hand by a razor, went berserk and punched his opponent into insensibility. The General's adversary, with the bicycle-chain, dropped to his knees and cried for mercy; and two others were borne down in a confusion of fists, and straining arms, and hacking feet. But the driver of Gamlie's car, dodging light-footed, escaped, and like a shadow in the gloom was lost in the moor's immensity.

'Well,' said the General, breathing more quickly than usual, 'what's the score?'

'Four prisoners,' said someone, 'and McKellaig has been knocked out.'

'Two got away, didn't they?'

'Just the two.'

'Poor McKellaig. — We must get him back to the village, but the rest of us, I think, ought to stay here till it's light, and then we'll beat the moor and pick up the other two.'

Four men made cradles of their arms and carried McKellaig to Nicholas's car, that stood fifty yards from the road; they replaced a couple of plugs, reversed, and slowly drove back to Laxdale Hall. Catriona was waiting in the library with bandages, sticking plaster, iodine, scissors, antiseptic gauze, whisky, glasses and a jug of water on the table. They put McKellaig to bed, and one of them went for Nurse Connachy. The others, with becoming modesty, accepted a little whisky, and with increasing amplitude described for Catriona the night's adventure.

On the hill the General told his diminished company to take what comfort they could in the poachers' vehicles, and wait for the dawn. He chose two of them to escort the prisoners, whom he proposed to march downstream and deliver into Nicholas's keeping. They could spend the night in the old mill, and Nicholas would have to find a guard for them.

'And I'll be back at first light, or a little before it,' he said, 'and then we'll look for the missing brace.'

'By God, and we'll find them too!'

'We'll make a clean sweep of it when morning comes.'

Exhilarated by victory and boasting a little, they stood in the glowing warmth of achievement, indifferent to the dark and the prowling wind; and the General led his bruised and woebegone troop of prisoners by the loudly running river to a night's confinement in the mill.

CHAPTER TWENTY-SIX

THE nearest police station to Laxdale was in the small town of Scatwall, some sixty miles away, that lay in fertile, pleasant country at the head of a long sea-loch. Here, about the same time as the *ceilidh* was interrupted by Peter McLeod's dramatic news of the poachers on the hill, the Inspector in charge was giving serious instruction to a Sergeant and a Constable. The motorists of Laxdale, he said, were still defying the law of the land. They had not only refused to pay their road-fund licences, but they had treated contumaciously the several attempts to serve summonses on them.

'Contumaciously!' he repeated. 'And that is a word that implies a total disrespect for law and order!'

They had replied, on one occasion, with a gross impertinence that could only be construed as contempt of court. The summonses had been mischievously redirected to another place called Laxdale — or something like it — in Iceland; and on a third attempt to serve them, it was said that they had been blown from the hands of the postman by a miraculous gale of wind and lost for ever in the vacancy of the moor.

But now, said the Inspector, he was going to take due precautions against the mischance of fortune and the notorious perversity of the Laxdale folk. There were new summonses, here on his desk, and they had to be delivered, each into the hands of an offending motorist, and no plea of mistaken address or a gust of wind would be accepted for a failure to do so. He wanted them to be delivered at daybreak, when the Sergeant and the Constable would find the offenders — man or woman — still in bed, and there could be no chance to escape or deny receipt of the summons.

The Sergeant and the Constable listened respectfully, and agreed with all he said. But when they went out they stood for some little time, without speaking, until the Sergeant gently expressed his opinion that the Inspector had been exaggerating the difficulty of their task, and the Constable — who himself came from Laxdale — as mildly agreed with him. Their conclusion was that they need not start so early as the Inspector desired, for no one in Laxdale ever rose until the sun was well above the horizon, and the fields had been aired and the mist driven from the sea. It was, then, a little after daybreak when their car rounded the first of the three hairpin bends on the precipitous road to Laxdale — the wetly gleaming mountain on the one side and the quietness of the sea-loch, like a misted sapphire far below them, on the other — and not until they were approaching the last of the constrained corners did they see, about half a mile in front, the hearse at the roadside with its bonnet nuzzling the hill.

'Now what is the meaning of that?' asked the Sergeant.

'It belongs to Willy John Watt,' said the Constable. 'But so far as I know he has never looked for custom on this side of the hill.'

'There is no one in it,' said the Sergeant.

'Indeed, there is no one visible.'

The Constable, who was driving, stopped beside the hearse, and to their great astonishment they discovered, on the floor below the driving-seat, a total stranger fast asleep. With the long leather cushion of the driving-seat, and Willy John's oilskin, Mr. Pettigrew had made himself as comfortable as possible in a confined space, and lay gently snoring with an expression on his face of bloated peace.

'He has been drinking,' said the Sergeant, stooping and sniffing the scented air.

'He has had a proper night of it,' said the Constable, picking up a bottle in which remained only a trickle of whisky.

'And who can he be? I have never seen the man before.'

'And what is he doing in Willy John's hearse?'

Softly snoring, his lips puffing out and retreating with a quiver, Mr. Pettigrew lay sound asleep, and the two policemen contemplated the mystery with minds that revolved in useless speculation, like engines without a gear-box.

'We must wake him up and ask him who he is,' said the Sergeant.

'Wait, wait,' said the Constable. 'There may be evidence against him.'

Hurriedly, but on tip-toe, he went to the back of the hearse, and unlatched the double doors. 'Come here!' he exclaimed. 'Come here, and look at this!'

The Sergeant went tip-toe too. He looked in, and saw the stag. 'God Almighty!' he exclaimed. 'He will be one of the poachers from Glasgow, that the General was complaining about. He will be the leader of the gang. That is why he is so well dressed.'

'He will be drinking a bottle of whisky every night of his life!' said the Constable.

'We have made an important capture,' said the Sergeant, and now with a firm step returned to Mr. Pettigrew, and taking him by the shoulders, shook him sternly. 'Wake up!' he demanded.

With a bubbling, grumbling noise — with incomprehensible remarks and little convulsive movements — Mr. Pettigrew regained a partial consciousness, and raising reluctant eyelids from bloodshot eyes, recognized the dark blue uniforms of policemen.

'A rescue,' he muttered. 'Splendid, splendid police force we have. Take me home, officer. I leave it all to you.'

'I want to know who you are!' said the Sergeant, shaking him again.

Mr. Pettigrew sat up, and grasped the Sergeant's hand. 'You'll be handsomely, handsomely rewarded for this,' he said. 'Take me home and you'll be handsomely rewarded. Help me up.'

With his arm round the Sergeant's neck, Mr. Pettigrew stood on the road, drooping and sagging, and sadly shaking his head. 'Splendid, splendid policemen,' he repeated. 'Take me home.'

'Should we not confront him with the evidence?' asked the Constable.

'We should,' said the Sergeant, and supporting Mr. Pettigrew to the rear end of the hearse, pointed to the stag and said, 'Can you give an explanation of that?'

214

Mr. Pettigrew peered into the cavity of the hearse, and laid a faltering hand on the stiff and hairy leg of the stag. 'It's dead,' he declared.

'Of course it is dead,' said the Sergeant irritably, 'but who put a dead stag in a hearse, and why?'

Mr. Pettigrew braced his muscles and stood erect. With a solemn movement he took off his hat and said, 'They must be going to bury it. Pious people in Laxdale, very pious. And mad as hatters, the whole bloody lot of them.'

He replaced his hat, and with unexpected assurance walked to the police-car. 'Is this your car?' he asked in the loud voice of one accustomed to obedience. 'Then please take me home as quickly as you can. I'm staying with General Matheson at Laxdale Hall.'

He got in, and stretching his legs lay back and went to sleep again.

'Now who can he be?' asked the Sergeant.

'If he is a gangster,' said the Constable, 'it means that the whole of Laxdale is in his pay.'

'I wouldn't put it past them,' said the Sergeant, 'but I am inclined to think that he is just a visitor who has been on a big spree. We had better take him to Laxdale, and when he is feeling better we will charge him with being drunk in charge of a hearse.'

'And stealing deer on the hill.'

'Yes, yes, there will be complications in the charge, and we shall need the evidence. You had better take the hearse down to the first corner, where you can turn it, and I will drive the car. We must go to Laxdale in any case, to deliver the summonses.'

CHAPTER TWENTY-SEVEN

THE receding night left a grey pallor on the hillside — a pallor that seemed, as yet, to owe nothing to the rising sun — but the General, walking with purposeful, long steps up the narrow path by the river, was unperturbed by the cold and cheerless vacancy of the scene. Marvell and Flett accompanied him, who had spent the night in Nicholas's command at the lower end of the river, and to them he was talking over his shoulder about his plans for the man-hunt and their prospect of success.

'Their car and the lorry,' he said, 'and my own car are still on the peat-road; but all three have been immobilized, and I told the cyclists to let the air out of their tyres and take their pumps away. If everybody has done what he should, our missing brace won't get away on wheels. But just in case someone has been careless, Nicholas has gone back to the village for his car, and Swanson is borrowing the Nurse's Austin, and they'll reconnoitre the road: I told them to go well over the top. And we, in the meantime, will beat downhill from the peat-road . . .'

Both Flett and Marvell were a little tired after their night in the heather, but the General's enthusiasm was unimpaired, his legs unwearied. He posted his beaters from the river to the road, where a reinforcement on bicycles had arrived, and in a long straggling line, under a mottled sky now gleaming with light like a net full of herring they began to search the moor. There were long intervals between the beaters, and the ground was cross-grained and broken. It was difficult to keep touch, impossible to maintain the line in military dressing. But the beaters had keen eyes and the countryman's quick sight for movement or an unfamiliar object in the landscape.

They had not gone far when a wild shout from somewhere near the river gave warning that one of the poachers had been flushed, and those nearest him broke into a run. Voice after voice was lifted in a hunting-cry, and the fugitive, looking back, saw five or six men pursuing him with ungainly speed. He hesitated; then turning away from the river, took advantage of a ridge that gave him cover to run head-down towards the road.

And now, from the beater nearest to the road, there came another shout: not fierce, to proclaim a new hunt, but high-pitched and shrill with dismay. Another, that sounded almost frantic with excitement, doubled the alarm; and the General, who was next in line, bellowed, 'Stop him, stop him! Oh, damnation, stop him!' — But there was no one near enough to obey, and he had to watch his own car being driven stern-first on to the road, where its bonnet was turned up-hill; and with sudden acceleration it disappeared from sight.

Gamlie had been as lucky as he was bold. After knocking McKellaig out he had waited in the darkness, not more than twenty yards away, and presently followed the bearer-party who carried McKellaig to Nicholas's car. As soon as they had gone he tried to start the Colonel's car, but discovered that two of the sparking-plugs had been removed. He walked to the road, and found a couple of bicycles; but both had flat tyres. His only chance of escaping, he decided, was to lie hidden till the morning, somewhere near the road, and by daylight look for a bicycle he could ride or a car that would start.

He returned to the Colonel's car to see if there was a rug in it, and set his foot on a small, solid, movable object. Willy John Watt, after taking out a pair of sparking-plugs, had left them, for convenience and to prevent loss, on the right-hand running-board. Fiercely excited, Gamlie refitted them, and was about to start the car when he heard voices nearby, between him and the road. He got out and lay flat in the heather, a couple of yards from the track. The new arrivals, three of them, were late-comers to the General's force, and disappointed to find no one at the end of the peat-road, to tell them where to go, they decided to wait in tolerable comfort in the General's car. Cold and savagely disappointed, Gamlie found a hiding-place in a thicket of wiry long heather, and waited for the morning.

His chance came, and he took it at once, when the General marshalled his beaters and sent the long line downhill. He knew that he had been seen, as he backed on to the road, but there was nobody to stop him. There was nothing to hinder him till he came to the winding, level stretch at the top of the hill, where he met the Sergeant from Scatwall coming up from the other side. The Sergeant recognized at once the General's old-fashioned Daimler, and halting abruptly in the middle of the road, got out and signalled to it to stop. He had a summons to deliver, and already he was unbuttoning his left-hand breast-pocket to find it.

Gamlie slowed to eight or ten miles an hour, for there was barely room to pass; but he did not stop. The Sergeant jumped back to avoid being crushed between his own car and the Daimler, and then, seeing a stranger at the wheel, leapt to the running-board and bent an inquiring face to the driver's window. Gamlie struck him on the chin with the heel of his hand, and as he accelerated the Sergeant fell backward on to the road.

A minute or two later, Nicholas drove up in his own clattering, square-cornered, ancient limousine, with Swanson in the Nurse's Austin close behind. The General and two of his beaters had waved to them from the heather, pointed uphill, and wildly signalled them to hurry. They had ridden roughly, lurching from side to side, springs banging; but slowing now to pass the stationary police-car, Nicholas saw beyond it the still body of the Sergeant, supine on the road. Horrified, he stopped behind the police-car, and got out. Swanson pulled up beside him, and while Nicholas lifted the Sergeant's head — his cap had fallen off — and felt for injuries, Swanson unbuttoned his tunic and found that his heart was still beating.

'He is only stunned,' said Nicholas with relief in his voice, 'and thank God for that! I thought it was a dead man on the road when I saw him, but it's just a knock on the back of the head. He fell on a stone.'

218

'It would be difficult not to, on a road like this.'

'That's so, indeed — but you'll need to be getting on, Mr. Swanson. Whoever did this to the poor man, and a desperate character he must be, is half way down the hill by now. But drive like the devil, and maybe you'll catch him yet — and I'll look after the Sergeant, for I know him well.'

'Well,' said Swanson, not liking much the prospect of pursuing a desperate man all by himself, 'well, yes. Yes, I suppose I'd better. All right, and — well, I'll see what I can do.'

He drove off in the Nurse's Austin, but at no great speed; and as soon as he had gone Nicholas took from the Sergeant's unbuttoned breast-pocket the buff-coloured summonses that he had been quick to see. 'It's not that I wish to be disrespectful to you, Sergeant,' he said, 'but I think these papers will do less harm in my possession than they would in yours.'

The Sergeant groaned, and from his own pocket Nicholas took a small flask, and unscrewed the top. He raised the Sergeant's head, and poured whisky into his slack-jawed mouth. To repair the shock to his own nerves he drank a little too, and was surprised to hear a familiar voice and to see behind him, when he looked round, the bloated face and curiously dishevelled figure of Mr. Pettigrew.

'What have you been doing to the policeman?' asked Mr. Pettigrew, with uncertain articulation; and swayed on his feet.

'Indeed, and it wasn't me that did it. But where have you come from, Mr. Pettigrew?'

'I was in that car, and when I woke up, the driver had gone. I think that's the driver.'

'And what are you doing on the top of the hill at this time of the morning?'

'I am not feeling very well. Is there anything in your flask?'

'Little enough,' said Nicholas, and took another mouthful before passing it to Mr. Pettigrew.

Mr. Pettigrew drank, and belched. 'Good luck,' he said.

'I'd better give the Sergeant a drop now.'

The Sergeant groaned again, and though he did not open his eyes, he was able to swallow. 'Is my head split?' he asked.

'There is no damage at all,' said Nicholas cheerfully. 'Your head struck a stone, and you were stunned a little; it is no worse than that. Can you sit up yet?'

The Sergeant opened his eyes, and Nicholas helped him up.

Mr. Pettigrew regarded him with ill-focused and unfriendly vision. 'I want to go home,' he said. 'You were going to take me home. And now you're sitting in the middle of the road, on the top of a mountain, drinking whisky. And what's the good of that? I'm cold, I tell you, and I want to go to bed!'

'I'll have a word with you presently,' said the Sergeant. 'Can you tell me who it was, Nicholas, that was driving the General's Daimler, and hit me on the chin when I tried to stop him?'

'He could be one of the poachers — but here's the General himself!'

Red-faced and breathless, pedalling hard and leaning across the handlebars of a bicycle with half-inflated tyres, the General appeared at the head of a small troop of heated cyclists.

'What happened to you, Sergeant?' he demanded. 'Did you see my car?'

'I tried to stop it, General, and got a blow on the chin for my trouble. But I would recognize the man who did it.'

'Mr. Swanson is after him,' said Nicholas.

'In the Nurse's Austin? He'll never catch him.'

'I don't understand what has been happening,' said Mr. Pettigrew, still tetchy, still confused by an irrational world in which even the hill-tops, to his disordered gaze, appeared to advance and retreat in nauseating undulation. 'I don't understand, and I don't want anybody to explain. I want to go to bed!'

'How did you get here? And why did you?'

'Well may you ask,' said Mr. Pettigrew sadly.

'Here is the answer to your question!' exclaimed the Sergeant, still sitting on the road, and pointing now to the east. 'He was in charge of the hearse, and drunk at that, when we found him.'

Surprised by the sudden appearance of Willy John's hearse on the hill-top, driven by a Constable from Scatwall, the General failed to observe Nicholas's greater surprise and evident perturbation.

Slowly the hearse approached, the Constable driving with grim propriety, and behind it came the Nurse's Austin with Swanson at the wheel.

'What's the news?' shouted the General. 'Did he get away?'

'I've got a passenger,' said Swanson, stopping and opening the door. 'Come and look at him.'

Huddled in the back seat of the little car, handcuffed and pale of cheek, but bloody about the nose and mouth, sat a defeated Gamlie; and beside him was the heavy, wet sack, full of clean-run salmon, that he had never abandoned.

'How did you get him?' asked the General, his voice soft and gratified. 'Tell me the whole story.'

'It's the Constable you've got to thank, for driving on the wrong side of the road . . .'

A little way beyond the crest of the hill, Gamlie in the General's car had met the hearse coming round a blind corner on the right of the road. On the other side the hill fell steeply to a narrow glen still full of morning mist. The hearse pulled out, and Gamlie tried to squeeze between it and the wall of the hill, but rammed a granite buttress. When Swanson arrived he found the General's car a crumpled wreck, and the Constable, in tears, trying to pull an unconscious man from behind a broken steering-wheel. Stricken to the heart by remorse, the Constable had confessed his fault; and Swanson had medicined him with praise. He had saved the day, retrieved a vital blunder, with brilliant decision cut off the fugitive's escape — and all for the cost of a ruined car.

'An old car,' said the General. 'Pity it wasn't licensed, I'd have got the insurance then. However, that can't be helped, and the main thing is that we've collared the whole gang now.'

Together, leaning into the car, they contemplated their prisoner, and Swanson said, 'He isn't badly hurt. He was winded, that's all. But I thought, for safety, he ought to be handcuffed.'

Gamlie said nothing, and the General made a thoughtful comment: 'It was lucky for us that the police arrived when they did. I wonder what brought them here?'

There were by now nearly a score of men on the road — a few

221

more were still riding uphill — and Mr. Pettigrew had deflected their interest from the last prisoner to himself. Remembering, without precision, something that had puzzled him earlier in the morning, he had walked unsteadily to the hearse, and opened the back doors.

It *was* a stag. His memory had not betrayed him, but he got little comfort from the sight. He still could find no explanation of what he saw. He touched again a cold stiff leg, the bristling hair on the slender pastern, and thought of death. In primitive times, and still in primitive places, death was attended with strange ceremonies, and to his befuddled mind came some recollection of the last few days, and a suspicion that here in Laxdale forgotten rites might linger still. He wondered if the stag had died a natural death, and laying hold of its thin, fleet legs, pulled it towards him. He pulled too hard, the stag slid out, and fell on to the road.

A score of fascinated spectators watched him as he stooped to examine it. He saw the slit in its belly where Nicholas had gralloched it, and looking up, said sadly, 'It had an operation.' Self-pity grew to see that other creatures had their sorrows too; and he began to cry.

'What's going on here?' demanded the General, pushing his way through the spectators. 'Good God, where did that stag come from?'

Still unbuttoned and dishevelled, but suffering now only from a headache, the Sergeant had been watching Mr. Pettigrew as though spellbound. 'It was him that brought it over the hill,' he told the General. 'When we first met him, early this morning, he was drunk, and in charge of the hearse; and when we examined the hearse, we discovered the stag. He would give us no explanation, however, and it was only a minute ago that I learnt who the gentleman is.'

'By God!' said Nicholas, with pious indignation in his voice ' we have learnt something this night! A gang of poachers on the river, and a gentleman who is a Member of Parliament stealing the General's stags on the hill. It shows you what the world is coming to.'

'Oh, be quiet, Nicholas,' said the General. 'What's been happening, Pettigrew? What have you been doing?'

'I was abandoned. I was deserted in the middle of the night.' Mr. Pettigrew wiped his eyes, and with a clearer vision regarded the General and the two policemen, the stag, the group of entranced and silent spectators. The chill shadow of returning sobriety touched him, and with a sudden apprehension in his mind, and sombre defiance in his voice, he said, 'About what happened next, I propose to say nothing at all until I have had an opportunity to consult my lawyers.'

'In that case,' said the General, 'I think we should all go back to Laxdale. You'll have to come with us, Sergeant, because we have five or six prisoners — a gang of poachers that we caught — and I want you to take charge of them.'

'I was on my way to Laxdale when I met with my accident,' said the Sergeant. 'I have a communication for you, General. A summons, in fact.'

'We can talk about that when we've had some breakfast. I'm too hungry to think about summonses, and I'm sure everybody's feeling the same,' said the General. 'Come along, and let's go home.'

Briskly and decisively he arranged the convoy — drivers and passengers for the cars — and the stag was replaced in the hearse. But still the Sergeant searched his pockets for the missing summonses while Nicholas watched him with interest and apparent sympathy.

'You were the first to come to my rescue,' said the Sergeant at last. 'Did you take anything out of my pocket, Nicholas?'

'Not a thing,' said Nicholas, 'for there was nothing left to take. You had come down on the flat of your back with such a bang and a thump that all your buttons were loosed, and your pockets burst open as if you'd been in an earthquake. It's a strong man you are, Sergeant, or the shock would have killed you. You ought to be thankful that you're alive, instead of fretting yourself about bits of paper.'

'You are the biggest liar north of the Highland Line, Nicholas!'

'That is a serious thing to say of anyone, Sergeant.'

'What have you done with the summonses?'

'You might as well ask a naked, new-born babe —'

'Come along!' shouted the General. 'You can't stand there arguing all morning. I'm hungry.'

I T was a considerable procession that returned to Laxdale. The General led in Nicholas's car, and following him came the Nurse's Austin, the laden hearse, the poachers' two vehicles, and the police car. They were accompanied by numerous cyclists, and received in the village an ecstatic welcome. Children ran alongside, hallooed, and pointing to the prisoners, shrilly laughed. Half-grown girls and maidens with their skirts awry, their hair un-brushed — new-roused from bed — waved sunburnt arms and cried their fierce congratulation. Old men blue-jerseyed, leaning on their sticks, nodded sagely in recollection of their larger battles over-sea, saluted, and approved the action in deep voices that carried echoes of Omdurman, the Modder River and Gallipoli. Stout women at their doorways exclaimed in loud relief and blessed their weary sons, and older women at narrow windows wiped their eyes, and felt the surging of their aged hearts, and cackled indis-criminately their praise and joy. The sun shone bright on white-washed walls, dogs barked, and the unshaven victors of the night looked proudly down and savoured triumph in the eyes they met, and waving arms, and old men's wrinkled fists.

The village would have begun to celebrate its victory at once had it not been for the General's insistence that breakfast should come first; and the prisoners must have their breakfast too. There was a derelict boat-building yard to the south of Shore Street where the prisoners could be housed — the four who had been fetched from the mill, and the two taken in the morning hunt — and the General saw that they had soap and water to wash themselves, porridge and tea for their sustenance, before he went to his own house and its comfort.

No one thought of work or business that day, but from the village there spread outwards through the parish a zeal for communication, and old unkindlinesses were forgotten, ancient feuds ignored, in the general desire to spread the news of Laxdale's triumph over brutal invasion. Much was exaggerated, and in the telling of it the battle changed its shape like clouds on a windy day. Mr. Pettigrew was sometimes represented as a villain, sometimes as a clown, and once or twice as the victim of tragic misunderstanding. Mr. Macaulay, it was said, had preached so eloquently to the prisoners in the mill that all of them had saved their souls in exchange for lost freedom. And what of Nicholas? asked others. There was no one but Nicholas who would shoot a stag under the General's eye, and only Nicholas would pick a policeman's pocket. But Nicholas, said some, has gone too far this time. — Was it not Pettigrew, asked others, who shot the stag, and stole the hearse? And the poachers were in his pay too. His was the mastermind . . .

It was about half-past ten when Andrew Flett came down from the Hall to look for Nicholas, and saw the village street like a stream broken by eddies, and in every eddy a little shoal of minnows fastened by the lips to the appetizing topics of the day. He found Nicholas in the middle of the biggest shoal, displaying the summonses he had taken from the Sergeant's pocket; and Nicholas came to ask what he wanted.

'I took some good photographs this morning — at least, I think they'll be good — and I was wondering if I could get them developed.'

'What photographs are they?'

'Of Pettigrew, mostly. Pettigrew and the stag. And the hearse, of course.'

'They should be interesting pictures, Mr. Flett. And maybe useful too.'

'Can I get them developed?'

'Yes, indeed. Alec Muir will do them. I'll take you to him myself, and he'll do them right away when he hears what they are.'

'I thought he repaired bicycles.'

'So he does, and many another thing too. He's a good photo-grapher in his spare time. He does all the weddings here . . .'

At the Hall Mr. Pettigrew had gone to bed, and Mrs. Pettigrew refused to let anyone disturb him. Her voice grew hard and de-fensive. A constrained but stubborn loyalty engraved upon her face incipient lines that no one had remarked before. — He was suffering from exposure, she said, and in no condition to answer questions. Defiantly she told the Sergeant who her husband's solicitors were, and he was perhaps unduly influenced by a London address.

The Sergeant had had a good breakfast, and the General had used him with all courtesy except in one particular, about which he had been as obdurate as Mrs. Pettigrew. He had written a full description of the night's affray, and submitting with patience to the Sergeant's interrogation, had answered his questions about the poachers with candour and a soldierly brevity. But when the Sergeant complained of his pocket having been picked, and accused Nicholas of the theft, the General's mild and handsome features seemed to acquire the marmoreally irresponsive surface of a Roman bust; and his refusal to promote or assist an investigation was frigid.

'I have only your word against Nicholas McLeod's,' he said. 'Neither his statement nor yours can be substantiated by witnesses, and it is not my business to decide who is telling the truth.'

'Because it is in your interest to conceal the truth!' said the Sergeant hotly. 'You are on Nicholas's side because you are both breaking the law!'

'Your duty is simple, Sergeant. It is to enforce the law. My duty, as a private citizen, is less simple. For in this country it is still, on occasion, the duty of a private citizen to call in question the administration of the law, or even to challenge the law's authority. But you and I needn't fall out over that. It's a matter that will be decided, eventually, by the proper courts — and I may tell you now that I don't intend to accept a Sheriff's judgment unless it concurs with my own!'

'And that isn't likely,' said the Sergeant.

'Perhaps not. And now, before you take your prisoners to Scatwall, I suggest a glass of beer as a mid-morning tonic.'

It had been decided to remove the six poachers in their own lorry. It would be a rough ride for them over the hill, but the Sergeant, whose chin was still sore from the heel of Gamlie's hand, and his head from a stone in the road, was not unduly sympathetic. He, in the police-car, would lead the convoy; the lorry, driven by a volunteer from the village, would follow; and the Constable, in Gamlie's car, would serve as rearguard.

The prisoners were embarked at the derelict boat-building yard, and the three cars drove eastward through a silent village. On either side of the street there were spectators of their passage, many of whom, in the early morning, had loudly hailed the victors of the night, and jeered at their dishevelled captives. But now, seeing the poachers as men defeated and already condemned, they stood in a grave silence, and without abating judgment, were compassionate . . .

Catriona had sat beside her father while he answered the Sergeant's questions. More intensely than he, she was gratified by his success, but with a divided mind she waited anxiously to learn if he had discovered McKellaig's complicity in the raid. She had said nothing of McKellaig's guilt, and she was tormenting herself with the thought that, by concealment of it, she was deceiving her father. But she and Nurse Connachy had put McKellaig to bed, and the pallor of unconsciousness, that turned his weather-beaten cheeks to the stained and yellowish look of old parchment, had moved and hurt her; he had obeyed her, and done what he could to retrieve his fault. He had not done much, in fact, but he had suffered in the attempt. And Catriona, when she perceived that her father had no suspicion of his treachery, felt more and more inclined to share McKellaig's baseness, and keep it hidden.

Nurse Connachy had the gift of self-confidence, and only a moderate opinion of doctors. McKellaig was in no danger, she said, but he had better go to Glasgow by the steamer tomorrow.

It was just concussion, she said, but nowadays, when people went to the doctor for no reason at all — because they were constipated, or worried about their children — even concussion was taken seriously. Though to a young man, living as young men should, she protested, it was no worse, nor less to be expected, than a common cold.

Catriona thought she might wait until McKellaig had returned from Glasgow before she made a final decision. In the meantime she would have to look for someone who could take, at short notice, the part of King Pentheus in the play. And it crossed her mind, when her mind was thus harassed, that her concealment of McKellaig's guilt might be nullified by Gamlie's revelation that he had had an accomplice . . .

At a quarter-past one Mrs. Pettigrew carried a tray to her husband's room, and persuaded him to sit up and take some clear soup and a piece of dry toast.

'My God, Sam,' she said, 'what a fool you are! Won't you ever learn to take care of yourself, and keep out of trouble? You're not so invulnerable as you think. Oh, I know you've been in trouble before, and wriggled out of it, or bought your way out, but you won't always be lucky. It isn't going to be easy to clean up the mess you got into last night.'

'My lawyers can deal with it,' he said. 'Or if they can't, I'll sack 'em and get a new lot.'

'Here in the country it may be different from what you're used to.'

'Human nature's the same wherever you go.'

'I'm not so sure about that. These people in Laxdale aren't like anyone I've ever met before.'

'They will be, before I've done with them. Six months after I've put them to work in Drumliedubbs, you won't be able to tell the difference between them and anyone else.'

'Do you still think you can persuade them to move? Oh, Sam, you're past praying for.'

'When I make plans, my plans have got to work.'

'Oh, God! Sometimes you seem like a great man, and sometimes like a village idiot . . .'

After lunch Mr. Crantit approached Mrs. Pettigrew with a complacent smile and an almost proprietorial air. He proposed a walk, and to his surprise and annoyance she refused.

'Haven't I any claim on your attention?'

'No, none that I know of.'

'But surely, Lucy! After last night —'

'A little fun and frolicking, when you're naturally excited, isn't enough to turn a casual acquaintance into an old family friend; and you needn't think so. No, I'm tired, and I'm going to sleep for an hour or two.'

In the library the General snored lightly in his chair, Swanson in another. Catriona and Mrs. Pettigrew went to their beds and slept all afternoon. Flett, walking in the wood, lay down in a sunlit hollow and fell asleep. Over the village the rain-washed air, like light in a crystal globe, was still and bright, and quiet as a May morning when the dawn-chorus of the birds has stopped. Old men, worn out by excitement, slept. Matrons relaxed, and over their knitting their heads dropped into slumber. Youths and maidens yawned, and looked for solitude, and lay down to dream. Even the children slept.

CHAPTER TWENTY-NINE

No one had made any formal proposal to celebrate victory over the invaders, no one had laid plans for a festive gathering. But by half-past eight at night there were ten or a dozen people talking and telling animated stories in Nicholas's shop; in the little room behind the shop an old man was singing, in a thin, small voice, to an audience of four or five, a cheerful song called *Ho Hoiligean, Ho my Heifers!*, and on the paved courtyard at the back of the shop, beside the long store-shed, a piper was playing *The Wind that Shakes the Barley* for the dancers of an eightsome reel.

The reel was concluded, and the dancers called for a foursome. But Morag McLeod, her cheeks flushed and her breasts high from the exercise, a little imperious in the pride of her skill, said to her partner, 'You could never do the foursome without making mistakes, Angus. I want another partner, and where can I find one?'

Angus took a half-smoked cigarette from behind his ear, and relighted it. 'All right, all right,' he grumbled. 'If I cannot dance well enough, you must look for someone who can. — And here is Mr. Flett: you had better ask him.'

'Can you dance a foursome reel, Mr. Flett?'

'I used to.'

'Then try again. It's a night for dancing, this.'

The piper filled his bag, and let out a long, drab note. Then his fingers took command of the air, and between the houses, in the darkness lighted by uncurtained windows, the tune of *The Black Snuff Mull* beat upon the walls and the dancers' ears, and filled their minds with its leaping pattern, their legs with impetuous but formal strength.

Nicholas came out to watch them, and when the reel was concluded he said to Flett, 'You dance very well, Mr. Flett. You might almost be one of ourselves.'

'I've got the photographs,' said Flett. 'Would you like to see them?'

'I would indeed,' said Nicholas. 'Where are they?'

In the light spilling from a window Nicholas solemnly examined a dozen snapshots of the morning's adventure, in five or six of which Mr. Pettigrew was exhibited in the most compromising association with a dead stag and an old-fashioned hearse. 'Glory to God,' said Nicholas, 'they are good pictures! They are the best pictures I have ever seen. I will have them enlarged and hung in the shop. Let us go indoors, Mr. Flett, and take a dram; and we will look at them more closely.'

Flett, a little doubtful, turned to Morag, who said, 'Go with my father, and I will see you later. You are a very good dancer, Mr. Flett.'

Nicholas opened the back door and showed Flett into a small room, somewhat darkly furnished in a late Victorian way, where by now there was an audience of nearly a dozen listening to the old man who sang. He came from the clachan called North Bay, three miles beyond Laxdale, and he was highly regarded by the older people for his knowledge of Gaelic poetry and music. He stood in a corner with his head up, his eyes half-closed, and his hands crossed; and his voice was thin and pure, it came down a beaked and generous nose, and moved the imagination like an off-shore wind at sea.

'Cha leon thu lach bhios air an t-snamh,
Chaoidh cha chreach thu h-alach uaip,'

he sang; and Nicholas whispered, 'It is a song about sport. There is a young man who is going out shooting, but before he goes he must take an oath that he will never shoot a sitting bird, nor a beast lying down, nor a suckling, nor the mother of a brood. He may shoot where he will, so long as he shoots like a gentleman and takes

232

no advantage of the weak. It was the old way in the Highlands, Mr. Flett.'

'Well done, well done!' he cried, as the man from North Bay finished on a quavering high note. 'That was a splendid song indeed, sung as well as ever I have heard it! And now, wife, it is time to give the folk a dram.'

'They have had a dram,' said Mrs. McLeod.

'Then it is time to give them another, and make it a good one. — Come, Mr. Flett, and we'll go into the shop, where the light is better.'

They went into the shop and saw a paraffin-lamp glowing through a midsummer heat-haze of tobacco-smoke, and sun-red faces, open mouths, and sea-blue eyes shining in the mist. The shop was crowded full with nine or ten men, three or four thick-waisted women, and Willy John Watt and Nicholas's boy Peter sitting on the counter between an elaborate, pyramidal structure of tinned meats on the one side, and a display of patent medicines and dentifrices on the other.

'Come in, Nicholas, come in!' cried Willy John. 'We have been talking about that terrible man, Pettigrew — a king of the under-world, they say — that was trying to steal the hearse from me.'

'But we put a stop to that, Willy John.'

'You did indeed, and I'm grateful to you, Nicholas. I lost a bottle in the hearse, but thank God I had another in the house. — Here, take a dram for your stomach's sake.'

He leaned forward on the counter, and handed a black bottle to Nicholas, and solemnly watched him drink. 'There is no comfort like it,' he said, 'and God knows it is comfort we are all in need of, what with bandits on every road, disguised as Members of Parliament, and the news I have just heard from Glasgow.'

'What news is that?'

Willy John took a letter from his pocket, and slowly unfolded it. 'Is it from your father?'

'From my poor father.'

'Then he's not dead yet?'

'He is not dead, thank God, but I was right enough when I told

233

you he was in great trouble. He is wearing on for seventy-three, Nicholas, and what do you think he has done now?'

'Is it the drink again?'

'It was that to begin with, and things went from bad to worse, and the end of it was he got married.'

'Your old father?'

'Himself, Nicholas. And here he is asking me the loan of £3 10s. to pay for his honeymoon.'

'Well, well!' said Nicholas. 'Is he not a man of great spirit? Drinking like a fish and falling in love like a fool, at the age of seventy-three! He is a better man than you, Willy John, and you ought to be proud of him. — Take a sup of that, and drink his health. And heaven help the poor woman he's married on.'

He took a half-bottle from an inside pocket, and handed it to Willy John; who drank, and passed it to his nearest neighbour. It went the round of the company, amid gruff and grateful murmurs of 'Slainte! Slainte mhor!' And a man with a kind, ingenuous face and outstanding ears asked diffidently, 'Do you think it true, that it was Pettigrew who killed the stag?'

'Never question the truth of that, Murdo!' said Nicholas. 'For a dead stag in a hearse is a very difficult thing to explain, and it was just providential that Pettigrew was there to take the blame. Oh, yes! We have had too good a day to spoil it with idle questions about who did this and who did that. We had a great battle on the hill, and we won a great victory. — Drink up, men, there's more where that came from. — And here is something else we should be thankful for: I found these bits of paper on the hillside after they had exploded out of Sergeant Ogilvie's pocket, when he hit the ground like a bomb going off. Oh, it has been a notable day in the history of Laxdale.'

With an expression of admirable solemnity, Nicholas displayed the police summonses; and stilled the quick chorus of applause by saying, 'They are mischievous things, these summonses. They cause trouble wherever they go, and I think we should get rid of them.'

He reached up, and covered the chimney of the lamp with them.

234

They caught fire, and he held them till they burnt down to his horny fingers. He dropped their fragments to the floor, and stamped out the last small flames.

'You are a great man, Nicholas!' cried Willy John, his lean shoulders jerking with excitement, and his chin drooping below his long moustaches as mouth and eyes all opened wide to contemplate life's wonderment. 'Oh, yes, yes! And my father is a great man too. Behaving like a young man, and a perfect fool, at the age of seventy-three. Oh, my father!'

He lifted his bottle to his mouth, and drinking deeply leaned back and farther back across the counter — and Nicholas's boy Peter, sitting beside him, gave his lifted leg a little kick under the calf that over-balanced him — there was no malice in it, only a boy's desire of experiment — but Willy John, feeling himself about to fall, clutched for support at the pyramid of tinned meats, in which there was no stability, and bringing them down in a clattering descent, slid over the counter into a crate of eggs.

He lay heels-up, bewildered, in a morass of ruddy yolks, and splintered shells and tralucent albumen; and his neighbours, handicapped by laughter and the smallness of the shop, were slow to help him. 'He has cost you four dozen eggs, Nicholas,' said one of them.

'Well, well,' said Nicholas, 'they were good, fresh eggs. There will be no stink on him.'

With a peal of the warning bell, the shop door was thrust open and a buxom young woman with a broad, freckled face and rusty-red hair came in. 'Good evening to you, Nicholas,' she exclaimed. 'They were telling me there is to be a *ceilidh* here tonight?'

'It is a catastrophe rather than a *ceilidh*,' said Willy John, taking off his coat.

'And what have you been doing, Mr. Watt? You are smelling like a custard.'

'Charge the eggs to my account,' said Willy John with dignity, and retired into the back room to have his coat cleaned.

'I brought Robin Oig and Malcolm from the Shore,' said the freckled woman, 'and they've got their boxies. — Come in, boys.'

Two young men came in, diffident and solemn of aspect. One was rook-haired, lean of cheek, with eyes like black olives; the other a flaring red, blue-eyed, shy but sturdy. Both carried accordions, and they stood within the door, ill at ease.

'There's no room for dancing here,' said Nicholas, 'unless you dance on the road.'

'And what's wrong with the road?' demanded the freckled woman. 'It's dry now, and the moon's coming up, and here are the boys to make the music!'

'Then try the road,' said Nicholas. 'There are worse places for dancing than the open air. But take a dram first, it'll sweeten the tune.'

'Come on, then,' said the freckled woman, wiping her lips. 'It's dancing we should be on a night like this!'

'Wait, wait,' said Nicholas, putting a hand on Flett's arm as the shop emptied, and the dancers from the courtyard behind went out to the street, and even the older people in the back room followed. 'Will you lend me the photographs, Mr. Flett? I am going to ask the General and Miss Catriona to come and see the fun; and I would like to show them the photographs. I might even show them to Mr. Pettigrew.'

'He's being very difficult,' said Flett. 'The General doesn't quite know how to deal with him.'

'Do you tell me that? After what happened this morning, I thought the spirit would be knocked out of him altogether.'

'He's tougher than you think. He says he was the victim of a plot, and he practically accused the General of trying to frame him — in revenge, of course, for Pettigrew's refusal to support your request for a new road.'

'What a man!' said Nicholas, half in surprise and half in reluctant admiration.

'I came away as soon as dinner was over, but the General and Pettigrew and Mr. Marvell were starting the argument all over again. About the road, I mean, and what Pettigrew says was a plot against him. Mr. Marvell and I are going tomorrow by the steamer — Mr. Marvell's broadcasting on Wednesday — but Pettigrew says

236

he's prepared to stay another week, and visit every house in Laxdale, and talk to every man, woman and child about the advantages of going to Drumliedubbs. The General doesn't want him to stay, of course, but Pettigrew's his guest, and I don't suppose he'd ever turn him out.'

'Is Marvell on our side?' asked Nicholas.

'I think he is, though he doesn't say much. He writes a lot, and he can talk well enough when there's only a microphone in front of him; but he's pretty silent among other people.'

'He is very interested in Miss Catriona, from the way he looks at her.'

'He'd eat out of her hands, if she offered him anything.'

'Do you tell me so? Well, that is all to the good, and may help a lot. Give me the photographs, Mr. Flett, and go you and join the dancers. I'll be back before long, and tell you the news.'

The full moon was floating low in a grapeskin sky when Nicholas took out his ponderous, ancient car to drive to the Hall, and on the white road between the houses some fifty or sixty people were dancing to the thin, gay music that Robin Oig and Malcolm from the Shore, with nimble fingers, squeezed from their accordions.

At the Hall there was no such liveliness, but in the dining-room three figures, still at table, sat almost as motionless, almost as enduring it seemed, as the sculptured effigies on Etruscan urns. Mr. Crantit had left them, soon after Flett excused himself, to join Catriona and Mrs. Pettigrew in the drawing-room; but Pettigrew and Marvell and the General remained, now locked in argument, now gravelled for lack of argument, or cornered by intransigence that went round the table with the port.

'If,' said the General, after a long pause, 'you would admit that for once you had been in the wrong, we might still find a compromise.'

Pettigrew took time to consider the new opening, and then replied, 'But I wasn't in the wrong. I never have been in the wrong.'

'I am prepared,' said the General, 'to re-examine the whole case from the beginning.'

'Oh, not again!' exclaimed Marvell.

'This is our last chance to reach agreement, and I'm ready to argue my case till morning. We're a remote community, I admit that, but we deserve consideration. In the last few years the inherited wealth of Britain has been re-distributed in subsidies of one sort or another — some of them open, and some concealed — to all the industrial parts of the country; but the Highlands of Scotland have been neglected, though no segment of the country has served Britain better than the Highlands, or bled more deeply in its service. And what we're asking for now is both modest and reasonable: we want better communications, and that's all.'

'I'm on your side,' said Marvell. 'I agree with you, entirely. But — oh, what's the use of talking? May I have another glass of port?'

'Help yourself.'

'You've got no argument but sentimentality,' said Pettigrew. 'Laxdale, and all the West Highlands, are of no more use to the modern world than the Sahara Desert. They're out of date, they've lived too long, they're just anachronisms. The world today needs production, and nothing should concern us that doesn't produce either capital value or goods for day-to-day consumption. The virtue and justification of man is that he can use tools; and if he doesn't use up-to-date tools, he can't pay his way, and there's no economic reason for his survival. On economic grounds, Laxdale has no claim whatsoever to assistance, or even to sympathy.'

'You regard people as handlers of tools,' said the General. 'As superior, semi-intelligent tools, that is. But I take a different view. I don't over-estimate humanity — I've met cowards and cads in plenty — but, on the whole, I like people, and I think they're entitled to live whatever sort of life they choose for themselves, so long as they don't become an infernal nuisance to their neighbours. I don't believe that anyone is spiritually entitled to plan other people's lives, or intellectually capable of doing so. The best we can manage is to put a stop to obvious folly and open iniquity, and try to give people a decent wicket to play on. And I tell you frankly, Pettigrew, that if you still think you can persuade Laxdale to transport itself to

Drumliedubbs, you're the victim of self-delusion, and it's a waste of time for you to stay here any longer.'

'And to strengthen your case,' said Pettigrew, 'you've brought in the police. You devised a plot to discredit me —'

'That is utter nonsense! I don't pretend to understand all that happened last night, but there was no plot against you, and I'm willing to use any influence I've got — which is much less than you suppose — to persuade the police to drop their charge. You're a guest of mine, and I admit a certain responsibility for the welfare of my guests. But I do ask you — not in return for favours, only in justice to your own intelligence — to reconsider our claim, and admit that we in the West Highlands are as much entitled as other people to decent roads and proper piers.'

'Not if you can't pay for them.'

'But I say we have paid — in human life and energy.'

'And nowadays,' said Marvell, 'there is a tourist traffic to consider.'

'I don't believe in commercializing idleness —'

Mr. Pettigrew was interrupted by an elderly maid who came in to say, 'Here is Mr. McLeod to see you, General.'

'Mr. McLeod? If it's Nicholas, bring him in.'

'It is Nicholas indeed.'

'Come in, Nicholas. I'm very glad to see you. Come and sit down. There's a clean glass here. You'll take some port?'

'Well, well,' said Nicholas, 'I wouldn't say no. It will be quite a relief after whisky. Yes, it is a nice refreshing drink, is port wine.'

'You've come into the middle of an argument, Nicholas. — Here's Mr. Pettigrew trying to persuade us that people are no better than screwdrivers and internal combustion engines, and only justify their existence when they're making a profit for other pieces of machinery; but I say that what a man does is primarily his own concern, and there's not much purpose in living if you don't enjoy life.'

'People can't enjoy life,' said Pettigrew, 'unless they're doing useful work, and drawing good wages — and have indoor sanitation, especially in winter.'

239

'But they do, my dear fellow. They do!'

'Only because they're ignorant.'

'Is Mr. Pettigrew going to recommend a new road for us, or a new pier?' asked Nicholas.

'I'm afraid not,' said the General.

'Most certainly not,' said Pettigrew.

'That is a great pity, and you are making a big mistake, Mr. Pettigrew. — But it's you I was wanting to talk to, Mr. Marvell, for I am told you are a famous journalist.'

'I wouldn't describe myself as such; but I do write for one or two papers.'

'Just so. And sometimes, when you are writing an article, you will need a photograph to illustrate it. And if you are going to write about Laxdale and the bad road we have, I thought you would like these photographs of Mr. Pettigrew and the stag he shot.'

'I shot no stag!'

'So you say — but here are the photographs.'

'Who took them?' asked the General.

'Mr. Flett.'

'They're slanderous, every one of them! I'll sue you, and any newspaper that publishes them!'

'They're good photographs,' said Marvell. 'They would reproduce perfectly.'

'Do you think so?' asked Nicholas. 'Well, that is very gratifying. And if I were a journalist, I would write a splendid article about Mr. Pettigrew coming here, like a missionary, to teach us how to lead better lives — and the photographs would show everyone how he enjoyed his trip.'

'So it's blackmail, is it?' said Pettigrew. 'You've come into the open at last? Well, other people have tried that, and no one has succeeded yet. And you won't succeed either. I can prove conspiracy, and I've got good lawyers who'll turn blackmail inside-out and make you weep for every word you've uttered.'

'There is no question of blackmail!' said Nicholas indignantly. 'All I was saying was this, and this only: that if Mr. Marvell wants to write an article about the man who refused to let us have a new road, he might like some photographs to show what sort of a man you are, Mr. Pettigrew!'

'And if I changed my mind, and promised to help you?'

'Then there would be no occasion to publish the photographs.'

'But you don't call that blackmail?'

'It is common sense. We wouldn't wish to expose you to ridicule if you were on our side.'

'I don't think you could sue for slander,' said Marvell, 'if we gave the photographs to the police, and didn't publish them until they'd been produced in court as evidence of your condition.'

'Give them to me,' said the General; and tore them up, and threw the pieces into the fire. 'I'll see Flett when he comes back, and get the negatives from him, and destroy them too.'

'Oh, General!' exclaimed Nicholas. 'Is that wise?'

'Mr. Pettigrew and I are now on the same side. You have brought us together at last, Nicholas. We both dislike the thought of blackmail — though our reasons are different.'

'Thank you very much,' said Pettigrew with a surly embarrassment. 'I'm grateful to you for that. Though blackmail, mind you, wouldn't have done your side any good! My lawyers would have seen to that.'

'You are throwing away our last chance,' said Nicholas mournfully.

'We're not entirely dependent on Mr. Pettigrew,' said the General. 'Mr. Marvell sympathizes with us.'

'A minority report won't help you much,' said Pettigrew.

'In a delegation of two,' said Marvell, 'you may have to overrate yourself to get a majority.'

'I've got the chairman's vote, if I need it . . .'

'Well,' said the General, 'is there anything else you want to talk about, Nicholas? What's happening in the village?'

'They are dancing on the road in the moonlight.'

'They are, are they? What a good idea. I think we ought to join them, for an hour or so. Catriona enjoys a dance, and so do I. What about you, Marvell?'

'There's nothing I'd like better.'

'Will you come and watch, Pettigrew?'

'I prefer comfort, thank you.'

'Will you go and tell the ladies, Marvell? I daresay Mrs. Petti-grew will be more responsive. — Cheer up, Nicholas, and have another glass of port. Can we all squeeze into your car?'

Catriona and Mrs. Pettigrew were quickly ready for the dance, but Mr. Crantit caused some delay by insisting on changing his evening slippers for a pair of tennis-shoes that would, he said, give him a better grip on the rough surface of the road. Mr. Crantit was very gay. He had been helping Catriona with a letter to Macaulay, in which she begged the minister to come to their rescue and play King Pentheus in McKellaig's place. Mr. Crantit had persuaded her to say that if he refused she would have to ask Mr. Pettigrew; who had, indeed, certain qualifications for the part. The letter had been sent to the manse by hand, and though Catriona was anxious about the effect of the ruse, Mr. Crantit felt sure of its success.

Brilliantly lighted by a moon so incandescent that it seemed to have burnt a hole in space, the village was magpie-hued, all sable shadow or milky walls — 'Black and white, a gentleman in evening-dress,' said Mr. Crantit happily — and on the long street, undulating slightly like a trout in a stream, stood a double rank of people, waiting for late-comers and their final arrangement into sets, to fill a hundred yards of the moon-powdered road with the high-leaping steps and brisk passage of Strip-the-Willow. Robin Oig and Mal-colm from the Shore were quietly fingering their accordions — not yet in the high compulsion of a dancing tune, but meditative, lightly pondering the air — when Nicholas, turning his car into the lane beside Alec Muir's repair-shop, jumped out and called, 'Wait, wait! Here are more for the dance!'

Marvell took Catriona by the hand at once, but Mr. Crantit, stooping to re-tie the lace of one of his hurriedly put-on tennis-shoes, lost Mrs. Pettigrew. She stood for a moment seemingly entranced by the lively parti-coloured scene, but her quick eyes were busy and she saw, standing alone, the shy poet Hector McBride, beautiful as Michelangelo's David, who was Dionysus in the play;

242

and boldly she claimed him for her partner. Swanson, by good fortune, found Morag McLeod almost beside him — Andrew Flett, for the sake of policy, was dancing with her mother — and the General was accommodated with the freckle-faced, buxom young woman who had brought the accordion-players to the village. Mr. Crantit, disconsolate, joined the spectators, and the dancers bowed.

From the head of each set began a movement both soaring and serpentine, as the leading pair danced to each other — rising like gamecocks to the assault, circling with a ritual disdain — and transferring their attention to the next-in-line, started a spiral pattern that presently involved all the set in swift, high-stepping, intricate movement. The bubbling, shrill music of the accordions, playing *Drops of Brandy*, propelled the dancers like shuttles on a loom, but lifted their heels, animated their shoulders and their waists, and raised their arms in triumphant gesture. On the white-washed walls on the lighted side of the street the moon drew, in enormous shadows, a wild caricature of the dance. Shadows leapt roof high and disappeared, shadows gesticulated in a clown's abandon, and elongated arms made antlers, arabesques, and floral patterns on the stone. The shadow-dance was supernatural, larger and more vigorous than life, but strangely it kept time to the music.

A Reel followed, and a Schottische, the Dashing White Sergeant and a Quadrille. The dancers were less easily tired than the shadows, for as the moon rose higher, the shadows grew less impulsive and their stature diminished. Sometimes the street was filled with dancers, sometimes a piper or a fiddler played to only a score or two. There were little festive parties in every house, and the dancers came in to eat and drink, and talk a while, and then go back to the music and the road. The younger ones, and some who were not so young, discreetly vanished from time to time into the darkness of a narrow lane, or the moonlit immensity of the beach, or the open *machair*. The beach had a music of its own, and the pulse of the tide, slurring on sand, was a motive of the incommunicable theme of the sea's estranging beauty. Andrew Flett — bullet-headed Flett, but for a little while made sensitive by love — and Morag McLeod heard it as they walked together on the beach;

243

and aware of the delicacy of living, and the fearful profundity of life, walked slowly, and as closely as they dared, but did not dare to touch.

They heard sea-music, and a drunken fiddler who had left the crowd to play in solitude the Eriskay *Love Lilt* to the moon; and they spoke with diffidence of common problems and their own transient affairs.

'I meant to be a schoolmaster myself at one time,' said Flett. 'I went to the Training College, in Aberdeen, and I taught for nearly six months till the war started and I went into the Army. And after the war I got a chance to go to the university and better myself, or so I thought, in the Civil Service. But I'm beginning to think I made a mistake.'

'It is not a bad life, being a teacher,' said Morag, 'if you can put up with children.'

'I'd like to be a country schoolmaster, in a place like this.'

'You could come here, and welcome. There ought to be two teachers in the school, but we can't get a young man to leave a big town and settle in Laxdale.'

'Would you take me, Morag?'

'You would have to ask my father about that.'

'I only meant as the other teacher!'

'And what else would you be meaning? My father is on the Education Committee of the County Council, and if he approved of you, it would be easy enough for you to get the job.'

'Would you like me to get it?'

'The school needs a new teacher — and it would be company indeed . . .'

Approaching them from the other end of the beach, blackly shadowed on the pale sand, they saw another couple, as close as they and like them held separate, within a span of desired contact, by the immense significance of life that the moon illuminated and the ocean whispered. They recognized Catriona and Marvell. They stopped, and turned about, and re-trod their footsteps in the sand. So also, abashed as they were by human encounter, did Marvell and Catriona.

244

Mrs. Pettigrew, however, was not at all impressed by the spectacular mystery of the universe. She was, quite simply, grateful for the brightness of the moon, which made it easy for her to see her way through the little seaside wood; and the lapse of the crumbling waves reminded her only of Blackpool. She was excited indeed, but very sensibly and straightforwardly, by the presence beside her of Hector McBride, the beautiful Dionysus of Catriona's play. McBride was a poet who had never dared speak his poetry to others. McBride, like every poet, had dreamed of praise, but never heard it until Mrs. Pettigrew praised him. The high moon exalted him, and in the soft phrasing of the little waves on the beach he heard a sly comment on the trombone-voices of a winter storm; it seemed, for a moment, that a corner of the curtain which hid all mysteries had been lifted, and in the light below it he saw the quick and confident loveliness of Mrs. Pettigrew, and recognized the dominating theme.

'Look,' said Mrs. Pettigrew, 'here's such a nice place to sit down and rest. There's a lovely view of the sea, and you can hear that drunken fiddler playing — what's it called?'

'The Eriskay *Love Lilt*.'

'I knew I'd heard it before . . .'

Mr. Crantit, with dwindling spirit, was dancing a Schottische with the buxom, freckle-faced young woman who had brought Robin Oig and Malcolm from the Shore to Nicholas's shop. It had been exhilarating, he admitted, to see the village — the whole parish, indeed — in such a festive mood, but now he was tired; and his own capacity for exhilaration had been exhausted.

CHAPTER THIRTY

A T Laxdale Hall, on the following morning, only the General
came down in time for breakfast. In the room that looked
upon the sea the long table was laid for eight, and on the
sideboard, on a copper warming-plate, sat lavish dishes of porridge,
and fried haddock, and scrambled eggs. But the General, walking
up and down, ate alone until the elderly maid came in to say,
'There's a policeman wanting to see you, General. He is Sergeant
Ogilvie, from Scatwall, and he says it's important.'

'Bring him in,' said the General. 'I'll be glad of company.'

The Sergeant came in, red-faced, and a little awkward.

'Have you had your breakfast?' asked the General. 'Well, sit
down, and I'll give you some porridge. You take porridge, don't
you? And there's some fish after that, or scrambled eggs. Do you
want tea or coffee?'

The Sergeant sat in the General's chair, at the head of the table,
and the General served him. 'And what's the matter now?' he
asked.

'It's serious this time,' said the Sergeant, wiping his moustache.
'And I thought I should tell you about it as soon as possible.'

'What has happened?'

'The leader of the poachers that you caught is a man called
Gamlie. He has a police record, and he has told us one or two things
that will surprise you. He is a man with a bitter mind, a revengeful
mind, and if he is to suffer, he is determined to make others suffer
too. — And the start of it is that he came here with the connivance
of your keeper, Norman McKellaig.'

'I don't believe it!'

246

'I doubted it myself to begin with, but I'm afraid it's true.'

'He's weak-willed, he's not very intelligent — but I can't think he'd be dishonest, unless he's got worries that I know nothing of.'

'Mrs. McKellaig's name, before she married, was Gamlie. This man Gamlie is a cousin of Norman's, and has given him a considerable sum of money.'

'What a fool he must be! And what a nuisance for everyone!'

'And my second piece of information,' said the Sergeant, 'is that Gamlie was in the habit of selling the salmon he caught to the Albany Palace Hotel.'

'What is the significance of that?'

'It's the big hotel that Mr. Pettigrew owns. Gamlie saw him on the hill yesterday morning, and recognized him. And if he's to go to gaol for poaching, he says, Pettigrew should go too.'

'Good God!'

'It's all to spite you, General. He thinks Mr. Pettigrew must be a friend of yours.'

'He's certainly my guest. — Go on with your breakfast, Sergeant, and I'll see if he's up yet.'

Left to himself, the Sergeant enjoyed a hearty breakfast, and before he had finished was joined by Swanson and Flett and Catriona. They were a little surprised to see him, but Catriona had a letter from Macaulay, which he had delivered himself, that gave her too much pleasure to leave room in her mind for any curiosity about other people's business. It was a very long letter, closely argued, and parts of it she could not understand; but the conclusion was satisfactory and plainly stated, and Macaulay was going to play King Pentheus.

The General returned, and was told the news. He was pleased but pre-occupied, and when the Sergeant had finished his third cup of coffee, he explained that they had business to do, and took him to the library. Pettigrew was waiting for them, with an expression less complacent than usual.

The Sergeant repeated his story, and Pettigrew said, 'Even if it's true, it doesn't involve me. I don't do the shopping for my hotels. That's my manager's job.'

'But you'll talk things over with your manager from time to time, I dare say,' said the Sergeant. 'Especially when there's an account for hundreds of pounds for a commodity that's been scarce and difficult to get.'

'Are you trying to lead me into making some sort of admission?'

'As I understand it,' said the General, 'Sergeant Ogilvie's only motive in coming here was courtesy. He discovered the possibility of your being charged with a very unpleasant offence, and as I am doubly interested — for you are my guest, and some of the salmon were probably mine too — he came to tell me about it. I think you should be grateful to him, not hostile.'

With discomfort now plainly visible on his face, with a twitching cheek-muscle, Pettigrew walked heavily to and fro — a little theatrically, perhaps — and over his shoulder, reluctantly, said, 'I apologize, Sergeant. I mistook your purpose.'

He asked several questions about Gamlie, and then said to the General, 'I'd like to telephone to the hotel, and speak to my manager. And I'd better have a word with my lawyer, too.'

'By all means,' said the General. 'You may find our local operator a little slow in putting a trunk-call through, but if you're patient she'll get your number eventually. We'll leave you to it. Come along, Sergeant.'

'And there's one other thing. — Will you tell Lucy to start packing? We'll be leaving on the steamer this morning after all.'

The General closed the door, and taking Sergeant Ogilvie's hand, shook it heartily. 'My dear fellow,' he said, 'you've done it! I thought we might never get rid of him. He was threatening to stay here indefinitely, to convert us all to his ridiculous schemes, and I couldn't see how to shift him. You've no idea how grateful I am to you. I'll get some fishing now.'

'He'll be off to see his lawyer,' said the Sergeant.

'Are you going to charge him with being drunk in charge of a hearse?'

'I think we'll let that drop. He did no harm, except to himself, and it wouldn't look well if he said that he got the drink at your table.'

248

'It was Willy John he got it from. Willy John says he left a bottle of whisky in the hearse, inadvertently.'

'Tell Willy John to send Pettigrew a bill for it — and we'll leave it at that.'

'That's very handsome of you, Sergeant. And now I must tell Catriona to inform Mrs. Pettigrew she is about to leave us. Poor Mr. Crantit will be sorry, and so shall I. I like her better than her husband — so long as she keeps her hands off me.'

A little before noon the visitors, half-surrounded by their luggage, stood on Miss Phipps's pier, and the ordinary difficulties of saying goodbye were much aggravated by constrained emotion. Mr. Marvell and Catriona could find no words at all to express their thoughts, and none to conceal them. They stood mute and clearly unhappy, and looking in different directions saw nothing anywhere to distract their attention from that which straitly held it. — Andrew Flett, his back to the dividing sea, looked hopefully towards the village and the school beyond it; but Morag had too strict a sense of duty to leave her charges for the sad luxury of saying goodbye, and hope faded in the midday sun. — Mrs. Pettigrew, though she had taken what amusement she could find in Laxdale, disliked the place and was glad to be going; but tried to conceal her pleasure behind a sprightly assurance of regret that she must leave so charming a spot for the sheer ennui of town-life; and Mr. Pettigrew, in contrast to the ebullient confidence with which he had come ashore, was now manifestly anxious to be gone, and unlike his wife made no effort to hide his feelings. — Mr. Crantit gave Mrs. Pettigrew his solemn promise that he would come to see her in London, and Mrs. Pettigrew made everyone uncomfortable by asking Flett to take a farewell photograph of them.

This embarrassment was prevented by the arrival of Norman McKellaig, on a stretcher carried by two stalwart young men, with his mother and Nurse Connachy walking behind. The General, with some reluctance, had told Catriona of McKellaig's dishonesty, and listened, with more astonishment, to her greater knowledge of it. 'What a fool!' he repeated. 'My God, what a fool!'

'I think, now, that we shouldn't blame him too much. At any rate, we shouldn't punish him. '

'Why not?'

'He's been punished already. He was punished beforehand, by his mother, and now he's got concussion.'

'Perhaps Gamlie knocked a bit of sense into his head. Let's hope so.'

McKellaig was looking much better. He had recovered consciousness the previous evening, and had a good night's sleep. The General concealed his displeasure, and wished him a speedy recovery; and Catriona, with more warmth in her manner, talked to him until it was time to go. The stretcher was handed down into the boat, the Parliamentary visitors followed, and the boat left the pier stern-first, turned, and headed for the steamer lying off-shore. Hands waved, and hats were flourished. The dull stammer of the engine grew fainter, and was heard only as an echo of combustion. Faces lost their claim to recognition, and when the diminished boat drew alongside the steamer, the parting was complete.

'And now,' said the General to Swanson, 'we can start fishing. We're going to have an early lunch, and in just over an hour's time we'll have our flies in the water.'

CHAPTER THIRTY-ONE

TWO days later, having borrowed a pair of rubber boots and armed himself with a gaff, Mr. Crantit declared his intention of helping Swanson to catch a salmon. Swanson, who took his fishing seriously, preferred to be alone; but as he and the General had already had good sport, he could afford a little unselfishness, and being unwilling to hurt Mr. Crantit's feelings, accepted his company without manifest reluctance.

There was a broken sky, with channels of light and blue firths dividing a mountainous archipelago of clouds. There was a mild, south-westerly breeze, and the river, though still running fairly strongly, was no longer turbulent. The flood-water had gone out to sea, and the pools were no more than tidily full. — A perfect day, thought Swanson, and felt a fisherman's excitement rising in his mind. His imagination filled like a balloon with eagerness to be at work, with little gusts of anticipation, with a hunger for the river and the pressure of water against his legs that was, perhaps, not unlike a salmon's own desire for rain-fed streams. He walked more quickly, and paid no attention to Mr. Crantit, who was talking about modern literature.

They came to The Cruive, and a few yards from the bank Swanson put his rod together, and pulling his green silk line through the rings, tied on a cast that he took from a copper damping-box.

'Which of these enchanting flies are you going to use?' asked Mr. Crantit. 'Here is one that I should find irresistible if I were a salmon. What do you call it?'

'A Silver Doctor.'

'And this — perhaps this is even better — this was obviously designed as an invitation to gaiety.'

'A Jock Scott,' said Swanson. 'But the General advised a Green Highlander.'

'A Green Highlander,' declared Mr. Crantit, 'must be the very embodiment of the pagan spirit, a symbol of fertility perhaps, a figure in a ritual dance. Let us try him by all means.'

'Are you going to fish?'

'Not yet, I think. I shall watch you, to begin with, and observe the proper motions.'

Mr. Crantit had taken a small trout-rod, belonging to Catriona, but he made no pretence to being skilled in its use, and admitted that he carried it merely to enhance his appearance as a sportsman.

Swanson, fishing from the bank, cast downstream, and steadily, shortening his line, drew his fly up and across the tawny swirl of water. He had been fishing no more than five minutes when, a moment after the fly broke the surface, the top of his rod bowed to the stream, his line straightened, and to the thin scream of the reel grew swiftly longer and was carried towards the bottom end of the pool.

'What's happening now?' asked Mr. Crantit. 'Good heavens, you've caught a fish! Well, I had no idea it was as easy as that.'

Swanson, with a look of fierce intensity on his mild and chinless face, was slowly following the fish downstream, and Mr. Crantit, brightly chatting, accompanied him.

The fish turned, the line hung slack, and Swanson reeled it in with nervous, hurrying fingers.

'You've let it go!' said Mr. Crantit disapprovingly.

But the fish, running up stream, leapt three times in quick succession, and then lay pulling doggedly, its head to the current. Swanson waded out, and with the current helping him, slowly drew it in, between himself and the near bank. The fish, though strong, lacked initiative. After two more runs and a brief tug-of-war, it suffered itself to be guided towards a belt of shingle where Swanson neatly gaffed it. It was a clean-run salmon of eight or nine pounds weight, with the soft sea-lice still on it.

'What a very simple process!' said Mr. Crantit. 'I always thought that catching a salmon called for heroic endurance and the dexterity of an acrobat. But anyone could do it, if it's no harder than that.'

Swanson, justifiably annoyed by Mr. Crantit's failure to recognize a faultless performance, said gruffly, 'Some are easy to handle, some aren't. It depends on the fish, and how it's been hooked.'

'Well, it's a handsome creature,' said Mr. Crantit, and taking a step backwards to admire it in a new perspective, set his foot on an outcrop of rock flush with the ground. There was a little crunching noise, and looking down, he saw that the agate ring at the tip of Swanson's rod had been crushed and splintered.

'Did I do that?' he asked.

'You did. By God, you did!'

'I'm very sorry indeed. But surely you shouldn't have left your rod lying where anyone might tread on it?'

'I usually fish alone — and I look where I'm going.'

'Well, I apologize, and I can't do more. I apologize humbly.'

'That's put an end to my fishing. I haven't got a spare top with me.'

'You have been careless! But I'll lend you my little rod, if you like.'

'Let me see it.'

It was a slim and pliant trout-rod, nine feet long, and Swanson decided to use it only because his judgment was obscured by anger. He drew the line off the reel, and made sure that there was plenty of backing. He tied on a lighter cast than he had been using, and a smaller fly; and cast across the pool.

The little rod was perfectly balanced, and seemed alive from butt to tip. It was a delight to handle it, and presently its grace and strength restored Swanson's temper. But there were no more fish in the pool, or none showed; and Mr. Crantit, abashed by his clumsiness, appeared to have lost his stock of conversation.

'Let's try the White Pool,' said Swanson. 'It's nonsense, really, to fish with a rod as light as this, but it's a little beauty, and I'd like to see if I can hold a salmon on it.'

'Oh, I'm sure you can. Keep a tight line — that's all there is to it, I'm told.'

Feeling that he had been restored to the anglers' communion,

Mr. Crantit recovered his spirits and remembered his interrupted disquisition on modern literature. They walked upstream and Swanson considered the White Pool with appreciative eyes. The water had gone down a little since the previous day, and a narrow strip of shingle showed along the near bank. He could fish nearly half of it without wading; but this meant that Mr. Crantit could stand beside him and continue his conversation.

'Much of today's writing,' he said, 'is hardly to be described as literature. I prefer to regard it as embroidery, and as embroidery some of it is very fine indeed. The best of our women writers do really beautiful work, and some of the young men ply nearly as sharp a needle, and are almost as nimble with their fingers. I like to think of them sitting in the lamplight and stitching away, drawing a fine thread, hemming a neat seam — and oh, so cleverly introducing the dark hues of guilt and aberration. Where would the critics be without those darker hues? — My dear fellow, you've got another!'

Swanson had seen a narrow, pointed head rise leisurely, too leisurely, to his fly, and lightly cast again across the stream to draw it in front of the waiting fish. Now the salmon, still in no hurry, took the fly, and slowly swam upstream. Swanson, not daring to strike hard, for a moment held his line and raised the tip of his rod. The salmon moved more quickly, but still did not seem perturbed. It lay gently pulling.

'Not a very big one, I should think,' said Mr. Crantit.

'It's a good fish.'

'Well, as I was about to say, the aim of popular criticism nowadays is not so much to examine the interest and assess the value of a man's work, as to delve into his subconscious to see what made him tick. In the insecurity of our lives today, we have, of course, a keener incentive than ever before to learn what makes our fellow-mortals tick; what made our predecessors tick. If we can discover the vital principle in them, we may cultivate something of the sort for ourselves. Something to help us survive. — Though, mark you, I often doubt whether the insecurity of life today is really greater than it used to be. Remember, in Victorian times, the widespread fear of hell and scarlet fever; both of which we have abolished. And if you examine all history impartially — now keep your head, Swanson. Keep cool.'

The salmon, lying head-to-stream above them, had been jerking savagely at the hook. A nagging, dangerous movement. You could almost hear it snarling, thought Swanson, and feared his cast would break at the eye. — But Mr. Crantit had not been aware of this hidden struggle. Mr. Crantit saw Swanson hurriedly reel-in as the fish turned and the line went slack, and then suddenly the reel was screaming and Swanson was following the racing fish downstream. The line went out, and the backing went out until the barrel of the reel showed through its remaining yellow coils; and Mr. Crantit, pleased with his forethought in borrowing rubber boots, followed Swanson into the river. Twice the salmon jumped high, falling on its side with a loud splash among the water-drops.

'A big one!' said Mr. Crantit happily. 'Don't let go, Swanson.'

The fish lay sullenly, and Swanson went a little further downstream and held it against the current.

'One of the very much overworked words in contemporary criticism — or shall we call it contemporary reviewing? — is *integrity*,' said Mr. Crantit, 'and it's often a great puzzle to know what the critic has in mind when he's talking about integrity. I have occasionally suspected that what it sometimes implies is a serious interest in homosexuality, and it is surely significant that whereas, in the brutal past, it was usual to describe the sexual heretics as "perverts", we now more respectfully speak of them as "inverts". Perversion is a turning away from what is right, but inversion suggests a turning-in to its very core and centre — and between *in*version and *in*tegrity there is, to the eye, a specious relationship. We poor extraverts, on the other hand, are merely those who have been left out in the cold. We have no status but extra-tegrity, and to the critics that is merely a dead-letter, like extra-territoriality in China. He's off again!'

The salmon had been lying near the bottom end of the pool, and Swanson and Mr. Crantit had slowly approached it. The fish headed first one way, then another, and Swanson held hard to persuade it away from the boulder-strewn, leaping channel below. The little rod was bent to a half-circle, and the fish came round and swam upstream again. Half way up the pool it leapt high, then desperately jerked at the line, three or four times, and made another run. Again the line went out till the drum of the reel was almost bare, and Swanson followed heavily against the current. But now, when the salmon stopped, and lay pulling, he had the stream to help him hold it.

'This is most exciting!' said Mr. Crantit. 'I've got water down my left leg, but I don't care a bit. — Now what was I saying? Ah, yes. And before I say anything else, please believe that I have no moral objection whatever to inversion of any extent, or perversion of any degree. No, indeed. Like the ever-to-be-regretted Menander, I call no vice unnatural. Nature is so catholic! I have sometimes wondered, indeed, if the cloud that you are under — the little trouble that you have run away from — was the result of sexual idiosyncracy?'

Tentatively Swanson put strain on his line and reeled-in two or three feet.

'If that is the case, you can not only trust my discretion, but rely on my wholehearted sympathy.'

The salmon shook its head, and swam strongly forward again.

'Well, some day you may feel inclined to admit me to your confidence. My own habits are conventional at present, but whether they will always be so, I should not like to say. I was born in the interesting city of Peshawar — my father was in the Indian Civil Service. I am flotsam of the *ci-devant* Empire — and many of the Pathans who came down to Peshawar for their entertainment used to tire of conventional pleasures, and seek new company, at the age of sixty or so. — I remember once commenting on this, at my club, and a young man, one of several to whom I was talking, at once inquired, in a voice like the mellow ousel fluting in the elm — what a poet was Tennyson! — "And how old are you now, my dear Crantit?" I was much flattered.'

The salmon made several short runs, with failing strength, and suffered itself to be pulled downstream till its long shape, dark in the water, was clearly visible. Then, with a powerful swirl, it turned away and headed for the opposite bank, where a fallen tree fouled the current: the only obstacle in the pool. Swanson again grew anxious, and used all the strength of the rod to keep it away from the sunken branches.

'Our great mistake,' said Mr. Crantit, 'is to wrap up this business of homosexualism in a frightened and forbidding silence. If we frankly admitted its existence, as an inevitable by-product of our civilization, we should strip it of the glamour which now so absurdly and rather tiresomely envelops it, and also – this is most important – we could find useful work in our society for many who feel estranged from it. My only surviving brother is a Regular soldier, and he, at the outbreak of the last war, was deeply impressed by the sterling qualities of two young temporary officers who were quite obviously pansies. They were the only subalterns in the battalion, he said, who felt any responsibility for the comfort of their men, and knew how to look after them. Later, in North Africa, he recommended both of them for decorations. Indeed, his experience of pansies, in battle, was such that he sent a memorandum to the War Office. – Is it dead?'

'He's finished, I think. Have you got the gaff?'

'Let me gaff him, please. I do want to share your victory.'

Keeled over, half on its side, the fish was slowly pulled in to shallow water, and Mr. Crantit reached eagerly forward with the gaff. Too eagerly, for he merely pricked the salmon, and sent it, with a flurry and splash, into mid-stream again.

'Damn!' said Mr. Crantit.

'It doesn't matter. He won't get away now.'

'Well, my brother, as I was saying, sent a memorandum to the War Office in which he reminded the Military Secretary, or some such person, of the Bantam Battalions in the first war – men who were too small for the ordinary line regiments – and recommended the formation, on similar lines, of Pansy Battalions for the second chapter of the struggle. They would regard themselves as an *élite*, he said, and their *esprit de corps* would be wonderful – '

'There now,' said Swanson. 'Take your time – you've got him!'

Embracing the salmon, Mr. Crantit splashed on to the shingle and laid it down for admiration. 'What a fish! What a monster!' he exclaimed. 'Twenty pounds, do you think?'

'No, not quite. Twelve or thirteen, perhaps.'

'On my little rod! I knew it was a good rod.'

'I'd have killed it a lot quicker on my own rod.'

'Still, time wasn't wasted. We've had an interesting discussion – '

'What were you talking about?'

'My dear Swanson! Weren't you listening?'

'Well, I heard you talking, of course, but I was really thinking about the salmon.'

'What a brutal sport it is, that can deafen a man to good conversation!'

'You were saying something about critics – '

'Please, please! Though you have hurt my feelings, there is no need to excoriate them. Shall we go home now?'

'I'm ready, yes. I was lucky to get a salmon on that rod. I'd lose another one.'

Silently, carrying a fish apiece, they returned to Laxdale Hall, and at the gates Swanson stopped and said with genuine remorse, 'I'm sorry for having been so very selfish. But if you were a fisherman you would know that even the Last Trump couldn't take your attention off a well-hooked salmon.'

Mr. Crantit was a good-natured man. 'Don't worry,' he said. 'The artist is constitutionally tough, he can stand a lot of neglect; and conversation is one of the arts – though it may be on its deathbed.'

They went in, and on a table in the hall where letters were left, saw two large, plumply filled manila envelopes, each decorated with a cluster of foreign stamps, that had been re-directed and were addressed to H. O. Pottinger, Esq.

'They're for me,' said Swanson, with a perceptible embarrassment.

'Pottinger?' inquired Mr. Crantit.

'It's a name I sometimes use. It's not uncommon in Orkney and Shetland.'

'They're from Venezuela. How strange to have correspondents in Venezuela. I never met anyone who came from Venezuela.'

'All right,' said Swanson. 'I'll tell you. I began to once before, didn't I? The General won't be back for another hour, at least —'

'And Catriona is rehearsing the good Macaulay. We are alone.'

'And with a brace of salmon for the larder, we're entitled to help ourselves to a drink.'

CHAPTER THIRTY-TWO

IN the library Swanson opened the large manila envelopes with a paper-knife, and from each took ten or a dozen letters that were, as Mr. Crantit observed, addressed to him in his own name. He examined the postmarks, and having found the letter for which he was looking, said to Crantit, 'Do you mind if I read this letter before we begin talking? It's the last one from my wife.'

'Is she in Venezuela?'

'No, she's in Shetland. But I'll explain everything in a minute.'

Thoughtfully, with a chess-player's expression, Mr. Crantit sipped his whisky-and-soda, and Swanson read his letter twice: running swiftly through it, then reading carefully.

'Well, that's all right,' said Swanson at last. 'They're all well, thank God.' And drank half his whisky at a gulp.

'And now for the explanation. I'm all agog!'

'It's a domestic story, essentially, and the easiest way to tell it — though it may bore you — is to begin at the beginning. And the beginning, the real beginning, is that I'm in love with my wife.'

Mr. Crantit raised his glass, and bowed.

'Then I made a lot of money.'

'And naturally the gods were jealous. Love and a fortune, too, is more than any man deserves.'

'The gods didn't meddle with me. There was no need. — I suppose you haven't read a novel of mine called *The King of Spain's Daughter*?'

'I have indeed, and very good it is. If it's the one I'm thinking of.'

'About three years ago an American film-company bought it for 25,000 dollars.'

'My dear fellow! That's about £8000.'

'Nearly £9000. And with that sum of money I bought, for my wife, a small estate in Shetland that had belonged to her family. Her father had once owned about 12,000 acres, but lost all his money and the land too. My father was an ironmonger who made quite a lot of money. Enough, at least, to send me to Cambridge and give me a motor car when I got married. But my wife's family is one of the oldest in Shetland — and I am, I admit, something of a snob.'

'I'm a roaring snob!' said Mr. Crantit. 'Every good man is. The life-force itself may only be sublime snobbery.'

'The old house came into the market, with a couple of sheep-farms. The house was dilapidated and the farms would only run a sheep to seven or eight acres, so I could afford to buy the place. I had to spend a lot on it, but I had been making a fairly handsome income for several years, before the windfall from the films, and I thought I could afford what I was spending. But I made the mistake of not including the 25,000 dollars in my income-tax return, because, in my opinion, it was a capital sale.'

'I have always understood,' said Mr. Crantit, 'that when you sell your work to a film-company you include not only your worldly reputation but your immortal soul.'

'They turned my novel into a musical comedy with a Moorish beauty-chorus dancing a hula-hula in the Alhambra, and the Duke of Buckingham losing his trousers in the bull-ring. Whatever I owned in the story, whatever property in it was mine, was certainly sold outright. But the Commissioners for Inland Revenue decided that my dollars were indistinguishable from the rest of my income, and charged me accordingly.'

'Didn't you protest?'

'I took it to court, and that cost something, and did no good. There was a long argument about it, and the final demand, the ultimatum, only came a few months ago.'

'For how much?'

'I had made a lot of money in the ordinary way that year, and what I owed in income-tax and sur-tax was, almost exactly, 25,000 dollars. Put it into pounds, shillings and pence if you like.

'Could you pay it?'

'Of course not. I had about £600 in the bank. I drew £300 and left home the next morning.'

'To go to Venezuela?'

'No, I don't like foreign countries much. But I told the Commissioners of Income Tax that I had to go to Venezuela to write about Juan Antonio Páez, and that I would settle my business with them when I came back.'

'Who was Juan Antonio?'

'I know nothing about him. I found his name in the Encyclopaedia Britannica. I chose Venezuela because it's got a fairly remote hinterland, and my brother's a mining engineer with an oil-company there. My wife writes to him, and sends on any letters she thinks I'd like to see; I send him a cable now and then, to give him an address; and he sends my accumulated correspondence to H. O. Pottinger.'

'But surely it isn't as easy as that to change your identity?'

'Pottinger was a crofter who lived near us in Shetland. Not a very nice man. He died of pneumonia a few days before I left home, and I helped his widow to tidy-up his affairs. He had just drawn his new ration-book, and I said I would return it to the Food Office the next time I went to Lerwick. But the next time I went to Lerwick I took an aeroplane to Aberdeen, train from there to Glasgow, and then by air from Renfrew to Belfast. I hadn't made any definite plans at that time, but I kept the ration-book and began to use the name of Pottinger.'

'Have you an Identity Card?'

'No one ever asks you for an Identity Card. I have my own passport in case I want to go abroad in a hurry.'

'How long did you stay in Ireland?'

'Two or three months. I finished a novel, and got some good fishing. I sent the novel to my brother in Venezuela, and he sent it to my agent in London. — Airmail's a great convenience when you're on the run. — And then, still as Pottinger, I went to the Outer Isles, and fished in North Uist and South Uist, and met the General.'

'And what does your wife think of all this?'

'She's lonely, but she hasn't got much time to worry, with five children all at home. Materially, she's all right at present. The bank holds the titles to the house and farms, and they'll guarantee a biggish overdraft.'

'But what are your plans? What are you going to do eventually?'

'I don't know. There's no point, you see, in deliberately trying to write a best-seller, to pay off the debt, because the following year I should have to pay enormous taxes on what the best-seller made, and be as badly off as ever. Perhaps worse. I see no way out of the difficulty. I may have to go to Venezuela after all.'

'Have you had no correspondence with the Inland Revenue people since you — ah! — absconded?'

'Not directly. They wrote to me in Venezuela, and my brother replied that my intention, so far as he understood it, had been to go to a village on one of the remoter tributaries of the Orinoco; to which there was no postal service. To prove that I really was in Venezuela I wrote an indignant letter about labour-conditions on the oil-fields, and my brother sent it to the *New Statesman*.'

'It's a fascinating case, and demands serious consideration,' said Mr. Crantit. 'A little more whisky? I see no easy or immediate solution of the problem, but in the very fact of your flight from the law I perceive real hope of your eventual significance as a writer. As I told you once before, our stock of respectability is strictly limited, and you, as a writer, cannot afford to waste your respectability on life. Keep it for your muscular sentences and comely paragraphs. As a nameless exile from society, with the tipstaffs at your heels, you may yet write a tale in such a plumed and virile prose — a language soaring like the albatross — as will carry it into the cloudless airs of immortality. On the whole, my dear Swanson, I am inclined to congratulate you on your misfortune.'

'You can't congratulate my wife. She doesn't enjoy being a widow before her time.'

'She is a good woman, and good women are bound to suffer. We can do nothing but sympathize. — What is the subject of the novel that you finished in Ireland?'

'The scene is Goa in the first years of the seventeenth century.'

'Nova Goa, where the pride of Portugal met the opulence of the fabled East and a many-tinted luxury flourished in a flower-bed of the vices? What a background!'

'My novel is a comedy.'

'An historical comedy? Good, that's unusual. But Luxury and Vice have at least minor parts, I hope?'

'There are three young men, living together, and too poor to enjoy either. But between them they can hire a servant, buy one good suit of clothes, and a silk umbrella —'

'The silk umbrella was the mark of fashion, the flag of high society?'

'It was.'

'And under it your three poor young men enjoy a series of over-lapping, complicated and humorous intrigues?'

'They do.'

'Against a background of Oriental luxury and vice. — My poor Swanson, it will be immensely successful.'

'It's a satirical comedy.'

'Ah, that's better. Satire should keep your circulation down.'

Having listened with exemplary patience, with generosity indeed, to Swanson's recital of trouble, Mr. Crantit felt it was now his turn to talk; and for thirty-five minutes, until the General and Catriona returned, talked with remarkable fluency on a variety of subjects, passing lightly from satire to some consideration of Camões and the Portuguese epic called *The Lusiads*, thence by natural passage to the older history of Goa under the Bahmani sultans, to the nearby kingdom of Golconda, and the curious effect of diamonds on the female mind . . .

The General and Catriona, having met in the village, arrived together; Catriona, after a successful rehearsal, emitting sturdy confidence, and the General, in wet and peat-stained clothes, in the difficult mood that propriety may induce when it suppresses an inclination to be amused.

'You should go and have your bath at once,' said Catriona. 'You're wet through.'

'I want a whisky and soda first, and I'm going to tell them about Nicholas. — But how did you get on, Swanson? Have a good day?'

'A brace. Eight and a half and twelve and a half.'

'Good enough!'

'And the larger on my little rod,' said Mr. Crantit complacently. 'On *your* little rod, that is,' he added to Catriona.

'Well, I must hear about that!'

With a commendable brevity Swanson described his afternoon's fishing, and the General said that he also had been lucky. He had shot two stags, the second after three and a half hours of the most arduous stalking.

'But I'll tell you more about it at dinner,' he said. 'It was really interesting, and for ten minutes before I got my shot I had to lie as still as a corpse on a bed of soaking peat with a fly on my neck and a hind staring straight at me and twitching her nose only fifty yards away. But I mustn't start that now — '

'Go and have your bath,' said Catriona.

'What's your story about Nicholas?' asked Mr. Crantit.

'Give me another whisky,' said the General. 'Well, I was coming down from the hill when I suddenly remembered the stag in the hearse, and realized that I didn't know what had become of it. — There was such a lot to think about, it went out of my head altogether. — So I looked in at the shop and asked Nicholas if he knew. And Nicholas, with an expression as innocent as a choir-boy, said he thought the stag belonged to Mr. Pettigrew, and he had sent it to him. He had tied it up, hung a label round its neck addressed to Mr. Pettigrew, M.P., at The House of Commons, Westminster, and sent it off in the same boat that took Pettigrew himself. — Oh, it's all very well to laugh, but it was sheer impudence to do such a thing, and Pettigrew may well think it was done on my instruction!'

Before dinner was over, however, the General was in a very good humour, and took a more tolerant view of Nicholas's parting gesture. He and Swanson now described their day's sport in considerable detail. The General did his own stalking — he had taken the

young man called Robin Oig and Nicholas's boy Peter as gillies —
and he held in perfect memory every shift of the wind and contour
of the high, bleak country where he had spent the day. Catriona,
a little nervously, had to warn him not to linger over his port.
'Mr. Marvell is talking at half-past eight,' she said.

'Marvell?' said the General. 'He never said anything while he
was here. Where's he talking now? And how does it affect us?'

'It's a broadcast,' she explained. 'About Laxdale.'

'It's the first I've heard of it!'

'I didn't tell you because I know how much you dislike books and
articles on the Highlands by people who only come to write about
them. But I think Mr. Marvell will be good — and it's nearly half-
past eight now.'

'Well,' said the General ten minutes later, 'he evidently feels
more at home in a broadcasting studio than he did with us. He
makes you seem almost taciturn, Crantit.'

'Oh, hush, please. He's only beginning!'

Before a microphone, indeed, Mr. Marvell was truly eloquent,
and his description of the natural beauties of Laxdale, of its mingled
grandeur and charm, was so just and warm-hearted that even the
General was manifestly pleased. And now Mr. Marvell was talking
with measured gravity, and urgency in his voice, of the general
problem of the Highlands.

'I speak as an Englishman,' he said. 'I am utterly and entirely
English, and no golden offer could ever induce me to be anything
else. It is as an Englishman — a materialistic, self-seeking Englishman — that I say we can no longer afford to neglect the Highlands,
because our stomachs need the beef that could be bred in those
deserted valleys and pastured on the lower slopes of those commanding hills. And as an Englishman of the other sort — the sort
that still remembers, though it is no longer the fashion to be proud,
our not-inglorious history — I say that it would be much to our
benefit if the Highlands were enabled to breed again, not cattle
only, but a lively and numerous population with the virtues that
helped so much to make our history —'

'Good for him!' exclaimed the General. 'Most young men nowadays won't admit that we've got any history except unemployment and Munich.'

'Much of our history is extremely discreditable,' said Mr. Crantit.

'Everybody's history is discreditable if you look for what's discreditable in it.'

'Oh, do be quiet!' said Catriona.

Presently Marvell returned to the subject of Laxdale. 'And I do so,' he said, 'not only because I lost my heart to it, not only because its problems are in some ways the problems of all the Atlantic parishes in the north, but because on Saturday — two days after tomorrow — the parish of Laxdale will become the scene of a truly heroic venture. The people of Laxdale are presenting, principally for their own benefit, it would appear, a Greek play . . .'

Catriona, flushed of face, sat bolt upright, and in her excitement her pulses beat so loudly that she could scarcely hear what he said next; and having half-heard, could only remember it as a splendid tune in her mind.

'So much for the play and its setting,' said Marvell. 'Of the cast I can say nothing, except that I am sure they will give a remarkable performance, and I wish that I could be there to see them. I cannot tell you their names, because the lady who is directing the play, and herself taking a leading part, has sternly decreed that all concerned in the production must be anonymous. She is a very remarkable person, and if I had not already spent all my vocabulary of praise on Laxdale's beauty, I could, without extravagance, spend it on hers — '

'What damned impertinence!' exclaimed the General.

'It is indeed a very public declaration,' said Mr. Crantit.

'He's nearly finished now,' said Catriona unhappily. 'Do let's hear the end of it.'

'I think I've heard enough.'

'He made a very good case for your new road,' said Swanson.

'Let us hear him out,' said Mr. Crantit.

'Well, if you want to.'

But Marvell was evidently reluctant to come to his conclusion.

They heard him say again, 'I wish I could be there,' and then his voice faded, and the ghostly whisper of an unfinished sentence was drowned in the clamour of Big Ben.

'Who wants to hear the news?' asked the General.

'The news!' said Mr. Crantit. '*We* are the news!'

CHAPTER THIRTY-THREE

THOUGH the General's initial pleasure in Marvell's description of Laxdale had been completely spoilt by the unmannerly reference to Catriona, the people of Laxdale were delighted by such a volume of public praise. Though they lived without the conveniences that Mr. Pettigrew thought so desirable, nearly every house had its wireless-set, and the whole parish had listened to the talk, and sat till midnight discussing it. Their bitter disappointment in Pettigrew was almost healed by Marvell's warm approval of their scenery and his appreciation of their needs; and they were naively gratified to think that both had now become public knowledge.

Catriona had called a full rehearsal for the following afternoon, and no previous rehearsal had been so lively or so confident. Mr. Macaulay, who was already word-perfect, declaimed his lines as though all Scotland were his congregation, and the whole cast was evidently performing to the invisible audience that had listened to Marvell's description of their venture.

'It went far too well!' exclaimed Mr. Crantit. 'After a rehearsal like that we can only look forward to an utter fiasco on Saturday!'

'Don't you believe it, Miss Catriona,' said Nicholas. 'We are just getting into the swing of it. Wait till Saturday, and we will show you what acting is!'

'Don't boast, Nicholas. Please don't boast! For the first time I'm beginning to feel nervous.'

'There's no point in being nervous,' said the General, 'until you see if we're going to have an audience.'

'I've never doubted that! From the very beginning I've been sure of an audience.'

'Maybe Mr. Marvell's broadcast will bring in a few,' said Nicholas comfortingly. 'But we will enjoy ourselves whatever happens.'

'I expect a large crowd,' said Catriona firmly. 'I think we should have more seats, and we must decide where the car park's to be.'

'The glass was going down this morning,' said the General, who still resented Marvell's reference to his daughter.

'But it was going up again at dinner-time,' said Nicholas.

'Not very much.'

The sky that morning had been bright and sinister with the sharp colours of autumn storm, and twice the harvesters in their small fields had run to shelter before violent showers of bitterly cold rain. But the wind was veering from west to north, and the afternoon was chill and clear. The stooks of gathered oats stood on a golden stubble, and behind the reddish hills that rose, above slopes grey-scarred with scree, to bald summits, the sky was a blue transparency. The actors, after their rehearsal, went back to work in the fields. Men who had cut their own crop bound a neighbour's sheaves. Rats bolted from the last strip of corn and were chased by excited children. Hector McBride put off the robes of Dionysus and took his dogs to North Bay to look for a couple of ewes that were limping with foot-rot. Kitchen-tables were furnished lavishly for harvest appetites, and in the village Mrs. McLeod was cleaning her windows and instructing Morag how best to rearrange the high-piled counter to impress the many visitors she expected. Willy John Watt was painting his front door, and a man in Shore Street, an old sailor, was tying signal-flags together to festoon the whole street. Everywhere in the parish there was liveliness and bustle, a sense of urgency, and ordinary, everyday tasks were done with high spirit and a sort of flourish. Nurse Connachy triumphantly reported that a young woman in one of the remoter crofts, married the previous Christmas, had been delivered of an eight-pound male child after a model labour of only two and a half hours.

But when it grew dark the barometer was going down again, the wind was backing, and morning broke in sullen hues. Nobody, however, would admit that the prospect had worsened. Reapers were out early, their machines clattering through the fields, and twenty women from the village were scrubbing and sweeping in the old mill to give the actors some comfort in their dressing-rooms behind the walls that would represent King Pentheus' palace. Nicholas McLeod and Alec Muir, having knocked down a chimney that stood at one end of the last miller's ruined cottage, and reduced the rubble to a seemly pile for the part it must play as the Tomb of Semele, were experimenting with a mixture of peat and damp straw to make a fire that could be depended on to emit a decent volume of ritual smoke at the proper intervals; and Nurse Connachy, as wardrobe mistress, made the final inspection of the costumes. The General, after shooting a stag in the morning, spent the afternoon planning and marking-out a car park, while Willy John painted large signs to indicate the way IN and a contrary way OUT.

When every reasonable preparation had been made — though there were still very few seats, no programmes, and no one had thought of charging for admission — a nervous lethargy supervened, and all the actors and most of their friends felt curiously tired and vaguely apprehensive.

The barometer, it was said, had begun to rise again, and the weatherwise stood at their doors and studied the sky. They got no promise of fine weather, however, till about ten o'clock, when the darkness cleared and stars of a quivering brightness began to show against a sky that was almost black but unobscured by gloom. Very high, and from a point between north and north-east — opinion differed as to whether it was nor'-nor'-east or north-east by north — a drift of transparent clouds, like the finest spinning of Shetland wool — floated gently below the brightest stars, and, as it seemed, between the dimmer ranks of the farther constellations.

'We're going to be all right!' declared the General, with confidence in his voice. 'There'll be a fine, frosty morning, and settled weather for at least forty-eight hours!'

271

CHAPTER THIRTY-FOUR

THE General's forecast had been correct. The sun rose on fields sparkling with the first frost of autumn, and the veils of morning lifted to show a sky as blue as a thrush's egg, and the old moon sleeping white on an azure bed.

For an hour or two, throughout the parish, there was a strenuous but almost furtive activity. As when a housewife dusts and polishes the ben-room to receive a wealthy cousin and his wife, come home on holiday from Canada or Australia, so now the whole village and all the outlying crofts made themselves trim and 'idy, settled window-curtains and swept the brigstones, to welcome with a proper dignity their expected visitors. But all that was finished by nine o'clock at the latest, and thereafter there was nothing to do but wait. No one had made any plans to work that day, or now thought of working. And hours of idle expectation travel slowly.

By midday, when not a visitor had arrived, a certain despondency was visible, and a few who were quick to pessimism were already saying that it was just as they had always expected, that no one had ever taken any interest in Laxdale, nor ever would. At five-and-twenty minutes past twelve, however, a small saloon car was seen coming down the road, and as it passed through the village there were eager faces at every window, and brightly inquisitive women and children in every doorway.

Guided by the signposts which the General and Willy John had set up, the car continued on its way to the car park on the *machair*, and its occupants, a family party from Inverness, got out and walked back, expectant of news and conversation, to the village. But now the village appeared to be deserted. Many of those who watched its arrival had been overcome by Highland shyness, and retired indoors; others, moved by Highland pride, felt it improper to show too much interest in Saturday tourists. The village street was empty.

Ten minutes later, two more cars drove in. Then a bus. A large American car, that filled the road, came at a quarter to one. Then a straggling convoy of five or six rather shabby vehicles, and a dazzling limousine. By a quarter past one there was a new arrival every two or three minutes, and Highland shyness had dissolved in a measure of excitement, Highland pride had retired to make room for the exhibition of simple pleasure. Half Laxdale lined the street to wave its welcome, and half was congregated round the car park on the *machair* to engage the visitors in conversation and watch them eat their picnic luncheons.

The real excitement began at half-past one, when two steamers approached the anchorage, reduced their speed, and stopped. The leading ship was either the *Lochboisdale* or a sister-vessel — but this was Saturday, and on alternate weeks the *Lochboisdale* called on Monday, Wednesday and Friday. She was not due today, nor due from the south'ard.

'It's the *Lochmaree*,' said Nicholas, with a long brass telescope to his eye, 'and the one behind her — by God, it's a tourist-steamer from the Clyde! They are making special excursions, and the whole of Scotland's coming here!'

At Laxdale Hall there was as much excitement as in Laxdale village, and the dining-room had been forsaken for the lowest terrace of the lawn, from which there was a clear view of the anchorage. Crantit and Swanson and Catriona stood mute and apprehensive to watch the arrival of their sea-borne audience — Catriona like a priestess at the moment of divination, exalted and terrified — but the General, forgetful of his scepticism, discarding his hatred of publicity now that publicity had summoned its forces, regarded the invasion as a challenge to be met, and estimating the number of spectators with a controlled enthusiasm, spoke of the afternoon's performance as a victory to be won.

'Catriona, my love,' he said, 'my dear Crantit! You've got the chance of a lifetime, and if I'm any judge you're going to roll 'em up, horse, foot and guns! I never hoped for anything as good as this!'

White-faced and miserable, but consecrated and doomed to their task, Catriona and Swanson and Crantit stood like the foremost infantry in their trenches, waiting for the barrage to lift them into battle, while the General, like a General, spoke of victory; but none of them, at that moment, believed in victory.

'We ought,' said Swanson, 'to eat something.'

'I couldn't,' said Catriona.

'Something to drink, perhaps,' said Mr. Crantit.

'No,' said the General, 'not a drop! — Now who's this coming?'

From the north-west, from the Gothic heights and the pigeon's-blue background of Skye, appeared a small motor fishing-boat at full speed — its yellow varnish gleaming in the sun, a bone in its teeth — and wheeling between the anchored steamers boldly approached Miss Phipps's pier, slowed and reversed, moved forward again when it found sufficient water, and gently came alongside. The General, staring through his field-glasses, exclaimed, 'I thought so! It's Donald Munro. He must have been staying in Skye. There's Ian Ross, and Lachlan, and Isobel; the whole family's there. — I wonder if they've had lunch? We ought to go and see.'

'It's time for us to go and change, and make up,' said Catriona. 'Oh, father!'

'My dear!' said the General. 'It's going to be a triumph for you. Fear nothing. That chap Marvell knew better than I did. He knew how to bring the crowd, and he's done it. He's a first-class fellow, Marvell, and I take back everything I said against him.'

'*Morituri te salutant*,' said Mr. Crantit.

'Don't talk nonsense,' said the General. 'I had an American wife, poor dear, and I know the proper answer to that: "You're going to slay them!" — Off you go, and I'll walk down to the pier and have a word with Donald Munro.'

'Who,' asked Mr. Crantit, putting off the moment of departure, 'is Donald Munro?'

'Well,' said the General, 'it isn't easy to answer that. He's rather

a great man, in one aspect, and a little bit wild in another. A little
bit unpredictable, you know. He was in the Navy during the last
war, and did very well; and now he's got a restaurant in Edinburgh.
The best restaurant in Scotland, if you ask me. And he does all
sorts of other things too, and knows everybody from the Lord High
Commissioner to the local constable's first cousin. But you'll meet
him after the play, and you can form your own judgment.'

The General kissed his daughter, with confident lips against her
trepidation, and knowing that trepidation always precedes a battle,
went down to the pier without diminution of his confidence . . .

Marvell's broadcast, and the warmth in his voice when he spoke
of Laxdale and thought of Catriona, had given her production of a
Greek play a new complexion. An idealistic venture suddenly became news, and before midnight Marvell had written articles for
three different newspapers in which, with small and easy variation,
he repeated what he had said in the broadcast; and answered by
telephone some half a hundred questions that the news-editors of
other journals had felt it imperative to ask. 'Without true love,
salesmanship cannot prosper, and without salesmanship neither can
love,' said Mr. Crantit, a little sadly, when in the course of time he
discovered how much publicity the Laxdale play had unexpectedly
been given.

By half-past two the round hillock, that was called The Drum,
was entirely hidden by the close-packed audience that sat upon its
northern slopes. Sergeant Ogilvie and a constable from Scatwall
had fortunately arrived, to assist in controlling the traffic, and two
policemen from Inverness to prevent Catriona from defrauding the
Revenue of Entertainment Tax. As no one, however, had thought
of charging for admission to a natural auditorium, the question of
Entertainment Tax did not arise, and with perfect good humour the
Inverness policemen, and those from Scatwall, served as ushers; and
the audience was marshalled and arranged with professional ease.

The performance began only ten minutes after its advertised time.
It began so casually — as it appeared — that very few of the spectators
realized it had begun; and all had the opportunity, in consequence,
to appreciate and comment on the very pleasing appearance of the

numerous Chorus, in robes of boldly contrasting colours, as it gathered on the level green between the hillock and the mill. — The village actors had been as excited as Catriona; but their excitement, unlike hers, had contained no fear of failure. They were naively confident, and as if an audience, large beyond the wildest anticipation, were no more than a modest recognition of their deserts, they confronted it with gaiety, and coming from up the river, and down the river, and behind the mill, walked to and fro, and talked, and talked to other groups, as much at home on their green stage as on the village street.

Then, from upstream, came a sound of flutes, and the audience, and the Chorus too, all looked towards a little band of gay musicians — Robin Oig and Malcolm from the Shore were their leaders — and in the midst of them a tall young man, in a violet himation and green-garlanded, of astonishing beauty. Shrilly hailing, the Chorus ran to meet him, and god-like he advanced, kind and contemptuous and taller by a head than all his worshippers. Raising his hand to keep them at a distance, he spoke:

'I have come again to Thebes!
You know me: I am Dionysus, son of Zeus
And my poor mother Semele,
To whom the lightning was both murderer and midwife;
The smoke still rises from her tomb,
And to recall her mortal contribution to my being,
I took once more the shape of mortal men
To walk by Dirce
And the fountains of Ismenus . . .'

With its clear, Highland articulation, the vowels prolonged and the consonants ringingly defined, the voice of Hector McBride held the attention of the audience throughout a long speech in which he threatened war against King Pentheus; and from the Chorus Morag came forward to reply, and pledge the love and loyalty of all women.

'I can hardly endure it!' muttered Mr. Crantit to Swanson, both of them watching privily from a glassless window in the mill.

'With bare arms and deerskin on her breast, she wakes the poet and the satyr in my mind; chiefly the satyr. I see rape as something infinitely desirable, even laudable, the unfulfilled purpose of my dilapidated manhood. Perhaps she isn't good — in the play, I mean — because she isn't Greek: she is Celtic, she is Deirdre, she is infinitely desirable. How I wish I had the strength of mind to rape her, or the physical attraction to make it unnecessary. I think I am going to cry. Have you a handkerchief, Swanson?'

Dionysus took his leave, and the Chorus, scattered on the lawn, sang small, fierce songs of worship and defiance, their Gaelic voices rising clear and thin to airs that a learned friend of Mr. Crantit's had assured him were in the Lydian mode.

'My lyrics sound very well,' said Mr. Crantit complacently. 'Though my heart is breaking for Morag, my mind, I confess, is titillated by my compositions. Art is always the traitor to emotion. — But I must go now, this is where Tiresias makes his entrance.'

'Give me your spectacles,' said Swanson.

'Take care of them,' said Mr. Crantit.

Mr. Crantit, as old, blind Tiresias, made his appearance some fifty yards downstream from the mill, crying querulously for attention:

> 'Where's the porter?
> Porter!
> The porter of the gate! —
> I want to see old Cadmus,
> Agenor's son.
> Tell him Tiresias is here . . .'

A massive figure, creating the impression of great strength crippled by age, came ponderously out of the mill, and Nicholas's voice boomed across the field:

> 'My good old friend!
> I heard the tune of wisdom in your voice,
> And recognized my friend . . .'

The two old men discussed the return of Dionysus, and the mere thought of him, and the beneficence of his rule, seemed to rejuvenate them. — Here Mr. Crantit had taken liberties with the text and, in the manner of Aristophanes rather than Euripides, introduced a little political comment. — But their conversation was interrupted by the marching beat of pipe and drum, and at the head of a troop of soldiers, Pentheus appeared.

The old men hid themselves under the west wall of the mill, and Mr. Macaulay, as Pentheus, summoned the Commander of his Bodyguard — who had halted, turned into line, and stood at ease upon their spears — and spoke to him with the genuine indignation of all the pulpits of the world, outposts of virtue in the swamps of vile humanity:

> 'They took advantage of my absence!
> I crossed the frontier
> On necessary business of the state,
> And when my back was turned the women pranced,
> Shook off the veils of civil modesty,
> And in their primal joy of life took to the hills —
> Our own wives and sisters took to the hills
> To worship Dionysus,
> Carrying wine,
> And ever watchful for secluded glades
> Where worship of that sort finds comparable worship
> And more wine . . .'

Mr. Macaulay was indeed impressive, and Pentheus, for a little while, held the field for bleak authority. But then the old men, tetchy Conservatives both of them, came out of hiding, and Tiresias delivered a counter-broadside:

> 'A wise man, choosing good occasion for his speech,
> Can hardly fail to speak well.
> You have a tongue that spends most lavishly
> As if the wealth of wisdom moved it,
> But in your words there is no pennyworth
> Of sense or reason,
> And a strong man void of sense
> Is all humanity's worse enemy . . .'

278

Mr. Crantit, who had shared the nervousness of Catriona and Swanson before the play began, lost all trace of diffidence when he perceived a packed audience committed, of its own volition, to listen to a speech a hundred and twenty lines long; and there was not only assurance but real feeling in his voice when he told Mr. Macaulay:

'It is not Dionysus' purpose
To shield a maiden's virtue.
If maidens have by chance some virtue, then their virtue shall avail
To keep them virtuous; there is no other means . . .'

Cadmus, in Nicholas's most persuasive voice, tried to reconcile Pentheus to the unalterable nature of humanity, and failed. Pentheus, in the indignation of a shallow mind, retired into his palace; and the old men, refreshed by old men's memory, went off to the hills. The Chorus took the stage again, and the Chorus, regrettably, became a little tedious in assertion of its own good sense. But drama came to its rescue, and Dionysus was brought in, a prisoner, by King Pentheus' soldiers.

Girls in the audience grew uncomfortable and warm to see his beauty so confined; and lively women of twenty-eight to forty-five invented fictions in which they rescued him from durance, and in the seclusion of their own homes gave him the comfort he deserved. Their elders, to whom sorrow was a nearer cousin, regarded him with equal longing but in a different mood, and in his beauty saw their private image of the sons whom one or other of our wars had killed. In a violet himation and clattering chains, Hector McBride looked indeed like a god distressed.

Pentheus came out to jeer at him, and after bitter argument Dionysus, humiliated and his long hair shorn, was led through the mill-door to his dungeon.

Shrill and distraught, the Chorus sang their grief, and Morag had a charming lament for the pleasant days of old when Orpheus with his lute made the trees dance with the dryads, and the fawn and the leopard listened in the shade; that Mr. Crantit had borrowed from a forgotten poet of the seventeenth century. Then, from his dungeon in the mill, came the voice of the god, and flame leapt among the smoke from the tomb of Semele. There was a sound of dissolving ruin, of iron protesting, straining timbers, and rushing water — the mill-lade, let flow for a few minutes in its old channel, turned the ancient wheel and shook the floor — and the stone pillars of the false doorway fell. Dionysus, unbound and glorious, came out into the light.

Stricken by fear, the many-coloured Chorus fell to their knees and hid their eyes; but Dionysus comforted them. Now it was Dionysus' turn to mock the silly king, and Pentheus in his rage had to face a power older than his own, and be rebuffed.

A Messenger appeared, genuinely out of breath, and with much excitement began a long speech that told of rebellious women who, in the hills above, were already practising forbidden rites, and exulting in their freedom. Their leader in rebellion was the old Queen herself, Agave, King Pentheus' mother . . .

The General, sitting beside Donald Munro on the slope of The Drum, said in a whisper, 'I'm frightened of the next bit. They're going to laugh, I'm afraid, and you can't blame them. The audience, I mean.'

'What happens next?'

'Hector McBride — that's Dionysus — persuades Pentheus to go and have a look for himself, and see what's going on in the hills. But for safety's sake he's got to be disguised, and dress up as a woman.'

'You mean Macaulay?'

'Yes.'

'By God, they'll laugh.'

'Well, perhaps it won't matter. Perhaps it's meant to be funny.'

The audience laughed without restraint to see King Pentheus dressed as a Bacchanal, and laughed the louder at Mr. Macaulay's fine assumption of indifference. But when Dionysus and the doomed monarch had gone, they were allowed to recover their composure, without a sudden demand for gravity, while they admired a dance.

The introduction of a dance was Catriona's idea. Mr. Crantit had written a lyrical piece for the leader of the Chorus which spoke of her delight in the King's discomfiture, but gave a rather frigid impression of delight; and Catriona and Mr. Crantit had both admitted that Macaulay, dressed as a Bacchanal, might start too much laughter to be easily stopped. Had Norman McKellaig been playing the part, the danger would have been slight, for he, under Dionysus' spell and decked in fawnskin and peplos, had looked so distraught and agonized that too much pity was the consequence they had feared. But Macaulay would not waken pity.

'Let the Chorus dance,' Catriona had said. 'The purpose of the Chorus at this point is only to fill in time, and suggest the passage of time, before the Second Messenger comes with the news of Pentheus' death. A dance is the obvious thing.'

'What dance do you suggest?'

'It must be fast and cheerful, it should look triumphant. But we haven't time, now, to invent a Greek dance, so it will have to be a Highland dance. I think *The Duke of Perth* would do. They all know it.'

So the Chorus, with great spirit, danced *The Duke of Perth* to accordion-music played, within the mill, by Robin Oig and Malcolm from the Shore . . .

Swanson considered his reflexion in a looking-glass, and wistfully observed how much he was improved by a short, brown beard. He, more than the others, had been made nervous by the great number of people who had come to see them, for in so large a crowd there might well be someone who knew him. He was not widely known, despite his success as a novelist, for outside Shetland he took no part in public life, he neither lectured on the modern novel nor attended literary parties, and he disliked having his photograph taken. But he had been afraid of recognition, until he remembered his beard; and now, bearded and prepared to make his entrance, he took courage from his reflexion. His face had been transformed by a handful of jutting hair. Not mild and recessive now, but arrogant and virile. He spoke a line or two, and his bearded jaw snapped proudly on the words. He put down the looking-glass and went out with confidence.

Unseen, behind the mill, he went upstream, and in a hollow by the river waited for his cue. Then, with purposive long strides, he hurried to the green stage and broke up the dance with tidings of doom. The King was dead, and he, a slave of the royal house, could tell the story of his last journey and most dreadful end.

He spoke of the bare hillside, and then the forest, and how, under Dionysus' spell, Pentheus had climbed a lofty tree to watch the Bacchanals at their dancing; and summoned by Dionysus the women had come, and pelted him among the branches. Their frenzy grew, and in the strength of their insane possession they took hold of the tree and tore it from its roots. Down fell the King, and like wolves the women pulled him limb from limb. Their leader, ruler of them all, was Agave, his mother . . .

'This is the part,' whispered the General to Donald Munro, 'that I dislike intensely. Catriona comes on in another minute, and it turns your blood cold. She's carrying his head . . .'

From the audience, indeed, rose a little tremulous sound of horror, and with a shudder they drew their breath in a momentary dismay to see the tall figure of Agave and her troop of Maenads. White-haired and dishevelled, her peplos torn and one side drenched in blood, Agave carried by its twisted locks the dripping simulacrum of a human head. She walked with inhuman stiffness, yet light upon the ground, as though in the cold aftermath of frenzy she hardly belonged to the living world, nor touched its earth. Her eyes, wide-staring, looked blank and sightless, and the Florentine perfection of her features would have seemed lifeless but for the quivering of her lips.

'If that's acting, she's a damned good actress,' said Munro.

'She's frightened,' said the General. 'She's dead-scared.'

Her voice, when she addressed the Leader of the Chorus, was low but clear, and her effort to control it gave it an unnatural calm:

> 'I heard a voice in the forest,
> O maiden dark with the sun,
> And I saw the beast thou abhorrest,
> And thy God ordered this to be done!

On the wild green heights of Cithaeron
Thy God demanded his due —
Take it, bestow thy care on
The head of the lion I slew . . .'

In silence they listened to the exchange between Agave and the Chorus, the whole audience catching as if by infection the intensity of her feeling; and as confidence swelled her voice, it grew louder to match the mounting strain of her madness, and the Bacchanals about her came and retreated in waves of excitement.

She boasted, horribly, of the strength of her hands, that needed no weapons to kill; and her boasting was interrupted by old Cadmus, walking slowly in his ruined strength, and followed by attendants who carried on their shoulders a bier swathed in black.

By the sorrow of Cadmus, Agave was given her sanity again, and saw what she had done.

Then Dionysus returned, and in the inscrutable purpose of the god, and in the radiance of his beauty, they found what reconciliation mortals may, who are caught in the toils of what they worship . . .

The green stage was empty, and still the audience sat, uncertain of their feelings, and doubtful as to how they should express their confused emotions.

The Chorus re-appeared — Chorus and Bacchanals, Soldiers and Attendants — and advancing from the mill in loose array, halted while Morag went forward three more paces, and deeply curtsied.

That this was not a Hellenic gesture, Mr. Crantit admitted; but Mr. Crantit insisted on it. 'We must do something conventional, and bring them back to earth. They'll be grateful, and respond. — Listen to that! They're applauding now. It's conventional to applaud, and it makes them happy to be conventional after an hour with Dionysus on the hills.'

'They're shouting for Dionysus,' said Swanson.

'Let us all go out and make our bow,' said Mr. Crantit; and now, seeing what they were accustomed to — a simple, human response, actors and actresses taking their pleasure in admiration — the audience applauded with even greater enthusiasm, and Mr. Crantit scarcely exaggerated when he declared complacently, 'This is a triumph indeed!'

A party of press-photographers demanded attention. They had arrived late, and the police had had some difficulty in keeping them off the stage during the performance of the play. Now, like men accustomed to obedience, they asked for poses, groupings, an attitude, or a background; close-up and movement.

The audience came forward from its hillock, and mingled with the performers. Catriona and Hector McBride were surrounded by admirers. Lesser performers had their measure of praise, their hands were shaken, some signed autograph-books. Swanson signed H. O. Pottinger twice, and walked to and fro with Mr. Crantit, both of them happy and relaxed now that the play was over. Swanson avoided the eye of a young man, neatly dressed in tweeds, who, with a pretty girl beside him, had two or three times shown some desire for conversation.

Mr. Crantit offered a cigarette. Swanson found matches. Little crowds still surrounded McBride and Catriona. They walked slowly, gossiping, and aware of ease.

'Take care!' exclaimed Mr. Crantit. 'Your beard's on fire!'

'So it is,' said Swanson, and pulled it off, and crushed the little ripple of flame between his hands.

'Mr. Swanson!' said an eager voice. 'I've been watching you! I was almost certain it was you, but the beard made a difference, of course. You don't remember me, do you?'

Swanson stood frowning at the young man neatly dressed in tweeds, who, too pleased by his discovery to notice the lack of welcome, proudly introduced the pretty girl who accompanied him. 'This is my wife. We've just got married, we're on our honeymoon, as a matter of fact. — Darling, this is Mr. Swanson.'

Swanson shook hands with her, and said, 'I must apologize for my memory, which gets worse and worse. I really can't remember your name.'

'Oh, I didn't expect you would. It's Parker, I work in Mr. Peters's office. — Mr. Peters, your agent, you know.'

284

'Yes, of course I know.'

'And I specially wanted to talk to you — if it was you, of course — because we've got the most marvellous news for you, and you may not have heard it, because we wrote to Venezuela. We thought you were still there.'

'Yes, naturally.'

'Did you get the letter, Mr. Swanson? The letter about the contract with B.G.M. for the film-rights in *The Silk Umbrella*. Mr. Peters sent a copy to B.G.M. at once, and they went right up in the air about it. They thought it wonderful — and so it is, I've read it myself! Well, they offered 30,000 dollars, and Mr. Peters was very pleased, and used the authority you gave him to sign the contract at once. That's the news we sent you, but we sent it to Venezuela.'

'How much did you say?'

'Thirty thousand dollars.'

'O God, my God!' cried Swanson miserably, and a gruffly genial voice said, 'Hold it! Keep still!'

They looked round to see a small and agile photographer who, having perceived an interesting group in animated conversation, had taken their picture.

'And now, gentlemen,' said the photographer, 'can I have your names, please?'

'Certainly not!' said Swanson.

'That's just modesty,' said young Mr. Parker happily. 'This is Mr. Olaf Swanson, the novelist . . .'

CHAPTER THIRTY-FIVE

'WHAT are you going to do for all these people?' asked Munro.

'I hadn't thought of doing anything,' said the General. 'They came to see the play, and they've seen it. They can't expect anything more.'

On the village street, in the meadows by the river, and on the *machair* there were several hundred people strolling aimlessly, unwilling to go home or return to the anchored ships, but incapable of finding occupation or amusement in a country whose inhabitants still provided their own. They had had a memorable outing, and clearly they wanted to prolong it; but they had no material excuse.

'What they'll really want, in an hour or so, is a good meal,' said Munro.

'They won't find an hotel in Laxdale.'

'I wonder if we could improvise anything?'

'I've got three stags in the larder. I can't think of anything else. Catriona asked me to shoot them in case a lot of people came and were storm-bound. I thought it fanciful myself, but that's what Catriona wanted, and she's got a stubborn streak in her.'

'What made her choose a bloody awful play like that?'

'Didn't you like it?'

'It was well produced and well acted — but I don't see how anyone could like it.'

'I think all Greek tragedies are, quite literally, both bloody and awful.'

'Then why did she produce a tragedy?'

'Oh, that's her mother's nature. People don't really die, Donald.

Not altogether. They live on in their children, or their work, or even in the rooms they furnished. And her mother was American, as you know, and they're a serious people, and less averse to violence than we are . . .'

Munro interrupted him: 'I've been thinking about those stags. They're just what we need. It's quite easy to dig a shallow trench in the *machair* and make a long fire, and I saw in the village a roll of coarse netting — sheep-wire — that we can grill them on, I think. I know the steward of the *Lochmaree*, and he'll let us have all the bottled beer he's got — '

'But what for? What are you proposing?'

'A barbecue, of course. It'll make a good finish to the day, and give them something to remember as well as that bloody play. Charge three-and-six a head — it's a mistake to give people something for nothing, they don't appreciate it. You ought to have charged admission to the play.'

'No one thought of it.'

'Well, we'll charge them for their supper, and they'll enjoy it all the more. What do you think?'

'Can you really manage to do all that?'

'I'll go and have a word with Nicholas McLeod and the steward of the *Lochmaree*. We'll fix it between us. The village is in the mood for a celebration, as well as all your visitors.'

'The village always is,' said the General.

Donald Munro went to look for Nicholas, and the General walked slowly towards Laxdale Hall. He was in acquiescent mood, relieved of the anxiety he had long denied, and grateful for the success of a play that he disliked. She's very like her mother, he was thinking, when he was overtaken by Swanson and Mr. Crantit, the former looking as distraught as if he had just escaped from a wrecked train, the latter plump and bustling in the importance of a man charged with sudden responsibility.

Though uneasily aware that his comment was, for some latent reason, irrelevant, the General congratulated them on their performance; and Mr. Crantit, exhibiting an ostentatious calm, accepted his compliments with a splendid affectation of patience.

'I'm glad, so glad, you liked it,' he said. 'But it's Catriona who deserves the credit. All credit is hers. We were puppets only. — And now, if I may turn the conversation to a graver topic, we have come, Swanson and I, to ask your advice and seek your help in a matter that, for Swanson, is of the most urgent moment. He is — through no fault of his own, as I see it — in a serious difficulty and considerable danger.'

'Danger?' asked the General.

'When you have heard the whole story,' said Mr. Crantit, 'you won't accuse me of exaggerating.'

'Let's go home,' said the General. 'I need a whisky and soda, after watching Catriona with that damned head, and if Swanson's in a pickle, he needs one too.'

Unnerved by recognition and exposure, and the disproof of his Venezuelan alibi, Swanson had resigned himself to Crantit's care. Crantit had prevented him, in his first indignation with the photographer, from starting a vulgar row that could only have made his predicament more conspicuous. Crantit had said he must make a clean breast of all his troubles to the General. And it was Crantit who related the whole sad story of married love, and public debt, and ignominious flight while Swanson, with a glass in one hand and his head in the other, miserably listened.

'And so,' said Mr. Crantit, 'he comes here, and very nobly — we're all indebted to him — he agrees to take a part in the play. And what's the consequence? He is recognized by an employee of his literary agent. His photograph is taken. A well-meaning young man reveals his name, and his fictitious domicile in Venezuela is irretrievably shattered. Worst of all, he is told that his last novel has just been sold to an American film-company for 30,000 dollars!'

'For how much?' asked the General.

'Thirty thousand dollars.'

'But good God, you can't possibly afford that! You'll be ruined, my dear fellow. As soon as those people in the Inland Revenue hear of that, they'll be after you like sharks round some poor chap who's fallen overboard. They won't leave enough of you for identification!'

'Swanson is well aware of that,' said Mr. Crantit. 'But what is he to do?'

'Clear out,' said the General promptly. 'Cut and run. When a position becomes utterly untenable, you retire while you can take your guns with you.'

'But where is he to go, and how? He's been recognized once, and his name is well known. Perhaps a hundred people have already heard that he is here. If he leaves by road, he may be seen. And could he go by road? There are only two cars in Laxdale — and the hearse — that are able to take him: Nicholas's and the Nurse's. But Nicholas seems to be busy, and the Nurse may be at any moment —'

The library door was opened, and Donald Munro looked in. 'I've made all the necessary arrangements,' he said. 'There are a few details to fill in yet, but they won't be difficult. They're digging a trench, and Nicholas is laying a fire, and Nicholas's boy Peter is selling tickets at three-and-six a time. I met a man who'd seen the play and didn't like the look of Pentheus' head, so I had a chat with him and discovered he was a butcher. I brought him back, and he's in the larder now, cutting up the stags. The steward of the *Lochmaree* has gone aboard to bring off all the beer he's got, and he thinks he can get some from the Glasgow ship too. So the main part of the business is well in hand, but I want two or three big pots to boil potatoes. Have you got anything that would do?'

'I dare say we have,' said the General. 'Yes, I expect we have, but I'm rather worried by another problem, just at the moment, so forgive me if I don't immediately grasp everything you've been telling me. The gist of it is that we are, in fact, going to have a barbecue?'

'You certainly are.'

'Well, really. You're a remarkable fellow, Donald. — But you haven't met my friends Mr. Crantit and Mr. Swanson, have you?'

Crantit and Munro began a lively conversation, while the General, taking Swanson aside, talked quietly with him at the other end of the room. — Mr. Crantit, who relished all who walked upon a level of their own, was much attracted to Munro, and solicitously asked how he had hurt his left hand, which was roughly bandaged.

'Gutting fish this morning. I was in a hurry, and the knife slipped. Just damned carelessness. I'd meant to dress-up a bit before coming over here, but I hadn't time, as it turned out.'

He was, indeed, rather conspicuously ill-dressed in corduroy trousers much stained with oil, a fisherman's blue jersey, worn threadbare across the chest, and a tweed jacket of considerable age. These drab and faded garments, however, served to emphasize his robust health — he was a little too stout for his old clothes — and the brightness of his complexion. His cheeks were so red that they subdued the russet gaiety of his hair, and the restless blue light of his eyes seemed to contend in vivacity with a sharp and questing nose. Among his friends his nose was famous. It was an exact and delicate judge in the matter of claret, and it led him unerringly, as the need arose, to articles of such varied use as a length of galvanized anchor-chain in a boat-builder's derelict yard, or a Chippendale chair to complete an imperfect set; to a spare magneto, or a setting of eggs for a broody Golden Pheasant, or a reliable man who could look after a motor-boat, was fond of gardening, and good with children. During the war, when he had been perilously engaged off the coast of Normandy, his nose had discovered a sunken ship with four-score cases of whisky in its after-hold, and then a complete diving appara-tus. Whenever his friends found themselves in unusual difficulty, or unable to obtain some obsolete, rare, or inaccessible article, they would say to their wives, or their wives to them, 'I think we had better ring up Donald Munro.'

It was, then, only to be expected that the General should presently say, 'I want your advice, Donald. Swanson here is in a very awk-ward position, and I don't quite know how to get him out of it. Help yourself to a drink, and I'll tell you the whole story.'

Gloomily Swanson endured a re-telling of his tale of misfortune, by the General this time; and Munro listened with interest and a growing sympathy.

'And then,' said the General, 'as soon as the play's over, this chap from London recognized him, and in all innocence gave him away.

Not content with that, he dealt poor Swanson a frightful blow by telling him that his new book had just been sold to some American film-company for 30,000 dollars.'

'Thirty thousand dollars!' exclaimed Munro. 'But you can't possibly afford to get as much as that!'

'The contract has been signed,' said Swanson.

'But if you use this new money to pay off your debt, you'll be worse off than ever in a year's time. When the Income Tax people have done with you, you'll be like a peeled grape.'

'He must get out of the country,' said the General, 'and as quickly as possible. And that, perhaps, is where you can help him.'

'Where do you want to go?'

'I can't go abroad,' said Swanson. 'Not immediately, that is. But Ireland is half way to being abroad, and if I could reach there —'

'I took a trawler into Londonderry often enough during the war. That's no difficulty.'

'But it's a tremendous favour to ask.'

'Let's think about it. — It's high water here at eight o'clock, and we ought to wait for a couple of hours after that to get the south-going stream. That means it would be getting light again by the time we were off Lismore — there's a tricky bit of navigation south of Lismore — but we'll have daylight by then, so that's all right. We may get a toss off the Mull: are you sea-sick?'

'No, never. But will you really take me?'

'I don't see why I shouldn't. — Can you put up Ian Ross and his family for the night?' he asked the General.

'Yes, and very glad to do it.'

'Well, that takes care of them. I'm pretty sure he's in no hurry to go home. He's never been in a hurry yet, I don't see why he should start now.'

'Who's in the boat with you?' asked the General.

'Old Tom Mackenzie. He's a good man, and it makes no odds to him where he goes. — And if we don't start till ten, or a little before that, I'll have plenty of time to see that the barbecue's properly run.'

'I don't know how to thank you,' said Swanson.

'Don't worry about that. I like a trip to sea, and there are several people in Londonderry I'll be glad to look up. — Now let's get busy with the barbecue. There's a tender-hearted butcher in your larder, and I'd like to take him a drink, if I may.'

With a sudden exhilaration — as though a gust of exhilaration had clapped him on the shoulder — Swanson went to his room to pack, and looking from his window blessed the sparkling sea. The sea was the old road to freedom, and still it served. How hopeless and remote from help must those poor mortals feel who lived in the innermost, dismal parts of some great continent! No wonder they were prone to panic, credulity, cruelty and intolerance. Only in islands or on the windy seaboard of the land were men assured of mercy and freedom, at the little price of daring to adventure on the waves. And let who cared to, call it escape, or that empty bit of neological nonsense, *escapism*. Surely to outwit one's captors was better than submitting, and Crantit was right when he said respectability was rationed, and must be used with care and circumspection . . .

Catriona knocked at his door.

'Father told me you were in trouble,' she said. — Sympathy made her grave, and gravity emphasized her beauty. — 'What can I do to help?'

'I think all the immediate arrangements have been made.'

'You're not very good at packing. I can do that, at least.'

Quickly, with a sort of indignant efficiency, Catriona packed for him, and said, 'I feel we ought to help you, after you've done so much to help us, and suffered in consequence. Shall I ask your wife to come here, and bring the children?'

'No, no. I'll find somewhere in Ireland she can come to. I'm feeling much more hopeful now. Donald Munro has given me confidence.'

'You can trust him at sea, he's a good sailor.'

'I'm sure he is.'

'Let me fold that coat again. — Have you anything else?'

'No, that's all.'

'Oh, I hate to see you going like this, and to think I'm responsible.'

'But you're not. I was bound to be recognized sooner or later. And don't think I regret coming here. I don't — not for a moment. It was an unforgettable experience to act in your play.'

'I shan't forget it. — Let's go down and see what there is for supper. You'll have to have supper alone with me tonight, everyone in the house has gone to the barbecue. But I couldn't face it.'

'I was so frightened,' she said, a little while later. 'Doubly frightened, frightened in different ways. It was only stage-fright in the beginning — everybody else had done so well, and I thought how dreadful it would be if I were the only one to fail — but afterwards, when I got over that, I was frightened of my part.'

'You frightened us all.'

'I never realized, till we were actually doing it, what a dreadful play it is. I don't think I understood it till today. Not properly.'

'And now?'

'It means that we're walking on a tight-rope, and if we stop walking and start thinking, we feel dizzy. Then we ask someone for a cure for dizziness, and the cure is quite horrible. So we look for a remedy for the cure, and that's worse still.'

'So we have to get back on the rope.'

'And keep our balance. That's why Mr. Crantit believes in a classical education, which really isn't practicable. — Is your wife well-educated?'

'No. She went to a school where they played hockey and cricket, and because she disliked both, I don't think she did much except dodge people.'

'Tell me about her.'

Willingly, and at considerable length, Swanson talked about his wife, and Catriona listened wide-eyed and sympathetic. Then, a little hesitantly, she said, 'Mr. Marvell has asked me to marry him. But I don't want to, because it would mean leaving Laxdale.'

'Are you in love with him?'

'I like him very much, and I'm terribly grateful to him, and I feel, perhaps, that he may need someone to look after him. — Is that enough?'

'As equipment for marriage,' said Swanson, 'an insufficiency of love is preferable to a superfluity.'

'Is that cynical?'

'Not if you want your marriage to last.'

'Oh, I should! Making up one's mind to ask for a divorce must be just as difficult as making up one's mind to get married. — Or would you say it's better to ask for a divorce on insufficient evidence, than to wait for too much?'

'That might make your life rather episodic. — Have you ever been in love before?'

'Not really, but several times I've been excited. Just as I am now. I haven't got a father-fixation, if that's what you're thinking.'

'Did you give Marvell an answer?'

'I told him I didn't know what to answer, and he said a girl never did until she'd been married for at least a year. He said love was psychosomatic — like the fashionable diseases, only nicer — and it took quite a long time to find out if you'd really got it . . .'

They were sitting in the library, still in such gentle conversation, when Mr. Crantit and the General, and his new guests, Ian Ross and his family, came in, loud-talking and exuberant, to describe the barbecue and its popular success. Six hundred people, said Mr. Crantit, chewing with a mediaeval gusto at collops of venison — pipers playing on either side of the burning trench, said the General — women and girls crying shrilly as they groped for hot potatoes in a pot — a bonfire of peats and driftwood flaming on the *machair* and spreading warmth — the popular, rich odour of bottled beer — charred meat upon the gridiron, eaten hot — and then the dancing, the spontaneous songs, the bonfire replenished, and up the long hill-road the lights of the departing cars opening and splitting the darkness.

'A very remarkable day,' said the General, 'thanks to you, my love' — Catriona spoke a little deprecatory phrase, quite formally — 'and thanks to Donald Munro, it's been given a memorable finish. But now, my dear Swanson, Donald's waiting for you at the pier.'

The General had borrowed Nicholas's car, and Mr. Crantit accompanied him and Swanson, and Swanson's luggage, to Miss

Phipps's pier. The luggage was put aboard, and Swanson shook hands with his host and fellow-guest. The General cut short his protestations of gratitude, and handed to Donald and Tom Mackenzie a haunch of venison and two bottles of whisky. 'You'll need some provender on your voyage,' he said.

The fishing boat's lines were cast off, and it stood to sea across the black inshore water that the dying bonfire stained yet with red and tawny hues, and the lighted ports of the anchored ships striped with pale and dancing streamers. In the little wheel-house Swanson stood with Donald Munro, and presently said, 'I'm on the run, and I'm going underground. It's the typical adventure of our time, isn't it?'

'You can often pick up a bit of fun on the way,' said Munro. 'I've never despised a little fun, even when·I knew it couldn't last and wouldn't leave anything but a headache. Can you steer?'

'Yes.'

'Keep that light fine on your port bow, and I'll go down and make some coffee.'

CHAPTER THIRTY-SIX

ABOUT six months later, on an afternoon of sun-shot storm in the middle of March, Catriona, in her own small sitting-room that looked upon the sea, regarded her rain-slashed window and the yellowish light beyond, and wondered whether she should write yet again to Marvell, or reply to the letter she had just received from Olaf Swanson. Since lunch-time she had written twice to Marvell, and twice torn the pages across and across, and put them in the fire; it was very difficult, she thought, to write well and interestingly when one did not know what to say.

She re-read Swanson's letter. He wrote from Galway. He liked Ireland, he said, but his wife did not. She resented the compulsory teaching of Gaelic in the school which their elder children attended, and she was perplexed by her inability to understand the people. 'She understands what they say, of course, but not what they mean. Their use of language is different from ours. We use words to state, and define, and assess, and clarify; but here they are used to suggest another possibility, to explore byways of the imagination, to praise or decry, to fantasticate — and unless you accept the usage, you may be irritated by it. I do accept it, and enjoy it, but only as an exile whose capacity for enjoyment is limited. That, however, has been of some advantage, for I have had time to work. I have begun a novel about the rebellion of 1798 and the French invasion under Humbert, which will certainly not be a popular success. There is a great deal of authentic material available, and most of it is extremely depressing.

'In addition to that, we have been planning our future, and by incurring some new difficulties, I think I may rid myself of the old ones. I used most of the money I got from the sale of *The Silk Umbrella* to pay off my debt to the Inland Revenue, and we have sold our place in Shetland. The Department of Agriculture paid a very good price for the house, which is to be used as some sort of hostel, and because I had spent a lot on improvement of the farms, we had no difficulty in selling them. It was a great sorrow to part with the place, which — though we ourselves had had it for so short a time — had previously been in my wife's family for nearly three hundred years; but we came to the conclusion that one is altogether too vulnerable nowadays if one lives ashore. So we are going to sea.

'I have bought a boat. She is a fishing-boat, a drifter, 65 feet long, that Donald Munro found for me. She is, perhaps, a little old, but apparently sound; and she is now being converted. There is a great deal of space in the fish-hold, so there will be plenty of room for the children. An old friend of mine from Shetland, a retired sea-captain, is joining us, and a cousin of my wife's, a very strong and healthy girl, is coming too. I am going to an engineering works in Belfast next week, to learn something about diesel engines.

'Our intention is to winter in the Mediterranean and spend summer in Irish waters and on the West Coast of Scotland. My wife, at present, is a little nervous about the sea, but she will get over that, and I keep telling her that even the Bay of Biscay in an autumn gale — which we shall try to avoid, of course — would be no more dangerous than living on land in our present conditions. I am putting together a small ship's library, a difficult job but interesting, and there are many other arrangements to be made. I am registering the boat — she is called *Vanity* — in Panama, which in various ways is helpful, I am told, though I don't like the Panamanian flag . . .'

With so much news to comment on, Catriona wrote rapidly for ten minutes, and then put down her pen to consider where she should start, and how arrange, her recital of the winter's events in Laxdale. The rain, in a grey occluding storm, thrashed the windows, and the squall drove a little cloud of peat-smoke down the chimney and out into the room . . .

'There has been so much happening,' she wrote, 'that the winter has really gone very quickly. One of the great excitements was a fire on New Year's Eve that completely gutted the store-shed behind Nicholas's shop. There was a *ceilidh* going on, so there were plenty of people to deal with it, and father quickly organized them into two long lines to pass buckets of water. They couldn't save the shed, but father was very good and thoroughly enjoyed himself. Nicholas wasn't really upset, because he had just taken out a new insurance on the shed, and he has plans made for a new one that will be much better. Mr. Macaulay preached a magnificent sermon on the fire, in which he compared it to the burning of Babylon, and warned the village against becoming too much addicted to commerce.

'Mr. Macaulay is a changed man nowadays. Very cheerful and sociable, and beginning to get fat. There is no doubt at all that he resolved some inner conflict by hitting you with a sword and knocking you into the mill-dam, for he has been in much better spirits ever since. And then, to complete the transformation, he had a great triumph over all the other ministers within fifty miles of Laxdale. They had protested, singly and at presbytery meetings, against the performance of the *Bacchanals* and his part in it; but he silenced them all by proving that the play was a terrible example of the evils both of rationalism and pagan license, and so, by implication, a mighty argument for the Church of Scotland which holds the narrow way between them. He has been invited to preach on this subject in at least a dozen different churches, and had such a wonderful success that several other parishes are going to produce Greek plays this summer. We, I think, shall be doing the *Electra* — if I am still here, that is. But I shan't tell you about my own affairs yet.

'There was, of course, great excitement after the play, when for a week or so we were all famous, and Morag and I and Hector McBride were asked to go and have screen-tests. None of us went, naturally, because Morag and I have no ambitions of that sort, and Hector is so good with sheep that it would be an utter waste for him to do anything else. He isn't nearly as shy as he used to be — I suppose the play cured him of that — and a month or two ago the *Scots Review* published five of his poems, which are very good indeed.

'The only person who succumbed to the allurements of the film-industry was Mr. Crantit! He went to Hollywood, with a vast salary, as historical adviser to a company that is making a film about Alexander the Great. But his engagement didn't last long. I don't quite know what happened, to bring it to an end, but he was so pleased about his success here that I think his ideas, and perhaps his behaviour, were a little too Dionysiac even for California. He was very sad and sorry for himself at Christmas, but early in January he wrote to say he had become Professor of Greek in some university in the south-west of America — I had never heard of it before, and I can't remember its name — and since then I have twice heard from him, and he seems well pleased with life. He has no less than fourteen students, and he says he has become a notable figure in the community. The local newspaper quotes him at least twice a week, and he has grown quite used to seeing his name in head-lines.

'The case against Gamlie and the poachers is still going on. When they first appeared in the Sheriff Court they had a very good lawyer from Glasgow to defend them, and they were released on bail. Neither McKellaig's name nor Mr. Pettigrew's was men-tioned, but the lawyer said there might be grave developments. What happened next was that father was charged with assault and wrongful detention of the four young men who spent the night in the mill. Nobody quite knows, apparently, whether a landowner is entitled to hit a poacher whom he finds poaching his river, or to arrest him; and in the particular case of father and the young man with the bicycle-chain — with whom he had a fight — it has been impossible to decide who made the first threatening movement. So there has been endless argument, and each side has appealed, and father has been put to a lot of expense. You can guess, as well as I, who has been paying the poachers' lawyers.

'But the case against the Laxdale motorists has been dropped, or postponed, I should say, "pending a full inquiry into the state of communications with and within the Laxdale peninsula". It is Hugh Marvell we have to thank for that. Twice before Christmas surveyors came to look at the road, and since then there have been divers exploring the sea-bed where the pier should be extended. Nothing, of course, has been decided yet, but everyone is very hopeful that something will be done.

'McKellaig has been forgiven and reinstated, and is now married to a girl with whom he had been corresponding, and who went several times to see him when he was in hospital. She has a lot of character, and is quite nice-looking, though she has a bad squint. McKellaig is happy with her, I think, but though he is rid of his old mother — she is living by herself in Shore Street — he is by no means the master in his own house. His wife rules him, more agreeably than his mother did, but quite as decisively. She will see that he does his work, however, and I wish I could say as much for Morag at the Schoolhouse.

'Andrew Flett resigned from the Civil Service, and Nicholas had no difficulty in getting him appointed headmaster of Laxdale School. He and Morag were married just before the New Year, and a new assistant teacher arrived, a girl who had just finished her training. But Flett and this girl between them are not half as good as Morag was by herself, and I am beginning to think that Flett came here, not only because he fell in love with Morag — there's no doubt of that — but because he is fundamentally lazy, and decided he could take things easily here. Morag, who might have been expected to keep him up to the mark, can see no fault in him, however, and was indignant with me last week when I said that I hadn't heard the children singing lately, and their drill wasn't nearly as smart as it had been in her time. It's quite incomprehensible how Flett has inspired such devotion, for to me he seems a very ordinary young man indeed.

'Poor Rory Mackenzie, you'll be sorry to hear, was drowned at sea — a great loss, that saddened us all — and Willy John Watt's father in Glasgow didn't long survive his marriage. But, on the other side of the account, Nurse Connachy has never in her life been so busy, and has had to get a new car. Our car was repaired, after the accident on the road, but until we got accustomed to it, it was a little difficult to steer.

'In January I spent three weeks in London, staying with an elderly cousin of father's, and saw a good deal of Hugh Marvell. It was at his suggestion that I went. At the theatre one night we met the Pettigrews, and I found it very difficult to sound and look sincere when I congratulated him on his honour. — He got a peerage in the New Year List, and is now Lord Drumliedubbs. — But he was completely unembarrassed and inquired for everybody at Laxdale as if he had nothing but the warmest feelings for them. She, when we said goodbye, gave me a vulgar but very friendly wink. She is certainly too good for him, but I don't know if you could call her really good.

'Hugh Marvell asked me to marry him again — I mean he asked me again — and promised that we should spend as much time in Laxdale as he could spare. I almost said yes, for I like him more and more, and it makes me very unhappy to think that I haven't yet made up my mind. I must do so very soon, and yesterday we had news that should really make my decision easier. My elder brother, who's in the Army, is going to Malaya, and his wife wants to come here with her two children. She is English, and devoted to the Highlands, and gets on very well with father, so really I shan't be needed . . .'

Savagely the wind howled over the roof, and the rain, as though stammering with rage, chattered at the window. But the sky was breaking, and between smoky clouds a light as pale as celandines revealed a distant, wetly shining cliff, and a turbulent but glittering sea.

'I must say *yes*,' wrote Catriona, 'I must! But I don't know how I can bear to leave Laxdale. Even the rain here is beautiful . . .'